*After this n*

## Dawn Caravan

For Ben Vecchio, everything has changed. His eyes. His diet. His new aversion to sunlight. But after a long sojourn in China, Ben realizes that the world he left behind hasn't changed as much as he feared. He wants to leave his old life in the past, there's one job remaining that just won't leave him alone.

Radu's mystery is too interesting—and too profitable—to ignore. The problem? Taking on this commission puts Ben in the path of his old partner, the one woman he's spent years avoiding.

Tenzin has been following Ben at a distance, hoping his ire might wane, but when he heads to Romania, her patience runs out. Ben is a new power in their world, and more than one vampire will be eager to test him.

Ben and Tenzin need to work together if they want to find the truth behind Radu, his mysterious clan, and the treasure at the heart of the Dawn Caravan. One last job, then it's finished between them.

Right?

*Dawn Caravan* is the fourth book in the Elemental Legacy, a paranormal mystery series by USA Today bestselling author, Elizabeth Hunter.

## PRAISE FOR ELIZABETH HUNTER

Ms. Hunter delivers. Every. Single. Time. I have the majority of her books and I am in awe of every book that she has penned and every book she has brought to life and here it is no different.

— KATE'S CORNER

...amazing, satisfying, endlessly entertaining read.

— NORMA, GOODREADS REVIEWER

[Hunter] writes mysteries that, beyond vampires and elemental powers, capture a human truth brought into perfect focus not despite the paranormal elements but because of them.

— KENDRAI MEEKS, BESTSELLING AUTHOR OF THE
RED HOOD CHRONICLES

While the treasure hunt is very entertaining, it's the emotions between these two, what's being said and left unsaid that is very powerful. ...this is Elizabeth Hunter at her best.

— NOCTURNAL BOOK REVIEWS

This book does not skimp on the excitement and intrigue, nor does it skimp on any of the sweetness and tenderness and joy that I have come to expect from an Elizabeth Hunter novel. I absolutely could not put it down.

— EBETH, GOODREADS REVIEWER

# DAWN CARAVAN

## AN ELEMENTAL LEGACY NOVEL

### ELIZABETH HUNTER

Cover: Damonza
Content Editor: Amy Cissell, Cissell Ink
Line Editor: Anne Victory
Proofreader: Linda, Victory Editing

Recurve Press LLC
PO Box 4034
Visalia, California
USA

*This book is dedicated to the
artists, activists, nurses, doctors, moms, garbage collectors, social
workers, gardeners, dads, chefs, librarians, aunties, postal workers,
farmers, census takers, grandparents, teachers, and all kinds of
neighbors who are working to make a better world.
Thanks.*

# CHARACTER GUIDE

**Arosh**—*fire vampire, age and origin unknown, ancient king in Eastern Europe/Central Asia, sits on Council of the Ancients, consort of Saba, former rival of Zhang Guo*

**Beatrice De Novo**—*water vampire, sired in last ten years, librarian and scribe of Penglai Island, resident of Los Angeles, blood-mate of Giovanni Vecchio, Ben's adopted aunt*

**Benjamin Vecchio**—*vampire, newly turned, born in New York City, antiquities dealer, antiquities locator, adopted nephew of Giovanni Vecchio, sired by Zhang Guo*

**Brigid Connor**—*fire vampire, sired in last ten years, security consultant for vampire in charge of Dublin, blood-mate of Carwyn ap Bryn*

**Carwyn ap Bryn**—*earth vampire from North Wales, one thousand years old, former priest in the Roman Catholic Church, leader of Bryn clan, blood-mate of Brigid Connor*

**Cheng**—*water vampire, born late eighteenth century in Guangdong, current governor of Shanghai, entrepreneur, former pirate, Kadek's sire*

**Chloe Reardon**—*human, midtwenties, born in Los Angeles, dancer, romantic partner of Gavin Wallace*

**Emil Conti**—*water vampire, born second century BC in Rome, governor of Rome, sire of Ronan*

**Fabia**—*human, Ben's childhood friend and day assistant in Rome, keeper of the Vecchio household in Rome*

**Filomena**—*water vampire, born in Naples, age unknown, governor of Naples*

**Gavin Wallace**—*wind vampire, born in Scotland, age unknown, entrepreneur, currently based in New York City, romantic partner of Chloe Reardon*

**Giovanni Vecchio**—*fire vampire, over five hundred years old, born in rural Tuscany, former assassin and partner of Tenzin, rare books and manuscripts dealer*

**Johari**—*earth vampire (formerly a water vampire), born in Zanzibar, daughter of Saba*

**Kato**—*water vampire, born in Greece, age unknown, sits on Council of the Ancients, grandsire of Giovanni Vecchio*

**Kamvasa**—*a moving safe house run in Eastern Europe by the Poshani people, also known as the Dawn Caravan*

**Kezia**—*wind vampire, terrin of the Poshani, sister of Radu and Vano, acolyte of Kali and vampire in charge of the Hungarian Poshani*

**Penglai Island**—*immortal island in Bohai Sea, seat of the Eight Immortals, largest seat of power in Eastern Asia*

**Poshani**—*a branch of the greater Romani people consisting of both vampires and humans ruled by three terrin, the keepers and guardians of the Kamvasa*

**Radu**—*wind vampire, terrin of the Poshani, brother of Kezia and Vano, client of Ben Vecchio*

**René Du Pont**—*earth vampire of the clan of Carwyn ap Bryn, over three hundred years old, thief*

**Saba**—*earth vampire, born in Ethiopia, age unknown, eldest known immortal, "mother of vampires," current queen of Alitea, Johari's sire*

**Sadia**—*human, adopted daughter of Giovanni Vecchio and Beatrice De Novo, sister of Ben, gelato critic, very high jumper*

**Tai**—*wind vampire, age and origin unknown, son of deceased Zhongli Quan, current servant of Zhang Guo*

**Tenzin**—*wind vampire, born approximately five thousand years ago in Central Asia, former assassin, former mercenary, former military commander, daughter of Zhang Guo*

**Vano**—*wind vampire, terrin of the Poshani people, brother to Kezia and Radu*

**Zhang Guo**—*wind vampire, born over five thousand years ago in Central Asia, eldest of the Eight Immortal Elders of Penglai Island, Tenzin's sire*

# PROLOGUE

B en woke in pitch darkness.

He smelled vinyl and leather.

Pine and the scent of fresh water nearby.

Fresh blood.

He touched his head, but the blow at the base of his skull had already healed itself. Scattered memories of jostling in a vehicle and heavy, unfamiliar accents. Flashing lights and the sound of truck engines revving.

He stretched out, searching for anything familiar. On his right was a ledge of some kind. He reached over. He was on a bed and there was a wall next to him, but it felt hollow. False. He slapped the wall and felt the edge of a familiar plastic fixture. It was the flat paddle of a light switch.

He pushed it and a small lamp turned on next to him, nearly blinding him with its low light.

In the newly lit compartment, Ben looked around.

Bed.

Small kitchen.

Square cupboards and plastic-covered bookshelves lined the walls. Was he on a plane? No, it was silent. He stood motionless and allowed the fear and panic to rise up so he could examine them clearly.

He took a deep breath and put his hands on the wall again.

Space. Some kind of insulation was packed behind the surface, but beyond that there was vast openness just on the other side. He reached up and felt the low ceiling. He felt the other wall and sensed the same.

In every direction, he was surrounded by air.

His panic began to calm. Just beyond these thin walls, his element waited for him. He could escape anytime.

A simple door stood at the end of the compartment, and as he walked toward it, he felt the floor swaying beneath him. It creaked and bounced.

What was this place? A mobile home? It was too small. A parked bus? Ben cracked the door slowly, reaching his amnis outward to sense any threats, but he was met by one single familiar energy signature a short distance away.

He pushed the door open and saw Radu standing alone on a hill under the swiftly darkening sky. The sun had set in the distance, and a lone Romani wagon was next to him, parked at the end of a cracked asphalt road where Ben realized his caravan had come to rest. That was the compartment where he'd woken, not a mobile home but a travel bus.

Radu turned and smiled ruefully. "I apologize, Ben Vecchio. This was not how I wanted to introduce you to the Dawn Caravan, but you left me no other options."

# 1

*Kashgar*
*Four weeks earlier*

A wood fire burned in the center of the courtyard, lighting the old stone house and the cobblestones that surrounded it, casting shadows on the brightly painted walls and throwing sparks into the cold night air. From the recessed loggia surrounding the central courtyard, vampires and humans lounged in the shadows. Some were feeding. Some were playing games of chance or discussing business matters.

Kashgar lived in the no-man's-land between the iron rule of the Eight Immortals of Penglai Island in the east and the authority of Arosh the Fire King in the west. It attracted those who wanted to remain anonymous and those looking to escape immortal authority.

Ben Vecchio was both.

That night he wasn't paying attention to the fire or the vampires around it. From his corner in the old house in Kashgar, he watched the woman on the far side of the courtyard.

Watched her as she watched him.

She could have been European or Central Asian. Her looks were ambiguous. Her eyes were large and dark. A crown of wild black curls surrounded a typically pale vampire face.

She clearly had some kind of status because behind her stood a guard who watched the courtyard with restless eyes. His hair was light brown and clipped short. He wore a plain black shirt and black pants. His height was average. His looks were average. Nothing about him stood out, but Ben's sharp gaze noticed every detail.

"Your tea, sir." A server set a pot in front of him, a glass vessel resting over a single flame. Saffron floated on the surface, its red petals bleeding gold into the simmering water.

The woman's lips were full and red, and she watched him from afar with unveiled interest. Ben suspected she'd fed recently based on the flush in her pale cheeks and her lip color.

Thinking about the woman feeding made his empty stomach twinge. He poured a glass of tea and concentrated on pushing the feeling down. He was two years immortal, and blood-hunger pangs could still drive him to distraction. It was his greatest weakness and his greatest challenge. Vampire hunger wasn't comparable to human hunger—or at least no hunger *he'd* known as a mortal. It was urgent and all consuming.

Ben hadn't fed in three nights, and he was starting to feel it. He'd been pushing himself, trying to stretch his control.

*"Do not become slave to your physical needs."* It was a constant refrain from his sire. *"If you are slave to your physical needs, others will be master of you."*

Of course, Ben also remembered the simple advice his sire's most loyal servant had given him. *"Don't push your luck,"* Tai had said. *"Vampire mistakes are messy."*

That night he felt Tai's wisdom in his bones, but the woman wouldn't take her eyes off him. It was hard to think about leaving the protected walls of the vampire safe house in the old city to hunt when he wasn't sure if he would be followed.

"Sir, would you like anything else to drink tonight?" The servant would have been near silent to human ears, but Ben wasn't human anymore.

Anything to drink? Ben scanned the compound. Several humans roamed around, the blood-red collar they wore a testament to their willingness to feed vampire guests. He wouldn't need to leave the compound to feed unless he wanted to, not with so many donors present.

It wasn't a hardship. There were women and men willing to offer their necks, especially when they were paid well. Many humans enjoyed the sensation of a vampire bite, which could range from excruciating to intoxicating.

Ben had spent the previous year learning how to feed with the least emotional transfer possible. He didn't want his reactions leaking into random humans who fed him; it wouldn't be fair to subject unsuspecting humans to his roller coaster of feelings. He might have gained control over his bloodlust, but his emotional highs and lows were enough to give even the steadiest human whiplash.

Most nights Ben felt like he existed in the world akin to an exposed nerve. He careened from ecstatic to angry to sullen in the space of an hour. Flying made him happy. Missing the sun made him angry. Silence gave him peace.

His stomach twisted, the server waited, and the mysterious vampire was still staring.

Saffron tea wasn't going to sate him.

Ben pointed his chin in the direction of a woman on the far side of the courtyard. "Her."

"Very well. I'll send Mer—"

"Don't need to know her name." He glanced at the server. "Just send her over."

"Yes, sir."

*Yes, sir.*

*No, sir.*

*It will only be a moment, sir.*

*Right away, sir.*

*My greatest apologies, sir.*

Ben supposed there were immortals who reveled in the deference, but it made his skin crawl.

*I was just like you.* He felt like shouting it. *I'm a nobody. A poor bastard who fell into the immortal world, constantly in debt to beings greater than myself.*

In debt to his adoptive uncle, Giovanni Vecchio, an immortal who plucked him off the street when Ben was twelve and gave him an education and a future. In debt to his Aunt Beatrice, a vampire who made sure he felt as loved as any natural child.

In debt to an immortal family who taught him how to protect himself and an ancient vampire who gave him vision.

Ben was in debt to vampire clients who had put their faith in him despite his mortal status.

And now he was in debt to others: a friend who betrayed him to save his life and a sire who gave him status he never wanted.

The mortal woman walked silently through the courtyard, her feet making no noise as they crossed the cobblestones. Her skin was a smooth light brown and her black hair was twisted up in a neat chignon that showed off a delicate neck marked with numerous healed bites. Her expression was carefully blank, but her hands didn't tremble.

She knelt on the plush carpet before him and looked up with hooded eyes. "Sir, do I meet your approval?"

Her lips were already flushed and her eyes were dilated. What had led her to this life? Why did she enjoy the feel of fangs in her neck and lifeblood being sucked from her vein? Her face told him nothing, but her lips told the story.

"Yes."

She rose and moved toward him, this time kneeling on the low cushion. "Would you like to feed from the neck or the wrist, sir?"

"Wrist." He kept his voice even, but he could feel her disappointment.

"Your wish, sir." She raised her wrist politely.

Ben turned to her and met her gaze. "Be comfortable."

Excitement flared in her eyes. "Of course, sir." She folded her legs to the side and leaned against the large back cushion before she held out her right wrist.

Through the entire exchange, the woman across the courtyard never took her eyes off him, and her bodyguard never looked at Ben directly.

Was she following him? Spying on him? Was she reporting to his sire?

To someone else?

Ben took the woman's wrist in his hand and warmed his skin to a nearly feverish degree. He saw goose bumps rise on the woman's arm, and a slight shiver ran through her when he put his lips to her wrist.

Since his hurried and violent congress with Tenzin immediately after his turning, he hadn't indulged his roaring sexual desires. Like his hunger, sex felt like a weakness. He'd never been a man led around by his dick, and immortality wasn't the time to start.

He didn't close his eyes when he bit into her wrist, but he sent a wave of amnis over her skin to give her the pleasure she wanted. The electrical current that controlled his amnis was powerful, far more so than what would be normal for a vampire his age.

Ben Vecchio was the son of an ancient king, the only son of Zhang Guo, the first child he had sired in over four thousand years.

Raw power flooded out of him and onto the woman, making

her gasp and arch her back in pleasure. An involuntary cry left her lips.

Ben took his mouth away. "Be quiet."

She didn't say a word, but she nodded. Her cheeks were flushed and her lips swollen. Her chest above the modestly cut dress she wore was red.

He put his mouth back to her wrist and licked up the drips of blood that had run down her arm, careful not to make a mess. Then he latched onto her vein and drank in leisurely sips, his eyes still locked on the woman across the courtyard.

*I see you. You see me. What do you want?*

The only response the vampire had was to raise a carefully groomed eyebrow in his direction. She watched Ben feeding from the human with clear interest, a small smile playing around the corners of her mouth.

The woman he fed from was silent next to him, but she twisted in pleasure, her body heavy against his. She was panting and tears leaked from the corners of her eyes. Her body shook with silent tremors of climax as Ben slowly fed.

Carefully. Deliberately. He felt the living blood splash against his throat like water tossed on a fire. Her taste reminded him of port wine. Rich. Sweet. He focused on the physical act of drinking. He focused on the sensation of his throat relaxing as the blood quenched his burning hunger. He fought the rising sexual desire that was inevitable.

He glanced at the woman who fed him from the corner of his eye. Watching her pleasure was the only release he allowed himself.

Was it a power trip? Yes. He gave humans pleasure and took nothing but sustenance. It was a trade he could live with. The woman gave her blood freely and received sexual pleasure and financial compensation in return.

She was exhausted by the time he finished feeding. She slid

down to the cushions and tried to lay her head on his lap, but Ben nudged her onto a pillow.

The woman looked up. "Nothing?"

"I'm fine." He licked his lips and ran a thumb over them. He couldn't abide dried blood on his lips. "Would you like some tea?"

She nodded.

"I'll order some." He looked back across the courtyard, but he didn't see his watcher or her guard. A sweep of his eyes around the dark veranda proved fruitless.

She was gone.

"Sir?"

Ben looked up to see the server standing next to him. He gestured to the woman next to him. "She needs tea."

"Of course." The server held out a tray. "The lady left this for you."

A cream-colored linen envelope sat on the tray. On the front was written a single name.

*Vecchio.* Not Rios, the name he was currently traveling under.

Ben snatched the envelope from the tray. "Thank you." He unfolded his legs and rose to his feet. "I'm finished here," he said to the woman. "Have a good night."

"You're leaving?"

Ben walked away without answering, the letter burning his fingers. He walked to the center of the courtyard where the fire was burning and opened it. Three words were written in the center of the page in thick blue ink.

*Answer your mail.*

No name. No address. No way of contacting the sender.

Ben read it again, looked at the paper through the light of the fire, and held it up to the heat, feeling a surge of satisfaction when the fire revealed a hidden message.

*Seriously, Mr. Vecchio. Answer your fucking mail.*

A smile threatened the corner of his mouth. He looked at the handwriting and committed it to memory, then threw the envelope and the letter into the fire.

~

"CARA, what's the time in New York?"

He didn't need to shout for his digital assistant to hear him. Cara was an artificial intelligence program designed for vampires who couldn't use more delicate human technology without shorting it out.

"It is 12:46 in the afternoon," Cara said.

"Place video call." He sat on the chaise next to the bed in his reinforced room and opened the heavy cover of his tablet.

"Encryption on?"

"Yes."

He missed the sleek electronics he'd used as a human, but vampire amnis was electrical in nature, a current running beneath the skin of vampires that connected them to their elements and interfered with modern electronic signals. For vampires to use technology, heavy cases and voice controls were essential.

"Video calling with encryption activated." Cara's smooth tones were as familiar as a friend's. "What number?"

"Chloe, mobile."

"You want to video call Chloe on her main mobile device. Is that correct?"

"Correct." He kicked up his legs and stretched.

The vampire body was different from the human one. On many levels, it was far more sensitive, but in other ways his nerves felt dulled. He no longer felt any soreness from a hard run or physical exertion. His muscles did not experience the minute tears that broke them slowly to be built up stronger with recovery. He was frozen in the exact physical state he had been two years before.

His lungs didn't pump when he climbed the side of a building or lifted something heavy. In fact, he didn't need to breathe at all.

But the brush of a callus against his skin could be excruciating. The temperature of the wind cut through his body like knives or caressed him like warm silk.

An electronic chime told him the call was connecting. He carefully arranged his face to speak to his assistant in New York.

"Ben?" Chloe's smiling face filled the screen. Her curly hair was tied back in a colorful scarf, and she was sitting outside in the sun. "Hey! I didn't expect to hear from you today. I'm having lunch with Arthur."

The small designer poked his head into the viewing screen and Ben angled his head so his transformed eyes weren't obvious.

"Come home!" Arthur said. "Everyone misses you like crazy. I know you and Tenzin had a fight, but stop being stubborn or you're going to give me wrinkles, and you know I'm too beautiful for wrinkles."

Ben couldn't help but smile. "I miss you too, Arthur."

Chloe shoved him away. "Are you calling for work?"

"Yes, but nothing related to a current client." He took a deep, unnecessary breath and did the thing he'd been avoiding for two full years. "Do you still have my last mailing address?"

Chloe's eyebrows went up. "Yes."

The last mailing address she had was directed to a box that was regularly delivered by courier to Penglai Island, the home of Ben's vampire sire.

"I think you need to send my mail."

## 2

The first time Ben traveled to Penglai Island, he'd been a resentful human, pissed off at his vampire partner for dragging him into another job where he might end up dead.

In the end, he hadn't been killed, but only because Tenzin had taken it upon herself to fly his mortally wounded body to her sire and had convinced Zhang to change him.

How? He still didn't know.

This time, instead of coming by boat, he flew through the air toward the golden jewel of an island set in the fog-covered sea. He was met by his sire's guards at the air perimeter of the island, and the guards stopped and bowed midair when they realized who approached.

"Master Vecchio." A guard with a familiar face moved toward him. "This marshal greets you with joy on your return. The wind is strong tonight."

"The wind is very strong." Ben searched his mind for the guard's name. "Duan Liping, it's good to see you again. Is my sire well?"

The man beamed. "The elder is in excellent health."

"Thank you for your greeting." It was far more than a greeting.

Zhang Guo and Zhongli Quan were the two wind vampires among the Eight Immortal elders of Penglai Island, and they were responsible for marshaling the air guard that protected the island, just as water vampires protected the seas. No one passed them without permission or invitation.

Well, Ben didn't need an invitation. Not anymore.

Though most of the elders had immortal children collected over many centuries, Zhang had only two. For thousands of years, he'd had only one. Tenzin had been it.

And now there was Ben.

As the immortal son of the founder of the island, Ben could come and go at any time, though he'd only spent a little time there since he'd turned. The first year of his immortal life had been spent training in Mongolia, and the second year had mostly consisted of him wandering wherever the hell he wanted, learning the limits and extent of his flying while he tried to avoid thinking too deeply about anything else.

He flew past the marshals and toward the large, square palace on the highest summit of Penglai Island. The traditional structure was divided between the eight immortals with Zhang holding the north-northwest corner as his own. Half the rooms had once belonged to Tenzin, but Tai had apportioned off several of them for Ben's use when he was there.

He flew to a training room with a retractable roof and saw a human servant stand up straight as he landed.

"Master Vecchio."

"Just Ben," he murmured, knowing it was useless to correct them. A part of him liked the formality. In a world that could be radically confusing, the structure of Penglai Island was blessedly welcome. Every type of vampire wore a different color robe, schedules were ruthlessly adhered to, and titles were respected. Servants addressed all vampires with respect and were respected in turn.

Everyone had their role, including him.

He'd landed in Penglai as the human, Benjamin Amir Santiago Vecchio, adopted son of Giovanni Vecchio, friend of Rome and Master of Iron in Lothian. He returned as Benjamin Amir Santiago Rios, Gan Jochi of the Kentii Mountains, Marshal of Penglai Island, bearer of the Laylat al Hisab, and Master of Iron in Lothian.

He walked to the bedroom Tai had made for him and dropped off the backpack he'd brought from Kashgar before stepping behind a screen and removing the dark pants and shirt he'd been wearing when he flew from Kashgar.

He used to think that Tenzin wore black as a statement, and maybe she did. Maybe that was part of it.

The other part was bugs.

So. Many. Bugs.

Flying, he'd discovered early on, was messy. Sure, once you got high enough, the bugs kind of died off, but takeoffs and landings? Lower elevations? They could be a nightmare. No one had warned him about that part, though he had a feeling that Tai and Zhang were laughing on the inside the one time he flew too low over a cabbage field in the middle of summer.

The black clothes went into the laundry that would be cleaned by silent servants, and Ben donned a simple grey robe. It was a uniform, but Ben didn't mind.

In this place, uniformity was comforting.

He stared at his grey robes in the bathroom mirror. Zhang wore white; all the elders did. The first time Ben had visited Penglai, he'd worn black. It wasn't only a warrior's color, it was the color of water, identifying him with his aunt and uncle's clan.

Now he wore grey like Tai. A concession maybe? He was Zhang's son but also Giovanni's. Or was grey simply the color Zhang had chosen for his household?

*I have no desire to separate you from your uncle or aunt. I* respect family. Nevertheless, you will not be permitted to return to them right now... You are not a water vampire or a fire vampire. You command the air.

Ben hadn't seen his family on anything other than a screen in over two years.

And Tenzin?

He hadn't seen her at all.

Memories of his human life were complicated. In the liminal space between waking and sleeping, they flooded through him, clearer than they'd ever been to his mortal mind. He remembered things from his childhood he'd never remembered as a human, facets of memories he'd hidden and locked away. Yet when he woke, even recent memories could be cloudy.

*"I need to tell you something."*

*"Tell me later."*

*"No, I need to tell you now. I need to tell you now, Tenzin."*

A tap came at the door.

"Enter."

It was Tai. The gracious vampire bowed and smiled when he saw Ben. "It's good to see you. How was Kashgar?"

"Does he know where I am all the time?" Ben buttoned his robe and straightened his collar in the mirror. Some humans thought vampires didn't cast reflections. Ha! Most vampires were incredibly vain. They'd languish in despair without mirrors.

Tai glanced around the room. "Zhang knows many people in many places."

"There was a woman there, at the oasis. She was watching me. She knew my name."

"Interesting."

"I thought so." He jerked his head toward Zhang's rooms. "So she wasn't one of his people?"

"Not that I know of, but he doesn't tell me everything."

"She told me to answer my mail."

"Ah." Tai raised a finger. "That I can help you with. It arrived yesterday." He paused and looked at Ben. "It's... substantial."

"I told Chloe just to send the important stuff."

"And I believe she did." Tai pursed his lips. "But you have to remember, you knew many vampires in your human life, and you were sired unexpectedly to a very powerful ancient."

And rumors flew fast and loose among the immortal. "Okay...?"

"Try to remember what our world runs on, Ben."

Ben shook his head. "Money?"

"Power," Tai said. "And favors. Both of which you are a source of now."

"Shit," he muttered. "Just how many letters am I looking at here?"

～

"Two hundred and thirty-seven?" Ben tried not to yell into the phone. "Chloe, why didn't you tell me?"

"Excuse me?" Her tone said she wasn't having even a little bit of it. "If you recall, I tried talking to you about your mail on a *weekly* basis. I said something every time I talked to you, and you kept brushing me off. Fabi's been sending things from Rome. Caspar's new guy... uh, Zan?"

"Zain."

"Yeah. He's been sending stuff too. You've been getting mail here, in LA, and in Rome. And it all comes to me, okay? I've been paying all your bills and dealing with your shit here, but it's not my job to answer things addressed to you. Did you even notice the piles were organized in chronological order?"

"I did notice that," he muttered. "Thank you. Did *she* take care of any of them?" He stopped short of asking if Tenzin was in New York. He didn't want to know.

Probably. Maybe. Maybe he wanted to know just so he could avoid her.

"Tenzin took care of anything addressed to the two of you or to the business." Chloe huffed out a breath. "But she's not going to touch your personal mail, Ben."

"Oh, *now* she respects boundaries?"

"I am not getting into this with you! Do not put me in the middle of your relationship issues."

"We don't have relationship issues because we don't have a relationship."

"I don't want to hear it." Chloe let out a long breath. "Seriously, every time I talked to you. Every *single* time I told you—"

"Yes, I know. You told me I had mail." Ben looked at the boxes of correspondence that had been delivered to the communications room in Penglai. "I just had no idea how much."

"One thing I noticed was that there were multiple letters from the same people. So it's possible that when you sort things out, it'll just be a lot of the same people writing you about one thing. It's not necessarily two hundred thirty-seven different things on your to-do list."

He murmured, "It's a good thing I'm in Penglai."

"Why? Because you have servants you can order around?"

"Yes." Zhang had many servants, and while Ben was usually reticent to ask for their help, this time he wasn't going to be shy. "My skin is delicate now, Chloe. I might get a paper cut."

She snorted. "Right. One suggestion?"

"Fire away. I promise I won't ignore you ever again."

"Promises, promises." He heard her shuffling papers. "There are probably tons of random requests. Tenzin explained that some of this is the vampire version of you winning the lottery. Every vampire you've ever met who thinks you like them—"

"Sadly, there's probably a lot of those."

"You weren't exactly known for being a standoffish human. Most of them are probably going to be 'Hey, my brother needs a kidney' kinds of things."

"Who needs a kidney?"

"No one probably. I just don't know what lottery winners hear. I'm guessing. Sort through the randoms, but the one you really, really need to deal with is Radu."

"Radu?"

"He sent a letter by private courier about six months after you went to Mongolia."

That stupid icon. Ben had forgotten all about it. "Don't you think she could deal with it?"

"He addressed it to you because you're the one who responded to him in the first place."

"Because Giovanni referred him to me." Ben didn't get headaches anymore, but if he did, he would name his headache Radu. The Romanian vampire had been trying to hire him for something like three years now to find a lost Russian icon.

But first they'd had to go to Puerto Rico to look for pirate treasure.

And then they'd had to go to the East China Sea to help out Tenzin's sire.

And then... Well, life—or undeath—happened.

"I'll deal with Radu," Ben said. "I may just lay things out for him and tell him we're not—"

"One thing you should know." Chloe cut him off. "With his last letter, he sent a down payment."

Okay, that was interesting. "How much of a down payment?"

"I'm not sure. But whatever the down payment is weighs about seven pounds and it makes Tenzin's eyes light up."

Both of Ben's eyebrows went up. "Gold?"

"Gold." Chloe cleared her throat. "I didn't send that part. International postage is a bitch."

"Right." Ben tapped his fingers on his knee. Did the woman in Kashgar have anything to do with Radu? She could have been Eastern European. And if he'd sent roughly a hundred grand of gold with a letter and been kept waiting for an answer for as long as Radu had, he might want the recipient to "answer their fucking mail" too.

"Okay," he said. "Radu first. Where's his letter in the pile?"

"I went ahead put that one right on top."

# 3

It took Ben a week to fly from Penglai to Los Angeles. He was still figuring out how to move efficiently through space, and he couldn't fly as fast as Zhang or Tai. But even with slower speed, the feeling was exhilarating; moving through the air was effortless. He was cocooned in his element and often he nearly slipped into a trancelike state, especially when he was going long distances.

Moving only at night meant he often had to take the long way around to avoid large bodies of water, but he didn't mind. Seeing the world from the air was awe inspiring.

As he flew from San Francisco to Los Angeles, he watched the lights below, dipping down to smell the familiar scents of salt water and kelp that were flung into the air with each crashing wave.

It was familiar and it wasn't. Ben was seeing everything through an immortal lens, and while the night's darkness was deep to humans, to Ben the reflection of the stars off the moon-pulled water was as bright as an early-morning sunrise. Nothing about the night was dark anymore. In fact, he often craved true darkness, which was much harder to achieve as a vampire.

As he flew south, the lights scattered and dimmed, twinkling sporadically through Central California until he reached Santa Barbara, where they grew brighter and denser.

As Ben approached the LA basin, the lights nearly blinded him. They lay like a thick blanket of stars covering the hills and valleys that made up the sprawling city of angels.

*Home.*

He spotted the pure white walls of the Getty Center and turned east, following the veins of light where cars sped through the city. He followed the foothill freeway and turned south in Pasadena, searching for a safe place to land.

There.

The familiar parking lot of the Huntington Library and Gardens caught his eye, and he was instantly oriented. There, the research library where his aunt had worked when she was still human. There, the alley of jacarandas that dropped lavender flowers on the asphalt where he'd ridden his bicycle as a boy, roaming the streets of San Marino and dreaming about the lives of the rich people who lived behind the walls and hedges of each compound.

Ben landed silently in the parking lot and walked toward the sprawling mansion a short distance from the library where his aunt and uncle kept their home. He passed the typical wildlife common in Los Angeles—possums hanging from trees; quick, striped skunks darting into bushes; clever cats slinking from one shadow to the next.

It was all familiar, yet nothing was the same.

When he reached the gate of the house, he rose and flew over it, triggering the silent alarm and switching on the video-recording equipment he'd set up after he graduated from high school. He waved at the cameras, then put a finger to his lips.

*Shhhh.*

Hopefully, whoever was guarding the place knew who he was, but it had been nearly three years since he'd been back in Los

Angeles. He'd been gone long enough that security might not recognize him.

He landed in the spacious backyard and spotted the recent addition of a trampoline in the corner near the house. There was a new gate around the swimming area and a bright blue bike leaning against the pool house.

Ben's heart gave three quick thumps as he sped over the lawn and paused beneath the window of the little girl who'd upended his aunt and uncle's life in various and delightful ways.

Sadia had been an orphan from the Syrian Civil War when Beatrice and Giovanni adopted her three years before. The first time Ben met Sadia, she'd been a wide-eyed, silent little girl with her thumb in her mouth, clutching a worn blanket. When she looked at him, Ben could feel her judgment and suspicion, and the wounded child inside him recognized it for what it was.

*"Do you know who I am?"*

She had looked at him with even more suspicion.

*"I'm your big brother now. And if anyone ever tries to hurt you, I will hurt them more."*

Maybe it wasn't the right thing to say to a little tiny girl days after she'd come into a brand-new home—Sadia probably didn't even understand what he was saying—but something in his tone of voice must have gotten through. In that instant, Sadia's eyes moved from suspicious to accepting; she had crawled into his lap the very next night and fallen asleep on his chest.

In the first difficult months after her adoption, Ben was often the only one who could make her laugh, and he'd done everything possible to keep in touch over video chats while he'd been away. But nothing was like *being there* when your little sister was five.

Ben tapped on the window, only to feel the cold barrel of a

gun pressing against the back of his neck. It was Dema, Sadia's scary-as-shit nanny.

"I'm surprised you didn't hear me," she said.

*I smelled you first.* He didn't say that. "I did hear you. I just know how much you love flirting with me like this." The quip was automatic. "Will you hide the gun before she comes to the window and sees you holding it on me?"

The feel of cold metal disappeared. "You really shouldn't sneak onto the grounds."

"You knew it was me." He looked over his shoulder as he tapped on Sadia's window again. "Besides, I'm *trying* to surprise her."

Dema holstered her weapon and straightened the sleek grey hijab she wore over her hair. "She's probably sound asleep. It's three in the morning, you know."

The curtain flew back, and Sadia's round little face appeared. She was rubbing her eyes and sporting a halo of messy curls. All Ben could do was smile. It had been weeks since they'd video chatted, and he swore she changed every time he saw her.

She blinked at him. Frowned. Blinked again. "Ben?"

"Surprise."

Her eyes went wide. "You came home?"

He nodded toward her door. "Put on a jacket and sneak out here."

Sadia's eyes lit up. "Come outside?"

"Yeah!"

Dema muttered, "She can't sneak out of the house. Do you know how many security features this compound has?"

"Since I installed most of them, yes, I do." He watched Sadia disappear behind her bedroom curtains. "Can you just go in there and help her 'sneak out'" —he used air quotes— "to see her big brother?"

Dema appeared unmoved.

"Please?"

She shook her head. "Don't make a habit of this, Mr. Vecchio."

"Mr. Vecchio?" He watched her retreating figure. "Really?"

A few minutes later, Sadia came racing around the side of the house with a bright yellow sweater flung over her pj's and ran straight toward him. Ben hesitated for only a fraction of a second.

Was he safe—*truly* safe—to be around this tiny, precious human?

"Ben!"

A flood of fierce protectiveness filled his mind and sharpened his senses. He noticed the chill in the air, the irregularity of the grass she ran on, and the shoelaces hastily tied. She could trip. She could injure a limb or her spine.

"Sadia, be careful." He reached down and scooped her up. There. She was safe in his arms.

"I can't believe you came home!" She was lisping a little through two missing teeth. "Do Baba and Mama know?"

Ben had no doubt that Giovanni and Beatrice were already aware he was on the grounds. They would have been informed by whoever was watching the cameras.

"I didn't tell anyone," he said. "I wanted to see you first."

"Really?" Her smile was incandescent. "Look! Did you see my tooth?" She pointed to the gap where her two bottom front teeth had been. "I lost two now, but Carina says they'll grow back."

"I remember. You showed me when we talked on the computer, remember?"

"Oh right." She wiggled down. "Want to see my bike?"

"Yes." Ben followed her to the bright blue bike on the patio.

"Right now it has extra wheels, but when I'm bigger, Baba can take them off and then I'll be able to go really fast." She looked over her shoulder. "Want to see?"

"Definitely." Ben crouched down and watched her take off on the little bike.

"See how fast I can go!" She was panting. "And I can go even faster in the front when Zain moves all the cars."

"Be careful, okay?"

"I will!"

Ben watched her pedal three large circles on the patio before she climbed off. He saw curtains twitching on the second floor and knew Giovanni and Beatrice had spotted them, but thankfully they held back from coming down to the garden.

"Want to see my trampoline?" She bounced on her toes. "We just got it, but I'm already really good."

Ben picked her up. He knew she didn't need to be held, but he couldn't help himself. She was so delicate but so full of life. His emotions were all over the place. He was happy. Ecstatic. He was sad he'd missed so many years. He wanted Tenzin to be there. He hated that he would never see Sadia in the sunlight again.

"I saw your trampoline." He swallowed his emotions and focused on her. "Do you know any tricks?" They walked toward the far corner of the garden where a blue-and-red trampoline rose in the shadows of oak trees. A large net surrounded it, presumably to catch any errant bounces.

"I know tricks like jumping really high and doing the splits—"

"Really?"

"*Kinda* doing the splits. And... mmm... spinning in the air." She held her fingers straight up and twisted them. "Like I kind of *jump*... and then I spin."

"That's amazing."

She absently tapped his cheek. "Baba said you can fly now."

He stopped in his tracks and forced himself to look at Sadia. "Uh... yeah. I can."

Her eyes were wide but unafraid. "Can I see your teeth?"

Ben had avoided the request when she made it over video chat, but he couldn't avoid it forever. Something about showing his fangs to Sadia made being a vampire even more real. That was who he would be from then on. A vampire to the world and to the smallest and most vulnerable member of his family.

"Do you really want to see them?" His voice was quiet.

She nodded forcefully. "Yes."

"You're not afraid?"

Sadia frowned like he'd spoken an unknown language. "Why?"

"Right."

Why would Sadia be afraid? Her father and mother were vampires. Her aunts and uncles were vampires. She'd been surrounded by them for years. Ben took a breath and opened his mouth. Just thinking about the scent of blood was enough to make his fangs lengthen.

Sadia stared and stared. In the end, she looked a little unimpressed.

"What?"

She sighed. "You don't have curvy fangs like Tenzin. Just the same ones like Baba and Mama."

Even the mention of her name after two years felt like a spike driving into his chest. Ben swept the net back and placed Sadia on the trampoline. "Sorry. They're just normal fangs."

"That's okay. They're nice anyway." Sadia began bouncing. "Where's Tenzin?"

Sadia loved Tenzin, and she mentioned her at least once a call. Though he hadn't seen or talked to his former partner in over two years, Sadia still linked the two of them in her mind, probably because Tenzin and Ben had been together when she was young.

Needless to say, he wasn't surprised she was asking about her.

"I don't know where she is, Sadi."

"Maybe she's at your house in New York. Look!" She jumped and spun in a circle. "See, I did a twist. Do you know you're the only one who calls me Sadi?"

"Excellent twist." He watched her. Watched the springs and

the net. "I'm the only one who calls you Sadi because I'm your only big brother."

She kept bouncing. "Why do you call Baba and Mama by their name and not baba and mama?"

It wasn't the first time she'd asked. "Because when they adopted me, I was a lot older than you."

"Oh." She attempted a move that looked a little like the splits. "Is Tenzin" —*bounce*— "coming" —*bounce*— "soon?"

"I don't think so."

"When I grow up, I want my fangs to be curvy like Tenzin's."

Ben smiled. "You only get fangs if you become a vampire, silly."

Sadia bounced over to him and rolled her eyes, letting her head fall back. "I know *that*."

"So you're saying you want to become a vampire?"

"Yeah!"

"Why?"

*Bounce.* "Because" —*bounce*— "my whole family" —*bounce*— "is vampires." *Bounce.* "*Silly.*"

"Right." She made it sound so simple. As if she was going to grow up and inherit the family restaurant or take over the farm. "Well, it's a very grown-up decision. You know that, right?"

"I know." She stopped bouncing and wove her fingers through the net, leaning to the side and letting her hair hang upside down. "Baba said I can only decide when I'm really old like you."

"I'm old?" He poked her in the side and she giggled.

"Yes. *Really* old."

"Well, you're my sister, so if I'm old, you must be old. And short."

She stood up straight and looked at him, her mouth hanging open in outrage. "I'm the second-tallest girl in my class!"

"Oh." He turned around and patted his shoulders. Sadia got the message and jumped onto them. "My mistake." He started walking back to the house with Sadia hanging on his back, swinging her legs and humming a song. "You must be very tall then."

"Ben?"

"Yes?"

"Are you staying home for a while?"

He considered how to answer. "I may need to go away for work next week, but then when I finish with that, I promise I won't stay away for so long again."

"Ever again?" She leaned over his shoulder. "Promise?"

He bumped her forehead with his own. "I promise."

"Good." She put her chin on his shoulder. "I miss you when you're gone."

"I miss you too."

"And I miss Tenzin." She sighed. "I love Tenzin so much."

Ben bit his lip. "I know you do."

"Is Tenzin coming soon?"

"I don't think so, Sadi."

"Why not? Is she working?"

"I think so." The lie slipped too easily from his lips, but he didn't know what else to tell her. "Has she video-called you?"

"Yes. With me and Baba. She showed me your birds in New York."

Ben stopped. "My birds?"

"Yeah. The pretty little birds that live in the glass house."

"Oh right." The spike twisted in his heart. "Those birds."

"I like their names." She giggled. "Tenzin said they were *love*birds."

"Uh-huh."

"Loooovebirds." Sadia couldn't stop the giggles. "'Cause they love each other."

Ben couldn't stop the smile at hearing her giggle so much. "I think you're tired and you need to go to bed."

"Do lovebirds kiss with their beaks?" She was still giggling in his ear. "I bet they kiss a lot, like Baba and Mama."

Ben shook his head. "I think you've been infected with a case of the sillies."

His words only made Sadia laugh harder. And for the first time in a long time, all was right in Ben Vecchio's world.

**4**

———

The De Novo-Vecchio predawn family celebration lasted until exactly dawn, when Ben abruptly fell into a deep vampire sleep. When he woke the next night, it was to a smell that was more welcome than the sweetest, freshest, most delectably pure blood in the world.

He sat up in the dark closet and inhaled deeply.

Dried chiles. Cumin. Corn. Sweet heaven and all the angels.

"Mexican food."

Ben nearly tripped over the bedsheets he stood so quickly.

Throwing on clothes and glancing at the clock, he realized that jet leg wasn't really going to be a thing anymore. Young vampires woke when the sun went down and knocked out when it rose. A few quirky ones like Beatrice and Tenzin woke during the day. And his uncle woke a little bit since he and Beatrice exchanged blood.

*You exchanged blood with Tenzin.*

He shoved that inconvenient voice to the back of his brain. It had only been once. Just the one time, and it would not be happening again.

When he left the room he'd used since he was twelve years

old, he was met by the cacophony of voices that was normal in a busy family home.

"Mama, I want juice."

"Is that the way you ask?"

"*Princesa*, here is some juice. Zain, give the baby—"

"Grandma, she has to ask politely. And she is not a baby. If you give in—"

"Thank you, Zain!"

"You are welcome, Miss Sadia." A deep male voice echoed down the hall. "Miss Isadora, what are you wanting to drink tonight?"

"A juice sounds good to me too."

Good Lord, had chatter in the house always been that loud to Giovanni and Beatrice? No wonder they'd tried to kick him outside so often. Though the voices were coming from the kitchen, Ben heard them like they were in the same room.

He walked through the familiar halls of his childhood, taking everything in with new eyes. Had he ever noticed the stunning swirls of blue in that ceramic vase? There were so many cracks in that oil painting! It nearly ruined it. No wonder Tenzin didn't have much use for stealing oils.

Ben walked down the hallway and stood in the kitchen doorway, crossing his arms and waiting for someone to notice him. Beatrice's eyes flew up to meet his, but he put a finger over his lips. *Shhhh*. She smiled and played along.

Sitting at the kitchen table like a queen before her court was Isadora De Novo, Beatrice's grandmother and Caspar's wife. She was overseeing the construction of enchiladas in a glass pan on the table while a dark-skinned man, his locks tied back with a bandanna, moved between the kitchen and the table, a neat apron wrapped around his waist.

"Now, no one needs to be eating any more snacks before

dinner." The man handed a glass to Isadora. "Miss Izzie, I'm looking at you."

Sadia spotted him. "Ben!"

"Benjamin?" Isadora's smile was wide and wonderful. "You're *home*." She said it with such relief Ben nearly started crying.

"Hi, Isadora."

Sadia raced over and climbed into his arms. "How's your room? Do you like your new closet?"

"Very much." Ben looked over at the recent addition to the household. "You must be Zain." With Sadia in one arm, he walked over and held his hand toward the young man. "Ben Vecchio. Really nice to meet you."

The corner of the man's mouth lifted as he shook Ben's outstretched hand. "Trust me, I've heard all about you. Welcome home." He moved to the stove. "Dinner should be ready in a half hour or so. I'm making chicken mole. Isadora's recipe."

"That sounds amazing. I haven't had Mexican food in like two years."

Zain smiled. "That's just wrong. We'll make fish tacos tomorrow."

"I like you already." Ben looked down as Sadia patted his cheek. "What's up, gremlin?"

"Zain drives me to school in the morning sometimes."

"You told me he's a very good driver."

"And when he fights with Dema, he moves *super*fast!" She made punching motions with her arms. "You should see him. His muscles are *really* big."

"Oh yeah?" He glanced at Zain, who was smiling and stirring the mole.

Superfast, huh? Ben bet Dema loved that. The minute he'd clapped eyes on the man, Ben had pegged him for far more than a driver. The way he moved had the same efficiency that Dema had, the same efficiency Ben had cultivated when he'd been human.

"Are you from LA?" Ben sidled over to the counter.

Zain looked up. "Houston originally. I've been here for about six years now. My mother worked for Caspar and Gio back in the day."

"When I heard he'd moved to Los Angeles, I ruthlessly stole him from Ernesto." A cultured voice spoke in a posh British accent from the door. "One of my finer negotiations, if I do say so."

Ben turned to see Caspar walking in from the breezeway. "Caspar."

"Of course, the hardest part was convincing Zain to move away from the beach."

Ben walked over, memories rushing like a waterfall.

"Come here and let me look at you." The old man was using a cane these days, and his shoulders were significantly stooped. But his voice and his eyes were strong.

Walking behind him came Ben's uncle, Giovanni Vecchio.

"Baba!" Sadia wiggled down and ran to her father to be picked up, carefully swerving around Caspar as Ben walked to meet him.

Caspar had been Giovanni's child once. Then his ward, his driver, his day person. His security and confidant. His friend. And one of the few people in the world Ben had trusted almost immediately, not that he'd made it easy on Caspar when he'd been a punk twelve-year-old convinced everyone was out to get him.

"I missed you." Ben stood in front of Caspar and the old man looked up. Once, Ben had been the one looking up.

Caspar clapped him on the shoulders and looked him directly in the eyes. "It's a fine thing."

*Is it?* Ben said nothing.

The old man patted his cheek as if he'd been reading Ben's mind. "A fine thing," he said slowly. "In the end you'll see."

"I really missed you." Ben put his arm around Caspar's shoulders and guided him toward the kitchen table.

Beatrice rose and took the glass pan of enchiladas to the

33

kitchen, sliding them in the oven as Giovanni moved to her and greeted her with a kiss. "Can I help?"

"Oh, please don't." Beatrice smiled. "We'd like dinner to be edible for Ben's first night home."

Sadia leaned on Giovanni's shoulder. "Baba made me macaroni and cheese last night."

"Did he?"

"Yes," Giovanni said pertly. "I did."

"Was it from a box?" Beatrice asked.

"Yes. A blue box. And it was this big" —Sadia held out her hands— "and I ate the whole thing."

Ben sat next to Isadora and leaned over to kiss her cheek.

"It's about time you said hello to me," she said. "Turning into an immortal better not have ruined your manners."

"I promise it hasn't. But it has spoiled my appetite."

Isadora dearly loved cooking gigantic meals for Ben when he was growing up. He ate like a horse, and Isadora delighted in feeding him.

"Then I will only say that it is a very good thing that Zain moved in." Isadora clasped his hand in her fine fingers. "I'm teaching him all my recipes, and he eats like a grown man and not a vampire."

"Good." Ben smiled. "What have you been painting?"

"Tenzin sent us a lovely picture of your birds, so I'm painting a watercolor for Sadia's room since she likes them so much."

Ben knew Isadora knew the whole story. He lowered his voice. "Why does everyone keep referring to them as my birds?"

Isadora smiled slowly. "Because they are."

HOURS LATER, with dinner dishes clean and small girls tucked into bed, Ben, Beatrice, and Giovanni sat in the family library, drinking scotch and talking about work.

Of course, it wasn't the main Vecchio library. That was in Perugia and contained a treasure trove of classical manuscripts and alchemical literature by humans and vampire scholars.

And it wasn't the Alvarez New World library that Beatrice had recently been consulting for. That would be a similar collection of historical literature and accounts from North, Central, and South America sponsored by Beatrice's many-times-great-grandfather, Don Ernesto Alvarez.

No, it was just their small family library that took up nearly the entire second floor of the mansion in San Marino.

What could he say? Ben came from a family of book nerds. Giovanni Vecchio might have once been a feared assassin, a fire vampire of ancient lineage and remarkable power, and Beatrice might have been renowned for her wits and political acumen at vampire courts all over the world, but in the end?

Giant, giant book nerds.

Giovanni was examining the three letters from Radu, the Romanian vampire who wanted to hire Ben. "You do realize he thinks he's getting both you and Tenzin, don't you?"

Ben bristled. "I realize that, but I'm hoping that with a little of your help, I can do the job myself and not need her."

Giovanni raised an eyebrow but didn't lift his eyes from the letters. "I did a little research on this icon when the job first came up. I confess, it's more interesting than most of the antiquities you and Tenzin go after."

He had to stop reacting to her name. It was everywhere, and he wasn't going to stop people from using it. She was too integrated into his family. "You're telling me Radu's icon is more interesting than a ninth-century sword preserved perfectly in blown glass, sitting at the bottom of the ocean for a thousand years?"

Beatrice let out a longing sigh. "I really need to see this thing."

Ben turned to her. "It's incredible. Seriously. Incredible."

"The icon" —Giovanni tried to steer them back on course— "is a rare one. I will give Radu that. But Russian icons—normally speaking—would not fetch the kind of money he's offering, which tells me that this job is more about sentiment than profit."

"Good." Ben paged through the file Beatrice slid across the table. "He won't quit paying until I find it."

"*Not* good," Giovanni said. "That means he won't be rational about it if you don't. It's personal. And from my initial research, there's a reason no one has been able to find it in a couple hundred years."

"Look." Beatrice nodded toward the closest library wall where a screen was slowly lowering. "I taught him to use PowerPoint presentations."

Ben frowned. "Did you give him a laser pointer?"

"Yep."

"Then may God have mercy on us all."

"Do not let Radu fool you." Giovanni continued, completely ignoring them both. "This job is far from the ordinary smash and grab you and Tenzin enjoy."

Ben looked at his aunt. "He's trying to use slang again."

"I know," Beatrice whispered. "Just let him. He thinks it makes him more relatable."

Giovanni switched on the projector with a long stylus that wouldn't short out the machine. "The icon Radu wants is the oldest known depiction of Saint Sara-la-Kali."

"Not familiar with her."

"She's not well known outside of a few rather insular communities. Sara's story goes back to the legend of the Three Marys in Southern France. Sara was supposedly their servant but a saint in her own right as well. This icon Radu is looking for was a double-sided icon." He tapped the stylus on his tablet, and a picture came up of a gold-laden icon of the Virgin Mary and Jesus. "On one side, an Eleusa-type icon of the Madonna, supposedly painted by Saint Luke the Evangelist. This *isn't* the one on your icon. It's a picture of something similar painted in the same style, also purportedly by Saint Luke."

"Wait, *the* Saint Luke? The one from the Bible?"

"The exact one." Giovanni tapped the stylus and another image popped up. "And on the other side—added far later, you'd have to suppose—was an icon of Saint Sara. This is a painting of the icon included in an art inventory dating back to the eighteenth century, but as you can see, the depiction is very detailed."

Ben leaned forward to examine the painting. The woman's skin was a dark reddish brown, and her hair was depicted in tight black curls clipped close to her head. She was beautiful and had the large, peaceful eyes of many Orthodox icons. But there was something familiar about her features...

"I've seen this before."

"I very much doubt that," Giovanni said. "The last time anyone saw the icon of Saint Sara-la-Kali was in Budapest in 1835." He flipped to the next slide, showing a picture of a gold-robed man draped in a red sash. "Before it was taken from the treasury of this man, Francis the Second, the last Holy Roman Emperor and later King of Hungary and Bohemia."

Ben leaned back and crossed his arms. "Okay, so maybe I haven't seen this *exact* icon."

## 5

"I think you should take the plane." Giovanni sipped a glass of golden scotch in front of the fire. "I know you can fly now, but the plane is faster. Plus it gives you a safe haven and a quick exit should anything become complicated."

The idea of flying around in his uncle's plane irked Ben, and he didn't understand why. He'd been touchy ever since he arrived home. It didn't make sense. Ben felt like a teenager again, overreacting to everything. Offended by the slightest suggestion he wasn't doing things right.

They were sitting in the library, having a drink and talking about life and work. It was a thing they had done a hundred—maybe a thousand—times before. And yet Ben couldn't relax. He felt uneasy. Constantly on edge.

He rubbed a hand over his beard and glanced at his uncle. "I know what you're saying is right, but—"

"But you don't want to." Giovanni smiled a little. "Because the plane is an extension of my territory."

*Oh.* Ben blinked. "Is that... Is that what's going on?"

Giovanni turned toward him. "I've tried to hide my reaction, but I'm not immune to it either."

Ben stood and paced in front of the fire. "So I'm going to be on edge in my childhood home from now on? That's not okay, Gio. I don't consider you a threat." Ben turned to him. "At all. Ever."

Giovanni stood and put a hand on his shoulder. "Be calm."

Ben saw the flames in the fireplace whipping back and forth wildly. He took a deep breath.

"I don't consider you a threat. I never would. These are our *instincts*, Benjamin. You are not human anymore. You were turned very recently by an enormously powerful and ancient vampire. Very few vampires can even imagine the changes your body and mind are going through right now, simply because of the power in your sire's blood. My amnis reacts because it knows you're a dangerous predator, and you're in proximity to my mate and my child."

Ben swallowed hard and had to fight back tears. Another over-reaction. "Should I leave?"

"Of course not." Giovanni pulled him into a hug. "You're not the first powerful vampire who's ever been in the house. Think about Carwyn or Tenzin. It's just the newness. Sadia and Beatrice have been around *Kato*, Ben. He's far more threatening than you are."

"What do we do?"

"Nothing." Giovanni pulled away and rubbed Ben's hair like he'd done when Ben barely came up to his shoulder. "We do nothing. Like so many things in this life, we acknowledge the feeling and we give it time. It's going to be rough for a while, but this feeling will pass. Our amnis will recognize each other as family, and we'll be easy with each other again."

Ben swallowed hard. "I am fighting the urge to punch you right now."

"Completely understandable." Giovanni released him. "Tenzin and I were uneasy around each other for decades. Of course, I was initially hired to kill her, so that didn't help."

The sound of her name made Ben flinch.

"Another instinctive reaction," Giovanni said quietly. "But a very human one."

"She betrayed me."

"I know that's how you feel."

Ben ignored the surreptitious response. "Do you talk to her?"

"I do."

Ben's eyes rose. "Does Beatrice?"

"No."

"Why not?"

"In all ways but blood, she is your mother, Benjamin. She is angry on your behalf."

"She and Tenzin were family once." Part of him was satisfied and another part mourned. "I don't want... I don't know what I want."

Giovanni looked to the fire. "You can love someone and still be angry with them."

"Are you angry with her?"

His uncle said nothing.

Ben felt his fangs lengthen. He willed them back. "Are you?"

Giovanni put a hand over his heart and turned toward him. His eyes were full of pain. "Did you see Caspar at dinner? Did you sense it?"

"What does Caspar have to do—?"

"He has everything to do with you and your anger toward her. With me and *my* anger. Because I am watching him die, Ben. And even though he has had a good and long life—the life he wanted—I will lose..." Giovanni cleared his throat. "I will lose a part of my soul when Caspar is gone."

Ben fought back his emotions. "But he made a choice and you respected that. I didn't—"

"No." Giovanni shook his head. "I know you didn't. But how

can I remain angry with her, Benjamin? How can I resent her for saving my son's life?"

"She knew." His fangs fell and he didn't try to stop them. "She knew how I felt. I made her promise so many times—"

"I couldn't have watched you die." The words rushed out of Giovanni's mouth in a quiet torrent. He clutched the hand over his heart into a fist. "Is that what you want to hear? Or *need* to hear? God forgive me, but I couldn't have watched you die when I knew I could save you. Would you have forgiven *me*?"

"You're my uncle." Ben swallowed hard. "It's not the same."

"But she was your friend. And I know there was more, but before anything else, you were her *friend*, Benjamin. She doesn't have many." Giovanni's eyes drilled into him. "She lost Stephen. She lost Nima. Did you think she could lose you too?"

Ben looked away. He couldn't face the raw pain in his uncle's eyes anymore. "You're saying I was selfish?"

"Maybe."

"She didn't have to take me." He walked to the table and threw back the glass of whiskey he'd poured earlier. "She didn't have to keep dragging me back. I was trying to get out, and she kept pulling me back."

"And you kept answering the call." Giovanni put his hands in his trouser pockets and stared at the fire. "She asked you to swim, but you dove into the deep end. Living that life was never only her choice."

Ben stared at his uncle, wanting to hug him. Wanting to fight him. Wanting to erase the words Giovanni had just said from his mind.

*You were her friend, Benjamin. She doesn't have many.*

"I'll take the plane," Ben said quietly. "You're right. I'll be able to move faster."

Giovanni kept his eyes toward the fire and nodded.

"I'm also going to ask Chloe to come with me to Bucharest, so it'll be more comfortable for her to fly privately."

"If Chloe goes, Gavin will go too."

Ben took a long breath. "I'm counting on it."

Giovanni looked at her. "Asking her to swim?"

"Yes. But unlike Tenzin, Gavin will make damn sure she doesn't jump into the deep end."

IT WAS early morning in New York and just before dawn when Ben managed to catch Chloe on the phone.

"Gavin's already on his way to LA." Her voice was cheerful. "He kind of figured you might need me, and he says it works out because he has three places in Eastern Europe he needs to check on anyway. I'll email Radu's people now and set up a meet for the two of you in Bucharest."

"I'll book you a flight tonight if that's enough time. You can take the red-eye."

"It's enough time as long as you're putting me in first class."

Ben smiled. "Of course I am."

She sighed deeply. "I do love working for rich people."

"And we'll take Gio's plane to Bucharest."

"I'm going to be ruined for economy flights," Chloe said. "I better stick with you from now on."

"You'll be support staff *only* on this, okay? You're not going to be sneaking through corridors and breaking into museums like you did in New York."

"You're so responsible now," Chloe said. "Fine. You know I'm not an adrenaline junkie like you anyway."

"I was never an adrenaline junkie."

Chloe laughed out loud. "You're adorable."

Ben ignored her laughter. "I'll book you a flight and text you the details. Pack for three weeks."

"Got it."

Chloe hung up, and Ben walked back to the garden where Beatrice and Sadia were swimming in the heated pool.

"Do it again, Mama!" Sadia's laughter flew through the air.

"Okay, hold your arms out."

Ben sat on a chaise and watched Beatrice lift her daughter into the air, raising a column of water under Sadia's arms and legs as the little girl laughed and wiggled.

"It tickles!"

"High enough?"

"Higher!"

"Just a little bit." Beatrice's face was glowing. "One, two, three... Dive!"

In an instant, Sadia pointed her arms over her head and puffed her cheeks out to hold her breath. The column fell back into the pool, softening Sadia's landing. The little girl flipped head over heels before she swam under the water like a fish, heading toward the shallow end.

"She's a good swimmer," Ben said.

"She is." Beatrice sat on the steps of the pool as Sadia surfaced. "Did you hear Ben? He was complimenting you on your swimming."

Sadia's smile was huge. "I can swim all the way across the pool. Want to see?"

"Yes."

She immediately flung herself into an enthusiastic crawl, her arms wheeling and her legs kicking as she moved through the water.

"Is she on the swim team?"

"Not yet." Beatrice leaned against the edge, her hair piled on top of her head in a bun. "Dema and Zain would be the ones to enroll her if she wanted to do it. Right now we're still keeping close to home or school."

Sadia attended the discreet and very private school that Ben had also attended as a child. It was run by and for the day people of immortal clans. All the children knew about vampires, and none of them had to hide their unusual families or parents' jobs from unknowing classmates.

"When do you think she'll be ready to hide things?"

Beatrice snorted. "Never? I've never met a blunter child."

"Not even me?"

"You?" Beatrice looked at him from the side of her eyes while she kept her focus on Sadia. "You were the opposite of blunt. You were the most politic teenager ever. You wanted to make everyone happy and get your way at the same time."

"Isn't that everyone?"

"Maybe." Beatrice narrowed her eyes. "But you weren't manipulative. You never did anything you thought would hurt people. You just... tried to cheerfully arrange the people in your life so you got the exact outcome you wanted."

Ben frowned. *But wasn't that how everyone worked?*

"Don't get me wrong, you were a great kid. But more than once, I caught you doing something, started to object, then realized you'd actually gotten me to give you permission in some tricky way."

Ben smiled. "I did get away with a lot."

"And your uncle didn't help. He treated you like a miniature adult. Tenzin—" She broke off and clapped for Sadia when she surfaced at the end of the pool. "Good job, Sadia!"

The little girl panted. "Okay, I'm coming back now."

"Then we need to go read before bed."

The little girl gave a pained expression. "Nooooo."

"Yes."

Sadia looked at Ben.

He shook his head. "Don't look at me, kid. I can't overrule her."

Sadia whispered loudly, "But you can fly me away and hide me."

Ben chuckled. "Tomorrow night."

She perked up. "Promise?"

Beatrice shrugged when Ben looked at her. "It won't be the first time she's flown."

"Because Tenzin flies me!" Sadia flung herself back into the pool.

"What were you going to say?" Ben asked. "About her?"

Beatrice looked at him, then looked away. "Just that..." Her voice was flat. "She never seemed to realize you also weren't an adult. She never treated you like a child."

Mentally, Ben couldn't help but think: *Since we've had sex, it would be super weird if she had. Definitely, majorly weird.* "To be fair, I wasn't exactly a normal sixteen-year-old."

He'd killed for the first time when he'd been sixteen. It wasn't the first time he'd seen someone die, but was the first time he'd killed someone.

"I know you weren't," Beatrice said. "But I tried to give you something approaching a normal childhood." She reached for Sadia and lifted the little girl out of the pool. "Is she a girl or a fish?" She turned her back and forth, pretending to check her neck. "Ben, do you see any gills?"

"I think she hides them." He walked over and pushed Sadia's dripping hair out of the way. "Where are they, Sadi?"

Sadia laughed. "I don't have gills."

"I don't know..."

She scrambled out of Beatrice's arms and ran toward the chairs.

"No running," Ben and Beatrice said at the same time.

"I'm not." She slowed to a very fast walk. "I'm walking fast."

"Okay, well fast-walk into your towel and then into the house please."

"Okaaaay." Sadia disappeared under a blue shark-shaped towel before she fast-walked into the house.

Ben turned to Beatrice. "She's so great."

His aunt smiled. "We were worried about attachment issues with her, but she's such a survivor. Stubborn as a little mule sometimes, but that's just who she is."

"She's great." Ben watched Beatrice. "Giovanni said you're not talking to her."

"To Sadi— Oh." Beatrice shook her head. "To *her*. No."

"When she visits—"

"I'm not going to fight with him," she said. "They've been friends for too long, and Sadia adores her. But I don't have to like it, and I don't have to hang around." She stood and Ben watched in mild fascination as she shook and the water fled from her skin. No towel. No drips. "I usually go to Dez's house when she comes."

"Does she visit a lot?"

Beatrice shrugged. "A few times over the past couple of years."

He stuck his hands in his pockets. "Why?"

"For the baby. Sadia loves her, and she asks..." Beatrice wrapped a deep blue robe around herself. "Giovanni says she's different."

"Different how?"

She shrugged. "Who knows? She's like five thousand years old, Ben. Do you really think anyone that old can change?"

"I don't know."

"I doubt it." Beatrice walked toward the house. "I highly doubt it."

## 6

Ben was sleeping when Chloe arrived the next day. He woke and heard her cheerful voice in the kitchen, chatting with Dema, Sadia, and Zain.

"And then at school I have three friends."

"Only three?"

"I play with everyone." Sadia's voice was cautious. "But friends are different."

"I think you're right," Chloe said.

"Dema says you don't have to be friends with everyone, just be polite."

"That's good advice."

Ben paused outside the kitchen door.

"Real friends..." Sadia took a breath. "Those are more special, and Lara Bright, I am not friends with her because she pushed my friend Jason down during free playing time and she's mean."

Maybe Ben needed to find this Lara Bright and have a talk with her...

"But what did you do when Lara pushed Jason?" Dema's voice was slow and steady. "Did you push her back?"

A long sigh from Sadia. "Yes."

"And did you get in trouble?"

"Yes, because I should have told a teacher and not pushed Lara harder."

Ben could hear the amusement in Chloe's voice. "You pushed her harder?"

"Yes."

*Good.* Ben approved of that tactic. Little Lara Bright wouldn't be pushing Sadia or Jason again if he had to guess.

"Tenzin told me that's what you need to do if there's a bully," Sadia said. "If someone hurts you or your friend, then you hurt them back more so they don't do it again."

Freaking Tenzin. Again. Ben scowled.

"And we'll talk about that tactic when you're older," Dema said. "But for now, when there is a teacher or responsible adult close by, you tell that adult, all right?"

"But what if—"

"No buts." Ben walked into the kitchen and rubbed the top of Sadia's head. "That was good advice from Dema, and I bet Baba and Mama agreed with it."

Sadia looked up with large, dark eyes. "Baba did, but Mama didn't say anything."

Ben muttered, "This family is full of vengeful females." He looked over to Chloe. "Hey you."

Chloe was looking at him, her lips pressed together. "Hey."

He could see some kind of emotion shimmering in her eyes, and he held out his arms. "Two years and I don't get a hug?"

Chloe blinked hard and walked over to Ben, throwing her arms around him.

"Big dumb boy," she whispered. "I missed you so much. Don't you ever go away for so long again."

"Missed you too." He pressed his cheek to her hair and inhaled her scent. Chloe smelled like vanilla and plain soap. She'd never worn perfume, but her scent was distinct and comforting. "I'm sorry I took so long."

She leaned back and looked up at Ben, examining him carefully. "The eyes are throwing me. They're more noticeable in person. Really bright."

"I'm still not used to them."

"You're paler." She patted his cheek. "Other than that, you look the same."

"You want to see my fangs?"

Chloe threw up a hand. "I've already seen them on the screen. Don't be weird."

Sadia was bouncing on a barstool. "They're just *normal* fangs. They're not curvy like Tenzin's."

Seriously? Sadia was going to end up giving Ben a complex about his boring fangs.

"Hey," he said. "Isn't it your bath time?"

"No."

"Are you sure?" Ben asked. "I can always throw you in the pool."

"No!" Sadia giggled and slipped down the barstool; then she ran into the living room. "Dema, get him!"

Dema eyed Ben before she followed her charge. "Great. Now she's going to want to swim."

Zain piped up from the kitchen. "Not before dinner."

Chloe shook her head. "That poor kid has like four parents."

Ben snorted. "Hardly. She has two parents and an assortment of adults who fawn over her. Nothing poor about that kid."

Zain smiled. "Gonna have to agree with Ben on that one, Miss Reardon."

"Please call me Chloe. I've been in and out of this house since I was fifteen, so I'm hardly a guest."

"Chloe then." Zain was eyeing her appreciatively.

Ben narrowed his eyes at Zain. "When's Gavin coming into town?"

"He should be here tonight," Chloe said. "Not sure what time."

"You know they have those GPS-tracker things."

Her eyebrows went up. "I'll have to suggest that. Sounds exactly like something Gavin would love."

Ben smirked. "It's just a suggestion. Those wind vampires are hard to track."

"Speaking of that, do you know where Tenzin is?"

Ben's smile fell. "Why would I know that?"

Chloe shrugged. "She left New York last week. Said it was something about work. I thought maybe she left you a message."

"We don't chat."

"Well, maybe you should. You know, she's not the same—"

"Not interested." Ben walked out of the kitchen and into the front garden.

The house in San Marino was built on two acres in the middle of the city. It was more of an estate than a house, and a tall stucco wall surrounded it. Green vines crawled over the walls, and dense trees and hedges sheltered the house from curious onlookers.

"Ben!" Chloe yelled from the house. "Come on. Get back here."

Ben crossed the gravel driveway. He wanted out of the house. He wanted to fly so fast the wind burned against his face, but before he could take off, he saw Gavin landing on the far side of the front lawn, just inside the gate.

Security rushed forward, but Ben intervened. "Wait! He's a friend."

The guard lifted a radio to his mouth as Gavin brushed off his shirt.

"Vecchio." Gavin offered him half a smile. "You still walk like a human."

"Thanks?"

"It's been a few years."

"Two actually."

"Over two. Have you lost track of time already?" Gavin's Scottish brogue was evened out. He had his company voice on. "Usually takes a hundred years or so for that to happen."

Ben stood at a distance, his hands in his pockets as Gavin's amnis pushed at his. He and the wind vampire had been friends for over a decade, but their elemental energy was unfamiliar. They poked and prodded, measuring the other vampire's power.

"Keep the heid." Gavin finally smiled. "Yer a powerful little bastard, aren't ye?"

The other vampire's amnis retreated so abruptly Ben nearly wondered if he'd been imagining it. Maybe that was the point.

"So." The Scottish vampire wandered over. "Is my woman here?"

"Yes. And she already brought Tenzin up."

Gavin offered him a shrug. "Tenzin's been around. This time you're the one who disappeared."

"Seems like it was my turn."

"And you'll get no argument from me. Be angry if you like, just don't expect me to be sorry you're alive."

"That's pretty much the reaction I'm getting around here."

Gavin slapped him on his shoulder. "It must be such a burden to be shackled with so many people who give a flaming arse you're alive. Where's Chloe?"

"The kitchen."

"Excellent." Gavin left him on the lawn and strode toward the house without a backward glance.

Ben watched Gavin leave. He spotted Sadia running through the backyard, Dema trailing behind her. He could hear Giovanni and Beatrice speaking quietly in the library and Zain making small talk with Chloe.

It was familiar. It was home.

It was suffocating.

Ben took off into the air, grateful for the soft cocoon of coastal fog that blanketed the San Gabriel Valley that night. He moved soundlessly through the clouds, moving by instinct and scent toward the heavy wisteria arbors at the Huntington Gardens.

Descending into the rose garden, he spotted the gates of the Japanese garden and walked toward them.

In the middle of the night, the park was serene. The only sounds were an owl hooting in the distance, a mockingbird call, and the quick flap of bats hunting through the gardens from their roosts in the palm trees.

Ben walked through the gate of the Japanese garden and sat under the wisteria arbor to survey the silent sanctuary. He'd spent summers here as a child. When he closed his eyes, he could see the sago palms and maple trees bathed in golden sunlight, the pools with darting koi, their tails cutting through the reflected sky.

*You will never see that again.*

*You will never see your shadow during the day or feel the sun on your skin.*

*You will never watch a sunrise or a sunset.*

It was a process, this litany. Like deliberately cutting off a limb that was already dead. Every now and then he forgot. Then he remembered and that limb twitched again, a phantom pain spiking through his heart.

*"I remember what I said that night. But I'm not that man anymore. I'm not a man at all. I don't know what I am."*

*"You are still you."*

Was he? Some nights he felt like himself, and some nights he was so filled with overwhelming anger he felt like he was choking on it. A year after he'd fled to Mongolia with Zhang, he flew out over the mountains and screamed as long and as loud as he could.

He felt better for a night. When he woke up the next night, the swelling rage nearly overtook him again.

*"All things have roots and branches. Every being has their end and their beginning."*

Zhang's words came back to Ben as he sat in the silence of the garden.

Roots and branches.

*"We don't have an end. We're immortal."*

*"All things have ends, and one immortal may have many lives. That does not mean there are no endings and no beginnings, but when one branch is cut off, another grows. You will have to find peace with your end before you can grow into your beginning."*

Roots and branches. Beginnings and endings.

His human life had ended. A branch cut off.

Ben stood and walked through the garden, over the bridges, and up to the teahouse, climbing to the Zen garden and the bonsai garden beyond.

*"Where one branch is cut, a bud will grow."*

*"So this life is a bud?"*

*"In a sense. If you want new growth, the old must be cut away."*

Ben didn't feel new. He felt shackled by his roots, but he was unwilling to pull away. He'd worked hard to find people and places that were his own. Cutting them off wasn't an option.

*"All branches grow from the same root."* Zhang was pruning his grape vines in Penglai. *"Cut off this branch, and the new bud comes. But it all comes from the same root. The root never changes. Will this branch have different grapes than the old one? Of course not. The root stays true."*

Ben walked along the path above the creek, through the dark canopy of camellia bushes, toward the Chinese garden in the distance.

*"You are still you."*

She didn't know. How could she? She was so old, the idea of her mortal life so remote it was a myth. The man Ben had been was dead, and the vampire he was now...

He didn't know who he was.

Ben passed through the camellias and walked under the cloudy sky again, the night sounds muffled by the clouds and the trees and the gurgle of running water.

He ducked under the round gate leading to the Chinese garden and took his shoes off, flexing his toes on the intricately patterned pebble mosaics that made up the garden.

A flash from the corner of his eye.

Ben froze as his eyes followed the moving shadow. He held his breath and listened.

Something was overhead. Something other than bats. Something...

A hint of amnis trickled through the air, the taste of cardamom and honey.

"Tenzin." Rage punched through him and he rose into the sky, arrowing toward the shadow, but it was gone.

The scrape of tile near the teahouse.

"Tenzin!" Ben snarled as he raced in that direction, only to see the shadow fly from the curving roof and toward the pavilion that overlooked the lake. The shadow darted under the bridge, the water rippling out from the speed of her flight.

"Dammit." She was too fast. "I know it's you!"

Why haunt him? Why follow him?

The shadow flew over the gates of the garden and through the night. Ben followed, the wind tearing through his hair as he raced behind. He wasn't fast enough; his control was too shaky. He felt the wind fighting him.

He thought he heard the echo of laughter as he passed through the alley of giant camellias leading toward a trickling stone fountain.

Ben hovered over the garden, listening to the water and the wind sweeping through the palm trees. The bats were back, flapping through the night as they feasted on insects.

"I know you're there." He didn't need to speak loudly. "And I don't know what game you're playing, but I'm not interested. Leave me alone."

Ben landed softly on the wet grass, realizing too late that he'd left his shoes back in the Chinese garden.

Shit.

Tenzin watched from her perch in the king palm tree near the desert garden as he took flight. He was getting faster and faster. His control was growing. She was glad he'd finally left Asia. Keeping tabs on him had been exhausting. He was far more adept at disappearing than she'd imagined.

It both frustrated and delighted her. Ben had never been boring in his human life, and he was proving to be a skilled opponent in his immortal one.

Very enjoyable.

Opponent for now, partner eventually.

She glanced at the bat eating a piece of fruit next to her. "He insists he wants to be left alone, but if that was truly the case, why did he chase me?"

The bat didn't answer her.

"Agreed." She drew up her knees and rested her chin on them. "He doesn't know what he wants." She glanced at the bat. "No, you're right. He does know, he just doesn't want to admit it."

He wanted her. For what, he was probably unsure. But he wanted her, and that was a place to start. Maybe at first he would only want her help. Maybe he thought he wanted revenge.

He'd see the truth eventually. She would be patient.

She had all the time she needed now.

## 7

Gavin was drinking a glass of whiskey in the front yard when Ben landed back at the house.

"I always forget how warm it is here," he said. "There's still snow in New York. *Snow*." He curled his lip. "I've got to convince Chloe to move. Houston. Los Angeles. Capri. I have a new bar in Spain she'd like."

"She loves New York." Ben fought to get his emotions under control.

"I know." He finished his drink. "How are you?"

"Fine."

"Yes, clearly." Gavin raised an eyebrow. "Funny, you have that enraged look you usually only get when you've been around your partner."

"Tenzin isn't my partner anymore."

"And yet you knew exactly who I was talking about," Gavin said. "She's still your partner, and you're fooling yourself if you think you can just avoid her."

"Did she fly to LA with you?"

"With me?" Gavin frowned. "Of course not. Do you know

how fast she flies? It's ridiculous and irritating." He muttered, "You'll probably be as fast as her eventually, you irritating knob."

"Missed you too." Ben stalked past the Scottish vampire.

"Giovanni wants us in the library," Gavin yelled. "You need some background on Radu."

"I already got the briefing on the icon."

"The icon?" Gavin smiled. "You still amuse me, sweet lamb. You think this is only about an icon? Everyone underestimates Radu." Gavin joined him. "It's not a mistake I've made."

"So?" Ben shook off the irritation Tenzin had provoked and focused on work. "He's offering way more than market value to find it. We knew it was sentimental."

"Sentimental is one way of putting it."

They walked in the house and past the empty kitchen.

Ben glanced at the clock. "It's late."

"Yes, that darling little mite was quite perturbed you weren't here to wish her good night." Gavin looked amused. "She's quite funny for a small human."

"I know."

"Does she ask everyone to see their fangs? I find her ease with vampires disconcerting."

Ben pushed through the swinging kitchen door. "Sadia has no fear."

"That explains her fascination with Tenzin."

Ben wiped a hand over his face and paused at the foot of the stairs. "Can I just go even one night without her being thrown in my face? I'm about ready to go back to Kashgar."

"Is that where you were?" Gavin nodded. "Good choice. What made you come out of hiding?"

"A woman."

Gavin lifted an eyebrow. "Really?"

"Not like that." He walked to the second floor. "She was watching me. She knew my name. Left me a note."

"Ah. Which said?"

"'Answer your fucking mail.' That's it. No name. No address. Just answer your fucking mail."

Gavin laughed as they walked into the library. "What did she look like? Little pixie of a thing with big eyes and too much hair?"

Ben froze. "How did you know that?"

Gavin took a seat near Chloe, who was sitting at the library table with Beatrice. Chloe had her laptop open, and Beatrice was pointing to something on a tablet.

"I would bet you a case of sixty-year-old Macallan that the woman watching you in Kashgar was Kezia. She's Radu's sister."

"Biological or immortal?" Giovanni spoke from the other end of the library.

"Maybe both," Gavin said. "The Poshani tend to keep the same bloodlines in the terrin."

Ben sat down near the fire. "And now you're speaking a completely different language."

"Yes he is." Giovanni walked toward them, holding a book he handed to Ben.

Ben looked at it. It was written in a Cyrillic alphabet. He handed it back to Giovanni. "I don't read Russian."

"It's not Russian; they just borrowed the alphabet. It became more accessible than the original Brahmi script." Giovanni sat across from him.

"Brahmi?" Ben asked. "As in ancient Indian?" He pointed to the Russian book. "And the connection between Cyrillic and Brahmi would be...?"

"Poshani."

"Is that supposed to mean something to me?"

"No," Beatrice chimed in. "Not unless you'd spent a lot of time studying immortal history in Eastern Europe."

"Fancy that," Ben said. "I haven't."

Giovanni said, "A now-obvious hole in your education that I'll have to correct with Sadia."

*That poor girl.* Ben winced on his baby sister's behalf.

Giovanni continued, "Gavin confirmed something for me that I suspected about Radu but wasn't sure."

"Which is?"

"Radu isn't your average vampire," Beatrice said. "He belongs to a particular community of Romani people who came from Northern India with the main branches of—"

"Romani?" Ben asked. "You mean gyp—"

"No." Beatrice threw a balled-up wad of paper at Ben. "Most Romani consider that word a slur; do not use it."

"It's also incorrect," Giovanni said. "Europeans didn't understand the origins of the Roma people and thought they were from Egypt, which is a mistake of course. They are Northern Indian both linguistically and ethnically."

"So Radu is a... Romani vampire?"

"Kind of." Beatrice flipped her tablet around to show Ben a sort of family tree. "He's Poshani, a completely separate branch. The Poshani origins are more myth than history as they don't follow a written tradition." She scrolled through slides that showed paintings of men playing lutes and pipes. "Some branches broke off over time—those were the human Romani people—but one group, the Poshani, were led by a man who was turned into a wind vampire."

Giovanni said, "The Poshani initially feared their leader, but he convinced them that this new form was a gift of Shiva and Kali, whom the Poshani revere."

"Shiva." Ben tapped his pencil. "The Destroyer. That fits with being a vampire, I guess."

"Shiva is often conflated with Rudra, a Vedic god associated with storms. More than one vampire believes Rudra was actually the first wind vampire, so that would be significant to the Poshani."

"Radu's a wind vampire?" Ben asked.

Gavin nodded. "He's cagey about it, but yes. He'll sometimes tell people he's earth."

"Okay, the Poshani are wind vampires." Ben wrote that down. "But why does Radu want the icon if the Poshani worship Shiva?"

"They have a blended religion," Beatrice said. "The Shiva and Kali connection is very old, but it threads through. The icon is a depiction of Saint Sara-*la-Kali*."

Giovanni said, "Whatever the individual sect or community, Poshani of all religions value purity of the elements and balance in all forms of life."

"Which fits with vampires," Ben said. "Okay, I'm seeing it."

"A note." Gavin held up a hand. "The Poshani as a community are both vampire and human. But all are *ruled* by wind vampires. Three, to be exact."

Ben scratched out his notes and corrected them. "Kind of confusing."

"It's complicated by design," Gavin said. "They don't talk about themselves with outsiders. They want to be misunderstood."

"Why?" Ben was fascinated.

"Human societies are not kind to those who don't conform to mainstream values," Gavin said. "The Poshani have a very strict code of conduct, but it wouldn't make sense to those outside the group."

Ben glanced at Gavin. "Reminds me of a vampire or two I know of."

"Our interests have overlapped at times, and I respect them," Gavin said, "even if I don't understand them. Their hospitality laws are sacrosanct, much like mine. The caravan, for example."

"The caravan?"

Beatrice showed him another picture on her tablet, a round wooden wagon painted with elaborate floral patterns, with no windows and only one small door. "The proper name is the kamvasa."

Ben reached for the tablet, but the picture started to waver. "Dammit."

"Gloves." Chloe threw some silk gloves at him. "The Dawn Caravan is the Poshani tradition of sheltering any vampire who meets their rules and pays their price."

Ben looked at the picture. "In one of those?" The wagon looked like a relic.

Gavin said, "Those are old-fashioned vardos. They have been updated and modernized of course, but the idea remains the same. The Poshani run a moving safe house called the Dawn Caravan."

Ben frowned. "How have I never heard of this?"

"It's intended to be something of an urban legend," Giovanni said. "Until Gavin confirmed it for me, I didn't really believe it existed."

Ben turned to Gavin. "And how do you know it's real?"

"Because I was a guest for a short time," Gavin said. "And that is all I will say."

*Come on, really?* Ben looked at Gavin.

Gavin shook his head slowly and decisively.

"From what I've been able to gather," Beatrice said, "if you want to disappear—and I mean disappear off the face of the earth..."

"Poof," Chloe said. "You don't exist anymore."

"...you come to an agreement with one of the terrin—the ruling vampires of the Poshani—and they name a price. There is no negotiation. There is no appeal. You tell them how long you want to hide—"

"Up to six months," Gavin said quietly. "But not any longer."

"—and they tell you the price. They have complete discretion and there is no set price. They can accept anyone or no one. There are no guarantees."

Gavin said, "Except—"

"Except," Giovanni said, "that if they take you in as part of the caravan, they will guard you during the day and keep you safe at night. They are brutal in their protection and have never lost a guest."

Ben's eyebrows went up. "Ever?"

"Ever." Gavin's tone was firm. "The agreement is nonnegotiable for both parties. Once you join, you do not leave unless they kick you out for violating their terms. You are there for the agreed-on contract. No more. No less."

"What's to stop someone from leaving?"

"You walk away, they keep their money and you can never seek their protection again," Gavin said. "And you forget they exist because you no longer exist to them."

Ben looked between Gavin and Giovanni. "Vampires abide by this?"

"How much is a sanctuary worth?" Giovanni asked. "The Poshani provide one, and our kind are willing to pay."

"And no one knows where you are?"

"Guests don't even know where they are," Beatrice said. "They pick you up and transport you to the caravan during the day. If you don't know where you are, you can't give yourself away."

Ben scrolled through the pictures on Beatrice's tablet, starting with the scanned letters from Radu, the pictures of the icon, and the pictures and sketches gathered about the Poshani. "Okay," he said. "What does the Dawn Caravan have to do with the icon?"

Gavin and Giovanni exchanged looks.

"When was the first time Radu contacted you?" Gavin asked.

"I'm honestly not sure," Ben said.

"Fall," Giovanni said. "And every time he sent a reminder or a courier, it was in the fall."

Gavin said, "Radu isn't predictable, but he does have some habits. And one of them is that you don't see him in the spring."

"Because the Dawn Caravan starts in the spring," Beatrice said.

Gavin said, "But now he's sending you reminders a few weeks before spring begins in Eastern Europe about an icon he's been missing for years."

"You don't think this is about a missing icon," Ben said.

"No, Radu isn't a liar. And he *is* missing this icon," Gavin said. "But let's say I don't think this is *only* about an icon."

"Can I ask something?" Ben looked at Giovanni and Beatrice. "Why did you both say Radu was such a pain in the ass? I kind of wrote him off as a nuisance. So did... everyone. Now you're telling me he's a lot more than that."

"Oh no," Gavin said. "Radu *is* a complete pain in the ass. But he's not stupid and you can't underestimate him. He's very clever. He comes across as something of a jovial fool because that's the persona he's created to set immortals at ease."

Ben noticed something in Gavin's posture. "You don't want me to take this job."

Gavin shrugged. "If you take it and you succeed, Radu will owe you a favor, and so will the Poshani. That's no small way to start off immortal life."

"And if I don't succeed?"

"Not really an option," Giovanni said quietly. "I told you the amount he's paying?" He shook his head. "Once you take this job, Radu won't accept a refund."

Ben mulled over the choices, and for the first time in years, he actually felt excited about a job. He wanted this. He wanted the challenge. Wanted the intrigue. And maybe, just maybe, he was spoiling for a fight.

"You can send the gold back," Gavin said. "Tell him things have changed. At this point, he'd have to accept that. Especially with you being newly turned."

"And if I want to take it?"

The Scot leaned forward. "Then I'm telling you—for yer own fucking health—to get over yer attitude and call yer damn partner."

# 8

Ben sat against a wall in an old warehouse in South Pasadena. He allowed his weight to rest on the ground, enjoying the memory of his human body in this place. How heavy it was. How it moved. How it ached after a long workout. How it thrilled with every duel.

Mirrors lined one wall, and empty weapon racks stood opposite. The training mats remained, a relic of an earlier and simpler time.

"I almost died once," he said quietly. "I didn't mean to. It was in Kentii, when I was learning how to fight in the air. Tai and I finished, but I stayed in the mountains. There was a storm. It was one of those early-spring storms that happen when you go high in the mountains. Ice and rain mixed together. The sky was so black, and I was so hungry. I hadn't eaten for three days. Stupid, I know."

She still owned the warehouse. He knew because they still received a bill from the city every month. There were odd artifacts of her existence scattered around the place, but the alcove where she'd once spent her days was empty. Her books were gone except for an old museum program from a special exhibit they'd attended ten years before.

"The sky was so black I lost track of time. I didn't realize I was starting to dream, that the sun was coming up. I saw you." He leaned his head against the mirrors and looked at the ceiling. "Or a vision of you, I guess. You talked to me, but obviously you didn't. So I guess I was talking to myself."

He fingered the black sash he'd tied around his wrist. It was something he'd found in his dresser at the San Marino house. A simple strip of cotton, one of the many she'd used to tie her hair back one of those countless nights they'd shared. She must have dropped it and he'd picked it up. When he held it to his nose, he could smell a hint of her skin.

"You whispered to me that I was a monster." He stared at the knot he'd tied over the inhumanly pale skin of his wrist. His skin didn't get brown anymore. It would never see the sun again. "Zhang found me right when I passed out. I probably would have been in a world of pain if he hadn't. Maybe burned up. I don't know, maybe not. That storm lasted for two nights. Do rain clouds protect you from burning?" He looked up. "Either way, I would have had a fun time recovering from those injuries."

Ben stood and walked along the empty racks, running his finger along the dusty wood. "I miss you, Tenzin. Maybe I miss who I thought you were. Maybe I miss who I thought I was too." He looked around the warehouse studio where he'd learned to fight with swords. He'd sparred with vampires and humans. He'd sharpened knives and debated combat like a seasoned soldier.

Like a *boy*.

He'd known nothing.

"Golden boy." He looked around the warehouse. "You used to call me that. I heard you. Was it an insult? I could never figure that part out." He walked along the mirrored wall, his feet sinking into the training mats. "For the longest time, I thought my child-hood ended in Rome when I killed that man. I don't know why I thought that, like taking someone's life was a kind of graduation in the vampire world." He paused and looked at his reflection, staring into his inhuman brown-and-silver eyes. "I was still a boy. Just a boy with blood on my hands. Killing never made me any smarter or any harder." He blinked. "Death did."

Ben walked away from the mirror, turning his back to his reflection.

"I know you're still keeping tabs on me. I smelled you in Xining. I'm pretty sure I saw you in the market in Seoul. I know you were in Kashgar, and I know you followed me here." He stooped and picked up a bag of her things she'd left around the San Marino house. "I'm leaving your stuff." He flew up to the alcove where she'd once rested. "Stop following me."

He tossed the bag into the nook and floated back down to the ground. "I'll even say please. If you ever really cared about me, Tenzin, *please* stop following me."

TENZIN LISTENED to him from the roof, absorbing every painful word.

*My Benjamin, anger still eats your soul.*

She wanted to hold him. Wanted to comfort him. Wanted to whisper in his ear that nothing could make him the monster he feared he'd become. He might be a little less shiny, but he was still her golden boy. He was still the light to her darkness; the only one she'd found in thousands of years. Was she selfish for wanting to keep it?

Yes.

Oh well.

He wanted her to stop following him? Fine. That was an easy one. She'd stop following him. She'd only done it because she was worried that he'd become careless about his own safety.

Now that he'd come home—his true home, not Penglai—and he'd seen his baby sister, seen his family, she felt more confident that he would take care of the life she'd paid for.

Because she had paid for it, though it was a price she never wanted him to know. Tenzin wanted nothing between them. No debts and no anger. Now that Ben was immortal, he could finally have the life he was meant to.

And when he came to her, it would be as her equal.

# 9

*Bucharest, Romania*
*One week later*

Ben woke to the unfamiliar. He smelled cinnamon and vanilla. Flour. Road tar. Someone was baking and it was raining outside.

He rose from the borrowed bed in Gavin's safe house, which lay in a luxurious basement below his whiskey bar. The whiskey bar was a newer establishment, trying to capitalize on the rich and growing international crowd in Romania's capital.

It reminded Ben of Gavin's bar in Houston. The lighting was low, the menu was extensive, and the vampire-to-human ratio was fairly even.

Romania and Ukraine fell in the slightly grey area of vampire territory between Saba's domain in the Mediterranean and the influence of Oleg in Russia with Romania being slightly more Saba's and Ukraine being slightly more Oleg's. Both earth vampires watched over the countries, but not closely, leaving local influencers with more power and less oversight. In situations like that, businessmen like Gavin and Radu became de facto authorities, offering safety to immortals who frequented their businesses.

Ben stretched and spent a few minutes practicing the tai chi forms Beatrice had reminded him were so important for focus. He closed his eyes and centered himself as he took stock of his immortal body.

Hunger, sated. He'd fed the night before from one of the paid donors in Gavin's bar as well as topping off right before dawn with a large glass of blood-wine.

Mind, focused. He was in Romania to meet Radu. He had a goal and three avenues to investigate that they'd identified before they left Los Angeles.

Amnis... uncertain. He kept waking in unfamiliar places with unfamiliar scents and energy around him. While human Ben was a longtime friend of Gavin's, vampire Ben's amnis was still becoming accustomed to the other immortal's energy, which Ben could only describe as... slippery.

Gavin was impossible to pin down, and Ben's instincts couldn't decide if he was a friend or a foe yet. Logically, Ben knew that was probably part of what made Gavin so successful in his business. He could set more powerful vampires at ease... but only so much. There was something fundamentally uncertain about Gavin's amnis.

Yep. Slippery.

Chloe, thank God, was a steadying factor. When the three of them were together, Ben could be at ease.

He punched in the security code with the stylus next to the PIN pad, and the doors unsealed. He walked out to the small living area outside his secure day chamber. Since the bar and the safe house were new, they had the most recent Nocht-compatible technology installed.

Ben woke his tablet. "Good evening, Cara."

"Good evening, Ben Vecchio. Your voice ID has registered

with this device. You have enabled two-factor authentication. Please speak or enter your ID code now."

Ben spoke his code in an obscure Mongolian dialect Zhang was teaching him.

"Authentication recognized. How can I help you tonight?"

"Do I have any new messages from today?"

"You have... ten new messages."

"Please display." He saw a tray with a thermos and several pastries on the coffee table. Nice. That must have been the vanilla and cinnamon he'd been smelling. He walked over and unscrewed the top of the thermos to find dark, steaming coffee.

"Good." He'd been half expecting blood, and that just didn't go well with cinnamon cake. He sniffed the coffee. Sweet. More like Turkish coffee than the American variety. He poured a bit into the small mug next to the cake and added cream from the tiny pitcher.

Okay, damn. That was delicious. He could get addicted to Romanian coffee if they stayed here long.

Someone tapped on the door.

"Cara, blank screen." Ben faced the door, coffee in hand. He could already smell Chloe. "Come in, Chloe."

She poked her head in. "Still really weird that you always know when it's me."

"Well, your..." No, he shouldn't talk about how she smelled. He'd always hated it when vampires talked about how he smelled as a human. "It's your steps. Maybe being a dancer, they're just more distinctive or something." He pointed to his ears. "You know, my hearing."

Chloe's dimples popped out. "It's okay. I know it's the smell."

"Sorry, it really is. I feel like an adolescent again, only this time I'm being led around by my nose."

"I live with one of you, remember?" She walked in and plopped on his couch. "It's okay. Let's go over tonight's schedule."

"Did Gavin want you heading to Radu's with us tonight?"

"Yeah. He said it would be good for me to be identified as" — she used air quotes and rolled eyes— "'his human.' And I get it, so it's fine. This city feels slightly..."

"Wilder?"

Her eyes went wide. "Yes! I was trying to compare it to Paris or Vienna, because the architecture kind of reminds me of both those places, but the vibe is completely different."

"Paris has really calmed down in the past few years," Ben said. "And no place feels as orderly as Vienna. I know exactly what you mean."

"Totally. I want to roam around, but I think I'll confine my roaming to daylight."

"And only with Gavin's security," Ben said. "I don't know anything about this place."

"Do you think that's why Radu wanted to meet here?" She pulled out her laptop. "Because he knows you don't have many allies in this part of the world?"

"Maybe." Ben sat across from her and tried not to think about the inbox he wasn't tending to. "Chloe, let me just..." He reached for his tablet and used an eye scan to open it. "I really need to read my email."

"No problem." She was already in her files. "When you're done, I have a question about the Corsican lead."

"Got it." He skimmed over the two messages from Tai. Nothing new in Penglai. He had one from Fabi, but it just looked like chatting. One from Giovanni with new information about the icon forger he'd found. "I'm forwarding this one to you. You can add it to the file on the forger."

"Okay."

He continued down to the bottom of the list to see an email from a BTA Art Recovery account. "Do we know a BTA Art Recovery?"

Chloe frowned. "Doesn't sound familiar."

Ben clicked on it.

*I will not follow you anymore.*

Ben dropped his tablet on the table. "Fuck."

"What is it?" Chloe looked up.

"Tenzin."

"What?"

Ben turned his tablet and showed it to her. "BTA Art Recovery is Tenzin."

"Huh. That's new." Chloe looked back at her own screen.

"You didn't know about this?"

"No. And I usually have to help her set electronic stuff up." Her voice dropped a register. "She's changing. Evolving. What will she do next?"

"This isn't funny." Ben was unaccountably annoyed.

Chloe bit her lips. "Uh, yeah. It kind of is. It's an email, Ben."

"An email that proves she was in LA." *And listening to me when I was at the warehouse.*

Fuck.

"So? You told me you knew she was there anyway."

"I thought she was."

Chloe shrugged. "And now you know. I don't know why you're pissed."

"Because..." He just was. "Forget it."

"Okaaaay." She looked up. "Did you want her to *keep* following you? Just email her back."

"Can we work please?"

"Sure." She turned her laptop around. "So here are the three leads we have. Now the Corsicans—"

"I know. It's slim. But if we follow what the forger said, it makes sense."

"But if this gang *has* the icon, why do they want to make forgeries of it?"

Ben thought back to Tenzin, a metalsmith in Venice, and a pile of rare medieval coins. "Just trust me. Sometimes people don't want to sell the original. And they're the only criminal organization in the vampire world that's shown any activity near Saintes-Maries-de-la-Mer."

"Okay, so that's one lead in Corsica, where I have never been—"

"And you will never go."

"Not even with vampires?"

"Especially not with vampires." Even Giovanni was cautious about the immortals in Corsica, who were a particularly ruthless fragment of the previous French vampire coalition that had shattered several years before. "You'd probably be fine as a human tourist, but since you're not an ordinary human tourist, don't go to Corsica. It doesn't really matter. It's last on my list anyway."

"What about Hungary?"

The second lead was Hungarian. "More probable. Radu has connections there via his sister, so we're going to focus on that one first."

"And Turkey?"

"We'll tackle that one second. We're looking at three places with strong Roma history and ties to the saint. I still say the Hungarian connection is the strongest."

Chloe closed her laptop. "Which brings us to tonight. Our meeting with Radu is at midnight. We're going to a club called Zarvă, which is Radu's place. It is *not* like Gavin's places."

"Did you visit?"

"I looked online, and I also asked Gavin. He made that face he makes when we walk though Times Square."

"Right." Unfortunately, Gavin's disgusted face could mean Radu's club fell anywhere between Euro-tacky and Jersey Shore spring break. "So what do we wear?"

"Wear black. Look handsome and dangerous. It shouldn't be that difficult for you."

The corner of his mouth turned up. "I don't look dangerous."

"Sure." Chloe gave him eyes that said otherwise. "Whatever you say."

"Since when do I look dangerous?" He batted his lashes at her. "I'm a friendly vampire."

"Benny, why do you think I went out with you in high school?" Chloe stood. "I was a rebellious kid, so you know it wasn't for your wholesome Midwestern demeanor."

THE THUMPING BASS spilled out of Zarvă, making Ben wish like mad for his human hearing back. Maybe noise-canceling head-phones. Earplugs. Anything.

Chloe walked between him and Gavin. She looked up. "Ha! You're both making the face."

Ben met Gavin's eyes. There was definitely a look, and it had a lot to do with the cacophony of sound emerging from Radu's club. "Have you been here before?"

"Not when it's been this crowded," Gavin muttered.

They made their way to the alley behind the club and the private entrance manned by a vampire bouncer who was taller than them both and had a head that was distinctly square and facial hair that looked straight out of an old Western.

Romania defied explanation.

A heavy metal door opened and steps led up to a distinctly muffled room that still thumped of bass.

"Vampire lounge," Gavin muttered. "This is new."

"Good idea though."

"Bummer," Chloe said. "No music at all?"

Ben looked at Chloe, amazed that she couldn't hear anything. Then he looked at Gavin.

The man shrugged.

"Was I that deaf?"

"Deaf?" Chloe asked.

"Oh no," Gavin said. "You were far worse."

"Bullshit." Ben walked up to a discreet hostess stand. "We're here to meet Radu."

The young woman was dressed in a strappy black cocktail dress and her red-streaked hair matched the leather booths in the dimly lit lounge. "You are Mr. Vecchio?" She spoke in heavily accented English.

"Yes."

She looked at Ben. "But I have only three in your party."

Ben looked at Gavin, then Chloe. "And?"

She offered him a strained smile. "I'm sorry. I am confused. Please, if you can wait. Please. Let me check with Radu."

She wandered off, leaving Ben, Gavin, and Chloe waiting in the lounge.

"Maybe it's a language thing?" Ben asked. "Do you speak Romanian?"

"No." Gavin was sweeping his eyes around the club. "Not picking up anything suspicious," he said under his breath.

"Neither am I."

The hostess came back, all smiles. "Please. My apologies. Please follow me." They followed her through the winding lounge. "It was a... missed understanding from me."

"No problem." Ben glanced at each booth they passed, taking note of faces and making mental notes to ask about a few who looked familiar.

*Hello.*

In the far corner he spotted the vampire guard he'd seen with the mysterious woman in Kashgar. The man was looking as nondescript as ever, but his eyes locked on Benjamin with clear recognition.

Ben knew the woman in Kashgar had been connected to Radu, but this obviously confirmed it. Ben nodded to the man as he passed, but the other vampire only observed him with a distant, unflinching stare.

Would his mystery woman appear from the shadows next? Ben wouldn't be surprised.

"Please." The hostess parted a curtain covering the corner booth. "It was my mistake. One of your party had already arrived."

*Fuck. Me.*

"Mr. Vecchio." Radu rose from the end of the booth, a handsome, dark-haired vampire with a barrel chest who was wearing a perfectly tailored three-piece suit. "Welcome. It is so good to finally meet you."

Ben barely registered what Radu was saying. Sitting silently in the booth next to him, wearing a blood-red dress, was the one mysterious woman Ben hadn't been expecting, though maybe he should have been.

After all, Tenzin did like surprising people.

## 10

Ben shook Radu's hand, never taking his eyes off her. Tenzin was pleased; it had been too long since she'd been able to look him in the face.

The eyes bothered her. She'd known they might change, but a part of her mourned. She missed the dark brown with gold flecks that had once been so warm.

What did the humans say? Tall, dark, and lethal? Something like that. Ben was all of that. He said nothing, and his inhuman gaze never wavered.

*You were born to be this.*

Gavin was the first to greet her and smooth over any rough edges. "Tenzin, we didn't realize you'd arrived in town already."

"I wasn't expecting to be here until tomorrow night." She glanced at Radu. "My apologies for confusing your human."

The confusion was completely part of the plan. She hadn't wanted to give Benjamin time to prepare. She needed to see his genuine reaction to being in proximity to her, and she'd been successful.

"No apology necessary." Radu sat and motioned Chloe, Gavin, and Ben to the other side of the booth. "I was making the acquaintance of your notorious partner, Mr. Vecchio." Radu glanced at her from the corner of his eye. "Such a fearsome reputation for such a delightful guest."

Why Radu was acting like he and Tenzin had never met before, she didn't know, but she decided not to challenge him in front of the others.

He was a disarming vampire, and that was the intention. Radu was a handsome man who'd been turned in the prime of his adult life. Not young enough to be a playboy and not old enough to be a mentor. He could be your friend, your partner, the one who had your best interests at heart. He was very good at his persona, mostly because Tenzin recognized that part of Radu actually believed it.

Ben finally spoke. "Tenzin likes to take people off guard."

"Yes, I do."

Radu laughed. "What do the Americans say, Mr. Vecchio? Mission accomplished?"

"Please call me Ben." He leaned back in the booth, cool and smooth as ice water. "Mr. Vecchio is my uncle."

Ben's immortal grace was lethal, confident, and as natural for him as breathing.

*You are so stunning.*

She didn't say it. He wouldn't appreciate it—certainly not among vampires he didn't know—but he was.

Tenzin felt her blood sing in his presence and wondered if Ben felt anything similar. Probably not. He was young and was likely flooded with far more sensation than she was. The sounds, scents, and sights of the club were meant to be overwhelming, and she could see that he was affected.

For Tenzin, the pulsing music and heavy scent of cedarwood and vetiver in Radu's cologne barely registered. Their host's power, carefully concealed as Gavin's was, simmered beside her while Ben's amnis was a roaring, incandescent flame. The fact that he did nothing to mute it marked him as a newborn, but one whom no one would confront rashly.

"Welcome to Bucharest, Ben." Their host put his hand over his heart. "Thank you so much for coming from such a distance. I am honored that you and Tenzin would consider this little personal item of mine worthy of your notice. I know you are very busy."

Flattery was Radu's forte and his favorite tactic, but Tenzin wasn't taken in. "Radu, this is our human assistant, Chloe." She motioned in Chloe's direction. "You cut your hair since the last time I saw you."

She smiled. "So did you."

Ben was sitting on the edge of the booth, staring at her openly. "New dress?"

Tenzin looked down at the dark red dress Arthur had made for her the previous month. It had nearly nowhere to put weapons, but her favorite tailor had managed to sneak at least one dagger in, which was difficult with the dress being very tight and very short.

"Yes. Do you like it?"

Ben stared at her. "Stunning."

"I've ordered a bottle of țuică," Radu said. "It's traditional here. My day manager's mother makes it." He turned to Chloe. "Don't buy the bottles they sell at the market. They're no good. The best țuică must be made in the home."

Chloe nodded. "I've heard that."

The waitress brought a tray with a gold-trimmed decanter and five small glasses. She poured for the table and passed the drinks around.

"To our health." Radu raised his glass. *"Noroc!"*

*"Noroc,"* they all repeated.

Chloe let out a hard breath, but Ben didn't even flinch when he finished his shot of the overwhelmingly strong liquor.

Tenzin knew that with him being a newborn, Ben's sense of taste would probably be blind for days after a drink that heavy, but Ben was savvy enough to know flinching wasn't an option.

He stood and slid one hand in his pocket. "Radu, I hope you don't mind, but can I steal Tenzin away for a dance?"

Radu grinned. "Of course!" He tapped his temple. "When partners have been separated, they must confer on strategy no doubt."

Ben said nothing, but he smiled calmly as Radu slid out to allow Tenzin to exit the booth.

She was wearing the low heels Arthur had insisted on. Cat heels. No, *kitten* heels. She'd refused to wear the ridiculous icepick shoes he'd tried to shove her into, even though she was impressed by their lethal possibilities.

Ben wasted no time grabbing her hand and hustling her out the door that led from the vampire lounge to the cacophony of the dance floor.

She pushed the sound away as Ben spun her around and fixed his hands on her waist.

Though he kept his expression even, his voice cut her. "What the hell are you doing here?"

*You sweet golden boy.* "You asked me to stop following you."

"And this is your idea of not following me?"

"I'm not following." A human bumped into her and she allowed her body to press into Ben's. He didn't push her away. "I'm *anticipating.*"

He froze, but it was only for the space of a human heartbeat. "So Radu thinks you're working this job with me?"

"You didn't think you could work this job alone, did you?"

"As a matter of fact, I did."

"Okay, you *could*," she said. "But it will be more fun with me. The Corsican mob owes me a few favors."

His smile was tight.

"That smile is not fooling anyone watching us," she said. "They can all see you are very angry."

"I can't imagine why." He spun them around so his back was to the windows of the vampire lounge and the front of her body was plastered to his.

*Bite him.*

She wanted to. She really wanted to.

"Pay attention." His voice was low and commanding. "We're not doing this. You're going to leave Bucharest, and I'll find some excuse for Radu."

Ben probably didn't realize he was doing it, but his amnis was running over hers, twisting and pulsing with the music. An involuntary shiver ran down her back. "Stop lecturing me. It's quite adorable that you think you can order me around. Especially when your amnis is telling me something entirely different than your mouth."

A lick of his energy hit her right between her thighs. Tenzin didn't try to stop the audible sigh of pleasure that that escaped her lips.

"Stop it," he growled.

"I'm not doing a thing." Her mouth felt swollen. "That is all you, Benjamin."

DAMN HER, damn her, damn her!

He knew it was him—he knew it was his amnis—but he couldn't seem to control it. His fangs ached in his mouth. The minute he'd seen her, felt her energy up close, Ben's instincts had taken control. He wanted to push her against a wall and ravage her. He wanted to bend her neck to the side and sink his fangs into her vein.

ELIZABETH HUNTER

He wanted to throw her across the room. He wanted to hit something.

"Careful." Her small hands slid up his arms. "Be calm."

He bit back a snarl. "It's quite adorable," he said, his voice hard, "that you think you can order me around."

"I would not try. My attempts have never been very successful."

"So why are you here?"

"Because Radu is a pain in the ass, but what you are walking into may be more than either one of us anticipated."

"How well do you know him?"

"I know him."

Ben swallowed hard and pushed past his craving for her. *Think, think, think.* "So why is he acting like you just met?"

"I don't know. Just like I don't know why Kezia was following you in Kashgar."

"Were you seriously following me the whole time?" A muscle in his jaw twitched.

"No. You lost me in Cambodia, and I consider that an accomplishment. I could not find you until you got back to Xining."

He slid his hand down her back, stroking the small of her back. He told himself it was to keep up appearances since they were definitely being watched.

It wasn't. He couldn't help himself. He wanted to put his hands everywhere.

She looked up at him, all stormy grey eyes and luscious red lips. He hated her and he wanted her so badly.

"I'm really not trying to push it, Ben. I've been giving you space."

A hard laugh burst out of him. "Your definition of space is unique."

"I know you're angry—"

84

He stared at the pulsing crowd of dancers over her shoulder. "Angry doesn't begin to describe what I feel about you."

Her hand slid up his neck and into the hair at his nape. She gripped it and forced his eyes to hers. "If you expect me to apologize for you being alive, you're going to be disappointed."

Ben kept his eyes locked on hers. "Why didn't you kill Johari?"

She blinked. "You asked me not to."

"When?"

She cocked her head. "You don't remember?"

"No." He really didn't remember.

Wait...

*You're lovely.*

Yes, he did.

*"You're lovely. Lovable. ...don't kill anyone, okay?"*

She pushed against him, starting to dance again. "Ben?"

His body moved with hers whether he wanted it or not. He wasn't dancing with her. It wasn't him, it was the memory of what they had been. The same memory that made his throat thick with emotion.

She pulled his head down. "Whatever you may wish to think, we are not finished, my Benjamin."

"Stop calling me that."

"I will not. Blood does not lie."

The song ended and Ben pulled away, keeping her hand firmly in his. "We need to get back and we need to be on the same page. You're leaving Bucharest; I'll make excuses to Radu."

"Are you listening to me? None of this is right. That's why I'm here, and I'm not leaving." She wore a placid smile as they made their way back to the lounge. "I will make no excuses to Radu. If you want me gone, you'll have to tell him everything."

His caution recoiled at the thought. "I hate you so much right now."

"If you think your hate will prevent me from doing what it takes to keep you safe, then you do not understand me at all."

"You're right." He opened the door. "I don't understand you at all."

"Liar." She held her hands out to Radu as they approached the booth. "Thank you for excusing us. It has been some time since we have been able to speak in private."

Ben slid next to Chloe as Radu rose to let Tenzin into her seat. "Tenzin wanted me to tell you about the Corsican lead first. We're quite optimistic."

Radu looked between them. "So you are officially accepting this job?"

"Of course. You've presented us with an irresistible challenge." Tenzin turned her smile toward Ben. "We're both quite intrigued by the possibilities."

GAVIN AND CHLOE waited until they'd entered the soundproof car before they started on the questions.

"Oh my God!" Chloe was nearly shouting. "What was that? What is going on? I feel so lost right now!"

"The atmosphere was..." Gavin cleared his throat. "...noticeable."

Ben stared into the sky where Tenzin had already disappeared. "Hopefully Radu thinks it was just repressed sexual tension or something."

"Oh, it was definitely repressed sexual tension," Chloe said.

"Holy shit. I have to admit, I was still kind of wondering if you two had slept together before tonight—"

"I wasn't sure either." Gavin looked at Chloe. "They have."

"They *definitely* have." Chloe leaned back into the seat of the sedan. "Why is she here? How does she know Radu—because he definitely knows her—*why is she here?*"

Ben cut his eyes toward Chloe and Gavin. "She didn't tell you she was coming?"

"No." Gavin shook his head. "I would have warned you."

"I know the three of you are *pals*." Ben's voice was bitter. "But if you—"

"Ben, we didn't know." Chloe's eyes were wide. "I know you're angry with her. And I even understand why, but—"

"But you're not." Ben knew that betrayal wasn't the right emotion, but seeing Tenzin had tossed him completely upside down. "You don't understand it, Chloe. Don't pretend you do."

"Watch your tone." Gavin's voice was a low warning. "What the hell do you expect, Vecchio? Were we supposed to be disappointed that she saved your life?"

"She *took* my life!" His fangs fell. "How am I the only one who sees that?"

Gavin leaned forward, blocking Chloe from Ben's view. "Did she plan it, Ben? Was it her own blade in your back? Or did she react in the best way she could when everything went to shit?"

"Since Tenzin is the one who kept dragging me into her damn problems and apparently she didn't want to let me die a normal death, she should have had a better plan when everything went to shit!"

Gavin laughed bitterly. "Dear God, I hope you never expect me to be as omniscient as you expect her to be."

"What does that mean?"

"It means that you expect too damn much of her." Gavin's jaw was clenched. "She's not a fucking god, Ben. She's a vampire, but she's human too. You're too fucking close to see it, and it's not bloody fair. She did the only thing she could think to do when someone she loved was dying. How do you not fucking see *that*?"

Ben rapped on the divider, and the driver rolled down the screen.

"Yes, sir?"

"Stop the car please."

Ben opened the door as soon as the vehicle came to a halt and disappeared into the night.

## 11

Ben walked through the pitch-black streets of Bucharest, a spring drizzle falling on his shoulders and dampening his hair, which fell onto his forehead in dark wet curls. He couldn't stop replaying Gavin's words in his mind.

*She's a vampire, but she's human too... She did the only thing she could think to do when someone she loved was dying.*

No, no, no, no. She could have taken him to the hospital. She could have listened to him. He'd begged her so many times—

*If you think your hate will prevent me from doing what it takes to keep you safe, then you do not understand me at all.*

Ben heard human footsteps behind him, at least three sets. He smelled their breath tinged with vodka, and their blood.

*Yes.* A fight was exactly what he wanted.

Ben turned right into an alley and allowed the men to follow him closer. He slowed down, waiting for them to approach.

They shouted something in Romanian. He recognized a few words, but they were slurred. All three were very drunk. Ben turned, his hands shoved in his pockets, and the men came to a stop.

One of them, the stumbling one on the right, blinked slowly three times; then with the instincts of the truly drunk, he turned and walked back down the alley.

"*Idioți*," he shouted.

Well, that didn't need any translation.

Ben stood at the end of the alley, calmly waiting for the men to get tired of mumbling insults at him and laughing.

The one in front held out his hand. "Tourist," he spat out in English. His head was shaved and he wore a military-style jacket with dirty medals all over the front. "Hey, tourist. Give me your money, ass hole."

"The accent needs some work." Ben was relieved he had some human jackasses to distract him. "I guess I can't say anything though. I don't speak a lick of Romanian, *stronzo*."

The man on the left narrowed his eyes.

"Does that translate?" Ben asked, stepping toward them.

The drunk on the left stepped back, but the man in the jacket didn't move. He puffed out his chest and took a knife from his pocket.

"Give me your money," he slurred. "See?" He held out the knife. "Ass. Hole."

Ben's arm moved so fast the man wouldn't even be able to see it. He punched out swiftly and caught the man straight in the throat. The guy stumbled back and fell, clutching his neck and wheezing. The man on the left turned and ran into the wall, righted himself, and then ran toward the street.

Ben walked over to the man in the jacket and picked him up by the collar. Then he shoved him against the wall, put his hand on the man's head, and let his amnis wash over him.

"Not so tough now, are you?" Ben kicked the knife that had

fallen out of the man's hand. "Not so tough without your friends and your knife."

Ben wanted to hurt him. He wanted to humiliate him. He wanted to move his thumb an inch to the left and gouge out one of the vacant eyes of the human predator who'd followed a stranger down an alley. He wanted...

"Give me *your* money." Ben bent the man's neck to the side, exposing the artery. "Ass. Hole."

The man was in a daze as Ben bit into his neck and drank. He didn't struggle or try to push Ben away. He was weak-minded and intoxicated on top of it.

The mugger's body odor was revolting. Ben took a few long drinks just to sate his hunger; then he sealed the wounds in the man's neck, let him go, and picked up the knife that had dropped on the ground. The human slumped to the ground with his eyes closed, and Ben kicked his feet out of the way, causing the man to fall to his side on the dirty street.

He'd be fine. The human would wake the next day with a hell of a headache and a nasty bruise on his neck.

And no knife.

Since Ben was feeling petty, he crouched down in front of the man and systematically sliced off every other medal on the jacket. Then he pocketed the trinkets, took the knife, and launched himself into the air.

He flew over the city, grateful for the cloud cover, and perched on the roof of an art nouveau palace with glass domes that overlooked a new building project made of tall, sweeping mirrored glass.

*What a weird and wonderful city.*

Ben decided that Bucharest fit his mood. He couldn't decide if he was happy, angry, or bitter most nights. He loved being with Chloe and Gavin again. It almost made him feel like himself. But he wasn't himself. Not anymore. And the people he thought would understand that, like Chloe and Gavin, didn't seem to.

He tossed the mugger's knife across the roof and dumped the cheap medals out of his pocket. Then he pulled out the heavy-cased phone he had to use now, and a wave of bitterness spilled into him.

He missed sleek electronics.

He missed driving whatever car he wanted.

He missed eating a giant chicken burrito and taking a nap afterward in a sun-warmed hammock. He'd never feel that again, and it pissed him off.

He rubbed an ache in his chest. Was it possible for vampires to get heartburn? It would serve him right for drinking vodka-infused blood from a wannabe-be mugger.

He pushed the button on his giant phone. "Cara, check the time in Dublin."

"Voice command accepted, Ben Vecchio. Checking time in Dublin, Ireland." Cara came back a second later. "The time in Dublin is 4:26 in the morning."

"Call Brigid."

"Do you want to call Brigid Connor's mobile number?"

"Yes."

"Calling Brigid Connor mobile."

The phone rang as Ben willed Brigid to pick up. The Irish fire vampire was the one person who seemed to understand his kalei-doscope moods. She was also the only other vampire Ben knew who'd been changed against her will.

"Ben Vecchio," she answered. "You're not in China, lad."

"No, I'm closer to your neck of the woods."

"Do tell."

"Romania."

"Working again?" She muttered something to someone. "Sorry, I'm in the office. Give me a moment."

"I don't want to interrupt."

"No, it's grand." She was walking. "I'll step outside for a moment. It's been a few weeks. Romania, eh? Is this the Radu thing? I'm glad you're getting that taken care of. I think it's been hanging on your mind."

"I know." He ran a hand over his forehead; the drizzle was turning to rain. "Am I ever not going to be angry about this, Brig?"

"About...?"

"Being a vampire. Missing the sun. Missing food. Having to drink human blood to survive."

"Ah." She closed a door. "Short answer? Yes. I have every confidence you will eventually not be angry about this."

That wasn't as comforting as it should have been. He kicked at a pebble on the roof. "I saw her tonight."

"Who?

"Tenzin."

"What? How?" Brigid sounded appropriately shocked. "Are you working with her?"

"She kind of... showed up in Bucharest before me."

Brigid snorted. "Savage bitch."

"Why are you laughing?"

"I mean... I know you're angry with her, I just can't help it. She's so fecking rude. Part of me has to admire it."

"Good to know you can find the humor in the situation."

Brigid took a deep breath. "Did she say why she's there? It seemed like she was keeping her distance."

"She was following me constantly."

"But from a distance." Brigid sighed. "What do you expect? You're one of her people."

"She decided that. Not me."

"Doesn't make much of a difference," Brigid said. "You're going to learn that. Some of that is just territorial instincts. You have them too."

Ben thought about his uneasiness in his own home with Giovanni and the itching under his skin on his uncle's private plane. "I know. I felt them in LA."

"And you'll adapt to it soon enough. Be able to understand when to ignore things and when to pay attention to them. So..."

"So what? That doesn't mean Tenzin can just barge into my life when I don't want her there."

"No, you are correct. You get to decide who is part of your life whether you're human or immortal. Well, other than your sire. You don't get much say about that. But she's not your sire."

"Thank God."

"Why thank God?" Brigid said. "Because you're in love with her? Or because you hate her?"

"I don't—"

"It can be both, by the way. You can hate someone you love."

Ben stared at the lights over the city, enjoying the drip of cold water that fell down his neck. "She said that she needed to be here. That the job is dangerous and something about it feels off."

"Okay." Brigid hummed a little. "Are you wanting my advice?"

Ben took a long breath and let it out. "Yes." He trusted Brigid. On a personal and a professional level.

"My advice is that if she thinks something is sideways about the job, you work with her. It's not personal, to quote a gangster movie, it's business. As far as your security goes, is there anyone you trust more?"

That was a loaded question. "Now that I have fangs, I guess not."

"Then you have your answer. You don't go into a fight with one hand tied—don't go into this job without all your assets. And she's an asset. As for what's between you two personally?"

"Yeah?"

"Set a boundary. This job and then you're quit. Make her

94

agree to it, and don't budge. This is the last job that was a holdover from before. She's got until the end of it to sort things out between you or say goodbye."

"And that's it?"

"I mean, you're going to live for who knows how many years, Ben. Might be worth it to keep a little bit of the bridge unburned if you know what I mean."

He shook his head. "How do you deal with it?"

"Which part?"

"The living-forever thing." Ben felt his throat closing up. "I never—"

"Aye, that was a sticking point for me too." Her voice got soft. "All I can say is... there's one or two things about your life that remind me of mine. And avoiding my problems never did me much good in the end."

"You think I'm avoiding something?"

"Yes, and before you ask, it's not my job to tell you. You probably need a therapist."

"Thanks for the advice I won't take."

"You're welcome." Someone called her name in the background. "Need to go. Call me in a week, lad, or you'll have me following you too. By the way, the fella and I may be heading to New York in the fall. Right! Laters."

Brigid hung up before he could get another word in. Ben stuffed his phone in his pocket and stared across the city.

Trying to have a conversation with Brigid was usually like jumping into a minor tornado for a moment, then jumping out naked and trying to figure out where all your clothes had blown off to.

*Work with Tenzin for this job.* Check. Fine. He could compartmentalize as well as the next guy.

*Set boundaries, but don't burn bridges.* Fine. That was all fine. Good advice.

Brigid thought he was avoiding something?

Tenzin. He was avoiding Tenzin.

*Because you love her or you hate her?*

Both?

How about because she'd betrayed him? She'd broken a promise.

*Were we supposed to be disappointed that she saved your life?*

Ben knew why everyone was happy. Even his closest friends and family understood why Tenzin had done what she did. And most of them, if they were being honest, were glad. They didn't understand why he'd been so reluctant to be a vampire in the first place.

But Ben had stared into monsters' eyes, human and immortal, and he knew what evil looked like. He saw the darkness in himself. He'd seen it flash hot and bright over the years. In Rome. In Shanghai. In New York. He'd felt the oozing blackness that crept through the darkest parts of himself and he knew—he *knew* —that taming that would be far harder than taming his thirst for blood.

*You're a little bastard.* His mother's slurred words across the kitchen haunted him. Five-year-old Ben didn't understand what it all meant, why his mom was lying on the floor with red eyes, her speech nearly unintelligible, but he understood what hate sounded like.

*You're such a little bastard.*

No. Done. She was gone and he was a different person. Ben Rios was well and truly dead now. He'd taken his last breath in a little stone house outside of Shanghai.

The Ben he would become? He was still working on that.

## 12

Ben woke the next night to the sound of Chloe in his anteroom and the smell of delicious Romanian coffee and some savory pastry. His mouth watered. He sat up and reached for the half-empty bottle of blood-wine on the table next to him. He'd drunk half the night before, trying to wash the taste of the Romanian mugger out of his mouth before he fell into day rest.

After finishing the bottle, he rose and pulled on a pair of loose-knit pants and a tank top. Unsealing his door, he walked straight to Chloe, who was already working on her laptop.

"I know you've probably got plans for the evening but—"

Ben pulled her up from the sofa and into his arms. "I'm sorry about last night."

She hugged him hard. "I don't want to make light of your feelings. I know it must have been a shock to see her."

Ben released her and sat in the chair across the table before he reached for the coffee thermos. "You could say that."

Chloe stared at him. "I don't know how you want me to react. It's harder to read you now."

Ben sighed. "It's harder to read myself now." He shrugged. "I don't always understand my mood swings."

"Okay." Chloe closed her laptop. "Just to give you a little perspective, I want you to imagine, for a minute, what it would have been like if it was me. If you'd gotten news from Gavin on the other side of the world that I'd been stabbed in the back—literally stabbed in the back—and there was nothing you could do to help. There was nothing you or Tenzin could do and Gavin was taking me to... his sister."

Ben made a face. Gavin hated his sister.

"Exactly," Chloe said. "And you didn't get any news for an entire day. Nothing. And then you found out that I was alive and a vampire and that was the only way to save my life."

"But that wasn't the only—"

"Stop." She raised a hand. "You don't know any of that. You only know that I was dying and now I'm okay. How would you feel?"

"Happy."

"But I hadn't decided that I want to be a vampire, Ben. It's a big decision, and I hadn't decided yet."

"Haven't decided is different than having your wishes overruled."

Chloe blinked shine from her eyes. "Gavin's right. You expect a hell of a lot from her."

"Yeah, I did." He woke his tablet. "Guess she's not the person I thought she was."

"That might be truer than you know." She opened her laptop. "I'm forwarding an email Tenzin sent me about the Corsican gang. Also, she wants to meet you at the club at ten if you have time."

"Radu's club?"

"No, the one here." She pointed down. "I think she may already be here."

"And yet she didn't barge into my room," he muttered. "Wow, she really has changed."

"Ben."

"Fine." He poured a cup of coffee. "I'll be nice."

Chloe looked skeptical. "If you really want to be nice, you'll share some of that coffee."

"Sorry," he said. "This coffee is part of my immortal territory now. You're going to have to get your own."

⁓

HE STARED at the clothes in his suitcase, debating what to wear.

*What the fuck does it matter, Vecchio? You don't care what she thinks.*

Except he did. It was foolish and petty, but he wanted her to want him. Wanted her to miss him and hunger for him like he hungered for her.

Had she taken a lover? Had she gone back to Cheng in Shanghai? Maybe she'd looked up René DuPont.

Ben picked out a pair of slim black slacks and a dark grey shirt that brought out the stone colors in his weird eyes. He rolled up the sleeves to show off his forearms. Tenzin liked his forearms.

He'd always kind of wanted a tattoo, but he never got one. Too late now.

Ben left his apartment and walked down to the club on the first floor, entering from the owner's hallway behind the bar.

It was the exact opposite of Radu's place, though the clubs were within walking distance of each other. Green velvet cushions softened the seats in the wood-paneled club. The long bar was burnished wood, no doubt bought from some establishment that had been in business for a hundred years. Soft music drifted overhead instead of pounding from speakers in every corner.

Human servers moved among vampire and mortal patrons, serving whiskey, blood-wine, and other cocktails. A small red pin on the collar of their button-down shirts identified which waiters or waitresses were available as donors if a patron requested it. He turned his head as one particularly attractive server passed him. She smelled like dark roses with a layer of something heady underneath.

*Divorce your hungers, one from the others. Blood hunger. Sexual hunger. Social hunger. Emotional hunger.* His sire's voice echoed through his mind. *All these are needs you must meet in their turn, but learning to understand their subtle flavors is vital to taming them.*

In a large booth halfway down the bar, Tenzin sat alone, reading something in a manila folder. She looked up and nodded as soon as he entered the room.

*What good does it do to tie sexual hunger and blood hunger together? Does it promote control? No. It only leads to loss of control when either appetite is whetted.*

Seeing Tenzin—being near her—caused nothing less than a cascade of hungers, one after the other.

Sexual hunger. He hadn't taken another lover since they had parted ways, and he was not suited to monasticism.

Blood hunger. His throat burned at the memory of her blood. He'd sampled humans across Asia and Europe now, and none of them touched the taste of her.

Emotional hunger. Maybe the deepest hunger of all. Seeing her the night before had been excruciating. Part of Ben wanted everything to be the same when nothing was. He wanted his best friend back. He wanted Tenzin to be the one guiding him through the complexities of this new body and new life. He wanted his partner.

Instead, the sight of her produced burning resentment and wave after wave of hunger.

*Be nice.*

*Nice* wasn't the word that came to mind.

*It's not personal. It's business.*

Ben sat and examined her openly.

Unlike the previous night, Tenzin was dressed for business. Gone was the blood-red dress and lipstick. She wore a tailored jacket the color of caramel over a maroon tunic. Chocolate-brown leggings and knee-high boots completed a look that Ben knew she had not picked for herself.

"You look professional," he said. "Did Arthur pick it out?"

She nodded. "I told him I had an important business trip to Europe, and he told me I was not allowed to pick my clothes."

"Sounds like Arthur."

She looked down with a small frown. "He did not give me any black clothes. I had to sneak some into my bag."

"Well, he doesn't know about flying and the—"

"Bugs." She smiled. "See? You know now."

Before he could respond to that, she said, "I ordered a whiskey for you. I saw one on the menu that I remembered you ordering at Gavin's bar in New York." She looked up. "I ordered it neat with a glass of ice water on the side."

What was she doing to him? "That was thoughtful. Thank you."

She folded her hands on the table, and Ben dragged his eyes from the nape of her neck, which was freshly shorn. She'd trimmed her hair again, the heavy black silk cut at a modern angle from her nape to just below her chin. He watched her hair brush her cheek as the server put two drinks down on the table.

When the server left, she said, "Thank you for meeting me."

"Thanks for giving me the option this time."

She raised an eyebrow. "You wouldn't have agreed to meet with me if I hadn't ambushed you last night."

Ben reached for his drink and the ice water, carefully pouring three fingers of cold water into his whiskey. He normally drank it with only a hint of water, but since he'd turned, whiskey was too intense without watering it down. Not that he'd be able to taste much after the rocket fuel he'd ingested last night with Radu.

"At least you admit it was an ambush."

"Of course it was."

Ben leaned an elbow on the table. "Do you have an abachee set with you?"

"That game." The corner of her mouth turned up. "How many times did he make you play?"

"I lost count."

Tenzin leaned forward and her eyes sparked with amusement. "I bet you lead with your horsemen."

She was right. "It's the swiftest offense. I bet you lead with your archers."

"Always. A long-distance attack endangers the fewest pieces on the board."

"Archer-led campaigns take forever."

"I am comfortable playing the long game."

*Yes, you are.* Ben cleared his throat and focused. It would do no one any good for them to fall back into old patterns and friendly banter. That wasn't who they were anymore. "So who wins? You or Zhang?"

She reached for her drink. "I capture his sun god every time."

"That's not what he says."

She waved a hand. "He's an old man with a horrible memory."

He cracked a smile, and Tenzin's eyes went soft. "Hello, my Benjamin."

Sitting across from her felt familiar and right and it hurt.

Ben swallowed hard. "I'd like to keep this professional, so why don't we talk about terms?"

"Fifty-fifty, like always," she said. "Neither of us has a personal stake in the icon."

"Agreed, but you are bringing the Corsican connection to the table."

Tenzin waved a hand. "That favor is long overdue. They will be grateful I am calling it in."

But that left Ben owing her a favor. "I'm comfortable with a fifty-five, forty-five split to account for the value of the favor."

She watched him. "If that's what you'd prefer."

"It is." He sipped his drink again. "Chloe and I have been going through the correspondence, and you've answered some of it yourself. Word has gotten out, and according to her, this is the last job on our books from New York."

Tenzin nodded. "It is."

"Given the circumstances, I'm willing to work as your partner on this." He kept his tone precisely even. He'd practiced before he left his room. "I make no guarantees or offers beyond that. Basically, this is a temporary thing, Tenzin. That means when we finish and I ask you to leave, you leave. And you do not follow me again."

Her eyes said *Or what?* but she didn't say it out loud. "I will agree to that if you agree that we will work openly and honestly as partners for this job. No vendettas. No resentments. No hidden agendas. I know you have anger toward me, but I do not want Chloe and Gavin caught in the middle of our quarrels."

"Absolutely." *I want to throw you against the wall behind the bar. And maybe fuck you on the ceiling.* "This is business." He sipped his whiskey. "Nothing personal."

"Agreed."

"If the four of us are going to work together, you need to fly with us on the plane. We don't have time to wait for you in every country."

Tenzin nodded. "That is fine."

Ben almost spit out his whiskey. Fine? Just like that? He'd had to threaten bodily harm to get her into a truck once! According to his uncle, she'd once punched a hole in the side of his carriage with her bare fists because it felt a little bit stuffy. She was agreeing to fly with them on the plane?

"Okay." He blinked. "Good."

"I know Gavin wants to stay with Chloe," Tenzin said, "but part of his passage through our world is that he is seen as a neutral party. If you'd be willing, I think it would be better if he and Chloe stay at his club in Monaco while we fly to meet Juvan and his brothers. It will only take an hour and a half to fly."

Ben jotted down some notes just to keep himself from staring at her. "Okay. That's a solid idea, and I can't imagine either one of them will have any objection to it. We can fill Chloe in on the Corsican meeting when we get back." Ben hadn't known Gavin had a place in Monaco, but it didn't surprise him. "How's the garden?"

She was silent until he looked up.

"The garden in New York?" he asked. "How is it?"

"Thriving. The glass house is finished, and the heating system is operational. I bought birds."

"Chloe told me. Sadia loves them."

Tenzin smiled. "She visited last summer."

"She told me. My little sister is kind of your superfan, you know."

"The feeling is mutual. She's an excellent child."

Ben couldn't take his eyes off her. *Did you have children?* He knew nothing about her human life, and seeing her uncovered a relentless curiosity. "Do you remember much about your human life?"

She froze. "Why do you ask?"

*Make it about me.* "I find myself wondering whether my memories of Sadia—from when she was very young—will stay with me."

"Ah." Her gaze relaxed a little. "Yes. I believe you will remember. Sometimes memories will escape you, but they always find you again."

Yes, he was a little bit afraid of that.

"So." He cleared his throat and finished his whiskey. "We'll leave tomorrow night, and we both feel comfortable with the business parameters of this job?"

"Yes." Her smile was polite. So damn polite he wanted to scream.

"Good." He held his hand out. "We agree. One last job and then... good luck to you."

"And good luck to you too." Tenzin stretched her hand across the table and Ben took it. Their hands met calmly while their amnis twisted and arrowed straight to Ben's groin. Twin desires nearly drowned him—his for her and hers for him—and his fangs lengthened and his cock swelled hard as a rock.

Ben dropped Tenzin's hand and reached for his notebook, forcing his aching fangs back into his jaw. "Why don't you brief me about the Corsicans? You said one was named Juvan and he has brothers? Is Juvan in charge?"

She raised one eyebrow, and Ben read the entire conversation in her eyes.

*So we are ignoring this?*

*Yes. We're ignoring it.*

*Didn't you say we should not avoid those things between us?*

*That was before. We're ignoring them now.*

"The Corsicans" —Tenzin's smile was amused— "are very entertaining."

"Entertaining in a really murdery, violent way?"

"Yes." Her eyes lit up. "But they enjoy karaoke as well."

## 13

Ben had been faced with a lot of unexpected twists and turns in his life, but seeing a stocky Corsican earth vampire absolutely killing it on a karaoke cover of "Born to Run" was definitely not on his bingo card for the year.

He leaned over to Tenzin. "You said they like karaoke, but I had no idea."

"Yes, they are very competitive."

This wasn't your drunken sorority-party version of the singalong. It was more along the lines of a singing competition, and participants were not making fools of themselves.

If anything, it made the gang even more creepy.

They'd landed an hour before on a brightly lit yacht floating off the north coast of Corsica.

Why a boat for earth vampires? Ben had asked Tenzin, and she'd waved a dismissive hand. *Rich men, whether they're human or immortal, like big boats.*

The three brothers, Juvan, Carlo, and Alcide, greeted Tenzin like she was an old friend, offered blood-wine to both of them, and then seated them on the top deck at the front of an ongoing karaoke party where Ben and Tenzin were clearly the guests of honor.

"I'm just glad we're guests and not participants," Ben muttered in Mandarin.

Tenzin's eyes went wide. "We *will* be expected to sing, Ben."

Oh fuck.

"Uh, no. I didn't agree to that because I don't sing."

"Everyone sings, Ben." She took a slip of paper from her pocket. "I have prepared a song. Everyone comes prepared with a song. It's karaoke."

"Do I have a history of enjoying karaoke? Have you *ever* heard me sing when I'm not drunk?"

She narrowed her eyes. "I suppose not."

"Exactly."

Alcide was finished paying tribute to the Boss, and a raucous round of applause rose from the gathered vampires and humans. The party was a fairly even mix between the two, though Ben noticed the vampire attendees were pretty heavily weighted toward the men who were dark, heavily stubbled, and dangerous, while the mortal attendees were pretty much all young, beautiful women.

*Lots* of young and beautiful women.

Another vampire was taking the stage with two others. They began a three-part rendition of "Sweet Caroline" that would have left Neil Diamond crying from the harmonies.

He leaned over to her, trying to ignore the instant burning in his throat and the tightness in his pants. "Tenzin, are you serious or are you trying to push my buttons? Do we really have to sing?"

"Not together. I am sorry, Benjamin, but I did not prepare a duet."

He blinked. "You're actually serious."

"Of course I am."

"You're singing?"

ELIZABETH HUNTER

"I do not know how I could have made it more clear." The crowd around them erupted during the "Sweet Caroline" chorus. "The Corsican vampire mob *loves* karaoke." She glanced around and looked back. "You can sing, Ben. I've heard you. You just don't do it when you are sober."

"Exactly."

"So pretend you are drunk."

"That's your advice?" He looked around the deck. "What am I supposed to sing?"

Tenzin clapped as the Neil Diamond classic came to an end. "Something you know. It doesn't have to be perfect, but you have to make an effort."

Of all the things his uncle, his aunt, his sire, and fifteen years of life with vampires had prepared him for, none of them terrified him more than the prospect of singing in front of a room full of judgmental and murderous strangers.

"Just take it seriously and try." Tenzin was rising to her feet as a chorus of friendly voices encouraged her to the stage.

"Tenzin!"

"Come sing," they called in mixed French and a language that reminded him of Italian. "Tenzin, we are waiting."

"I can't believe you're doing this," Ben said.

She turned. "Your turn next."

"Right." He was going to be sick.

She took to the stage and scrolled through the music choices on the small screen on the left side of the stage; then she tucked her hair behind her ear and raised her face to the crowd.

She was wearing black, as he was, a formfitting sleeveless tunic and a pair of leggings. She wore no jewelry in her ears or around her neck, but her forearms were layered with thin, yellow gold bangles. She had four stilettos hidden in her black boots and three small daggers in her tunic.

She was beautiful, dangerously elegant, and the sexiest woman he'd ever seen in his life.

The background music started, a chorus of humming he recognized immediately.

*Fuck me.*

Tenzin immediately launched into a simple and haunting version of Billie Eilish's "When the Party's Over." She didn't look at him, but every word pierced his chest like one of her knives.

He couldn't think. He couldn't look away. Like him, the audience was rapt, hypnotized by her soft, breathy voice. It took everything in Ben to keep from flying away.

He couldn't fly away. Until this was over, she held him captive.

Tenzin turned her eyes to him as she finished, her gaze direct on the final chorus. She seemed to pay no attention to the crowd, which erupted into applause. She walked away from the microphone, off the small stage, and sat next to him as if she hadn't just destroyed him with a song.

"Your turn," she said quietly.

The crowd fell silent, waiting for him. No one called his name, but they were all looking at him.

"Ben." She lifted her eyes to his. "You have to try."

"Right." He swallowed the emotion he'd been holding back and rose, walking slowly to the front of the room.

What on earth was he supposed to sing that he wouldn't murder?

He stopped at the edge of the stage and looked over his shoulder. What else?

He leaned toward the microphone, heard the dangerous crackle and hum of concern from the crowd before he leaned back quickly. "Sorry." He cleared his throat. "Since this is my first time singing with our hosts" —he nodded generously toward Juvan and his brothers— "I thought I would sing a favorite."

He entered Louis Armstrong's name on the specially designed machine and was relieved to see "What a Wonderful World" come to the top of the list.

Perfect. He could half-speak that one, and the swelling background music would cover a multitude of sins.

As soon as he broke into the familiar lyrics, the audience gave a little clap of encouragement and he heard approving murmurs around the room.

He didn't look at her. He wouldn't. But in his mind, he was in every room, every alleyway, and every club floor where they'd ever danced together.

*"We always dance to Louis. That's the rule."*

They were next to a canal in Venice. In their apartment in New York. Hiding in an alley in San Juan.

His heart ached with the memories. Back then she'd felt right in his arms. He never knew what she'd do or say, but he knew that no matter what, she'd have his back.

*I would never kill you, Benjamin. I would sooner kill myself.*

She scanned the crowd, watching for threats. Though the Corsicans had greeted them as friends, she'd seen their reaction to Ben. They were wary, and wary allies made for unhappy accidents.

Juvan sat down next to her. "He's not good."

"Believe me." She turned to the stocky vampire. "He is very good. He just doesn't sing well."

The corner of Juvan's mouth turned up. "I'd heard the rumors that you'd taken a mate—"

"Ben and I are not your concern."

"—but I ignored them of course." Juvan's eyebrow rose. "We all know a bloodthirsty hunter like Tenzin would not endanger herself with such a raw and uncontrolled consort."

"I find it interesting how you have judged him." She turned back to the stage. "You are incorrect."

"In what way?"

"In many ways."

"No one dismisses his power. We're not fools."

"Do you think I would take a liability on as a partner, Juvan?" She glanced at his brothers. "He is not my blood relative, so I'm not swayed by my emotions." She smiled. "It's business."

Everyone knew that Juvan had turned his brothers for sentiment. Some viewed it as a foolish decision, but Tenzin knew that emotions could be more powerful and dangerous than the most logical calculation.

"Let him finish the song; then meet me in the conference room," Juvan said. "He's not good, but he's not playing a fool. I will talk to him."

"I would be disappointed if you didn't."

"THE ICON of Sara-la-Kali is famous for being impossible to find." Juvan spoke in French, but his accent wasn't anything like Ben had ever heard. "It disappears and then it shows up. Disappears again. It is reputation more than market prices that determines the value."

They were sitting in a plush conference room surrounded by windows and armed guards. While the party continued outside, this section of the top deck had been reserved for business. Ben and Tenzin had been ushered into the room where Juvan and Alcide were waiting for them. Both had greeted Ben with a deference he knew he wouldn't have received as a human.

Ben wasn't human anymore, which was both a strength and a challenge. He was used to going into negotiations like this while being underestimated. Ben had learned to work those preconceived notions to his advantage. He *liked* being underestimated.

Now he was a powerful predator, and though the men were earth vampires, Ben knew his amnis shouted across the room. Learning to cloak it the way Tenzin and Giovanni did would take time.

"You hired the Dominican to paint three forgeries." Ben paged through his folder. "Why three?"

"Why not?" Juvan shrugged. "We were going to sell them to humans."

"So not on the open market?"

"No, no." Juvan's brother Alcide waved a hand. "Only to criminals."

Tenzin asked, "Is there a market for forged icons in the human criminal class?"

She was next to him at the table. Ben had a feeling she might have been taking notes for future business opportunities. Selling forged icons to mobsters for hard cash would be exactly the kind of thing Tenzin would find hilarious.

*Not your problem anymore.*

"More than you might think," Juvan said. "Most human criminals are extremely stupid, so the gold that's on icons makes them think they are worth more than their actual value. If the story is good and we put up enough resistance to selling the piece, they always buy. Icons have become a good source of income for us."

"Interesting." Tenzin sipped a glass of blood-wine. "Of course, if you hired the Dominican, then you must have photographs. He won't work without them."

"We did."

"Really?" Tenzin cocked her head. "Then you weren't selling it to humans."

Juvan and Alcide froze.

Ben kept his lips glued together because he had no idea why a photograph... Ohhhhhh. Right.

The icon had disappeared from public records long before photography had been able to record it, so no living human had ever seen it. Which meant absolute accuracy—which necessitated an expert forger working off photographs—would only be important for an individual who had actually seen the icon in their lifetime.

In other words, a vampire.

Juvan and Alcide exchanged a look.

"We were," Juvan said. "On my honor, we would not have tried to pass a forgery to an immortal. Too many opportunities for the transaction to go wrong."

Alcide said, "We don't need the money or exposure. It wouldn't be worth the risk."

Ben asked, "So why did you need the pictures?"

"We didn't *need* them. We had a written description and references. Our partner offered them, and we saw no reason to say no."

"Partner?" Ben said. "So this wasn't your own idea?"

Juvan and Alcide narrowed their eyes.

Tenzin put a hand on Ben's arm. "He means this wasn't *only* your idea of course. Tell me about your partner."

Alcide cursed under his breath, and Juvan spread his hands. "Are you going to tell us about your client?"

Tenzin smiled. "You know we can't do that."

Alcide said, "So you must know that we cannot tell you either."

"You can't tell me a name," Tenzin said. "But surely you can give me something." She looked out the window of the yacht. "I would consider it a favor."

Juvan and Alcide both perked up. Giving Tenzin the meeting was fulfilling their favor to her. Offering information would gain them a new favor from one of the most powerful vampires on the planet.

"She gave us the pictures, but we don't have a name," Juvan said. "Only a bank number and a voice on the phone."

"Voice?"

"Female," Alcide said. "Immortal. The accent wasn't recognizable."

Which was often the case with older immortals. They usually traveled too much and lived in too many places for their accents to be classifiable. Added to that, they often spoke versions of languages that had long ago become extinct.

"A guess?" Ben asked. "Even a region would be helpful."

"I would say..." Juvan pursed his lips. "Eastern Europe. Perhaps Austria or Hungary."

Wildly different languages, but it gave them a place to start, and they did have a Hungarian lead.

"How did the pictures come?" Ben asked.

"Delivered by courier. A man."

"Age?"

Juvan muttered, "I am shit with human ages, but he was experienced. I would say forties or fifties."

"Language?"

"English." Alcide was catching on. "But he did have an accent."

"Was it familiar?"

"Russian but not Russian," Alcide said. "If you know what I mean. He sounded like he learned English from a Russian."

So the courier was a man in his forties or fifties who learned English from a Russian and worked for a vampire in either

Hungary or Austria. Since Hungary was in the former Soviet Bloc, Ben guessed the Hungarian connection was the next one to follow.

"This has all been so interesting." Tenzin picked up her blood-wine again. "And the concert was excellent."

Juvan glanced at Ben. "I like him. He's not the best, but he respects the microphone."

"Thanks," Ben said. "I think."

"You're welcome." Alcide slapped his shoulder. "It is all about respect."

## 14

Ben and Tenzin were silent on the flight back to the mainland. Ben ran through every piece of information he'd gathered along with all the new revelations from the brothers.

The Hungarian connection. That was the one. He'd been thinking they should go to Ankara next to explore the lead in Turkey, but after their meeting with Juvan and Alcide, Ben was definitely thinking Hungary was the lead to follow.

"They liked you," Tenzin said.

They were flying above the clouds, an oddly silent and peaceful place over the twisting wind currents that rose from the heated surface of the sea.

"They didn't like me," Ben said. "They like you. They tolerated me."

She appeared to think for a moment. "That is possible."

"Probable." He flew silently for a few minutes. "How did you earn a favor from them?"

"I spared their lives."

Ben glanced to the side. "Who wanted you to kill them?"

"Your uncle."

Okay, he hadn't been expecting that. "Giovanni? Why?"

Tenzin narrowed her eyes. "You do realize they're very horrible criminals, don't you? They traffic in drugs, guns, even in humans."

*And I just serenaded them with Louis Armstrong classics.* "Okay, better question, why *didn't* you kill them?"

"I thought your uncle was overreacting. And he'll admit he was now. Juvan helped Lorenzo kidnap Beatrice years ago. He lent some of his men to Lorenzo when they went to Houston."

"I can see why Giovanni would be kind of pissed about that."

"But they never had anything to do with Lorenzo's little schemes," Tenzin said. "They were work for hire. Your uncle sees that now."

"And that made a difference to him?"

"Of course. Don't forget that your uncle was an assassin too. For many years, he didn't have much of a conscience. He had rules, but not a conscience."

Ben tasted bitterness in the back of his throat. "So that's going to be me eventually?"

Tenzin looked genuinely baffled. "Why would that happen to you?"

"Don't you lose your human morals after a while? Justify things you normally wouldn't because you're so... above humanity?"

Tenzin raced in front of him, stopping him on his flight path. "Why do you think that?"

"Because—"

"I do not understand this about you, Benjamin. I truly do not. Your uncle's sire was a madman who actively killed Giovanni's empathy for others, but he still retained a core of humanity. My early immortal life was horrible, and I..." She stared at a spot over his shoulder, her eyes piercing the darkness. "I cut off parts of myself to survive it. But that was us."

Ben stared at her. What was she saying? Tenzin never talked

about her past like this. She didn't look back. He couldn't remember how many times she'd told him: *If I look back, I will go truly mad.*

"You cut off parts of yourself to survive?" He swallowed hard. "What does that mean, Tenzin?"

She shook her head. "It means that you are not me. And you haven't had to do that. I would *never* have let him take you unless I knew he had evolved. I wouldn't have allowed it."

"Tenzin—"

"This isn't about Zhang. Or me. You are yourself. And I know you are angry with me, but you have to think past that now."

"No, this *is* about you." *I don't want to talk about me.* "You want me to reveal everything when you give me *nothing*. What do you mean, Tenzin?"

She ignored him. "Does Carwyn have a conscience? Does Beatrice?" Her face was twisted with an anger Ben had never seen before. "Think of the countless men and women of honor whom you know. Baojia. Brigid. Lucien Thrax." She seemed to stumble a little on Lucien's name. "Your *friends*, Benjamin."

He felt a burning in his chest. "You were my friend."

She looked him straight in the eyes. "I am still your friend. I will always be your friend whether you want me or not."

She turned and flew toward shore, leaving him alone in the dark clouds, the wind cutting through his clothes and lashing his skin as a light rain began to fall around him.

TENZIN LANDED on the balcony of Gavin's house in Monte Carlo. He had a top-floor apartment in a historic building with updated amenities and vampire security. It would have cost him millions and millions of dollars, or many favors.

Did Gavin have a conscience? It was slightly grey, but yes. He definitely did. He had a code of honor that he stuck to. Immortals could depend on him. And while some high-minded philosophers like Carwyn didn't approve of Gavin's policies, his safe spaces allowed many disputes to be resolved without blood or collateral damage. That was a valuable service to vampires and humans both.

Gavin Wallace wasn't pure of heart, but he'd earned the love of a pure-hearted woman. That had to mean something.

Chloe was sitting on a lounge chair reading a book. She glanced up when Tenzin landed on the ledge. "Hey, how was your night?"

"Ben is brooding again." Tenzin hopped down. "I do not understand him."

"You'd be bored if you did." Chloe turned a page. "What now?"

"Why does he think becoming a vampire is a recipe for inhumanity? Why does he think he's going to become some kind of monster?"

Chloe looked up with wide eyes. "You know, you really need to work on the small talk. 'Hey, how was your night? Is the casino nice? How much did Gavin drop in frightening fashion on games with ridiculously large cards?'"

"I do not have time for small talk." She walked over to Chloe and dragged a lounge chair next to hers. "I have until the end of this job to make this man see reason. Why does he think he's going to become some kind of monster now that he is a vampire?"

Chloe set down her book. "You know what he did to my ex-boyfriend, right?"

Tenzin stared blankly at her. "Do you?"

"Yes. He eventually told me. He broke Tom's fingers and his knee. Some... other stuff. He basically got a list of the injuries Tom gave to me and systematically, over a period of months, inflicted every single one on my ex. Not in anger. It was pure, cold revenge."

Tenzin said nothing.

"You know it's in him," Chloe said quietly. "That cruelty—the capacity for it—it's there. He plays at being light and funny, but you've seen it. You recognize it too."

Tenzin knew it was there. She'd sat next to him through some of the darkest times. "But it is not in his heart," she said. "That's why he eventually told you about Tom. That's why he could never become like me."

"You're very hard on yourself."

"You don't know all the things I've done." *And you never will.* "I'm being honest."

Chloe let out a long breath. "So... his parents were awful. He'll never tell you how much, but they were really awful. Those scars on his arms are not from goofing around with friends when he was a kid." Chloe pulled her knees up to her chest. "When Giovanni adopted him, I think Ben decided that he was going to be *perfect.* The best nephew. The best friend. The perfect student. Everything under control. Because he was never going to be like *them.*"

"And becoming a vampire puts some things out of his control."

"Yes." Chloe cleared her throat. "You're so brilliant and wise. Don't you see how scared he is?"

*Scared?* Ben was frightened?

"But he's not supposed to be afraid anymore. That was the point." Tenzin rose and began to pace. "That was the whole point."

"I wish I could snap my fingers and make it different, but people don't work that way."

Tenzin walked toward Chloe and knelt in front of her. "No one can manipulate him now. His mind is his own. He was sired by one of the most powerful vampires on the planet. That was the *point*, Chloe. For Ben to not be afraid."

Chloe brushed back a piece of Tenzin's hair. "I know that's what you wanted. But fear is one of the things that keeps us humble. It makes us human."

"It can also make you dead."

Seeing Ben afraid had broken something in Tenzin. His fear broke open a rage she had not felt in thousands of years. That rage had burned her from the inside out, hollowing her out until something new was forced to grow.

Chloe smiled, but it was sad. "I can't force him to see your perspective. And neither can you. He's going to be angry for a while, and he's probably going to do a lot of things you don't understand."

*I love you. I love you so much. And I'm dying, so you need to know that.*

Tenzin turned away from Chloe and watched the waves rise and fall in the midnight sea. "I am trying."

"You mean your New Year's resolutions?"

Tenzin—in her new spirit of openness—had tried to explain to Chloe that she was becoming something new, but most of it hadn't translated very well.

"Yes. My resolutions."

When Ben's human body had died, a part of Tenzin had died with it. The mercy he'd demanded of her had forced Tenzin to look inward.

Which she *hated*.

She was a weapon, a blade in her sire's hand. A creature created to be used by others.

Over millennia, she had sheared away the parts of herself that could be hurt. If she was a weapon, she would be a weapon only for herself. She wouldn't only be feared, she would be worshipped.

Now Tenzin wanted to be more.

She had humbled herself before her father. She'd crawled across cobblestones on her knees. She'd pledged fidelity to a sire she hated in order to save the life of the one human who had never seen her as a weapon or a goddess.

He had only seen her.

*You're lovely. Lovable. You're worthy of that.*

She was trying to awaken parts of herself that had been strangled by the past. It was irritating as shit.

"Humans are so infuriating."

Chloe said, "He's not human anymore."

"Then vampires are so infuriating! I don't know what he wants from me."

Chloe sighed. "The problem is, he may not want anything from you. Not for a long time."

She tapped her foot on the marble tiles. "I can be patient."

Chloe nodded. "Uh-huh."

Tenzin turned to Chloe and narrowed her eyes. "You said something that means yes, but your face says the opposite."

"You're just... not the best at waiting for things you want."

Tenzin flopped back on the lounger and scowled at the stars. "Why should I wait for something to happen when I can make it happen faster?"

Chloe reached down and stroked Tenzin's hair. "Because you can't change someone's heart."

"I can try."

"Well, yeah. I guess that's the whole point, right? Just remember, hearts can be stubborn things."

Ben had loved her once, so Tenzin was counting on his heart

being very stubborn. Stubborn enough to keep loving her even when he was angry.

Chloe kept stroking her hair.

"You're petting me like your cat."

"I know. I really miss Pete. I kind of wish we'd brought him with us."

"Glad I could help."

## 15

Ben landed on the roof of Gavin's club in Monte Carlo, absently noting the muffled noise of the casino in the building below.

Vampires, Ben had learned, enjoyed gambling as much or more than humans did. There must be something about centuries of life, vast amounts of money, and boredom that caused them to dabble in games.

Go figure.

He walked to the hostess, who hadn't batted an eye as he landed on the balcony. She was human, though Ben could see more than one vampire working in the club. Unusual, but then not all vampires were rich.

"*Bonsoir, monsieur.*"

"*Bonsoir,*" he replied, also in French. "Is Mr. Wallace in the club tonight?"

"May I tell him who is inquiring about him?"

"Ben Vecchio."

"Thank you, Mr. Vecchio. I'll let him know you're here."

There was no use trying to be anonymous in Europe. He'd

already spotted several vampires he knew from Rome and more than one he'd seen in New York and London.

Come to think of it, most of the vampires he spotted hadn't seen Ben since he'd turned. He'd been more than a bit of a hermit in Asia. He was attracting a few looks, and he hadn't even thought about it.

*Oh well.*

Gavin walked out from the interior of the club and onto the open-air patio where Ben was waiting. "I see we're not being circumspect anymore."

Ben shrugged and kept his hands in his pockets. "Let them stare."

Gavin glanced at the open stares many vampires in the club were sporting before he led Ben to a smaller alcove with a table and two deep benches. "The stares used to drive you crazy."

"People are going to look their fill whether I want them to or not," he said under his breath. "Better to let them get a good eyeful, smother the rumors, and be done with it."

Gavin was clearly amused. He leaned back and stretched an arm across the back of the bench. "You picked a fairly prominent location for your coming-out party, my friend."

Ben assessed the club with a critical eye. "It's fancy."

"I like the weather."

"Gotta love the Mediterranean nights. They're never too hot."

"Very true." Gavin nodded. "So, any developments?"

Ben glanced around. "Is talking in the club—"

"We worked sound masking into the audio system." Gavin kept his voice low and even. "I mean, don't shout, but you haven't been hearing everyone's gossip, have you?"

"I can't really concentrate on much over the casino noise."

"Exactly." Gavin tipped his glass toward a speaker embedded in the wall next to him.

Huh. Clever. Ben nodded. "Cool." He was craving a drink. "As for developments, it's looking like Hungary."

"Are you sure?" Gavin waved over a server and ordered a very expensive bottle of champagne.

"Fairly sure."

"Looking at it, I was leaning toward Turkey."

"Hungary definitely seems higher on the list."

"And you're sure they've seen the original?"

"No, but they've seen photographs."

Gavin's eyebrows went up. "That is notable."

"Tenzin thought so too."

"How did things go with her?"

The server brought back crystal champagne glasses and a cut crystal glacette with ice and a bottle of Dom Pérignon. She opened the bottle and poured two glasses, setting them in front of Ben and Gavin.

"*Santé.*"

"*Santé.*"

They clinked glasses, and Ben sipped the dry, sparkling wine.

"To your immortality," Gavin said. "May you not waste it as long as I did."

Ben's eyebrow went up. "Oh?"

"Yes, Tenzin gave me quite a lecture a few years ago about all the dawdling I was doing. Apparently creating an international club and entertainment empire was a bit of a waste. Who knew?"

"She did apparently." He drank his glass and poured another. "Fuck, I hate not being able to get drunk."

Gavin raised an eyebrow.

"What?" Ben said. "It just took the edge off sometimes, you know?"

"I know. What did you think of the Corsicans?"

"They're interesting. They really love Tenzin."

"That doesn't surprise me; she saved their hides from your uncle."

"She told me. So Hungary. Can you leave tomorrow night?"

"I can. This visit was more of a check-in than a real work trip. My manager here is very good."

"He or she would have to be."

"She, and yes." He looked around the club. "This club has seen more than its share of immortal summits."

"Not that you can tell me about them."

"Of course not."

"Does it bother you?" Ben saw a water vampire Emil Conti had been trying to track down in Italy for a few years. The man was a thief and had assaulted a human on Conti's staff, nearly killing her. Yet here he sat in Monte Carlo, openly chatting with business associates and beautiful humans.

"I like who I like" —Gavin followed his eyes but said nothing about the Italian vampire— "but business is business. Safe haven is assumed in my clubs unless you cross me or those under my protection. Neutrality may not be palatable to some, but it's necessary."

Ben shook his head. "What does it say about me that it makes sense?"

"It says you appreciate disagreements being settled without bloodshed."

"Right."

"What has you in a mood?"

*I am still your friend. I will always be your friend whether you want me or not.*

"Tenzin thinks she did the right thing, doesn't she? Not just the selfish thing" —he looked at Gavin directly— "the right thing. The *righteous* thing."

"Yes. And she's right."

"How can you say that, knowing how I feel?"

"Because look at you." Gavin leaned forward and refilled his champagne glass. "Look at yourself, Ben." His voice was low. "Your power fills this space like the bass thumping in Radu's club the other night. That's how big it is. Most vampires would walk in here with an attitude if they wore that much power. Even if they were young, they would flaunt it. And yet here you are, quietly drinking a glass of wine with me, speaking politely to the humans in my employ, nodding at immortals you only know socially and acknowledging everyone, not only those who can benefit you."

"And?"

"You were born to be this." Gavin sat back. "Don't glare at me when you know it's the truth. You—the man you were—has not been changed by immortality. If anything, it's made you a little more humble. And that's extraordinary."

"So you're saying Tenzin knew what was good for me better than I did?" Yeah, that really didn't sit well.

"I'm saying that if it hadn't been her who had to make the decision, you'd already be at peace with it. You're angry because you don't want to admit this is who you were meant to be."

IT MIGHT HAVE BEEN early Saturday morning for Ben, but it was still Friday night for his baby sister, which meant that he owed her a video chat.

Ben sat in his safe room at Gavin's and powered on his tablet. In seconds, a ringing sound filled the room.

"Ben?" Sadia's little face popped onto the screen. "You called!"

"I told you I would."

"Every Friday night."

"As many as I can." Ben knew not to make promises he might not be able to keep. "I will do my best."

Sadia's screen jumped and shook. "Wait a minute."

"Where are you taking me?"

"To my fort."

He smiled. "Your fort?"

"Yes." The shaking stopped but the picture wasn't as bright.

"Where are you?"

"I told you, in my fort." She craned her neck. "Dema and I built it in the playroom, and we used blankets and some of the poles from a camping tent and it's really cool." She looked up. "Can you see?"

"I can see the inside a little."

"It's really cool." She propped her chin on her fists. "Do you have a fort?"

"I don't."

"Where are you?"

He looked out the window at the glittering lights of the boats docked in the harbor. "I'm not too far from Rome."

"Really?" She switched to Italian. *"Piacere!"*

Ben smiled. *"Ciao, sorellina."*

"Are you going to Rome? Are you going to see Fabi?"

"Not on this trip. I'm going to a new place I've never been tomorrow."

"Is it going to be fun?"

"I hope so."

"If it's not" —she rolled over and looked at the tablet upside down— "just come home."

"I'll keep that in mind." He smiled. "I do have to work though."

"I know." She kicked her feet in the air. "Do you see my feet?"

"I do."

"Mama said Dema is going to buy me new shoes because I grew out of my old ones."

"Are you getting really old while I'm gone? Am I going to recognize you when I see you again?"

She giggled. "Yes. I'm going to be old enough to be a vampire soon."

Ben tried not to wince. "Okay, silly, just remember—"

"It's only, only allowed for grown-ups." She rolled back over. "I knoooow."

He stared at her precious round face and her missing teeth. He tried to imagine what she would have done if he'd died in China. Would she still remember him? Or would he only be a faint memory now, reserved for pictures in her childhood home?

"Sadi?"

"Yeah?" She was reaching for her feet behind her back.

"Why do you want to be a vampire when you grow up?"

She nearly caught her toes, but she toppled over in the dark blanket fort. "'Caaaaause Mama and Baba are vampires. And you are. And when I'm grown up, then I'll be a vampire too and then Mama and Baba and you and me can be a family forever."

Ben had the urge to hug the screen, but it wouldn't be as satisfying as hugging Sadia. "That makes sense."

"I know. And Tenzin will be in our family too." She was reaching for her toes again. "And Dema and Zain, but they won't be vampires."

"You've got it all planned out."

"I know! Don't you think it's a good idea? Mama says it's good to plan things."

"Yeah, she's right." Ben was fighting the urge to cry. He cleared his throat. "Tell me what you learned in school this week."

Sadia launched into a litany. She loved reading books, and she extra loved playing on the giant grand piano in the music room. She did not like Latin and said it was boring and Mandarin was more fun because she already had a screen friend in Hong Kong she could talk Mandarin with, but none of her friends knew about Latin even though Baba loved it best.

His baby sister switched fluidly between English, Italian, and Spanish, though she sometimes confused things in Italian and Spanish. She spoke Arabic with Dema but never with Ben. She was quick, curious, and had more than her share of attitude.

Ben refused to think about himself at Sadia's age. She lived in a different world than he had, and Ben was happy for it. She chattered like a bird, nothing at all like the suspicious, wounded toddler he'd first met. She was cautious with those outside her family, but within, she was a glittering star.

Ben could feel dawn approaching. "Sadi?"

Her blinks were also getting long, and she'd lain down in the blanket fort, resting her cheek on her arms. "Yeah?"

"I need to go to bed, and I think you do too."

"Okay." Another long blink. "Baba said you were with Tenzin."

"Um. Yeah, she's here."

"She's there?"

"Not right here. Not this time."

"Next time?"

Ben was hoping that by next week Tenzin would be out of his life, but how was he supposed to tell Sadia that? "I'll tell her to call you, okay?"

"Okay." Sadia yawned. "Love you forever, Benny."

"Love you for always, Sadi."

He ended the video call and tried to contemplate a world where he didn't get to see Sadia grow up. Where he wasn't able to watch over her.

*"I didn't want to die yet."*

*"You won't."*

# 16

The flight to Budapest took a little over two hours, so Ben, Tenzin, Gavin, and Chloe used their time the next night to go over Ben's notes about the Hungarian collector.

Ben put the man's picture in the center of the table. "Gergo Farkas is pretty notorious with human authorities. *Collector* is a generous term. He does collect and he does deal on the legitimate market now, but he started out as a thief. Probably retired now."

"This guy?" Chloe held up the picture. "He looks like a bookkeeper."

The nondescript man in the photo looked like he was in his early seventies and was wearing a dull brown suit and a tweed cap.

"Don't be fooled by his appearance. He's successful because he skates under most radars. He wants to be forgettable."

"Farkas is more than successful. He's brilliant." Tenzin was glowing. "Such a beautiful thief. Some of the best work I've seen from a human. He stole the Caravaggio Nativity, and it was not ruined like they said. That part was fiction."

Gavin said, "Really? I thought that was two men?"

"No, it was Farkas and a partner. A woman. No one ever found it."

"I thought the mob had that one," Ben said.

Tenzin waved her hand. "Not even close."

Ben glanced at the photo. "Farkas's residence has been a mystery for years, even among his close associates. The only reason we have this location is because apparently, someone very private and very mysterious owed my aunt a favor."

Gavin looked at the map spread on the table. "How far outside of Budapest is this?"

"No more than an hour by air," Ben said. "I think it's best if Tenzin and I go in by ourselves."

"Agreed," Tenzin said. "Chloe, we'll keep in touch with you via Cara."

"Sounds good to me." She leaned into Gavin's shoulder. "I bet there's a safe, comfy place I can hang out."

"Of course, dove." Gavin was still looking at the map. "So you're breaking into Farkas's house."

"Yes. It's near Lake Balaton." Ben put more pictures on the table. "An old baroque mansion with a winery attached. Farkas runs the winery now. Claims to be totally legitimate of course, but access to the house is limited. As far as I can tell, there are no pictures of the interior. No plans of any kind on file at city or county offices. He doesn't get visitors. He entertains a little, but it's all at the winery, not the house."

"Big old house like that," Chloe said. "Lots of walls. So many possibilities." She nudged Gavin. "If you want to go..."

"No, it's fine." Gavin stared at the pictures. "Totally fine. I don't need to go."

Tenzin said, "You can come if you want."

Gavin looked at Tenzin, then at Chloe. "No. It's fine."

Chloe broke into peals of laughter. "Oh, you *so* want to go break into the old art thief's house!"

"No." Gavin straightened his tie. "I'm a legitimate businessman now. Not some thieving rake."

"Well, we're not thieving rakes." Ben looked at Tenzin, then back to Gavin. "We're going to break in the thieving rake's house and then... *recover* an icon that rightfully belongs to Radu."

Chloe asked, "And we know it belongs to Radu how?"

"Because" —Ben cleared his throat— "he told us so."

Chloe pursed her lips. "Just admit that you have different standards about stealing things from a thief than you do from a normal person. I completely understand that justification."

Ben spread his hands. "I mean, Farkas obviously stole it from someone, right? If it's there, it's Radu's icon. And Radu knows the entire history of the thing and he's Poshani, which means that his people pray to Sara-la-Kali, so obviously the history of the thing..."

Tenzin was frowning at him.

"What?"

She turned to Chloe. "If you're an art thief, then you have to expect people to try to steal from you. It's only fair."

"Agreed," Chloe said. "That makes sense to me."

Ben turned to Tenzin. "So do you expect people to try to steal from you?"

"Obviously. Why do you think I move my gold regularly and keep very little art?"

"Are we ignoring your jewelry and armor collection?"

She waved a hand. "That's more fashion than art."

"The armor is fashion?"

"It is if you ask me."

"Arthur loves the armor," Chloe said. "Even though he's a little creeped out by it."

"Do we have any blueprints at all?" Tenzin asked.

"Nope. I scoured online archives but couldn't find anything. It's possible there's something in the local county records, but I figured it would be just as easy to break in and look for ourselves."

"Sounds good."

Chloe and Gavin went to the galley to grab a snack for Chloe, leaving Ben and Tenzin at the table alone.

"I talked to Sadia last night," Ben said. "She wants you to call her."

"Then I will do that."

"Do you talk to her often?"

"I try to call at least once a month."

"Why?"

Tenzin looked up with wide eyes. "Does it bother you?"

"I'm just—"

"You know what? I don't care if it bothers you." Tenzin looked back at the pictures of the house. "You cannot keep me from speaking to Sadia if she wants to speak to me. I love her."

"I'm not trying to keep you from Sadia."

"Good."

Ben could tell she was pissed. "You need to stop assuming the worst about me."

Tenzin looked up. "Why? You assume the worst about me constantly."

"I do not."

"Of course you do."

"I don't—" He raised a hand. "Okay, look. I don't want to fight about this."

"You don't want to fight because you weren't winning," she muttered.

"No, this is supposed to be just business, and it's getting into the personal." He gathered up the papers. "We agreed to keep it business."

"Our lives have been entwined for over ten years," Tenzin said. "Do you really think we can keep anything only to business at this point?"

"Doesn't matter." His throat felt tight. "That was the agreement."

Tenzin stared at him for a long time. "So it was."

She rose and left him alone with his files.

THEY'D all agreed to stay in Gavin's house in Budapest since he had plenty of room for them all, and with any luck, they'd only be there for a night. Knowing that Tenzin was going to be not-sleeping in a room right next to him was messing with Ben's mind.

He wanted to talk with her. He didn't know what to say. He probably shouldn't talk to her, but he found the urge to just be in the same room with her was nearly impossible to resist.

Was it her blood? Was this because he'd taken her blood and his amnis wanted her? Ben felt slightly desperate thinking about the end of this job. In a matter of days, they'd be finished and he'd have no excuse to be near her. What would he do? Where would he go?

He had no obligation to return to China to be near Zhang because his sire had asked nothing of him.

He had no obligations in Los Angeles except with family.

When he thought about his future, the only thing he wanted to do was what he had been doing. He wanted to look for lost art for clients.

Ben found her in her room. He knocked on the door and waited for her to open it, but all he heard was a clatter of what sounded like plastic hitting the floor.

"Tenzin?"

She opened the door, her cheeks flushed. The sight sent an immediate surge of arousal to his groin even though he knew she'd probably just been having blood-wine.

"What?" She was irritated. She glanced down at the sudden tent in his pants. "I don't have time for that right now."

"I wasn't... What was that?" Ben found her irritation oddly comforting. "Did you break something?"

She spun and looked at a scatter of yellow plastic on the ground. "This... thing! It's driving me crazy."

He walked into the room and stared at the mangled plastic and circuitry. "Is that the new Nintendo portable console?"

"Yes. If I wear thick gloves, it's too clumsy. If I wear thin gloves" —she held up her hands in light pink driving gloves— "then it breaks in under a half an hour!"

He looked at the stack of boxes next to the bed. "How many of these things have you wrecked?"

"This is the third."

"Tenzin."

She kicked the pieces toward the wastebasket. "What else am I supposed to do? I'm going crazy waiting. Why aren't we flying to Farkas's house tonight?"

"Because tomorrow he has an event at the winery and no one will be home."

She let her head fall back. "So we just sedate him or something if he's in the house. Come *on*, Ben, you're a vampire now. You have amnis."

"Which I'm not going to use on humans unless I absolutely have to." The familiarity of the argument was soothing. "I don't know why you find this surprising."

She sat in a chair and glared at him, her arms crossed over her chest. "I would just like to point out that the man who was convinced he was going to turn into a monster if he became a vampire is still the man with an overdeveloped sense of honor toward humans who don't deserve it."

"This isn't an honor thing. It'll just be easier—"

"Tell the truth—you don't even like hunting, do you?"

He leaned against the doorjamb and crossed his arms, mirroring her posture. "Why would I need to when there are perfectly willing human donors available when I want to drink?"

A slight flush came to her lips. "I bet they love you."

"I tip well."

"That's not why they love you."

"Tenzin..."

She said nothing, but the raised eyebrow said enough.

"I don't have time for this."

She laughed. "Yes, you do. You have time, Ben. Plenty of it now."

"Are you trying to piss me off?"

She opened her mouth, then closed it. "Hmm."

"Are you actually thinking about what you're going to say?"

"I am attempting in this new life to be more introspective." She pursed her lips. "So far the results have been mixed."

"What new life?"

She turned her eyes to him, and Ben felt a sudden sense of vertigo. Her eyes were ancient. Too often it was easy to write her off as a mercurial, easily distracted magpie.

She wasn't.

Tenzin was an immortal over five thousand years old. She'd been born in a time before history was written. She'd seen the land reshape itself and civilizations rise and fall.

He was a child compared to her. Everyone was.

Tenzin walked over, nudged him to the side, and closed the door.

Ben was frozen, still leaning against the wall with his arms crossed over his chest.

"Do you know how many nights it has been since you were changed?"

"About two—"

"Eight hundred twenty-six." She looked up. "I counted."

"Why?"

"Because we both lost important things that night. You lost your human life, and I lost the one human who truly saw me and wasn't afraid."

His chest felt tight. "Nima?"

"Nima loved me, but she always feared me."

The urge to touch her was impossible to ignore. He reached out and ran a finger under her bottom lip.

Tenzin closed her eyes and let her mouth fall open. Her fangs were long and curving. They never retreated; she couldn't hide like Ben could.

"What else did you lose?" he asked quietly.

"Peace."

In that, at least, they were the same.

"I can't give that to you," Ben said. *I'm still looking for my own.*

"I know." Tenzin opened her eyes. "It's not your job."

*I miss you.*

*You're the other half of me.*

*You broke my heart, and I don't know how to forgive you.*

Ben swallowed the words he wanted to say. "Tell me about this new life."

"Are you sure? This really isn't business."

"Just tell me."

Tenzin took a few steps back and hopped on the bed. "Chloe calls them my New Year's resolutions."

The corner of his mouth turned up. "Is this some kind of self-improvement thing?"

She cocked her head. "Not yet. Right now I'm just trying to find the dead parts."

A low, silent part of his heart screamed. "Dead parts?"

She didn't say anything.

"This is what you were talking about before, isn't it? The parts of yourself you had to cut off to survive."

"Yes."

"Are you going to tell me?"

She smiled a little. "Why would I do that?"

"You were my best friend for ten years, Tenzin."

"Exactly. Why would I do that to my best friend?"

"Talking—"

"Saying something aloud doesn't make it more or less horrible. I know that talking is helpful to some people, but it's really not useful for me." She leaned back. "It's nothing personal. If I felt like it was useful, I would tell you."

"Have you ever told anyone?"

She was clearly struggling with how much to tell him. Ben dragged a chair over and sat. He didn't say anything; he just waited.

"Beatrice knows the basics. I told Nima some things before she died."

"Why?"

"She was dying and she asked me to tell her. So I told her a story. It was for her, not for me."

Ben had a feeling that Nima had seen far more than Tenzin gave her credit for. "So what are your New Year's resolutions?" *How do you find the dead parts, Tiny?*

"To look inward more." She looked at a point over his shoulder. "To think about how situations make me feel and not just react to them."

"Let's just consider the Nintendo carnage a slip and not a complete fall off the wagon."

She snarled. "Mobile gaming options for vampires are limited and highly imperfect."

"You're preaching to the choir now."

"When did you join a choir?"

Ben shook his head. "Never mind. Tell me more about the resolutions."

"Nima left her journals with me, and that is one thing she mentioned, that I needed to not react to things instinctively."

Ben let out a long breath. "That's got to irritate you."

"So much." She narrowed her eyes. "So very much."

Ben smiled. "It's good though. That's a good one. Giovanni was always really good at reinforcing that. Live deliberately and not by instinct."

Which was the only reason he was all the way across the room and not on the bed, tearing Tenzin's clothes off. Being with Tenzin created a gloriously messy set of emotions. He was relieved. He was angry. He was happy. He was very horny. And he was hungry.

While Tenzin appeared completely nonchalant.

"It is a good idea," she said, "otherwise I would not be doing it." She looked straight at him. "But that does not mean I regret having sex with you. That was instinctual, but a good instinct. Is that why you came to my room?"

"What? No!"

"Because I know you're aroused."

"No. That's not..." He'd initially come to talk to her about the New York house, but he'd gotten distracted by Nintendo carnage and New Year's resolutions and... Tenzin.

"Okay." She swung her legs. "Did you want to—?"

"Right." Ben jumped to his feet and headed toward the door. "Um... we have a big night tomorrow, so I'm going to... leave." He turned at the door and her annoyingly perfect eyebrow was arched again. "Bye."

## 17

---

Tenzin stretched back on the bed and reached for the journal she'd brought with her. It was one Nima had written during a particularly turbulent part of their life together, just after Nima had decided she would not turn.

As Tenzin felt the sun rise, she closed her eyes and allowed her mind to drift in the fluid space that had become her favorite part of the day.

It wasn't exactly sleep, but it was close. She felt the touch of a single familiar finger slide across her cheek.

"He still loves you."

She turned and saw Nima lying next to her. "Do you think so?"

In her dreams, Nima was young again, flush with life and possibilities. This was the Nima before human religion had turned her mind away from immortal life. Her skin was smooth and her eyes were dark brown with flecks of gold that reminded Tenzin of amber. She loved staring into Nima's eyes. Her face was constantly changing, but her beautiful brown eyes remained the same.

"Look at you." Nima's smile was a brilliant crescent moon.

"Your hair is so short."

"Do you like it?"

"It suits who you are now." She scooted closer. "I would miss braiding it though. I always loved to braid your hair."

"I am sorry."

"Why are you sorry?"

Tenzin thought. "I do not know."

"Yes, you do."

"I did not deserve your love."

Nima's smile turned soft. "My love for you was a gift. It required nothing in return."

"You deserved more."

Her eyes teased. "I know I did."

She stroked the soft, smooth skin of Nima's cheek. "I am sorry I was not who I am now."

"You couldn't be," Nima said. "You needed to remember that you are human."

"I am not human."

"Oh, my lovely Tenzin." Nima's hand cupped Tenzin's cheek, and her thumb brushed over her skin with a featherlight touch. "I was angry and I was wrong. You are the most human of them all, for you have known weakness. If you remember, it will only make you stronger."

"I miss you."

"He misses you."

"But I miss *you*."

"You miss him."

Tenzin closed her eyes. "I wish I had been more for you."

"You were only who you could be in that moment. Now you are someone else, and he loves who you are."

"Sometimes I think he only loved an idea of me."

"What are any of us but the idea of a person in someone else's mind?" Nima pressed her forehead to Tenzin's. "Don't forget: ideas are powerful things."

~

THEY FLEW under the clouds on a moonless night, their black clothes invisible in the night sky. If anyone saw them from below, they would only see a shadow passing over the stars as they flew southwest of the capital.

The mansion where Gergo Farkas made his home was a restored baroque castle that sprawled across a hilltop overlooking Lake Balaton. Lush forests covered the hill behind the house while gracious vineyards blanketed the slopes in front. All the fields draped down toward the emerald-green water of the lake, one of the most cherished tourist spots in Hungary.

The house was fully restored with bright yellow and cream plasterwork arches and intricate wrought iron running along numerous balconies.

Ben and Tenzin floated at a distance. Ben was looking through a pair of binoculars while Tenzin surveyed the land around the house.

"The north balcony," Ben said. "The windows don't look secure."

"We'll see," Tenzin said. "I've heard that Farkas knows about our kind."

"But how much?" It was one thing to know vampires existed. It was a whole other matter to know the intricacies of vampire life along with their strengths and weaknesses. "For now it doesn't look like he's expecting any thieves."

"That could be a clever trap to lure us in."

"Or it could be he's an overconfident old man convinced of his own security." Ben tucked the binoculars away. "North balcony."

Tenzin spread her arms out. "You lead, and I shall follow."

Ben sped down to the wide balcony that overlooked the hills and the vineyards. He landed softly and waited for Tenzin to join him. They moved silently over the balcony, which was paved with star-shaped stones.

Ben waited for Tenzin to reach the window, and it did look suspiciously open.

Tenzin narrowed her eyes. "Strange." She pushed open the window without another word. "Let's go."

Ben followed, ducking his head as he entered the wide hallway that led along the north balcony. It was a classic long gallery with artwork hanging on both walls, interspersed with windows and french doors leading to the balcony. Doors leading to what were probably bedrooms came at regular intervals.

Ben turned right and followed Tenzin. She was out of sight, already turning the corner to the west gallery, which overlooked the front facade and grand entrance of the house.

He didn't hear a pin drop. There were no humans in the house, no pets either if he had to guess.

Maybe a turtle. Turtles didn't make much noise.

"Tenzin?"

She paused in front of a giant painting and looked up. "Do you think I could take this one?"

Ben glanced up. "No."

"It would match Chloe's room. He probably stole it in the first place."

"Tenzin, it's like six feet tall."

"*Midnight Labyrinth* was bigger."

He pulled on her sleeve. "Let's just go."

"Fine." She started walking again. "No one is home, but something feels off."

"I feel the same way." He rushed through the gallery, scanning all the walls. "You see anything?"

"I don't even see anything stylistically similar to the icon.

145

These are all modern."

"Agreed." He reached the landing that led to the grand staircase and halted. "Oh, I get it."

"Organized by era." Tenzin ran her hand along the edge of a rural landscape. Romantic-era paintings lined the staircase, leading down to a neoclassical nude sculpture.

"Icons are going to be on the second floor maybe?"

"Depends. We'll start there." She was looking around the massive entryway. "Something isn't right."

Ben froze and whispered, "What?"

"Something about the house."

"There's no one here."

"I know." She floated to the center of the room, turning in place. "Come here."

"Tenzin, we should really look at the second floor."

"Just come here. There's something, and I can't quite tell..."

Ben floated out from the gallery landing to the center of the room. He had a distinct sense of discomfort. "Okay, I feel it now."

"It's too... small?"

It was a ridiculous statement on the surface—the house was enormous—but that was exactly the same feeling Ben had. The proportions of the rooms were off. "Let's keep going. I think we're going to find something on the second floor."

"Okay."

Tenzin and Ben floated down to the second-floor landing where, instead of a gallery leading around the house, a massive ballroom took up the east half of the residence. Rococo and baroque-era canvases covered the walls of the ballroom, and the ceiling was painted in brilliant Easter egg colors. Decadent gold plasterwork dominated the space.

"I have the same feeling here," Ben said. "This room is massive, but it should be bigger."

"I may know what's going on." Tenzin walked to the marble

fireplace at the north side of the room and put her hands on the wall next to it.

"What are you doing?"

"Come here." She was a black shadow against the pale blue wall. "Feel here."

Ben put his hands on the plaster. It was smooth and cool, the paint was perfect, and gold sconces lined the walls at eye level.

"Do you feel it?" she asked.

"I don't know what I'm supposed to be looking for."

"The space." She put a hand over his. "Feel the *space*, Benjamin. The air will talk to you now if you know how to listen. Don't listen to what is there. Feel for what is not there. Feel for the void."

Voids were everywhere, but as soon as she said it, the disquieting feeling settled and he understood. "There's a passageway."

"More than that." Tenzin smiled. "From the expanse I'm sensing, there are entire hidden rooms."

Ben turned around in the ballroom, then raced out to the entry hall. "That's it. That's why it feels off. It's too small on the inside."

"Now we just have to find an entrance." Tenzin started to search for the seams around the molding. "There will be multiple entrances."

"So clever."

"And safe." She pressed in and a panel pushed out. "Jampot."

"Wh-what?" He pressed his lips together to keep from laughing. "Jampot?"

Tenzin looked confused. "Eureka? What's the thing you say when you find something? I forgot."

"Jackpot."

"Right." She pushed the panel in and pushed it to the side. It moved silently on hidden tracks. "Jackpot. Let's look for the real treasure, shall we?"

147

"Let's." Ben ducked his head to enter the passageway.

Tenzin was right. It was far more than a narrow hallway. This was a comfortable, though by no means grand, room meant for the same purpose as the ballroom. Sconces lined the walls, and comfortable sofas were arranged along the walls. There was plenty of room for dancing or walking.

Unlike the formal ballroom though, the art here was much more eclectic. "This is his real collection." Ben looked at the walls. "The art outside is the public collection."

"I thought you said no one came to the house."

"As far as I know, they don't. But this is definitely the private collection."

Not only were there numerous erotic art pieces on the walls, there were three-dimensional art pieces, masks, and modern art.

"Wait." Ben took a second look at a mask. He leaned closer. "Peepholes."

"Really?" Tenzin pushed him out of the way. "Oh, that's clever."

"Or, you know, *creepy*."

"Kind of both."

Looking through the eyes of the masks, the room beyond was visible. In this case it was only the empty ballroom, but in other circumstances, it would be the perfect place to spy.

Tenzin left the room and walked toward what would be the center of the house. She was as happy as a kid in a candy store.

"You love this, don't you?"

She turned and her eyes were dancing. "It's very cool." She beckoned him with a finger. "Come look."

The pattern followed through the entryway. A wide hallway lined with sconces encircled the massive walls of the grand entrance, and narrow stairs led to higher and lower floors.

"This is a labyrinth," Ben said. "You know what this reminds me of."

"Yes." Tenzin flew up a wall and into sheer darkness. "An immortal designed this."

"Without a doubt." It wasn't only the lack of windows that gave it away. Ben spotted a few quirks he'd come to recognize in vampire homes.

There were no clocks on the walls, but there were many mirrors, mostly at the end of hallways and at junctions. Vampires didn't like surprises, and they didn't much care about time.

Ben had the feeling if the icon was in Gergo Farkas's home, it was going to be in these passages.

"See anything like the icon?"

"Not yet, but I know we're on the right track."

"Unfortunately," he muttered, "this place isn't organized in any way."

"That is very true."

It was going to take much longer what with twice the number of walls to check.

Farkas's private collection followed no rhyme or reason. The only common decorating theme was the masks, and all of which he'd checked so far had proved to be hiding peepholes into rooms.

The shadow rooms on either side of the ballroom connected via the entryway, branching off there to run down the center of the house between the entryway and the rooms on the north and south ends. On the north side, Ben found a large library and what looked like offices.

On the south side, connecting through the entryway, were private salons and game rooms designed for amusement. A room devoted entirely to jigsaw puzzles and model making. Another with a pool and snooker table.

Each shadow room reflected the use of the room beyond. Game rooms and private libraries with rare books. Ben spotted more than one edition that would make his aunt and uncle drool.

"Anything like an icon yet?"

"No." Tenzin landed in front of him. "I have an idea."

"What is it?"

"Most of these European palaces had a chapel attached. Usually tucked away. Very private."

Ben looked around at the rare book library. "So if all the shadow rooms reflect the use of the rooms beyond..."

"Find the public chapel," she said. "Then look for the private one."

Ben and Tenzin exited the shadow rooms near the entry on the second floor.

"Where is the library?"

"Through here."

Ben and Tenzin entered the wide and impressive room. Beatrice could have spent hours there, but Ben didn't have that kind of time. "Look." He pointed to a small, gilt-edged door between two massive built-in bookcases. "There."

"Jampot."

"That's not a thing, Tenzin."

Ben and Tenzin walked through the small door and under an archway, only to be immediately assaulted by the scent of incense.

Tenzin sniffed. "Yep. Definitely an Orthodox Christian living here."

"Okay." Ben spun in the middle of the intimate chapel, the floor tiled in an intricate mosaic and the ceiling painted with sacred art. "What are we looking for?"

Tenzin began gently pressing on walls. "We're looking for the real chapel."

Ben began to copy her movements, and within a few minutes he heard a quiet click behind him.

"Tenzin?" Ben looked over his shoulder, then turned to scan the room.

She was gone.

## 18

Tenzin waited a few minutes in the sacred silence of the private chapel. She turned in the center of the room, enjoying the scent of incense and wax. She spotted a familiar face in the far corner and walked over to greet her.

"Hello, Kali Ma." Tenzin put her right hand over her heart and bowed. "It has been too long, mother."

The painting hanging on the wall was a relatively modern depiction of the goddess, her skin the color of charcoal ash and her four arms round and fat with bounty. One of her right hands was up in a position of blessing and the other held a handful of pink flowers. In the left hands, she carried a curved sword and a bloody severed head.

Her long black hair fell down her naked body in a wild, untamed waterfall. Delicate fangs peeked from behind her lips, and a golden crown adorned her head. The painting was framed in gold and an altar had been built beneath it.

Mother and devourer. It wasn't the first time Tenzin had encountered the goddess, and it wouldn't be the last. Kali was beyond time. Some vampires believed she *was* time.

Tenzin looked at the Christian sister whose picture they had come for, resting patiently in her golden frame, her eyes only hinting at the sacred and ferocious feminine she represented to her devotees. As Tenzin surveyed the chapel, she recognized other familiar faces.

Parvati and Durga.

Dana.

Kybele.

Pele.

Ala and Ishtar.

Tenzin glanced back at Kali Ma before she went to fetch Benjamin. "I haven't forgotten you, Kali Ma. But you haven't caught me yet."

She pushed on the panel leading out to the chapel and invited Ben inside.

"Hey." His eyes widened when he poked his head inside the chapel. "Oh wow."

"This is the place he truly worships." Even as she said it, Tenzin knew it wasn't true. This place wasn't for Gergo Farkas. There was a profoundly feminine energy in the space, and it came from both the worshippers and the worshipped.

She gestured to the small icon hanging near Kali's right hands. "I believe we've found your icon."

Ben stepped inside the room, and his vibrant, masculine energy filled the space.

Tenzin glanced at Kali Ma, pleased that she felt no imbalance. Ben was the best kind of male, utterly confident in who he was while humble enough to respect the feminine.

Ben stood in front of Sara-la-Kali. The icon was modest next to the gilt-edged painting of Kali. The woman was depicted in the flat perspective common in Eastern European art. Her skin was medium brown and her eyes large, dark, and round. She wore a soft pink scarf around her hair, the base knotted at her nape, and her right hand was raised in a gentle blessing.

"There she is." Ben's voice was soft. "Damn."

"What's wrong?"

"It probably sounds strange, but I really hate to move her. She seems happy here."

Tenzin smiled. It was good to see his reluctance. "She won't mind."

He glanced over his shoulder, amused. "I don't think she'll care one way or the other, but it's obvious that Farkas holds this icon in enormous esteem." He turned in a circle. "This is a very... deliberate collection."

"It is." Depictions of the sacred feminine from all parts of the world were everywhere. Creation and destruction. Life and death. Hindu, Christian, druidic, pagan, and more. Her eyes locked on a small triptych on the altar to the right of Kali. "Yes, it's quite obvious that this isn't simply... art."

Could it be?

*Oh, you clever vampire.*

Tenzin smiled at the Renaissance painting. "Take the icon. Sara-la-Kali belongs to Radu and his people."

"Are you sure?"

"Quite sure. You will not offend her." She stepped forward to examine the triptych. The patroness who had commissioned it was pictured to the left of Mary, raising the same hand of blessing that Sara and the Kali offered.

Yes, she was a very clever girl.

How had she concealed their relationship so well? Tenzin had studied Gergo Farkas, and not a hint of immortal connection had come to light.

Where was this leading?

*Was that why her brother...?*

"Oh!" Pieces of Radu's plan started to fall into place, but there were still a number of holes. What an odd, roundabout way of—

"Tenzin?"

Oops. She'd forgotten about Ben.

Tenzin turned. "Hmm?"

"What's going on?"

Would he see? Probably not. She gestured to the triptych. "I was just admiring this one." If he noticed it, she'd fill him in. If not... he'd figure it out soon enough.

Ben shook his head. "We're not taking any other pieces from this place. I feel bad enough taking the icon."

"Oh no, it's fine." She waved a hand. "I'm not going to take anything else. Well, maybe..." She picked up a small pink posy that had been laid on the Kali's altar. Kali Ma wouldn't mind. Tenzin wanted to press an offering in Nima's journal.

"A flower?" Ben asked. "I doubt Farkas is going to notice."

He gently lifted the icon from the wall and placed it in the case he'd brought with them. It was only about a foot and a half long by a foot wide. He secured the icon, placed the protective layers over it, then strapped the case onto his back.

"Okay, we better go."

He was focused now. All he was thinking about was securing the prize and returning it to the client. He wasn't seeing the larger puzzle, but he would. Soon.

"Right." Tenzin turned, pressed her hands together, and bowed toward Kali Ma. Then she reached into her pocket and took out the only offering she'd brought, a lime-flavored candy she'd grabbed from Gavin's club the night before. She placed the candy on the altar, murmured a mantra, and bowed once more.

Ben was frowning. "What are you doing?"

"I'll explain later." She pushed the panel open and walked into the baroque chapel. "Come on. Radu is waiting."

BEN SAT in his room in Budapest, drinking a glass of blood-wine and staring at the icon he'd stolen from a human thief to give to a vampire one.

*All's fair in love and war.*

And art theft. Ben was fine with that. Farkas was a well-known thief, and he'd left his house unprotected. He couldn't be surprised that decades of privacy, layers of aliases, and dense Hungarian bureaucracy had not been enough to protect him.

Nope.

Something else was bugging him. It wasn't only Tenzin's odd reaction in Farkas's chapel. It wasn't the eclectic mix of deities in the worship space. It was the house itself.

Which vampire designed it? Was it a coincidence? Had Gergo Farkas happened to buy a house that had once belonged to a vampire? It was possible. He could have found the passages after he bought the property and decided the house had belonged to a criminal or a kinky aristocrat. It might even have been why he liked the mansion in the first place.

But that didn't explain the mirrors.

The carefully placed mirrors were the thing that was bugging him. Paranoid human or cautious vampire?

*I'll explain later.*

Tenzin said that a lot, but she didn't always follow through. What had she been looking at in the chapel? What about the triptych had caught her eye when there were so many other, more valuable, pieces of art in the house?

Why had she been so quick to leave when this was their last job and she clearly didn't want to cut ties with him?

Because once they were finished with this, the two of them were done. Going their separate ways.

Finished.

And she seemed totally fine with it.

Ben rose and walked to her room. Tenzin was hiding something, and he was going to find out what it was.

He knocked on the door.

Tenzin opened it, and her lips were pale.

Ben frowned. "Have you not been eating?"

She shrugged. "I forgot."

"Tenzin—"

"I don't get hungry like you do, Benjamin. It's not the same for me."

"When was the last time you drank anything fresh? There's a pub two floors below this with donors."

Her eyebrow went up. "Are you my mother?"

He crossed his arms over his chest. "Fine. Forget I said anything."

"Okay." She started to close the door, and he stopped it with his foot. It was so easy to fall into familiar bickering patterns with her, he'd almost forgotten why he came.

"I didn't come to nag you about eating regularly."

"Good." She tried to close the door again, but he didn't move. "Why did you come?"

*To seduce you, strip off your clothes, and make you drink from my neck.*

Nope. Bad idea. That was *not* why he was there.

He cleared his throat. "It's later."

"And?"

"There was something going on at the house earlier when we found the icon. You said you'd explain later."

She frowned; then her eyes lit in awareness. "Ah. Yes. I have been reflecting on that."

"Thinking instead of reacting?"

"Yes." She raised a finger. "Exactly. Thinking instead of reacting. And I think..."

He waited for longer than he usually would. "Yes?"

"I think I'm not going to tell you after all." She pursed her lips and nodded. "Yes."

And just like that, she'd pissed him off again. "So there's definitely something else going on? Something I'm not seeing?"

She nodded again. "Yes."

"Possibly the thing about this job that was throwing you off to begin with?"

"Yes! That's probably what it was. Good catch."

"But you're not going to tell me."

"No."

"Even though we're partners."

She pointed down the hall toward his room. "You have Radu's icon, so we're not partners anymore."

Ben blinked in surprise and felt his heart give a quiet thunk.

*"...we're not partners anymore."*

"We're not partners anymore." He forced the words out. "Just like that?"

"That was what you wanted." She closed her eyes. "You said, 'This is a temporary thing, Tenzin.' You were very clear."

It was the fact that she seemed totally unperturbed by it that set him off. "I also said that you should go when I asked you to go, not before we were finished."

"Ah." She gave him a rueful smile. "I see."

"What? You see what?" He leaned against the door to keep it open.

"You want me around, but you don't want to be my partner. Not *really* my partner. You just want me to... hang around, waiting for you to decide what you want."

It was exactly what he'd accused her of doing countless times. "Seems fair for you to have a turn," he said sharply. "Besides, you're the one withholding information."

"It may seem fair, but it's not. I never sent you away."

"No, you just ran away instead of talking."

"And then you ran away." She spread her arms. "An eye for an eye. I'm here now. Do you want to talk about what happened in

Puerto Rico? Or what happened in Penglai? Or why I guarantee neither of us has had sex since we went our separate ways?"

Ben felt cold and hot all at the same time. "I didn't come here to talk about that."

"Fine." She tried to close the door but couldn't because his foot was in the way. She narrowed her eyes. "Don't make me, Benjamin."

"I'm amnis resistant now, remember? And according to Zhang, I'm probably just as strong as you are." He leaned closer. "You can't *make* me do anything."

She took his movement a step further and leaned into his space.

Ben's body roared to life. His amnis leapt toward her. He could feel the air whisper in the space between them, and every cell in his body begged him to reach out.

*Step closer. Consume her. Take everything. She is yours.*

"That instinct you're feeling right now? You think I don't feel it too?" Her voice was low and quiet, barely over a murmur. "I have not let another being take my vein for over four thousand years. I have killed any who tried. My blood and my instincts are shouting at me that you are *mine* in every way, yet for two years now, you have kept me at a distance. You have no idea what this is costing me."

He stared at the fine strands that grew along her hairline. The pores of her pale skin. The minute creases next to her eyes. He looked at her and saw everything in a way his human eyes never could. And he still wanted to be closer.

He drank her scent and felt like drowning. "You took my blood too."

Tenzin looked up and boldly met his eyes. "Yes, I did."

"Why?"

Fine lines appeared between her eyebrows. "Why do you think?"

His chest felt like it was cracked open. "Just tell me."

Tenzin floated up his body, and Ben forced himself to remain frozen. He felt her lips an inch away, running along his jawline and down his neck, pausing where his vein lay shallow beneath the skin. If she opened her mouth, her fangs would draw blood.

"Why would I tell you what you already know?" She warmed her breath before it touched his skin, sending pinpricks of pleasure in a wave down his body.

"I told you everything that night," he whispered. "I bared my soul."

"Yes," Tenzin said simply. "You offered your love to me, then you demanded that I watch you die."

Ben's breath stopped; he couldn't speak.

Tenzin's voice held pain. "I knew you had cruelty in you, Benjamin. I didn't think you would use it on *me*. Not like that."

"That's not what I did."

"That" —she pulled away and there were tears in her eyes— "is exactly what you did."

She put a hand on his chest and pushed him away. Ben didn't resist. He couldn't. He backed into the hallway, his arms still crossed over his chest while his blood screamed at him to reach out and take her, hold her, keep her close.

"I'm leaving tomorrow at nightfall." Tenzin stared over his shoulder, the tears still visible in her eyes. "Goodbye, Ben."

Then she closed the door.

He heard nothing for a long time, only the sound of her breath moving slowly in and out of her lungs, then her footsteps receded from the door and there was silence.

## 19

Chloe caught Tenzin before she left the next night. "Where will you go?"

"Back to Bucharest." She stuffed a new video game console in her backpack next to her gloves and a Cara-enabled tablet. "Can I stay in the same place?"

Chloe nodded. "You have the code?"

"I do."

Gavin had his regular apartment over the club in downtown Bucharest. He also had a safe house where Tenzin had stayed that few knew about. It was only accessible by air, built into an old Soviet-era warehouse on the outskirts of the city.

"How long will you be in Romania?"

Tenzin said, "No more than a few nights. I need to contact a few people; then I will probably disappear for a time." She pulled an envelope from the pocket of her tunic and handed it to Chloe.

"What is this?"

"I emailed instructions to you about the safe in New York. The letter is for Ben." She met Chloe's shocked eyes. "If a year has passed from this day and I have not spoken to you, give this letter to Benjamin."

Chloe said, "You're scaring me."

"Don't be scared." She touched the woman's shoulder. "I don't expect anything to happen to me. I'm quite hard to kill. But I think this is necessary. It shouldn't take more than three to seven months."

"Three to seven months? That's oddly specific."

"I think the snow will come in October."

Chloe let out a strangled laugh. "Yeah, this is weird and cryptic even for you."

"I know." She frowned. "I am not going to stop working on my New Year's resolutions, but for now I may have to pause my progress."

"Okay." Chloe nodded. "Again, nothing about that makes sense."

"Hopefully I'll be able to tell you in three to—"

"Seven months." Chloe waved the letter. "I got you."

"Are you and Gavin going to return to New York soon?"

"I think he said last night that he needs one more night to work here, then back to Romania for Ben's meeting with Radu, then back to LA to drop off the plane, and then we'll head home from there."

"I see." Tenzin thought rapidly. "I can't decide if Gavin should accompany Ben to meet Radu. I think maybe he should."

"I don't think he was planning on it. Radu has no leverage on Ben at this point. He prepaid for the icon with all that gold, so all Ben needs to do is drop it off. Pretty straightforward."

"Yes, all that gold..." Tenzin turned to Chloe. "Tell Gavin there is *nothing* about Radu that is straightforward. I warned Ben not to underestimate him, but I ended up doing it myself. Ben won't take me seriously."

Chloe fisted her hair in her hands. "You need to start making sense, Tenzin!"

"I know." She quickly leaned forward and kissed Chloe's

cheek. "You are a true friend to both of us and I love you." She hugged Chloe quickly. "You know that, correct?"

Chloe's expression told her she hadn't known it. "I love you too. Please be safe."

"Of course." Her fangs peeked out when she smiled. "I'm finally having fun again. But don't tell Ben I said that."

"That you're having fun with something that's obviously life-threatening? Yeah, I think I'll keep that to myself."

"Ben likes to pretend that he doesn't also get excited by dangerous situations. I don't understand that about him, but I have decided not to challenge his sense of self for a while."

"Okay." Chloe shrugged. "Sure."

"I'll see you in three to seven months." Tenzin slung her backpack over her shoulder. "Hopefully."

BEN WOKE from his day rest and he was starving. He hit the intercom inside his sleeping chamber.

"Yes, Mr. Vecchio? Can we help you this evening?"

Gavin's household staff was amazing. "Can I get a thermos of preserved blood heated and sent to my room?"

"If you'll give us ten minutes, we can have fresh delivered."

"Sweet." He swallowed back the burning in his throat. "Just leave it on the table. I'm going to stay secured until it's delivered."

"Thank you, Mr. Vecchio."

Ben had excellent control, but he really didn't feel like growling at room service when they delivered his blood, and with the way his throat was feeling, that was highly probable.

What had set him off so much? He tried to think back to the drifting place before he truly woke.

Right. Sex dreams about Tenzin. That would do it.

He was still confused about why he dreamed at all. According to Brigid, it wasn't normal or natural for a new vampire to dream. When she went out, she was out. No consciousness at all. She said it was one of her favorite things about being a vampire.

But Ben wasn't that way. He hadn't slept like that since the first night he woke.

The first night he woke... and drank from Tenzin.

He refused to think that her blood could have affected him that much; it was one time.

Nope. Wasn't an option.

It was probably something about Zhang's blood being so old. It was far more likely that was the explanation.

He lay back down and waited for the intercom to chime again, and an uneasy tremor ran down his spine.

Ben sat up and stared at the wall. The realization hit him with an unexpected slap of anger.

She was gone.

He knew it like he knew blood would sate his thirst. He knew it like he knew the wind would hold him if he jumped off a building. Tenzin was gone and his amnis ached.

"Mr. Vecchio?"

"Yes?"

"Your evening meal has arrived."

"Thank you."

He couldn't identify how he was feeling. He rose and gave the server a few seconds to depart. He pulled on a pair of cotton pants and a T-shirt. Then he leaned against the door and closed his eyes, thinking about the dream he'd left behind.

They were flying over a forest, a blanket of thick trees below them. They were pressed together, their bodies moving as one while the air cradled them.

Not a sex dream really. Something far more intimate.

He walked into the living area and found the thermos on the table. He gave it a quick shake—fresh blood coagulated quickly—

and opened the lid to drink it straight from the thermos, ignoring the tall black mug the server had placed on the tray.

God, it was so good.

As a human, he'd always imagined blood hunger would be the same as human hunger, but it was far more intense. It was closer to being drastically thirsty than hungry, but sating that thirst was more satisfying than drinking water. It was a full-body sensual experience that was second only in pleasure to sex.

Sex and blood drinking? Well, that was probably part of the reason Ben hadn't wanted to touch another women since his one night with Tenzin. He couldn't imagine the intimacy of blood exchange with anyone else, but he couldn't imagine finding any sex without blood drinking satisfactory in the least.

He finished the thermos and set it down on the table, wiping the traces of blood from his lips with his thumb. He felt the warmth traveling from his throat, down the core of his body and into his limbs as he woke from daily torpor.

She was gone.

Left.

*You asked her to leave*, his mind taunted him.

*"...this is a temporary thing, Tenzin. That means when we finish and I ask you to leave, you leave. And you do not follow me again."*

So... she was gone. And he had work to do.

Ben walked to the bathroom and started the shower, waiting for the steam to fill the small room. One of the more surprising things about becoming a vampire was the constant, invasive cold.

While it was true that he could heat his body with amnis, he hadn't quite gotten to the point where it was automatic. It took effort to create an average body temperature, which meant that if the surrounding environment was cool and there were no humans around to fool, he usually didn't make the effort.

But Ben hated being cold. It reminded him of childhood

winters in New York when the landlord would shut off the heat in their building and his breath would freeze in the air as he lay in bed, wishing he could stay under the covers.

Basically, Ben now understood why so many vampires—not just the northerners—had saunas and steam rooms in their houses. He sat in the bathroom enjoying the warm, wet air surrounding him and thought through his next steps.

Return to Bucharest. Gavin had another night of meetings, but Ben didn't need to be there and it was only a couple of hours to fly on his own. Did he want to just take off? He was sure Gavin's place was still safe even without Gavin.

Yep. Best to just leave.

Meet with Radu and hand over the icon. Unlike some of his jobs, this wasn't going to be hard. Nothing about the icon appealed to him. It was nice enough, but Ben didn't understand the sentimental value, and while it was a beautiful example of early Orthodox art and it had a fascinating history, it wasn't something he'd become attached to. It really was just a job.

The last job.

*"That was what you wanted. You said, 'This is a temporary thing, Tenzin.' You were quite clear."*

Yes.

*Yes.* This was what he wanted. Ben shook off the feeling of loss.

Except she hadn't even seemed sorry. Or angry. Or sneaky, which would tell him that she had no intention of actually leaving him alone.

It didn't matter.

He'd leave tonight for Bucharest and call Radu to meet the next night at his club. The vampire had already paid, so nothing else needed to happen. At the end of the night, this had really been one of the more straightforward jobs he'd worked, and he hadn't even had to wrangle about payment.

Payment in advance.

Investigate icon.

Call in favors from Corsicans to confirm a sneaky tip from associate of his aunt.

Break into cool thief's house.

Retrieve icon.

Return icon.

And that was that.

Aaaand he hadn't been able to talk to Tenzin about what they were going to do about the New York house. No matter. After he finished in Bucharest, he'd head to Rome for a while. He was overdue for a visit with Fabia, and he could chill in the Eternal City with Ronan and his old friends for a while. It would be good to be among familiar faces.

Would he need a formal introduction to Emil's court now since he was under the aegis of Penglai? He buzzed Chloe.

She picked up after two rings. "Hey, sleepyhead."

"Hey, yourself. Can you remind me when I'm finished in Bucharest to call Giovanni and ask if I need a formal letter of introduction to Emil Conti in Rome?"

"Are you going to Rome?"

"I thought I'd head over there after I'm done in Bucharest and give Fabia a visit since I'm on the continent. You and Gavin should come too. There's plenty of room in the house, and you and Fabi could shop. She'd love to take you around."

Chloe was suspiciously silent instead of enthusiastic. "Give me a minute." She hung up and a knock sounded at his door a few minutes later.

"Hey." He opened the door, and she immediately walked in with a frown on her face. "What's up?"

"Tenzin is gone."

"Yeah, I know."

She looked like she was going to ask something and then

changed her mind. "Okay, I have no idea what is going on, but she seemed really determined that you shouldn't meet with Radu on your own. She thought Gavin should go with you."

"Why?" He sat on the edge of the couch. "There's not going to be any trouble with payment. He's paid in advance. I'm going to drop off a painting. That's it."

"And I told her that, but she said not to underestimate him."

Ben rolled his eyes. "Yeah, she likes to keep people on edge. At this point, I think she thinks it's adorable, but it's not. It's just annoying. I'm going to fly to Bucharest tonight and I'll meet with Radu first thing tomorrow night. Then I'm going to head to Rome."

"I really wish you'd wait for Gavin."

Ben stood and kissed Chloe's forehead. "I'll be fine. I'm not being rash. I've completely thought this through and there are really no dangers in meeting Radu at a club I've already visited in a city where I have a safe house."

"But Ben—"

"At times like this, it's actually convenient to be a vampire everyone worries about." Ben started unplugging his devices and packing his backpack. "Trust me, Chloe. Radu is not stupid enough to mess with the son of Zhang Guo or the nephew of Giovanni Vecchio. He'd have vampires from half the known world pissed off at him over a minor work of art."

She stared at him a long time. "I really don't like this."

"And don't forget." Ben folded a long-sleeved black shirt and tucked it in his backpack. "If anything gets too dangerous, I can just fly, fly away."

*Two nights later...*

167

Ben woke in pitch darkness.

He smelled vinyl and leather.

Pine and the scent of fresh water nearby.

Fresh blood.

He touched his head, but the blow at the base of his skull had already healed itself. Scattered memories of jostling in a vehicle and heavy, unfamiliar accents. Flashing lights and the sound of truck engines revving.

He stretched out, searching for anything familiar. On his right was a ledge of some kind. He reached over. He was on a bed and there was a wall next to him, but it felt hollow. False. He slapped the wall and felt the edge of a familiar plastic fixture. It was the flat paddle of a light switch.

He pushed it and a small lamp turned on next to him, nearly blinding him with its low light.

In the newly lit compartment, Ben looked around.

Bed.

Small kitchen.

Square cupboards and plastic-covered bookshelves lined the walls. Was he on a plane? No, it was silent. He stood motionless and allowed the fear and panic to rise up so he could examine them clearly.

He took a deep breath and put his hands on the wall again.

Space. Some kind of insulation was packed behind the surface, but beyond that there was vast openness just on the other side. He reached up and felt the low ceiling. He felt the other wall and sensed the same.

In every direction, he was surrounded by air.

His panic began to calm. Just beyond these thin walls, his element waited for him. He could escape anytime.

A simple door stood at the end of the compartment, and as he walked toward it, he felt the floor swaying beneath him. It creaked and bounced.

What was this place? A mobile home? It was too small. A parked bus? Ben cracked the door slowly, reaching his amnis outward to sense any threats, but he was met by one single familiar energy signature a short distance away.

He pushed the door open and saw Radu standing alone on a hill under the swiftly darkening sky. The sun had set in the distance, and a lone Romani wagon was next to him, parked at the end of a cracked asphalt road where Ben realized his caravan had come to rest. That was the compartment where he'd woken, not a mobile home but a travel bus.

Radu turned and smiled ruefully. "I apologize, Ben Vecchio. This was not how I wanted to introduce you to the Dawn Caravan, but you left me no other options."

## 20

Ben sat across from Radu, a bottle of blood-wine between them. He was trying to keep calm, but anger pushed at him. Tenzin had been right. He shouldn't have met Radu alone. He'd been lulled into a sense of normalcy by Radu's familiar face and the small number of guards with him.

He hated when Tenzin was right.

"I really hate to pull this one out," Ben said. "But do you know who the hell I am?"

Radu smiled. "I am very aware."

"Tell me why I shouldn't fly away right now." Ben leaned back and crossed his leg over his knee.

"Again, I deeply apologize for the unfortunate way I had to bring you here." Radu opened the bottle in front of Ben. "It was not my wish."

"Your guard hit me on the back of the head hard enough to knock me out." Ben hadn't even known that was possible.

"He disoriented you just before daybreak, and as I said, it was not what I wished. Devan was perhaps a little too concerned when you said you were leaving for Rome, and he will make restitution for his actions."

"You still haven't answered my question." Ben watched Radu pour a generous amount of wine in both glasses. "Why shouldn't I take off right now?"

"It will be to your benefit to stay and hear my offer. If, after this drink, you don't agree with me, I will bid you farewell as well as leaving you with a chest of valuable items" —Radu nodded at a small belted travel chest near the door of his vardo— "as a thank-you from me and my clan for your generosity of time and your forgiveness."

Ben glanced at the chest, then at the blood-wine, then at the vampire across from him. "You're going to pay me to listen to you over a glass of wine?"

"I value your time." A smile touched Radu's mouth. "If you had, perhaps, valued mine as highly, this abduction wouldn't have been necessary."

"I'm going to go ahead and argue this abduction definitely *wasn't* necessary."

A hint of Radu's jovial smile touched his lips. "When I contacted you three years ago, I had time to spare. That time has run out."

Okay, Ben did feel a little guilty about putting the man off for three years. Maybe it was worth giving Radu another ten minutes. He looked around the clearing. "No guard?"

"I know you are an honorable man." Radu raised his glass. "Good fortune and safe roads, Ben."

He took his glass and lifted it. "Good fortune and safe roads." He waited for Radu to drink; then he drank after him. "None of this makes sense. You got your icon. I wasn't asking for any more money. Why am I here?"

"In a way, your own cleverness compelled it." Radu sipped his wine. "The icon was a puzzle, Benjamin Vecchio. One that others had not been able to master. The real reason I wanted to hire you is far more complicated."

"You have another job for me?"

"Yes. One much more profitable than the first."

Seeing as Radu hadn't gone cheap on the icon job, Ben was intrigued. "Details?"

Radu examined him. "I must have your confidentiality."

"I don't know what the job is yet."

"I'm not asking for a commitment, I'm asking for your assurance that—no matter what you decide—what is spoken between us will go no further."

Ben could live with that. "Unless it endangers me or anyone under my aegis, you have my word." Technically, he didn't have anyone under vampire aegis—he was way too young—but he might have someone someday, and vampire commitments and promises didn't have expiration dates.

"That is a fair promise," Radu said. "I accept your assurance." He finished his glass of wine and poured another. "How much do you know about my people, the Poshani?"

"My aunt filled me in on the basics of your history."

"Half of what she told you is probably wrong." He waved his hand. "We often seed stories among scholars to obscure the truth. We're very private."

"Are you the leader of the Poshani?"

"I am one of three." Radu took a drink. "Remember that. We Poshani are highly suspicious of authority. No one person is given everything. The three terrin are chosen by the previous terrin, but if confidence is lost at any time, the mortal and immortal members of the Poshaniya will overthrow that member and choose another."

"Okay." Ben drank his wine. "So your leadership is in trouble somehow in a way that I can help. What valuable cultural treasure did you lose?"

Radu grinned. "See? I knew I chose the correct man."

"I find things, Radu. The only reason you'd need my help is if you'd lost something that the terrin is supposed to guard and people would be majorly pissed about it. It's not a hard guess."

"You are correct of course, but I did not lose this particular artifact. It was stolen from me."

"I'm going to guess that doesn't help your position." Ben set his glass down. "Lost it or let it get stolen. Either way, you didn't guard it well enough."

"You are correct. And this is where the kamvasa comes in."

"The Dawn Caravan?" Ben had to admit he was intrigued.

"The Dawn Caravan was my idea. We were always so effective at staying hidden, I thought. If we could hide in plain sight, why not offer this service—a safe house—to others willing to pay?"

"Makes sense."

"My sister and my brother—the other terrin—were not in favor of this. They eventually gave me their support because too many of our mortal families were struggling in the human world."

"Among the Poshani, the mortal and immortal members are equally supported?"

"Of course." Radu spread his hands. "We are helpless during the day without our darigan. And the mortals would be vulnerable to predators, both human and immortal, without the Hazar."

"You only employ Poshani?"

"We are the only ones we truly trust," Radu said. "Even about you, I have reservations."

"I understand."

"But your position makes you the most trustworthy outsider capable of this task. You represent two great houses, neither of which would own you if you were not a man of your word."

"Thank you." He examined Radu's expression. "Why not find this yourself?"

"I have tried for many years. I have narrowed the search, but I am at an impasse and need an outside perspective."

"I'm also guessing that you don't want your brother and sister to know that you lost whatever it is that was stolen."

Radu raised an eyebrow. "My sister knows something was stolen—she's the one who helped me test you—but she does not know all the details. My brother knows nothing, and it must remain that way."

Ben had a feeling there was no love lost between Radu and his brother. He poured another glass of wine from the bottle. "Okay, I'm intrigued. What is it you need to find?"

"It's a goblet," Radu said. "Carved in the ninth century from a single giant emerald."

Ben set his glass down and sighed.

Dammit. An emerald goblet? There was no way he could fly away now. That was just too cool and unique.

"Okay. Tell me the rest."

THEY HOVERED over a picturesque clearing in the middle of a dense forest. The landscape was made of empty hills for as far as the human eye could see. Dirt roads snaked through the country-side along with the occasional mobile phone tower.

Twenty state-of-the-art luxury campers and trailers circled the clearing in the forest. There were trucks and vans. A large fire was burning in the center of the circle, smaller ones in the outer loop, and in the distance, Ben saw a dozen air vampires hovering over the encampment.

"This is the Dawn Caravan?" Ben kept his voice low. "Where are we?"

"Don't ask questions I cannot answer. The location of the caravan is known only to the head of the darigan. It is the humans who decide where we go every day, not the vampires. The caravan moves every night from the spring to the fall. It ends when the snow starts to fall and we retreat to our winter camps."

"And anyone who has been sheltering with you—?"

"The longest any immortal is permitted to stay is a season," Radu said. "We will not take responsibility for them during the winter, and the location of our winter camps remains a secret for the Eastern Poshani alone."

"There are different clans?"

"Three clans, but we cooperate and travel in each other's territory."

"Okay."

"The Eastern Poshani, my people, run the kamvasa. We have not lost a guest in over five hundred years."

"Impressive." Ben scanned the camp. "So a vampire pays you a set amount—"

"Payment depends on the vampire," Radu said. "Sometimes payment is in treasure, sometimes in favors. It depends on the individual."

"But you make a contract. A set period of time and a set amount. Total protection during that time?"

"We provide a comfortable caravan" —Radu pointed to the silver-grey vehicles in the distance— "protection, blood, and a level of entertainment."

"What kind of entertainment?"

"Stories, dancing, music." Radu shrugged. "The normal amusements."

"What about modern electronics?" Ben was already thinking about how he was going to communicate with Chloe so she didn't completely freak out when he wasn't there in Rome.

"Patrick Murphy in Ireland isn't one of us," Radu said. "But he comes from Travellers. He understood our unique needs and created a mobile network with security."

Probably some kind of virtual private network users could

access that wouldn't reveal location. It was ingenious really. If guests didn't know where they were, they couldn't inadvertently reveal it to anyone, even someone they trusted.

"I'll need access to the internet," Ben said. "I don't work alone. The icon? I had help finding it." From Beatrice and from Tenzin.

Tenzin.

Of all the times for her to take off, this one was not ideal.

"Of course," Radu said. "I expected that you had research assistance from your uncle's clan. That will not be a problem, though I need the exact nature of the theft to remain confidential."

"I should be able to manage that."

"The nature of this mystery will be a bit different."

Ben was really wishing Tenzin hadn't taken off. From a work perspective, her insight would be invaluable. Plus he had a feeling that Radu's friendly demeanor masked a ruthless leader if a threat emerged against his people.

*Note to self: don't become a threat to the Poshani.*

"When was the goblet stolen?"

"Between eighty to ninety years ago."

Ben blinked. "You can't narrow it down more?"

"It stays in my personal treasury." Radu pointed to the traditional vardo being pulled to the edge of the clearing by a pickup truck. "I'm not a greedy gadjo who spends his nights counting my treasure. I had no reason to examine it when I assumed it was secure."

"Not even a glance?"

"There was a replica put in its place. Good enough that a glance wasn't enough to register a forgery."

"I see. Do you still have the forgery?"

"Yes."

Ben was already narrowing down his options. A forgery meant this wasn't a crime of opportunity. Someone hadn't stumbled across an emerald goblet and not been able to help themselves. This was planned, deliberate, and familiar.

"You said you'd narrowed it down," Ben said. "How?"

"I have pursued every guest we had during that window of time. Most were easy to eliminate, but there were five who stood out. Five who would know the value of the item they stole *and* the significance."

"And what is the significance?"

For the first time, Ben saw Radu's anger simmering behind his dark brown eyes.

"The emerald goblet is one of three that were given to the oldest of our people, a chief who was turned into a vampire by an ancient immortal king. The goblets were a gift from a Persian ruler to our chief, and they passed to his three immortal children. One made of emerald, one of citrine, and one of ruby."

"Three terrin. Three goblets. I'm getting the idea."

"My sister is the keeper of the citrine, and my brother is the keeper of the ruby. The Poshani will host the Vashana festival in three weeks' time, but this year is the Vashana Zata, which only happens every hundred years. The current terrin must present their goblets to the Poshaniya, and if they choose a successor—as I have considered doing this year—they must pass their goblet to them as a sign of leadership passing from one power to the next."

Oh shit. "Did you say three weeks?"

Radu nodded slowly. "As I mentioned earlier, Benjamin Vecchio, I am running out of options."

## 21

Ben and Radu strolled through the camp, the Poshani leader nodding to groups as he passed. In the background, a band of musicians played traditional music nearly to the point of being too loud.

"The volume of the music and position of the players provides a level of privacy," Radu said softly. "But know that ears are everywhere."

"I understand."

Two vampires were playing a game of chess on a table set up near the fire. Another was watching as a group of human men and women practiced an elaborate dance.

The camp had the feeling of a traveling village, with cooking smells drifting through the air and music ringing through the night. A few children played along the outskirts, and a lazy dog lounged near a fire.

"It's very welcoming," Ben said. It was the highest compliment he could think to give Radu, who valued hospitality so much.

"Thank you." The vampire beamed. "We like to think of ourselves as providing an important service to our guests."

"Do you hide anyone?" He kept his voice nearly silent.

"Yes and no. Do we hide those whom some might consider criminals? Perhaps. It is not our way to judge others. If you have done our people no harm, no harm will come to you. But all three of us—Kezia, Vano, and myself—have discretion to choose or reject guests. The safety of our people, including the vampires who stay with us, is our top priority."

Ben glanced around. "So according to everyone here, who am I?"

"You are another guest who has paid me a great deal to make him disappear." Radu's voice remained low. "You wouldn't be the first powerful newborn who has sought our protection while they come to terms with their new life. We don't take the bloodthirsty of course. But after the first year, some find shelter with us."

"Good to know." Ben saw a familiar face across the camp, the strange woman who'd been following him in Kashgar, along with her plain-faced vampire guard.

*Oh, hello.*

Her eyes rose as if she could hear him, and the corner of her mouth turned up. She was even more enchanting in firelight, a sphinx of a woman with mysterious dark eyes and an enigmatic expression.

Radu followed his eyes. "I believe you met Kezia in Xinjiang."

"*Met* is stretching it." He pulled his eyes away and continued scanning the campsite. "Is there anyone else I know?"

Radu's mouth turned up at the corner. "I cannot tell you that."

"Why not?"

His face was all innocence. "How could I possibly know all your associates?"

Of course he'd answer that way. "Do I have my own caravan?"

"Only the finest," Radu said. "Very private and equipped with the latest technology for the Nocht platform."

"Great."

"It is also soundproof and secure from listening devices. We provide a bug sweeper if you want to verify. Feel free to conduct business there. Or... entertain guests. It will be your home while you are here."

"I'll keep that in mind." Ben wasn't planning on doing any *entertaining* while he was working, but he appreciated the privacy nonetheless. "I need to call Chloe, my uncle, and my assistant in Rome tonight. She's expecting me."

"Of course."

"Where's my bag?"

"In your caravan. I'm afraid we had to remove the tablet computer, but it's being kept safe for you. We've also provided some more clothing than what you had with you."

"Seriously, Radu?"

"We are only considering your comfort. You'll have the latest equipment to work on. The best blood and wine." Radu patted his shoulder. "Everything in your caravan is for sale. We can negotiate a fair price should you want to keep anything."

He was very good at what he did. Ben almost forgot he'd been kidnapped.

They walked to a long travel caravan that was built on the chassis of a Mercedes truck. As they approached, steps extended toward them and lights switched on from invisible motion sensors along the side of the bus.

"This will be your home for the next three weeks." Radu walked ahead of Ben into the caravan. "This is our newest unit. You're only the third guest who has used it."

Ben couldn't *not* be impressed. The bus was equipped with leather interior and wood cabinets lining the sides. Sections of the caravan had been expanded to create more floor space in the living area. The windows had been blocked by modern art canvases and bookcases lined by plastic to keep the books from shifting when the bus moved.

"The day chamber is in the rear." Radu pointed toward it. "Completely secured from the interior."

"And what's to stop someone from taking a chain saw to it in during the day?"

"That's where the darigan come in." Radu continued to push buttons and move levers to exhibit the amenities of the caravan. "You're welcome to meet them if you want, but meet them or not, they will do their job, protecting you with force if necessary."

"Great." He sensed something nagging the edge of his amnis. There was someone nearby whom he'd met before. Radu's sister? No, he didn't know her well enough.

Radu was explaining the engine with great enthusiasm when Ben held up a hand.

"Yes?"

"Who else is here? Which vampires?"

"The vampire—?"

"The five you narrowed it down to. Which vampires are we talking about here? I must know one of them."

Radu leaned against a leather couch. "Let's see. There is Tatyana, who is not old enough to have stolen it, but she's inexplicably wealthy and currently hiding from Oleg. Not a likely suspect."

"And who are the other four?"

"If we are counting Tatyana, there are six guests, but only five real suspects. It took quite some wrangling to arrange their visits all at the same time."

"Who else?"

"Madina is the first suspect. She's been recently ousted from power in Central Europe, but she stayed with us in the 1930s."

He didn't know a Madina. "Who else?"

"Fynn. He's German, but he's been living in Argentina since the Second World War for exactly the reasons you imagine. He visited the caravan in the 1940s, and his character is despicable."

"But you invited him back?"

Radu looked surprised. "Why wouldn't I?"

"Okay, who else?"

"Darius is the oldest vampire here and not likely as a suspect, but I included him because he knows more about the history of the goblets than we do, *and* he stayed here during the same period. He's Persian and very, very secretive."

"Sounds like Darius is a man who knows things," Ben muttered. "Who else?"

"A French thief, René DuPont. He was with us—"

"He did it." Ben blurted it out, then regretted it. "I mean, I've run into René before. He's a very likely suspect."

Fuck. He didn't really feel like tangling with René. Not only was the thief clever, he knew how to spark Ben's temper, which had grown far more hair-trigger since he'd become immortal.

Plus René was an asshole.

"Okay," Ben said. "That's four suspects, and who's the fifth?"

Radu pursed his lips together. "A degree of impartiality will be needed for the last suspect."

"Okay." So he definitely knew this one. That was probably why his amnis was starting to go haywire. He was nearly coming out of his skin, and Radu—

"It's Tenzin."

"Tenzin what?" Ben flexed his back; his amnis was crawling up and down his spine.

"Tenzin…" Radu frowned. "Tenzin is the last suspect."

Ben barked a laugh. Then he closed his eyes. "Of course she is."

COULD SHE HAVE DONE IT? Was Tenzin capable of stealing a fabulous carved-emerald goblet that was probably worth millions and had a cool legend attached to it? Of course she was. In fact, she was probably the most likely suspect.

Ben strode through the campsite, following Radu's instructions and the pulsing beat of his elemental energy, which was coursing over his skin in giant horny waves. His amnis knew she was close, and it craved her like a drug.

He was going to kiss—no, *kill*—her. He was going to kill her. She had to have known something was up in all this. That's what she'd been holding back last week at Farkas's mansion. That's what she hadn't told him. She'd been cryptic and evasive and this was why, because she must have figured out that the icon job was only a ruse.

He pounded on the door and felt every rap in his erection.

How was he supposed to function like this? His body was betraying him. The moment he'd smelled her scent, he'd gone hard.

*You are not a teenager.* He imagined glaring holes through her body. She'd shout at him and deflect, then refuse to apologize for being stubborn and cryptic and withholding important infor—

"Come in. It's unlocked."

Ben yanked at the door and it swung open, only to be met with Tenzin hanging upside down from a bed mounted from the ceiling.

She was insane. And adorable. And he'd missed her like crazy, even after only a few days apart. Seeing her in Bucharest had been like an alcoholic getting a sip of whiskey when he wanted to down the whole bottle.

"Aren't these buses cool?" She grinned, and her adorable fangs gleamed in the low lamplight. "We need to get one of them in America."

Ben slammed the door shut and marched over to her. "This is what you were hiding?"

"The bus?"

"No!" He kept his voice low. "This thing with Radu. Did you know he was going to kidnap me? Is this what you weren't telling me in Hungary?"

"Hmmm." She stayed hanging upside down. "Sort of."

"What kind of answer is that?"

"The only one I'm going to give you right now."

Ben grabbed Tenzin's cheeks and kissed her hard, giving in to the instinct that had been scraping at him since he'd seen her at the club in Bucharest. He'd thought she was gone, and now she was back.

He wanted her. Fuck, he wanted her so much. Every cell in his body was hungry for the taste of her. He sucked her tongue into his mouth, nicking the end so her blood flooded his mouth and his senses.

She groaned and reached for his neck, dragging him closer.

Ben slid his hands down her neck and across her shoulders until he cupped her small breasts in his hands and squeezed. He wanted to pull her shirt up and feel her skin. He needed the contact. He ran a hand down to her waist and slid his fingers beneath her leggings, tracing the rise of her pelvis and the smooth skin of her hip.

The sound she made in her throat was halfway between a purr and a snarl.

He dragged his hands up her body again and broke their kiss, keeping both his hands on her cheeks. Her mouth was open and her lips were red. A drop of her blood lingered at the corner of her mouth, and he licked out and captured it.

The smell of her desire nearly buckled his knees. "You drive me absolutely fucking crazy."

"I missed you too." She brushed her thumb over his lower lip. "Did Radu tell you I was here? Is that why you came with him? He couldn't take you if you didn't want to be taken."

"I came for the job. I came because of the goblet that René probably stole."

"Goblet?" She rolled over, and her hair fell in her eyes. She puffed her breath up and the hair tucked itself behind her ear.

"Don't pretend like you don't know."

"I didn't know they were missing one of the goblets." Her eyes gleamed. "Which one? Is it Kezia's or Radu's? It wouldn't be Vano's; he wouldn't ask for help."

"Was it you?"

She shook her head. "What kind of question is that to ask someone you just kissed? Quite well, I will add. That was nice."

"Because it's you, it's necessary."

"The kiss?"

"The *question*, Tenzin."

She ran a finger along his bottom lip. "You're so stern right now. Is this because René is here? It's not René this time."

"You're pissing me off."

She floated down from the hanging bed and planted her feet in front of him. "You don't really think I stole this."

"If you did, just give it to me and I'll get it back to Radu. You can take off and we'll never speak of it again."

"I can't take off. I've agreed to be here for three weeks. You can't leave the Dawn Caravan before your stay is over, not if you ever want to come back. Those are the rules, Benjamin. Didn't they tell you?"

"You're here for three weeks?"

She smiled. "You know what's happening in three weeks, don't you? The Vashana Zata is a big deal. A giant festival where they choose the future terrin. That's why Radu, Kezia, and Vano are all here."

"How did you know about the festival?"

She ignored him. "You don't want me to take off." She whispered, "You need me to help you find the goblet."

The fact that he'd been thinking about that no more than half an hour before didn't assuage his anger at all.

"I know all the vampires here better than you," she continued. "Well, except for Tatyana, but I'm figuring her out. I can tell you when they're lying. Even more, I can tell you all the things that Radu won't."

"Radu's not telling me everything?"

"Of course he's not." Tenzin tapped his lower lip, and Ben let his fangs fall. "Do you want to have sex?"

"That's not why I came to your caravan."

"That's not a yes or no."

"Then no."

"Liar." She glanced down at the tent in his pants. "But we can pretend you came to tell me I was annoying you."

"Driving me crazy."

"Right." She held up a finger. "Yes. Driving you crazy."

He was going to have to do it. They were going to have to have a giant fight in front of God and a dozen strange vampires before this was over. There was no way he could work with her on something in such close quarters without exploding eventually.

"Well?"

"Well what?" His voice was rough.

"Was there anything else now that you've told me I drive you crazy?" She floated up to him until they were eye to eye. "I am here to listen. I'm not going to say I am 'all ears.' That is a horrible saying that creates a grotesque mental picture."

Everything Ben wanted to say was caught in his throat.

*I still love you.*

*I also hate you.*

*I miss you too.*

*I dream about you.*

*You are the only one I want, and that makes me unbearably sad.*

The last thought killed the remnants of Ben's desire. "I'm going to investigate this," he said. "And I'm not going to play favorites."

She looked disappointed. "Fine. I don't have anything to hide. Once you eliminate me as a suspect, we can work together."

"That's not how this is going to go."

"On the contrary," Tenzin said. "According to the deal we struck, we were going to work together through the end of Radu's job. Since Radu's job never really finished, then here we are. Business partners again."

Dammit, she was right.

"I don't think Radu invited you here because he wanted us working together."

"Radu didn't invite me at all," Tenzin said. "Kezia did." She reached for a colorful copy of a magazine entitled *Birds & Blooms* on the kitchenette table. "If you'll excuse me, there's an article about creating bee-friendly urban gardens I wanted to read."

Ben backed out of the caravan, and Tenzin blew the door shut with a flick of her tiny hand.

## 22

"Where are you?" Chloe was practically yelling at him. "You were supposed to be in Rome two days ago. Do not do this to me again, Ben! Do I need to send Gavin after you?"

Ben put a hand over her mouth on the screen, but that just made the screen wobble. He pulled his hand away. "Chloe—"

"She told you not to go without Gavin, but did you listen? No! 'She's being dramatic, Chloe. She likes the attention.' Do I need to call Giovanni?"

He rolled his eyes. "Of course you don't."

She held her hand up to her forehead. "Because I've had it up to here with both of you! It's been two fucking years! The two of you love each other, and I know you have issues, but you refuse to talk. You just passive-aggressively lash out at everyone around you, and I'm sick—"

"Chloe!"

"What?"

Ben couldn't remember the last time she'd been this pissed off. "Tenzin is here. We're stuck in this very small camp together for three weeks. So your wish has been granted. We'll either figure things out or we'll kill each other. Happy?"

"I'm honestly fine with either outcome at this point." She sat back and crossed her arms over her chest. "Sick of it."

"Up to here." He held his fingers to his forehead. "I got it. I'm fine. She's fine. Neither of us is in any danger, and we're still working with Radu."

"But the icon—"

"I can't tell you all the details, but think of the icon as a kind of dry run. Now we're working on the real deal."

"The real deal? And you can't tell me anything?"

"I can't tell you what we're after, but I can ask you to look into some names for me."

Chloe pulled out a notebook. "You're going to figure things out with Tenzin?"

"Yes. I can't promise you it's going to work out the way you want it to, but—"

"I don't really care— No, that's a lie. I want our happy family back in New York. I want my friends back. I want both of you to be happy. But I'm a big girl and I realize I don't always get what I want." She picked up a pen. "What do you need?"

He stared at her, the girl who'd been his first friend in high school, his first girlfriend, his first love, and then one of his best friends. "Chloe?"

"What?" She looked tired.

"I'm sorry we put you in the middle of our shit. I really love you and appreciate everything you do."

She blinked hard. "You were gone for two *years*. And I know you glossed over a lot of the hard parts during that time. I don't know if you've talked to Gavin or if you've talked with anyone—"

"I have. I promise."

She nodded. "I love you both. I want you to be happy, and I just don't understand..." She cleared her throat. "I don't understand why you think you're so different now, when to me you're still the Ben Vecchio I always knew. You have fangs now, but you're still you."

"Thanks for saying that." He didn't feel the same. Not even close.

A tear slipped down Chloe's cheek. "None of us could stand living without you. Is that so wrong?"

"No."

"Okay." She swiped at her eyes. "Give me names and as much background as you have and I'll start searching."

"Thanks."

She probably wouldn't find much, but she'd ask Gavin, who might give him more. He gave her the names and tasks to keep her busy and to make her feel like she was helping.

Chloe did help. She helped every time she called him Benny or teased him or reminded him he wasn't the monster he saw in the mirror anytime he could bear to look at his reflection. She helped every time she prodded Ben and Tenzin to figure things out.

*"You offered your love to me, then you demanded that I watch you die."*

Tenzin was right.

And she was wrong.

She was both those things at exactly the same time, and how did he reconcile that? How did he forgive a human impulse when the results were eternal?

He checked the time in Los Angeles and called Sadia.

Dema answered the video request. "It's you."

"Yes, it's me. Is she there?"

"It's almost dinnertime."

"I won't keep her on the screen too long."

Dema nodded and stepped away. "Sadia, Ben is on the screen for you!"

Ben heard the thunder of miniature elephants; then Sadia was leaning on the little desk where her screen lived. "Ben!"

*"Ciao, sorellina."*

*"Ciao bello."* She rested her chubby little chin on her hand. "Where are you?"

"I don't know exactly, but I'm very safe, so don't worry."

"Are you coming home soon? Baba said you were going to Rome. We can go to Rome and see you there if you want."

He touched her flyaway hair on the screen, but just like with Chloe, the picture wobbled. "I'm working for the next three weeks."

"Three weeks is long."

"I know. I didn't think it would be so long either. After that, I'll try to come for a visit, okay?"

She sighed. "Okay. Is Tenzin with you?"

"Yeah, actually she is."

"Where?" Sadia's eyes lit up. "She didn't call me back, but I sent her a picture of me on my bike."

"She's not here, here, but—"

"Can you get her?" Sadia stood and danced at her desk. "I want to see her."

*Of course you do.*

"Okay," he said. "How about tomorrow night? Would that work?"

She nodded, then looked over her shoulder. "I have to go."

"Dinnertime?"

She threw her head back and groaned. "I think I smell broccoli."

Ben stifled a smile. "Listen, when I was your age, I had to eat a lot of broccoli."

"Does it help you become a vampire?"

"Uh... yes. Because it makes your body really strong."

She nodded, her mouth set in a grim line. "I'll eat the broccoli."

"Good. It's really important."

"Okay." She raised her hand to touch the button; then she stopped and held her little finger up. "Tomorrow night with Tenzin?"

If he didn't deliver, he'd never hear the end of it. "I'll do my best."

"Okay." She looked over her shoulder. "I'm coming." She looked back to the screen. "I love you. Bye."

Sadia hung up without waiting for Ben to respond. It was one of those little things she did that reassured him.

She didn't wait for Ben to respond because she knew he loved her. Sadia knew she was loved. She knew he'd do anything for her. There was not a doubt in her mind.

Ben had never had that assurance when he was five. Not even close. But Sadia did, and he was a part of that. On nights where he felt especially bitter about never seeing the sun again, he reminded himself of that.

"COMPLETELY WRONG AND COMPLETELY RIGHT," Brigid mused over the phone. "Yes, that sounds like roughly half the decisions you have to make as an immortal."

"Tanks." He mimicked her accent as he moved a pawn on the chessboard, playing both sides. "Tat's so helpful."

"Feck off." She laughed at him. "I don't know what you want me to tell you. We don't live in a black-and-white world. Sometimes there aren't any good answers to a problem."

Ben tapped the white knight on the chessboard. "If Carwyn was human and dying, would you—?"

"Faster than you can fecking blink."

The words tumbled out of Brigid's mouth at such rapid speed, Ben had to rewind to catch her meaning. "You would?"

"Without a second thought."

"Even if he didn't want to be a vampire?"

"I think even if he hated me forever, I'd do it," she said quietly. "Even if I had to do it myself and it killed the love between us, I'd do it. I'm not proud for saying it, but God's truth, I can't give you another answer."

Hearing her answer brought a bitter taste to his mouth, so Ben was surprised when the spike in his heart eased just a little. "Why? How are you so sure?"

Brigid took a long time to reply. "My life was very dark for a long time. And then... this man came into it. This infuriating, glorious madman came into my life, and it was like seeing the sun break over the horizon—to put it in human terms." She cleared her throat. "So it's just to say I'd do anything to keep that sunshine, Benny. *Anything*. Because thinking about a world where Carwyn ap Bryn didn't exist at all takes me to such a dark place in my soul that I wouldn't emerge from it."

Ben had nothing to say.

"Do you understand what I'm saying?" Brigid's voice was intensely quiet. "Those of us who have been wounded cling to what gives us light or peace. Even if it's not the right thing. Even if it hurts. Because the other option is not an option."

*"She did the only thing she could think to do when someone she loved was dying. How do you not fucking see that?"*

"I get you." Ben picked up the black queen and held the piece to his lips.

"Do you?"

"Yes." He set the queen down on the board, moving her into

position next to the black knight. "I understand what you're saying."

⁓

HE WALKED across the camp and knocked on her door an hour before dawn. The fire had burned down to embers, and the immortals had retired to their day chambers. The only movement he saw in the blue predawn light was from the scattered figures of the humans on the edges of the encampment and a cat slinking through the long grass.

This time Ben waited for Tenzin to come to the door.

When she opened it, Ben's body had the exact same reaction it always did, but something in his amnis had settled. The frantic, desperate feeling she'd provoked earlier was gone.

She said nothing. She leaned against the door of the trailer, blocking the entrance.

Ben asked, "Will you come to my caravan tomorrow night so Sadia can say hello to both of us?"

"Of course I will."

"Okay." Ben didn't know what else he wanted to say, he just knew he didn't want to say goodbye.

Brigid was right.

When you'd been wounded, you held on to the things that gave you light. Even if they weren't good for you. Even if they hurt.

"I don't know how to *not* be angry with you," he said quietly.

"I know." She opened her mouth. Closed it.

"New Year's resolutions?"

"I told Chloe I might need to pause them, but I don't think I have to," Tenzin said. "At least not with you." She stared over his shoulder at the horizon. "I told you I would wait."

"It's been two years."

"And?" Her eyes drifted to his. "I have waited longer for things I want."

Desire twisted in Ben's belly, and Tenzin smiled.

He couldn't hide his irritation. "Do you always know when I'm horny?"

"Yes, I always have."

"Yeah? Well I knew too." Ben thought about all the times he'd caught her looking at him with pure female appreciation. She loved looking at his body. "Want me to take my shirt off?"

"Yes." She crossed her arms and raised an eyebrow. "Anytime you would like."

Fuck. "Well... I'm not going to, because I'm not an exhibitionist."

"A very damaged bedroom on Penglai Island says otherwise."

Ben's fangs dropped. If he could have blushed, he would have. "That wasn't exhibition."

"Well, it was not quiet."

"Tenzin—"

"In fact, several vampires approached me later that night and asked if either of us had been injured." She narrowed her eyes. "I now realize they were probably trying to embarrass me."

"I can see that was supereffective."

"I do not get embarrassed by sex. Every animal in the world mates, Benjamin. I have never understood cultures that try to hide it."

He raised a hand. "Can we just agree that wrecking entire rooms and parading around naked isn't something we need to make a habit of doing?"

"If those are parameters you want to set in our relationship, I am comfortable with them."

"They're not *parameters*. I'm not saying we're going to... We just don't need to..."

Tenzin frowned. "I truly do not know what you're trying to say."

*Neither do I.*

Ben took a big breath and let it out slowly. The air smelled like woodsmoke, fresh grass, and human sweat. "I don't know how to not be angry with you, but I'm really tired of being angry with you. You're in every part of my life. You're my uncle's best friend. We share an assistant. And my baby sister thinks you walk on water."

"I'm a wind vampire; I don't walk on—"

"It's an expression, Tenzin! She thinks you're amazing and she adores you. So I'm *tired* of being angry with you, but I don't know..." He swallowed the anger that rose. "I don't know how to *not* be angry with you."

"You're like Giovanni. He was never very good at holding a grudge."

Ben thought about his parents. "I can hold a grudge."

"No. If you truly are done with someone, you cut them out of your life completely. When you are very angry with someone, you are cold, but if you are really and truly done with someone, it's as if they don't exist at all."

She was right.

"Sometimes I hate that you know me so well."

The corner of her mouth turned up. "Trust me, the feeling is mutual." She stepped back. "It's almost dawn. I'll see you tomorrow night."

## 23

The next evening, Ben was greeted by the sound of music at sunset, a raucous, intoxicating melody that reminded him of wine-filled nights, dancing, and firelight. He threw on a fresh shirt and left his trailer, searching for the source of the music, only to find a brand-new landscape surrounding him.

The night before, they'd been camped on a hilltop, surrounded by a lush meadow edged by oak trees. Now he was standing in the middle of a forest, the scent of pine was everywhere, and a stream trickled through the middle of the camp.

Caravans were parked among the trees, but in a small clearing, a fire burned, musicians sang, and tables were set up while the scent of roasting meat drifted through the air.

Radu was sitting at the table with the sandy-haired vampire guard who was usually attached to Kezia. The Poshani leader stood and waved Ben over. The other vampire left without a word.

Ben walked toward him, his eyes moving everywhere at once.

"Do you move every day?" He sat in the chair Radu pointed toward, the one the guard had just vacated.

"Not every day, but when we get a new guest or one leaves, we must change location."

"And no one has ever found the camp?"

Radu pursed his lips. "I cannot say that *no one* has ever found it. But if they have, they have been wise enough not to take advantage of that information to cause any trouble. We take a different route every year so as not to be predictable."

"I see." Ben looked around. "This is beautiful."

The woods reminded him of some bohemian fairy-tale dream. Tasseled hammocks hung between trees, and colorful lamps dangled from branches above them. Thick rugs were spread on the ground near the fire, along with cushions and baskets of fruit and wine.

"We are in the business of providing a comfortable sanctuary for our guests," Radu said. "We take the job seriously."

"The club in Bucharest?" Nothing could have been further from the fairy-tale forest than the pulsing disco in the heart of the Romanian capital.

"The club is what the humans want. And it's what vampires who want humans want." Radu shrugged. "We pay attention to our customers. Here, we create a more traditional Poshani experience."

Ben opened the bottle of a blood-wine in the center of the table. "It's not a bad way to live. Join me in a drink?"

Radu held out an empty glass. "Happily. But you are incorrect. It is not just 'not bad,' it is the most excellent way to live." He looked around the forest. "Among your friends and family, new earth under your feet every night. Humans weren't meant to be so settled."

"You're giving away your element, Radu. I'm sure earth vampires would disagree."

Radu's eyes twinkled. "Indeed I am. Is it so obvious?"

"To one of the same element? Yes. Maybe not to others."

Radu tapped his temple. "Ah, but you're a clever man."

"I'd better be." Ben's eyes swept the gathering, examining the immortals and humans he saw. Though the tables were relatively close together, the music prevented any eavesdropping, which was probably part of the reason they played it.

The first person to catch Ben's eye was a waif-thin blond vampire with round blue eyes and a worried expression.

"That is Tatyana." Radu caught the direction of his gaze. "The newborn who's on the run from Oleg."

"Did she tell you that?"

"She didn't need to." Radu smiled. "I like her. She has a very Russian sense of humor."

"Hmm." Ben saw an older man with a pocked face and olive-brown skin sitting on his own. More correctly, the man was sitting in an isolated pocket of introversion while humans and vampires tried to tempt him with something he ignored. "Let me guess," Ben said. "Darius?"

"Yes, that is Darius."

"If these vampires are the ones you've narrowed down, how did you get them all here?"

"I sent them an invitation."

Ben blinked. "And they just arrived?"

"I made excuses of course." His eyes shifted. "Now, Fynn is an interesting case."

"The Nazi vampire?" Ben didn't know if he was guilty of the goblet theft, but everything about the man told Ben he was scum.

He was wearing a suit the color of oatmeal in the middle of the forest and flicking the servers away from him with a casual disregard that Ben found enraging.

"Please tell me he's paying a lot of money," Ben muttered.

"I cannot tell you exact details, but he's paying a substantial amount." The corner of Radu's mouth turned up.

"Good." Ben liked Radu more for the half smile. It told him Radu was milking Fynn, and that made him happy. "The woman near Tatyana?"

"Madina," Radu said. "Very smart. Very opportunistic. She was getting a little too imperialistic according to rumors, so Arosh asked her to leave Samarkand."

"He asked her?"

"He asked her... forcefully. I believe she accepted my invitation so quickly because the offer of safe haven was appealing."

"Good." This was the kind of information he needed more of. "Why would she steal the goblet?"

"I have two theories: pure greed or leverage."

"Greed is greed, but leverage?" Ben looked at Radu. "What does she want from you?"

"Safe haven for now, and later? Possibly a new community to rule? She comes from nomads too. I don't think being terrin of the Poshani would be undesirable to her."

"If she wanted to use the goblet as leverage, wouldn't she have approached you by now?"

"She *has* approached me."

"With the goblet?" *Why am I here then?*

"No, with sex. She made a sexual advance toward me."

*Thanks for the info?* "Which has what to do with the goblet?"

"I don't know." He narrowed his eyes. "But she is an excellent lover. Perhaps she means to entrap me."

"That's..." *Too much information? Unlikely?* Unfortunately, more than one vampire considered sex just another weapon in the immortal arsenal. And most of them were very good at it.

Tenzin was good at it.

"I think" —Ben cleared his throat— "that if she had the goblet and wanted to use it in some kind of bargain, she would've made her hand a bit easier to read."

"Perhaps," Radu said. "You suspect René DuPont. Why?"

Ben wanted to swallow his exclamation from the day before. "I only know he's a skilled thief. But he also takes contracts for others. If René took the goblet, I suspect he's already sold it or handed it over to a buyer and the goblet is probably long gone."

A flicker of anger burned in Radu's eyes. "It is far more than a goblet."

"To you," Ben said, "yes. But to another, it's a priceless artifact." He saw the object of their conversation lounging on a cushion near the bonfire with a slim, dark-haired woman Ben recognized. "Your sister Kezia."

Radu glanced at René and Kezia. "What about her?"

"She's clearly friendly with René. Could her loyalties—?"

"Not even a sliver of a chance." Radu was clearly confident. "She would never betray the Poshani."

"I see." Nevertheless, Ben watched Kezia and René, watched them flirting and playing coy with each other, watched them whisper and laugh.

After a minute's scrutiny, René glanced up and saw Ben watching him.

"Vecchio!" The French thief broke into a wide smile. "Fancy meeting you here." He leapt to his feet. "And all grown up too."

René sauntered over to Ben and Radu's table.

"Hello, René." Ben desperately wanted René to have stolen the goblet, but he had a feeling that Tenzin was right this time. René DuPont had the look of a man without a care in the world. He didn't even appear to be scheming.

It made his face look all wrong somehow.

"I see you recovered from that time Tenzin threw you off a building," Ben said.

"And I see you've shed that irritating mortality, yet kept the same *lack* of humor." René cocked his head. "Such a disappointment."

"Must be the title of your sex tape," Ben muttered.

All the vampires looked confused, but a familiar laugh cackled from the trees.

René lifted an eyebrow. "If Vecchio is here, he must be following Tenzin." He slipped an arm around Kezia's waist. "You know Tenzin, don't you, *chérie*?"

Kezia said, "Of course I do."

"The boy follows her like a faithful puppy. It's quite adorable."

"Hey, René," Ben said.

"Yes, Vecchio?"

"Remember the times I beat you—*twice*—when I was still human and you were a vampire?"

René's lip curled just slightly. "You have different memories than I do."

"Clearly. The funny thing is" —he addressed himself to Kezia — "René always seemed to be a step behind me, even when I was mortal. Can you imagine how far behind he'll be now that I'm a vampire?"

Kezia's mouth curled into a smile. "You like playing with fire, young Vecchio?"

Ben rose and stepped close to both of them. "Fire doesn't concern me. Just makes me think of home."

"Hmmm." Kezia looked him up and down appreciatively. "So I see."

He felt her approaching and knew instinctively what she would do. Tenzin flew toward them and landed on Ben's back, curling her arms around his shoulders and her legs around his waist possessively.

Was she making it look like she was claiming territory? Yes. Did Ben mind?

Not... really?

It was a power play, but a good one. Tenzin might be one of the suspects on Radu's list, but Ben wasn't willing for any adversary to see them as divided. They had their problems, but those were no one else's business.

He ran a hand from Tenzin's ankle up to her knee. "Hey, Tenzin. How'd you sleep today?"

"Metaphorically?"

"Of course."

"Very well, thank you." Tenzin laid her cheek against Ben's neck. "Hello, René. Hello, Kezia."

"Tenzin." René looked slightly ill, and yet he couldn't take his eyes off Tenzin. His lips were flushed. It was a weird combination.

"My dear Tenzin." Kezia greeted her with a smile. "I am so glad you accepted my invitation."

"I was surprised to receive it, but there was no way I would turn it down. I wouldn't want to miss a minute of this," she said. "I'm just glad Radu invited Ben too."

Radu rose. "Forgive me for leaving this delightful group, but I must attend to other guests."

"Cool." Ben's fingers were running across Tenzin's ankle. "We'll catch up later."

"Let me know if you have any further questions about your accommodations."

"You bet." Ben wasn't looking at Tenzin, but every cell in his body was tuned to hers. "So René—"

"I heard so many rumors about your adventures in China," René said. "I imagine only half of them could be true."

"Did you hear that Ben found the Laylat al Hisab at the bottom of the ocean," Tenzin asked, "where it had lain for a thousand years? But he found it completely intact, stored in the glass vessels created by Harun the sword master, along with countless other gold treasures valued at many millions of dollars."

René pressed his lips together.

"Because that happened," Tenzin said, playing with a curl of Ben's hair. "It was fun."

Ben turned to her. "Did you want to make that call at my place?"

"Yes."

Ben turned to Kezia and René. "You'll have to excuse us. Personal business."

Kezia smiled. "Of course. I'll just let my imagination run wild until René fills me in on all the details." Her eyes swept up and down Ben's body one more time before she glanced at Tenzin, smiled with a hint of fang, and turned back to the fire.

Ben gave René a flippant wave and turned toward his caravan. He said nothing more until he reached the bus. He kept Tenzin on his back until he walked inside and shut the door. "Okay, you can get down now."

Tenzin floated off his back and landed in front of him. "Kezia would like to have sex with both of us. Just in case you didn't understand what that look was about."

"Yeah, I got it." It was pretty obvious. "Just not into it."

Tenzin nodded. "I will add that to the previous parameters."

"This is not..." He closed his eyes and willed the erection away. "Can we not start a conversation about this when we're here to video call my baby sister?"

"That's fine," Tenzin said. "We can talk about it later."

"Or never. That's okay too."

She patted his cheek. "I don't know what René was talking about. You have a wonderful sense of humor, Benjamin."

## 24

"So then!" Sadia leaned on the desk and kicked her legs up behind her. "Kara and Owen were the last ones, and they jumped in the pool and went all the way to the bottom!"

"Really?" Ben shook his head. "That's really dangerous."

"I know!" Sadia's face was glowing as she told them about her swimming party. "All the way in the deep end. That's where Dema threw the hoops."

Tenzin said, "The deep end is very deep."

"I know! But Kara grabbed the red and the yellow ones—those were her colors—and she swam all the way up and she popped up" —Sadia jumped up— "and then swam to the steps, and that's how she won the race."

Tenzin asked, "What did she win? What was the prize?"

Sadia lifted her shoulders. "We didn't have a prize. We were just racing."

Tenzin frowned. "No prize?"

"That's cool." Ben squeezed Tenzin's knee. No doubt the idea of a competition without something shiny at the end was messing with her brain. "You don't need a prize. Sometimes racing is just for fun, right?"

"Yeah." Sadia was bouncing again. "And on the trampoline, I totally won."

"Of course you did," Tenzin said. "You are superior to other human children."

"But I came in last on the bikes since I just got mine and I don't have practice like my friends. And that's why I didn't win in the diving race."

Tenzin opened her mouth, but Ben jumped in. "Which is fine, because you're going to ride your bike a lot, right? With Zain and Dema? So you can get better on your bike and have more fun."

Sadia nodded. "And pretty soon I'm not even going to need the extra wheels anymore and Baba can take them off and then I'll go" —she pointed her fingers into an arrow and zoomed them across the screen— "superfast!"

Tenzin turned to Ben. "So she is not holding a grudge against her playmates for besting her in the race?"

Ben shook his head. "Everyone is good at different things, Tenzin."

Tenzin pursed her lips, and Ben could practically read her thoughts. What was the point of competing unless you were good at *all* the things?

"It's *fun*." He spoke quietly and grabbed her hand so she wouldn't say anything more. "It's fine."

"Hmm." Tenzin watched Sadia on the screen. "Sadia, you are taller than the last time I saw you."

"Yeah, I'm very tall now. When are you going to be in New York again so I can come see the birds?"

"I cannot give you an exact time right now, but I will call you when I reach home unless it's during your sleeping hours."

"Good." She sat in the purple chair at her desk. "Ben are you going to New York too?"

"I don't know. But I'll come visit you in LA." He and Tenzin were both putting off the New York conversation. Technically, the house belonged to Ben, but he'd bought it with the intention of letting Tenzin make it her home, and she had. She'd decorated the second floor, installed a training area on the first floor and an elaborate garden on the roof. Her name wasn't on the deed, but it was her home.

Yeah, New York was complicated.

Sadia let out a long yawn.

"I think it's bedtime for you, kiddo."

"It's not though. It's dinnertime almost."

"Broccoli again?"

She nodded. "Are you sure you have to eat it to be a vampire?"

"Yes," Ben said.

"Absolutely not," Tenzin said. "That is not necessary."

Ben quickly muted the call. "Tenzin, I'm trying to get her to eat vegetables."

"By lying to her?"

"Yes. It's a solid strategy. Trust me."

Tenzin reached over and unmuted the call. "Sadia, you do not have to eat vegetables to be a vampire, but you *should* eat them because they will make you healthy, and your health is important for future training."

Sadia's eyes were wide. "What training?"

Ben just sat back and watched them. *This should be interesting.*

"Swords mainly. The nutrients in vegetables like broccoli will be important for building lean muscle that will enable you to wield weapons more effectively. Your natural body type does not indicate a particularly muscular frame, so you will need to be deliberate in your diet and exercise regimen."

Sadia's eyes were the size of saucers. "Real swords?"

"Yes."

Oh, he'd be hearing about this one from Giovanni and Beatrice, but what could he say? It was Tenzin. And honestly, she was probably right. Sadia would probably start learning the basics of sword handling by her early teens like Ben had.

Sadia's face brightened. "I can eat broccoli."

"Good." Ben jumped in. "Just eat the broccoli. It's good for you. Don't tell Baba and Mama about the swords."

"Okay!" She turned and yelled, "Dema, Tenzin is gonna teach me swords!"

Tenzin bit her lip to hide the smile. "Well, she didn't tell Baba and Mama."

Sadia turned back to the screen. "Okay bye. I love you, Tenzin."

"I love you too."

"Hey," Ben protested, but the screen went dark. He turned to Tenzin. "Nice."

"Don't be jealous. You didn't offer to teach her swords."

HE SPREAD his notes on the table in the caravan. "I don't have a board here, so we'll have to make do." He stood and taped a paper with Darius's name on it to the cabinet on the far left. "Darius."

"Old but not ancient earth vampire." Tenzin stared at the name. "I'd say maybe fifteen hundred years old. Near East. He knows about the goblets and their significance. I don't see a motivation for him to take the goblet though, even if he had opportunity. He's not hungry for power. If he took it, it would only be for sentimental value, and that's a dangerous play with Radu."

"Okay." Ben stuck another paper up. "Madina."

"*Very* possible," Tenzin said. "She's been ruling Samarkand and the surrounding territory for nearly one hundred years, but Arosh became annoyed with her and now she's out."

"Out of what? Territory? Time? How much did she piss Arosh off?"

"Enough that she will want to lie low for a century or two. They've been lovers—of course, what female in Central Asia hasn't slept with Arosh? —but he's pretty angry with her for cutting one of his children out of a trade deal."

"Have you?"

She looked confused. "Why would I get involved in a trade deal?"

"Have you had sex with Arosh?"

Tenzin raised an eyebrow. "Do you really want to know?"

"Actually, no." Ben turned back to the paper. "So Madina is kicked out of Samarkand and what? She's now looking for new territory? A new job? The Poshani seem pretty insular. From what Radu said, they're not going to follow a leader from outside the clan."

"Of course Radu would say that because he wants to believe it. But if she had enough support and could make a good case, it's not out of the question. She's very rich, and they have many young people. Money matters."

"And taking the goblet would help her case?"

"It's a divine symbol of leadership. Of course it would."

He marked Madina's paper with a star. "Okay, so she's the lead suspect so far."

Tenzin leaned her chin on her fist and tapped her lower lip with a finger. "I'm so curious about Tatyana."

Ben dragged his eyes away from her mouth. "Me too." He taped a paper with Tatyana's information to the cupboard.

"Why is she here?" Tenzin asked. "She's younger than you are. Is she Radu's pet? Purely a distraction?"

"I'll try to get to know her a little tomorrow night." He tapped her name. "Maybe play up the 'fellow new vampire' thing."

"Good idea."

Ben turned and realized Tenzin was staring at his ass. "Hey."

She lifted her eyes. "Yes?"

"Uh... never mind. What do you know about Fynn?"

"Almost nothing. He seems generally evil, but I don't know anything about him. You might ask Carwyn and Brigid. They're more knowledgeable about immortal politics in South America."

"I will." He put up a paper with Fynn's name and a large question mark. "And finally..." He wrote TENZIN on a piece of paper and stuck it to the wall. "There's you."

"Are you serious?" She sat up straight and smiled. "You're really going to investigate me?"

Ben sat at the table and started taking notes. "Known thief."

"*Accomplished* thief." She leaned over the paper. "Make sure you write that. 'Known, accomplished thief.'"

"Noted." He kept writing. "Multiple connections to human and immortal criminal networks. Military experience. No known ambitions to rule, but she does enjoy causing general chaos and breaking things."

"Who doesn't?"

"For reference, see Naples and Puerto Rico."

"Those were both more convenient timing than intentional chaos."

"Political alliances are... disparate."

"That's one way of putting it. Or you could just write the truth: I have none."

"Bullshit." He looked up. "You're loyal to your father. You don't want to be, but you are. You're loyal to Giovanni." *You used to be loyal to me.*

She stared at him long enough that Ben wondered if she'd managed to master mind reading.

Finally she shrugged. "Giovanni doesn't have any political ambitions."

"You're loyal to Cormac O'Brien. I know you've done him favors over the years and he's done them for you. For most people, a favor is just a favor, but not for you."

"Cormac is the vampire in charge of the city where I currently reside. If I didn't like him, I'd find someone to replace him. But I do like him, so I can do him favors every now and then. It's not political."

"No, you're right, it's personal." He set down his pen. "Subject has no political ambitions, but she enjoys playing God with people she claims to care about."

*That* pissed her off. He could tell by the minute tightening of Tenzin's jaw.

"Everyone plays God with people they love," she said evenly. "You lie to Sadia about vegetables and call it love."

"Did you just compare a white lie about vegetables with all the lies you've told me over the years?" Ben blinked. "They're not even in the same *neighborhood*."

"Wrong." She leaned her elbows on the table, mirroring his posture. "It is exactly the same thing."

"So you took me to your father and overruled my wishes to remain human because you knew it was good for me?"

"No, Ben, because I know *you*." Her cool facade cracked, just a little. "You keep lying to yourself, but this was always where you were heading. You lived among us, demanding to be seen as an equal. And for the most part, you succeeded, but the first time you lost a step, the first time your knees started to ache in the morning, the first time you felt your body breaking down, you would have turned to your uncle" —she snapped her fingers— "and made the same choice I had to make for you that night."

"Maybe you're right. Maybe I would have. But you didn't *have* to make any choice that night, Tenzin. You could have saved my life if you'd taken me to a hospital, and you know it."

"So I should have left you with the humans?" Her fangs fell. "You think I should have watched them cut you up and piece you together like a patchwork garment?" She snarled. "Hoped and prayed they didn't fumble with your *life*? Human healers are butchers. I *knew* Zhang could save you. Anything less was an unacceptable risk."

He gripped the edge of the table to keep from striking out. "What did you give him to save me?"

"He owed me."

"You gave him something. What was it?"

"It doesn't matter."

"Yes it does!" He rose, cracking the table as he stood.

Her expression was unreadable. "Why do you care if you're so angry with me, Benjamin? Why does it matter what I gave him?"

"Because..." Because he didn't need another debt in his life. He didn't need another person he loved sacrificing important things to save his dumb life. "It just matters, Tenzin."

"You're right," Tenzin said softly. "It matters because you're alive." Tenzin rose and floated toward him until they were eye to eye. She put a warm hand on his cheek and traced the arch of his eyebrow with a single finger. "You are *alive*."

She repeated it like a mantra.

"You live, Benjamin Vecchio, and you owe your life to no one. Not me. Not Zhang. You will live however you see fit. You will protect those who matter to you and follow only the commands of your conscience." Her voice fell to a whisper. "You will go where you want and you will love who you will, so be angry with me for as long as you want. I know I did the right thing."

Ben felt his heart break open, because he saw the history of Tenzin's life through her wishes for his.

She had owed her life and loyalty to Zhang.

She had lived at the will of the powerful.

She had protected the unworthy and been bound to the command of others.

Ben couldn't deny what he felt for her even if he didn't know what to do with it.

He loved her. He'd never stopped.

~

BEN TOSSED a tennis ball in the air and caught it, over and over like a baseball. "Patterns," he muttered as he examined the names on the cupboard.

Brigid was on speakerphone. "What?"

"Patterns. We fall back into them, whether we want to or not."

"Are you talking about you or Tenzin?"

"I don't know yet." He stared at Tenzin's name. "Maybe both."

"What happened?"

"I'm dangerously close to understanding her point of view."

"That *is* dangerous."

Ben tossed the tennis ball and caught it again. "Is that vampire morality taking over? Am I going to become one of those monsters who justify anything if it gives me what I want?"

"Do you even know what you want?"

"Probably not." No, that wasn't right.

He *wanted* Tenzin. He wanted to grab her, drag her to his trailer, take her blood, and bind her to him so thoroughly that when he breathed in, she breathed out.

"I do know what I want," he said. "I just don't know if what I want is good for me."

## 25

Tenzin was waiting outside his door at dusk.

Ben buttoned his pants and rubbed a hand through his messy hair as he descended the steps. "Are you saying you actually can't break into these things?"

She nodded toward the two guards standing a short distance from his trailer. "Not without bloodshed, and that's one of my New Year's resolutions."

"Not killing people?"

"Not killing people unless I have a reason for it that you could justify."

Ben stopped in his tracks. "Wait. That *I* could justify?"

"Yes." She floated toward him. "I like being in a place where I don't have to hide." She slowly flipped in the air. "It's lovely here, don't you think? Maybe this is how all vampires should live."

"Yeah, it's nice." He glanced at the bonfire, newly lit in the forest clearing. The music was already going—a trio of guitarists were playing a mellow tune near the outdoor kitchen. "Why am I the person who decides if you should kill someone or not? I don't want that responsibility."

"I'm not going to call you or anything." She looked irritated. "I am simply pausing and asking, 'Would Ben kill this person in these circumstances?' The answer is usually quite clear."

"Right." Ben found that incredibly disturbing. He'd become the unwilling leash on Tenzin's homicidal tendencies, and he didn't even know where she was most of the time.

"It's a good system for the most part, but you can be a little too forgiving at times." She paused. "Not with me of course. With other people."

"So we're talking about forgiveness now?" This felt like a continuation of their argument last night. "Why should I forgive you when you haven't asked for forgiveness?"

She smiled. "It's an interesting quandary, isn't it?"

"It's a genuine question." He stopped walking. "Are you sorry for what you did?"

She looked away, then looked back. "What do you think?"

"No."

"Correct. To be sorry for what I did would mean that I regret that you're alive, and I will never regret that you're alive and being a brother to Sadia and a friend to Gavin and a son to Giovanni and Beatrice."

"I could have been all those things as a human if you hadn't dragged me to Penglai in the first place."

"You could have also had all those things as a human if you'd listened to me and not trusted Johari."

Damn it. He couldn't argue with that.

He'd beat himself up a thousand times in his own mind, asking why he hadn't seen the clues or paid attention to Tenzin's advice. "Well, at least Johari and Saba didn't manage to throw Zhang and Arosh into another war by stealing the sword."

"Yes." Tenzin looked away. "Have you seen Tatyana yet tonight?"

Something pricked at his instincts, but he was tired of self-examination. Confronting Tenzin was exhausting. Once you forced yourself inside her head, she made a frightening amount of sense.

Which just... messed with his mind.

"Radu says Tatyana's been hanging out near the human cooks."

"Really?" Tenzin landed on the ground and turned toward the outdoor kitchen. "Wait." She stopped.

"What?"

Tenzin dropped her voice. "You were going to investigate her using camaraderie."

"It's not that mercenary," Ben said. "I just want to get to know her. She seems like the odd one out in all this."

"I agree. You should befriend her so she will trust you."

"Do you have to put it that way?"

"Yes." She glanced up at Ben. "Someone has to keep you honest."

"And apparently someone has to keep you from stabbing." He nudged her toward the tables where blood-wine was already being poured. "Go. I'll join you later."

"I smell René."

Ben stopped and turned. "Just so we're clear, if you are ever deliberating about killing René DuPont, the answer will always be yes."

"Why would I need to kill René? He's harmless."

"He's annoying."

Tenzin shook her head slowly. "You can't just kill people because they're annoying, Benjamin."

"Not people." He started walking again. "Just René."

TATYANA MIGHT HAVE LOOKED like a lamb in the woods, but she was by far the most openly suspicious vampire he'd ever met.

Her sky-blue eyes narrowed. "Did Oleg send you?"

Ben frowned. "All I said was 'hello, I'm Ben. I heard you're from Russia.'"

"You didn't answer the question." She was stirring a large pot hung over an open fire. The fire didn't seem to disturb her.

"Okay." He spotted the sheen of moisture on the back of her hand. Ah, that's why she wasn't afraid of the fire. She was a water vampire. Interesting. "Oleg did not send me."

"Good."

The scent of peppers and garlic filled the air, and Tatyana continued to ignore him, speaking to the women in the kitchen with a clearly fluid grasp of the dialect they spoke.

"You're very good at languages," Ben said. "I've been trying to figure it out."

"Poshani?"

"Yes."

Tatyana glanced up. "You're probably trying to fit it into a Romantic or Slavic paradigm," she said. "Which would be your mistake. The Poshani language is primarily North Indian with opportunistic borrowing from Hungarian, Turkish, and Farsi."

Ben grinned. "You're a language nerd." His aunt would approve. "How did you get to be a vampire?"

She was clearly confused by his enthusiasm. "None of your business. Do all Americans smile so much?"

"Probably." He held a hand out. "Can I help?"

She looked at the spoon stirring the deep red stew. "You're a wind vampire?"

"I am."

"Then cool the stew. It's getting a little hot."

Easy enough. Ben channeled a swirl of air over the pot, but it splashed on one of the women's dresses.

"Stop." Tatyana waved a hand. "Just stop."

She might have been as young as Ben was, but she was

217

surprisingly good about concealing her power. He got nothing from her other than the urge to back up and give her space. She was definitely putting out "don't touch" vibes.

"So if you don't want to talk about yourself—"

"I don't." She glanced at him. "I know who you are. You didn't need to introduce yourself. Everyone knows who you are."

Ben leaned on the trailer behind him. "That's so annoying."

She waved. "Your profile isn't exactly low, Benjamin Vecchio, son of Giovanni Vecchio, immortal son of Zhang Guo, mate of Tenzin—"

"Wait, what?" His stomach dropped.

Tatyana raised an eyebrow. "She is not your mate?"

Shit, how did he answer that question? "It's complicated."

Tatyana grimaced, and Ben knew she wasn't a stranger to complicated relationships.

"Oleg?" Ben asked.

Tatyana said nothing, but the look she shot him told Ben that he wasn't far off.

Ben stepped closer and lowered his voice. "Okay, level with me. Does everyone assume Tenzin is my mate?"

"Yes." The twitch at the corner of her mouth was as close as she'd come to a smile. "Is she not?"

"Tell me about Oleg."

Her mouth twitched again. "It's difficult to remain hidden in this world, isn't it?"

"Which is so weird, because the humans aren't supposed to know about us."

"Be serious. Don't you think most of them know?"

Ben remembered Chloe's shock when she'd woken up to see Tenzin hovering, fangs out, in their loft in New York. "I think there are a lot of people who don't know a thing."

"Then they're blind." She glanced up. "Did you always know?"

"No." He debated how much to tell her, but he decided to offer something to see if she'd open up. "I was twelve. I picked a vampire's wallet."

"You tried?"

"Succeeded. Not to brag, but I did. He tracked me down and ended up adopting me."

"That's interesting." She glanced up again. "I was in university."

"Same as my aunt."

"I doubt that." She took a breath. "It wasn't a pleasant revelation, but I overcame it."

"So Oleg isn't your sire?"

She let out a string of unintelligible curses that got the humans laughing. "No. Praise God he is not my sire," she muttered. "That asshole."

"Clearly you're a big fan."

"He's a manipulative son of a bitch."

"Aren't they all?"

Tatyana looked up. "You tell me. You've known them longer than I have."

Ben didn't know how to answer her. When he was with Tenzin, he found it easy to call himself a monster. But when he was confronted with calling his aunt or uncle a monster, he felt strangely protective.

"You'll find your people," he said quietly. "Eventually you'll find them."

"I hope so."

She put on a good front, but Ben sensed nothing but fear from her. "So what brings you to the Dawn Caravan?"

"What brings anyone?" She lifted the spoon and waved the scent of the stew in front of her face. "I heard about it. I needed to get away. I needed..." She shrugged. "It seemed like a good idea."

What had she been about to say? What could the Dawn

Caravan have that would draw a vampire on the run? Ben glanced around.

Poshani women and children. The young ones ran between the trailers and buses in the swiftly dimming light as human guards roamed the perimeter and vampire guards hovered overhead.

Ah. Of course. "You're afraid of him."

"Of who?" She looked up with blank eyes.

"You know exactly who I'm talking about."

"Sorry, I really don't."

She was afraid of Oleg, hiding in a place where protection was guaranteed and Oleg the fearsome Russian fire vampire wouldn't dare trespass even with all his influence and wealth.

Ben had a feeling that Tatyana had booked her caravan for the whole season.

"What will you do when winter comes?"

Her eyes were all innocence. "Be on my way of course."

Ben wasn't so sure that Tatyana was an innocent. Maybe she hadn't stolen the goblet initially, but what if she happened to find it in her possession? Surely the Poshani would trade anything for their priceless treasure even if it meant bending the rules for a vampire on the run.

"Here." She held out a bowl of stew. "Wipe that smile off your face and eat."

"Does my smile really annoy you that much?"

"You look like a crocodile," she muttered, "with too many teeth."

Ben hadn't laughed that freely in months.

Tenzin looked up when she heard his laughter. Glorious. What had the young woman said?

For the thousandth time, Tenzin debated her strategy. Perhaps she was wrong to follow him so closely? Perhaps he needed to take a few immortal lovers so that he wouldn't regret—

No.

Her amnis recoiled at the thought, as did her memory. He already belonged to her. She just had to be patient.

Benjamin loved her, and his anger was natural. When he let his temper cool, he would return to her. What was two years? The blink of an eye. The snap of her fingers. Two years was nothing.

*Two years was everything.*

She hungered for him. When they touched, his amnis roared over her like a crashing wave while hers waited like a tiger. She had to resist the urge to sink her teeth into his flesh and never let go.

She wanted to drown in him, not listen to him laughing at the jokes of another woman.

Her fangs ached in her mouth.

She sipped the glass of blood-wine Radu had poured for her and watched the humans dancing in front of the fire.

"I know you suspect me," Tenzin said to Radu. "But I am not your enemy. If I was, he wouldn't even be here."

"You're very confident you can control him."

"Control him?" She smiled. "It doesn't work that way with Ben."

Radu glanced toward the kitchen. "I haven't seen a newborn like him in a very long time."

"You haven't seen a newborn like him *ever*." The wine was delicious with a hint of berry flavoring the iron tang of blood. "He is unique."

"Those we love always seem unique."

"Do you know what happened to all my sire's other sons?" Tenzin leaned forward.

Radu said, "The world was once a much more violent place. Wars, famines, conflict—"

"I killed them all," Tenzin said quietly, staring at Radu. "And I didn't do it for power. I didn't want their land or their authority. I didn't want their people or resources."

Radu stared at her, unflinching. "Why do you tell me this?"

"I'm not after your throne, but others are."

"Others are always after my throne."

She glanced at Ben. "We all see what we want to see, Radu. If we take a step back, sometimes the picture becomes clear."

## 26

He flipped his pencil in the air, end over point. "Who are the two most likely culprits?"

"Based on what we know so far?" Tenzin was playing some app on her tablet with a rubber-tipped stylus. "Madina and Fynn."

"Not Darius?"

"Not Darius. I told you, no ambition."

"I really want it to be René," he muttered. "Are you sure it's not René?"

"Yes, Benjamin. Very sure."

"Why?"

It had been a week since he'd joined the Dawn Caravan, and Ben felt no closer to understanding the dynamics at play. He was confident that Tenzin didn't have the goblet, but that left Madina, Darius, Fynn, René, and Tatyana as suspects. He wasn't ruling anyone out.

"René is as confused by all this as we are," Tenzin said. "I can read him well enough to know. Kezia invited him like she invited me, but she's more interested in seducing you now, and René's more than a little put out. He doesn't like you either."

"Shocker." Ben drummed his fingers on the table. "Not that I don't love the idea of spoiling René's party, but I really don't think Kezia is into me." He was staring at the makeshift board they'd created on his cupboards.

"She is." Tenzin looked around the trailer. "Do you have a printer?"

"Yes." He pointed to the corner.

"Good."

The machine started to hum, but Ben reached for the tennis ball again and started tossing it up and down. "So if Madina and Fynn are the most likely suspects, we need to break into their trailers."

Tenzin looked up, her eyes dancing. "Really?"

"Yes, really."

She clapped. "I thought you were going to be honorable, but I agree. We really do need to break in." She hopped to her feet and walked to the printer.

"Day isn't an option for me anymore, so we have to find a way to distract them as a group, and then the two of us can slip away."

*And have sex!*

No. Nooooope. Ben had managed to wrangle his libido under control, but spending every night pretending to be Tenzin's partner was exhausting. She was as openly affectionate as she'd been before everything went to shit, which meant Ben had to be equally affectionate. And then as soon as they got behind closed doors, the tension was nearly unbearable.

Still, his amnis was happy. His amnis was happy just being in the same room as Tenzin.

Tenzin walked to the cupboards and put three sketches on top of their suspect board.

"Why are you putting pictures of Radu, Kezia, and that weird Poshani guard up? What do they call them? The Hazar?"

Tenzin pivoted to Ben and pointed to the guard. "You think this is a Poshani guard?"

"Yeah."

She smiled a little. "That's not a Poshani guard. That's Radu and Kezia's brother, Vano."

"What?" Ben sat up straight. "That guy is the mysterious brother?"

"Yes. Why did you think he was a guard?"

"He was acting like one in Kashgar, standing behind Kezia while she watched me. It was odd, but I assumed he was her guard. He's kind of..."

"Nondescript?"

"Yes. Then I saw him in Bucharest at Radu's club—"

"Because it belongs to both of them," Tenzin said. "Vano is based in Ukraine, but he has invested with Radu in several properties. He's been here longer than we have."

"Weird." This meant something. "What does this mean? What am I missing?"

Tenzin raised an eyebrow. "You can't tell which vampires are in charge and which ones are guards?"

"No, no, no..."

*My sister knows something was stolen—she's the one who helped me test you—but she does not know all the details. My brother knows nothing, and it must remain that way.*

Ben stood. "Vano knows. Radu thinks Vano doesn't know anything about the goblet being stolen, but he was in Kashgar with Kezia, looking for me."

"So Vano knows something is up?"

"If he knows what we do, he has to have figured out that Radu lost something important."

"The icon?"

"Possibly." Ben started to pace. "But if we were still looking for the icon, then why would I be here?"

"Kezia is wondering that herself. She's the one who set up the icon theft." Tenzin used air quotes around the word *theft*.

"What do you mean?"

Tenzin frowned; then she looked a little embarrassed. "I did forget to tell you."

"Tenzin!"

"What?" She motioned between them. "There's been quite a bit of tension if you hadn't noticed. Kezia's picture was in that Renaissance triptych I spotted in the chapel."

"She was a patron?"

"That was her chapel. Farkas is *her* human."

Ben's mouth dropped open. "Farkas is her—"

"I'm guessing a former lover? Current lover? He's not that old. Or maybe he was just her errand boy, gathering pretty objects as she happened upon them."

"So the house did belong to a vampire."

"Oh yes." Tenzin hovered in the air, sitting cross-legged as she floated in front of the sketches she'd made. "I'd guess the house belongs to her."

"So Kezia knows about the icon."

"Yes. She set up the job with Radu to test you," Tenzin said. "But does she know about the goblet theft?"

"Not according to Radu." Ben paced in front of the pictures. "She does know something is missing."

"She might suspect the goblet since the ceremony is coming up."

"And if she confided in Vano, she might have told him about the goblet."

"Possibly."

Kezia and Vano.

Radu and Kezia.

Kezia and Farkas.

Farkas with a vampire.

Was everyone scheming behind everyone else's back?

*Click, click, click.*

"I know what's bugging me. I know what's not right." He spun toward her. "I really do think faster now; Beatrice wasn't lying."

"Of course she wasn't. What is going on?"

He walked to the board. He took down Fynn, René, Darius, Tenzin, and Tatyana's pictures.

"What are you doing? I'm not a suspect anymore?"

Was she disappointed? Ben tossed the pictures over his shoulder and stared at the three portraits Tenzin had drawn. "I know what's been bugging me about this whole job."

"The fact that it's too cozy?"

"No, the tension." He spun around. "Can't you *feel* it?"

She rolled her eyes. "And you used to accuse me of being obtuse."

"No, not between us." He snapped his fingers and felt the air snapping back at him. "That rippling... something. It's just under the surface. The humans are tense and wary. Kezia and Radu are constantly poking at each other. The guard—Vano—is slinking around."

"What are you trying to say?"

"It's Puerto Rico," Ben said. "It's Naples."

The light went on behind her eyes. "You think there is some rebellion in the works?"

"I think one has to be. All the signs are there." Ben turned back to the three pictures remaining on the board. Radu, Kezia, and Vano. "This isn't a theft; this is a coup."

Tenzin rose and stood next to him, staring at the pictures. "So these are the trailers we need to break into? Radu is not going to like that."

~

"YOU MUST BE JOKING." Radu was unamused. He glared sideways at Tenzin before he leveled his dark eyes on Ben. "I told you that you would need to be impartial."

Tenzin leaned forward. "What motive would I have to steal the goblet?"

"It's a beautiful and valuable one-of-a-kind treasure," Radu said.

"Point taken." Tenzin leaned back. "He's right—if I got a chance to steal it, I probably would."

Radu snorted. "Surprisingly self-aware."

Tenzin spread her arms wide and smiled with fangs in full view. "I'm evolving."

Something about her expression made the idea of Tenzin evolving absolutely terrifying. Judging by the expression on Radu's face, he felt the same.

Ben reached out and took her hand. "Tiny, I don't think Radu actually thinks you took the goblet." He looked at Radu. "Admitting that one of your own family members may have it out for you is difficult."

"My brother and sister had nothing to do with this." Radu wore a tense smile. "But just to prove that to you, I will create an amusement tomorrow night, something involving all the guests. I will instruct the Hazar to allow you passage through the camp without harm."

"Thank you," Ben said. "I promise we'll—"

"There will be no *we*." Radu cut him off. "*You* may search the trailers if you can get past the safeguards," he said. "You alone.

Tenzin will stay with me." Radu's mouth was set in a firm line. "Because I still think she is the one who took it."

Tenzin and Ben exchanged a look, and Tenzin nodded. "I will stay with Radu."

"Fine." Ben wasn't happy, but he understood. Tradition was everything to Radu. The idea of violating his siblings' privacy went against everything he believed in.

"I'm not a busybody," he said. "All I'm going to do is look for the goblet. Don't forget, you're the one who brought me here."

"To find a thief, not accuse my family."

"I will go where the evidence takes me," Ben said. "If Vano knew nothing about the theft, then why was he in Kashgar?"

A shadow flickered in his dark eyes. "To accompany our sister."

"You know there's more to it than that," Ben said. "Radu, I'm trying to help. Think. Look around you. Who benefits most from your loss of legitimacy?"

He didn't answer, but he didn't avoid Ben's eyes. "I appreciate your honesty, Ben Vecchio."

"I won't lie to you." He glanced at Tenzin. "And I didn't dismiss her outright. But I can tell when she's lying."

Tenzin snorted. "No, you can't."

"Really?" Ben raised an eyebrow. "The ship in Puerto Rico?" The place she'd told him she was leaving for China and that it had nothing to do with him.

Tenzin narrowed her eyes and looked away.

～

Why did he persist in irritating her? She was showing admirable restraint as it was.

Ben had no idea how much gold Tatyana had hidden in her

caravan. But was Tenzin stealing it? No. Radu kept a chest full of gemstones in his vardo. Had she taken a single one?

Well yes, she'd taken a rather nice sapphire, but then she put it back.

*See? Evolving.*

She was doing remarkably well on her New Year's resolutions. Did Ben give her any credit? No. He continued to act as if she hadn't changed at all.

And he still had iron control over his sexual urges, which was very frustrating.

*"Tell me this has nothing to do with me. Look me in the eye and tell me this has nothing to do with you and me and what happened in that cave..."*

Why had he brought up Puerto Rico? Three years had passed since that happened. Was he still angry that she'd left? If she hadn't, she would have lost control, just like she had in the cave. She would have hurt him. She'd nearly killed him while he spent his dying breaths reassuring her that it was okay.

Oh no. She'd needed a long break from the temptation that was human Benjamin Vecchio.

He'd been slowly wearing down her control for years, picking at her, making her lower her guard, trying to reveal the human beneath the vampire she'd become.

Ben thought he knew her, but he had no idea.

"Tenzin?"

Radu was gone. The two of them sat alone at a table on the edge of the forest with a candle burning between them and an open bottle of blood-wine.

She turned her eyes to him. "Why do you try to humanize me?"

Ben looked surprised. "Because you are human."

"I'm not." Something in the center of her chest ached. "You

should be honest about who I am, Benjamin. Otherwise, the person you think you love will only be an illusion."

The smile he gave her was halfway between bitter and sad. "I know who you are."

"Do you?"

Ben leaned on the table. "I think you tried. I do. But the last job finally made me understand how you saw me as a human. So maybe this was all inevitable."

"Do you think I thought I was greater than you? Better somehow as a vampire?"

"I know you did."

"You're wrong." She leaned forward and ran a finger along his jaw, reveling in the contact, the energy that embraced her, even as he held her at a distance. "You were always too good for me, Benjamin. I never deserved your admiration or your friendship, much less your love." She gently touched her lips to his. "Shining boy. White knight. You should have been more afraid of me."

"I couldn't be."

"Are you afraid now?"

His lips remained parted. "No."

"You should be. I'm trying to remember who I was," Tenzin said. "But the parts I had to cut away were all the soft, gentle things. I'm not sure what's left."

He grabbed her hand. "If you take off before this is finished—"

"I'm not." She took a breath and let it out slowly. "I've been following you for two years, Ben. You haven't figured out why?"

"I'm waiting for you to tell me," he said. "You call me a white knight, but we stopped playing chess the minute I stopped being human. I need to hear the words, Tenzin, because I'm tired of trying to read your mind."

*You're lovely. Lovable.*

Lovable. She'd had to look it up to make sure she understood the nuance. *Love* was a very imprecise word. *Lovable* meant "deserving of love or affection," which was a circular definition and not at all precise, but it told her one thing: Ben thought she deserved love, whatever that meant to him.

What did it mean to her?

Tenzin looked toward the bonfire. "English needs better words."

"Then find another language to tell me how you feel," he said. "You find the right words to tell me, and I will learn the language."

## 27

When Ben opened his caravan door to the dusk sky, he was in an entirely new landscape. His trailer was parked on the crest of a hill where the earth sloped down into rolling fields of poppies and tall grass. For as far as Ben could see, not a vehicle or a human habitation was in sight. A pair of rabbits stared at him from the edge of the grass as they munched on thin stalks of what looked like wild oats.

The sky was a brilliant velvet blue that reminded Ben of the deepest ocean. Stars were just starting to peek from behind the clouds, and the scent of fire and roasting meat filled the air.

He turned to the left and followed the scent around a copse of oak trees toward a meadow carefully mowed down to make room for the Poshani settlement.

"Good evening."

Ben turned to see Tenzin walking with René.

*Is she trying to piss me off?*

Ben felt like they'd been getting somewhere the night before— he thought they'd had a meaningful moment—but maybe that was wishful thinking. Maybe all of this was wishful thinking.

René looked like the cat that had blissfully chowed down on

the canary as he bent down and kissed Tenzin on the cheek. "*Au revoir, chérie.* Shall we meet for a drink later?"

"No." Tenzin stared at Ben. "Don't bother me until tomorrow night. Or maybe the next one."

René chuckled. "As you wish." The smile he smothered was smug and satisfied.

Ben waited for the Frenchman to be well away before he spoke. "Seriously?"

Tenzin lowered her voice to barely over a whisper. "I told him what is really going on with us."

"You mean—"

"He knows we're not really mated. That we've been estranged for a couple of years." Tenzin frowned. "More like three if you count the time between Puerto Rico and Shanghai."

"Why?" Ben struggled for words. "Why would you do that?"

"I have my reasons."

"Which are?"

The frown didn't leave Tenzin's face. "I know I need to share things with you, but it is very cumbersome to feel like I have to explain myself to another person. Shall we get some blood-wine?"

Ben took her arm and steered her back toward his trailer. "Food can wait."

"I am quite—"

"You're going to tell me what's going on." He opened the door and nearly tossed her inside. "I know you probably have a reason for informing that man about our business, but I don't know what it is and I don't know if it's a *good* reason. So spill."

Ben crossed his arms over his chest, blocking the door as Tenzin looked around the trailer.

"You removed all your notes."

"I remember them."

She smiled. "See? Better memory too. I told you—"

"We're not going over all the user upgrades to my body and

brain I'm still getting used to, Tenzin. Tell me why you told René about us."

She sat, leaned her elbow on the table, and rested her chin on her hand. "I needed some relationship advice."

Ben's mouth dropped open. "What?"

She smiled. "I'm joking. But that face you're making right now is excellent." She looked around. "Where is your tablet? I want to take a picture of it."

He shook his head. "René, Tenzin. Tell me why you told René."

"Ah." She settled back in the chair. "Do you know how long he's been here? Four weeks already. Far longer than Radu invited him for."

"Why would René take time out of his intense schedule of scheming and duping human women to— Ohhhh." He uncrossed his arms and sat across from her. "You think he's planning something."

"Of course he is. Radu invited him on the Dawn Caravan because he suspects that René might have stolen the goblet. But why did René accept? He's in no need of shelter right now. None of his jobs are particularly hot."

"So why did he take time out of his regularly scheduled scheming to hang out in rural... wherever were are—"

"I'm fairly certain it's Ukraine. I think we're out of Romania now."

"Whatever." Ben found the concept of borders becoming less and less relevant now that he had access to every country by air. "So René's planning something."

"He knows Radu lost something," Tenzin said, "since he didn't make a secret of hiring us. Then he invites an odd company of immortals to the Dawn Caravan right before a large festival, along with Kezia and Vano, the other leaders of the Poshani. He knows something is going to happen."

"It's risky for René. If he stole the goblet from Radu, his contract would be broken, and he'd be an earth vampire at the mercy of some very unfriendly people."

"But René knows he didn't take anything, so he is not concerned. He does know something odd is going on and something valuable was lost. He's smart enough to look past that. What will the state of security on the caravan be when its leaders' attention is so divided?"

"Oh." Ben saw it in an instant. With Radu distracted by his missing treasure and both Kezia and Vano occupied with shifting power dynamics... "So René's planning to flat-out rob the caravan."

Tenzin nodded. "It's quite a good plan. I used something similar when I robbed Wangara."

Ben frowned. "Who?"

Tenzin tapped her fingers on the edge of the table. "Not a who. It's quite a large complex of gold mines in West Africa. See, at the time gold had gone down in value because of Musa's hajj, so repurposing a large amount of it during a religious festival was actually beneficial to the economy."

Ben lifted an eyebrow. "You robbed a gold mine to benefit the economy?"

"Obviously." She shifted in her seat. "But we're not talking about me. We're talking about René, who definitely has plans to rob this caravan."

"Stupid."

"Highly stupid," Tenzin said. "I agree. But he's gathered quite a lot of good information that I feel like we could use."

"Like what?"

Tenzin slid a piece of paper across the table. "Like the combination to the lock on Kezia's caravan. I copied it from a notebook in his trailer that he thought he was hiding." She smiled. "He's adorable. Kezia is old-fashioned."

Ben looked at the paper. "A combination lock?"

"Combined with a tumbler. She trusts the Hazar far too much."

"Apparently." A tumbler lock could be picked with a simple set of picks he'd practiced with when he was ten. "Okay, I'm supposed to do this tonight, right?"

"Yes." She angled her head toward the door. "I believe Radu is gathering your distraction as we speak."

"Fun."

"I better go." Tenzin rose. "I don't want Radu to doubt my innocence. Wait at the back of the crowd until the Hazar join the festivities. Then search Kezia's trailer."

"Got it."

CLUTCHING the paper in his pocket, Ben walked to the kitchen trailer and sat down for a plate of kebab, rice pilaf, and a delicately spiced eggplant dish. He wasn't ravenous, but he ate more than he'd been expecting. Then he drank a full glass of blood-wine, thanked the cooks, and wandered toward the bonfire in the middle of the poppy-dotted meadow.

As he walked, he watched the dynamics of the campsite. Instead of observing the vampires, he watched the humans.

Children. There were far more children than he'd realized the first night he came. Ben wondered if they kept the younger Poshani out of the way when a new vampire joined the caravan. That would make sense. But now the children emerged from campers and travel trailers. They rode horses across the meadow and tossed balls at each other from horseback in a game that looked a little like polo without the mallets.

The crowd near the bonfire was growing, drawing occasional vampire attention, but mostly human. Ben heard a loud bang, then a zip of fire, and a bright stream of light shot into the sky. It disappeared into the darkness for a brief second before it exploded into a massive shower of sparks.

Ben smiled. Fireworks.

The crowd clapped in appreciation.

As he approached, he saw the ground around the bonfire had been meticulously cleared of grass or anything flammable. Most of the vampire guests were sitting in plush chairs at the center of the crowd while servers offered glasses of wine or plates of fruit. Tenzin had already joined them, sitting close to Radu with René on her left side and Kezia on her right. She glanced at Ben, then quickly looked away.

On the far side of the crowd, near Kezia's trailer in the distance, Ben saw Tatyana watching with an amused expression on her face.

Ben wandered over. "This is nice."

"Yes," she said. "Quite a show for the little ones."

"For grown-ups too."

She looked around. "One errant spark and this all goes up in flames."

"Such an optimist."

"A realist."

Ben glanced at her hands, then at the small stream that ran along the edge of the forest. "Keeping an eye on things?"

"I'd be a fool not to," she said quietly. "Even water vampires can burn."

"True."

"Still..." She shrugged. "Radu asked me to keep an eye out for any errant fire, and I was willing. There are not many of my kind in the camp."

"You're generous to help."

"I've become quite good at putting out fires." She glanced at him from the corner of her eye. "I used to work for Oleg."

"I see."

"I very much doubt that, Benjamin Vecchio." She raised a hand, and a basketball-sized blob of water rose from the nearby creek. "But I'm ready when I need to be."

He gave her his biggest grin. "Good vampire."

"Ugh." She curled her lip. "Put it away. I'm not in the mood for your teeth."

Ben laughed. He liked Tatyana. He liked her cranky nature and her obvious humanity. He liked that he caught her smiling when children ran past and there was a cat who followed her around the camp, clearly knowing that eventually Tatyana would give him food.

*Why are you here?*

Was she on the run? Hiding out? Or here to bargain for a shot at staying hidden beyond the season by fencing a priceless cultural treasure? Could she be part of Vano's or Kezia's schemes?

"Vampire life is complicated," Ben muttered.

"So it is." She looked over her shoulder. "The Hazar are coming to watch. Radu will call them down."

Ben looked up and saw the shadowed silhouettes of wind vampires guarding the perimeter of the camp. "Seems like you've gotten to know the ins and outs of this place pretty well."

"I'm observant," Tatyana said. "Some of us don't come into immortal life with riches, connections, and extraordinary power." She glanced sideways at him. "We have to watch for our opportunities."

Ben's curiosity was driving him crazy, but he knew he had to focus. Now was not the time.

"Come closer. Put out your lights." Radu lifted his voice and shouted at the Hazar. "I don't want to worry about burning our fine guards. The fire will keep others away tonight. Why don't all of you watch from the ground to protect yourself?" Radu caught

Ben's eye for a fraction of a second. "It will only be for a few minutes."

*Understood.*

As the crowd grew denser and torches and lights were doused, Ben fell back, eventually leaning on the corner of a camper trailer parked next to Kezia's.

Another zipping firework.

Another cheer from the crowd. Darkness, then explosion.

Ben saw no hovering shadows, and no one was looking his direction. He ducked between the trailers and dove under Kezia's caravan. Then he emerged on the far side and examined the door.

Another pop. Another gasp of delight.

The combination lock was simple, no electronics, and the tumbler was far from a challenge. He managed to open it within a minute.

He cracked the door and felt a nearly imperceptible trip line pull tight.

Aha. Slipping his fingers along the edge of the door, Ben felt for the device and disabled it with a razor blade and a piece of tape. It wasn't a sophisticated device but a basic hack that would alert Kezia when someone entered her trailer.

He was buying time. Probably five to ten minutes at most.

Like Radu, Kezia lived in an old-fashioned vardo, but there was nothing rustic about it. Silk wall hangings covered where curtains normally would be. The woodwork on the walls was carved and painted, and gold trim lined the cupboard doors and ceiling beams.

In an intricately designed living space like this one, there were a hundred places to hide something small, which was what Ben was looking for.

He surveyed the space, deliberating the most obvious place to start.

Not the desk or office area.

Not the closet or the vanity.

The sleeping area.

She'd want to keep her treasures close. Ben walked to the platform bed at the far end of the trailer and poked his head past the drapes. It was a cozy space with thick wall hangings that blocked out all light and would keep the custom wagon warm when it was cold in the winter.

Not that Ben saw Kezia spending a ton of time rolling through the winter in her vardo. She was far more likely to be spending the winter in the Crimea or on the Mediterranean or wherever Poshani royalty liked to hang out.

In the corner of the sleeping area, there was a small altar. Ben was only mildly surprised to find the famed icon of Sara-la-Kali there.

Of course the icon was Kezia's. Of course it was. He should have seen it before Tenzin told him; the chapel had nearly screamed *female*! Leaning closer, he saw the small triptych Tenzin had spotted that clued her in.

It was a devotional, a private type of scene meant for a bedroom or personal chapel. There was a picture of the Madonna and Child being tended by the angels, and painted into the faces of the angels was the patroness who had commissioned the piece.

Kezia.

Her large eyes and dark curly hair were unmistakable. That was what Tenzin had seen in the chapel. That was what made her say yes to Kezia's invitation to join the caravan. Kezia had been part of it since the beginning. Ben wasn't sure if that made her more or less likely to be the one angling for power, but it was something to remember.

A cursory search of the sleeping area revealed no signs of the goblet, so his first theory was out the window. After searching the overhead and underbed cabinets, Ben slid his hands underneath the edge of the mattress and ran them along the sides.

Halfway down the right side of the bed, he felt a faint seam in the wood.

*Gotcha.*

He pressed down and heard a latch click somewhere across the vardo. Sitting up straight, he searched in the area where the click had occurred.

He thought about Kezia. Proud, vain Kezia wouldn't bend down. She wouldn't crawl. Ben dismissed the lower cabinets.

He opened all the storage cabinets he'd searched before.

Wait.

*Don't think like you. Think like Tenzin.*

Ben headed to the closet. If Kezia was anything like Tenzin, she wouldn't only have coins and gold goblets in her safe, she'd have jewelry in there too. He sat at the small vanity and pulled open the drawer.

Lipstick. Bottles of perfume. Hairpins.

And the seam of a false bottom in the drawer.

## 28

Sliding back the false bottom, Ben saw that it didn't contain a chamber but another lever. He pressed it and heard another click, but this time the sound was right under his nose.

A decorative panel beneath the vanity popped out from the wall. Ben reached up and slid it to the side, revealing an eight-by-eight-inch-square cabinet built into the vardo wall.

"Clever."

He listened for the sound of fireworks, but he heard none.

The cabinet was like a small wall safe. Contained inside were stacks of gold coins, a silver dagger as long as his hand, a stack of old documents and—nestled in the far back—a worn silk purse no bigger than an aluminum can.

He reached for it and felt the weight of gemstone against his fingers. Ben opened the purse and let a carved gemstone goblet slide into his palm.

The sight rendered him stupid for a solid minute.

The artifact was incredibly beautiful. The sides were polished and carved with writing he couldn't place. Not Arabic. Farsi maybe? It was small, no bigger than a demitasse glass, but made of pure gemstone the color of sunlight.

Ben grabbed a piece of paper from his pocket, placed it over the inscribed base of the goblet, then looked for any powders or pencils he could... *There!* An eye shadow. He tapped the tip of his finger against the dark powder before he rubbed it delicately over the writing.

He didn't need to know everything it said, but he wanted to show it to Tenzin. She'd be able to identify the writing and the age.

He examined the goblet from bottom to lip, wishing he had the convenience of a mobile phone to snap pictures.

Dammit, being a vampire was so irritating sometimes.

He heard voices in the distance and put the goblet back, placing it in the exact position he'd found it in the first place. He carefully closed the panel and the drawer. He stood and put the vanity bench where it had been.

Then he backed out of the living area and crept toward the door, looking for something he could use to hide his scent. Most vampires, whether they could get drunk or not, kept a bar in their living area.

Kezia was no different. Ben saw the nearly full bottle of premium vodka on the edge of the bar. No, not smelly enough.

There! So much better. A half-full bottle of peppermint schnapps would hide his scent nicely. He unscrewed the top and tipped it over, making sure the splash landed in the middle of the rug he'd stepped on.

The scent of alcohol and peppermint was overwhelming. Nearly gagging, Ben left the trailer, making no attempt to reset the tripwire. She was going to know someone had been in her stuff; he just didn't want her to immediately identify him.

He passed two other camping caravans before he ran into his first person.

"René." Ben smiled, grateful the vampire had become his unwitting accomplice. "How are you?"

Ben's friendly demeanor immediately set René on edge.

He narrowed his eyes. "Why do you ask?"

Ben stuffed his hands in his pockets, hiding the paper with the inscription. "Being polite, old man. Chatting the chat. Working the room."

René curled his lip. "I have no idea what you are talking about."

Ben tried to look sad. "And that's why you're always going to struggle with multilevel marketing."

"What are you talking about?"

"Never mind," Ben said. "Do you know where Tenzin is?"

"Yes." The smugness was back. "I just left her caravan."

Ben patted his shoulder. "How nice for you."

Leaving René to try to unscramble his friendliness, Ben walked to Tenzin's trailer and knocked on the door. She yanked it open from the inside and pulled him in.

She narrowed her eyes and twitched her nose.

"Tenzin, what—?"

"Shhhh." She rose to smell along his chin and his neck. Then she spun him around and sniffed his back. "Good."

"What the hell was that?"

"You covered your scent with peppermint. I thought you were trying to hide something."

"Hide what?"

She landed and walked to the table. "Nothing."

"Clearly not nothing." Ben followed her. "Tell me—"

"You were searching Kezia's trailer. It was entirely possible she could have interrupted you. Then you would have had to lie about why you were there and possibly offered to have sex with her."

Ben blinked. "That seems like a leap."

"Not really. She wants to have sex with you—with both of us really—"

"Yeah. You said."

"If she'd caught you searching her trailer, that would be the most obvious ploy to cover what you were actually doing."

Dear Lord, she had an active imagination. "So you thought I was going to get caught and I was going to have sex with Kezia just to cover my tracks?"

"It's possible." She didn't even look embarrassed.

"So you were sniffing me because...?"

Her voice was barely audible. "Because I do not want you having sex with Kezia."

Oh, this was nice. "We're not together. I can still smell René in this trailer." He put his hands in his pockets and strolled toward her. "Do I need to sniff you?"

"Not necessary."

"Maybe it is." He leaned down, put his face in the crook of her neck, and inhaled deeply, trying not to groan.

Tenzin smelled like dust and sunset and cardamom tea. She smelled like sexual desire and a little bit of kerosene.

"Were you polishing swords today while I was sleeping?" he whispered.

"Yes."

Ben opened his mouth and let his fangs slowly scrape against her skin. Her flesh prickled underneath his mouth. "Why don't you want me to have sex with Kezia? We haven't been together in over two years. Are you jealous?"

"I am... territorial."

"Because you've taken my blood?"

"No, because you've taken mine."

His mouth hovered over the silk skin where he'd bitten her two years before. He remembered the exact place. The exact taste. The instinct to sink his teeth into her neck and take her inside was overwhelming. He bathed in the scent of her skin, her blood, and her desire.

Ben let his breath wash over her, moving it down her body to touch every exposed inch. "I'm not the only vampire to ever take your blood."

"No."

"You had a mate once."

Tenzin froze and her amnis retreated in a blink. She raised a hand and pushed Ben firmly away. The blank expression on her face unnerved him.

*You are a shitty person.* His conscience screamed at him, and he stepped away. Why had he said it? Why had he even brought it up? *Because she's not the jealous one; you are.*

Yep. That was it.

Ben stood up straight. "Tenzin, I'm sorry. I shouldn't have brought him up."

She was quiet for a long time, staring into space. She didn't seem upset; more pensive. "Stephen and I..."

He was *such* a dick. "It's fine. It's none of my business."

She frowned. "Yes, it is."

Ben didn't know what to say.

"If you had a blood-bound mate in your past, I would consider it my business to know about that person," Tenzin said. "To know why you were no longer bound."

"I already know he died. You don't have to talk about it if you don't want to."

Tenzin looked at Ben with a frown. "It wasn't what you are thinking. Stephen and I cared for each other, but it was a strategic mating. A political marriage, if you want to think of it that way. I didn't love him the way that Beatrice and Giovanni love. Not the way..."

*Not the way WHAT?*

He shut up since he'd already made an ass of himself enough for one night. "I'm glad the two of you cared for each other. I'm sorry he died."

"I'd been sleeping." Her voice was soft. "For a long time I'd been sleeping. Stephen woke me up." She smiled. "And he made me laugh."

"That's good."

She kept her eyes on him, and Ben sat in the feeling he sometimes experienced in the silent space between waking and dreaming when he saw Tenzin's image in his mind. Her expression moved from one second to the next between very young and indescribably ancient.

He sat with the knowledge that tempted and terrified him about forging something new and untested with her. *If you know her, you will know everything.*

## 29

Since Ben had run out of time after searching Kezia's trailer, he followed Vano the next night. Ben chatted with Tatyana as they strolled through the camp. They talked, and he subtly steered her from one place to the next, always keeping his eyes on Vano.

"Where did you grow up?" she asked him.

"I thought you said I was famous."

Tatyana shrugged. "You're mildly famous *now*. No one really talks about your human years."

"Really?" He watched Vano lift a Poshani child onto his back as he chatted with three burly men around a small fire. "I'm kind of bummed about that. I tried really hard to make a reputation for myself when I was human."

"Why?" She sounded horrified.

"For business. It's not easy being the human partner of a famous vampire."

"You mean Tenzin?" Tatyana shrugged. "I don't know that I would call her famous."

"Infamous?"

Tatyana smirked. "Feared. Admired a little. But mostly feared."

"Is it the military stuff in the past or the assassin thing?"

Tatyana's eyes went wide. "Military stuff?"

Ben's eyes followed Vano as he walked among the humans in the Poshani camp. "Don't worry about the military stuff. She's retired now. So it's the assassin thing. I get that, but I know her. She'd never take a job to kill someone who was an innocent."

"Are you sure?"

"Yes. She has a thing about powerless people." He glanced at Tatyana. "Besides, what vampires do you know who are innocent?"

"Me of course." She offered him half a smile. "You would not count yourself?"

"Innocent?" Ben thought about the man in Rome. About a thief in Shanghai who'd done nothing but get caught up with the wrong people. He thought about the hundreds of innocent bystanders he'd probably left in his wake, never wondering how they fared in the chaos he and Tenzin routinely left behind. "I'm far from innocent," he said. "In fact, I might be the guiltiest one here. At least other vampires are honest about being monsters."

Tatyana rolled her eyes. "Self-pity is so boring. You've been given riches, eternal life, a powerful sire, and a fierce mate who obviously loves you very much. Why on earth are you complaining? Think about the choices you have."

Ben was watching Vano shake hands with two men with long beards and furtive expressions. They were wary, watching for errant eyes.

He hardly registered speaking. "I didn't choose this."

"What?"

Ben looked down and realized he'd said it out loud. Shit.

No denying it now. "I actually didn't choose to be a vampire. I was dying and Tenzin took me to my sire, but I never chose to become a vampire."

Tatyana didn't look shocked. "So you lost one choice and gained a thousand others. I didn't choose this life either; that is the nature of the world. We make the best of it, Ben Vecchio."

Ben focused on Tatyana after Vano disappeared into one of the men's camper van. "You didn't choose this?"

"No." She glanced around and lowered her voice. "Since you told me the truth, I will tell you. I was working for someone dangerous. I didn't know they were dangerous at the time of course; I was only a bookkeeper. Such a boring job, right?"

"Uh-huh."

"I found something unusual that ended up being a big deal." Her expression was bitter. "My sire changed me to keep her secret. So I would have to be loyal to her."

"Where is your sire now?"

"Dead." Tatyana's expression cleared. "Oleg killed her, but I helped." Then Tatyana gave Ben the first true smile he'd seen from her. "That feels very good to say."

"That you helped to kill your sire?"

"Yes. She was a horrible person, and I'm glad she's dead." Tatyana took a deep, cleansing breath. "Yes, that feels very good."

"Glad I could help."

She looked around at their surroundings. "And I'm glad I could help give you cover while you followed Vano. Do you want to tell me why you've been watching him?"

"Not really."

"Okay."

BEN STAYED WATCHING for Vano long after Tatyana abandoned

him. He waited by the fire until Tenzin joined him to get an update.

"Have you broken into his caravan yet?"

"I don't even know which one is his." Ben scanned the ring of more traditional Poshani homes. "Kezia's was fairly obvious, but I can't pin this guy down."

"He sleeps in a modern camper." Tenzin nodded toward a sleek grey caravan on the far end of the guest caravans. "You haven't seen him coming in and out of that one?"

"I've seen him near it."

Tenzin held her hands out near the fire. "That's his."

Ben examined the trailer. "He's a little different than his brother and sister."

"Vano is the practical one." Tenzin turned her hands to warm them. "He doesn't have clubs; he owns factories. He owns a caravan company as a matter of fact. And two rather large horse ranches, but that is traditional. I believe Radu has horses as well."

"How else is Vano practical?" Ben found himself leaning closer to her.

"He spends more time with the humans." She spoke very softly. "Have you noticed that?"

"Yeah, I really did. Who are the Poshani who travel with us?"

"The darigan?" Tenzin glanced around at the ring of campers, trailers, and trucks that surrounded the central vampire camp. "They are humans of Radu's clan, charged with protecting the vampire guests and moving the caravan during the day. You have one driving you around every day when you're sleeping, just beyond that reinforced wall."

"I knew that." He frowned. "I don't actually know who it is though."

"Your driver? It could be any of them." Tenzin waved a hand. "They don't care. You're cargo to them. Rich, precious cargo they'll protect with their life, but cargo. The Poshani only care about their own."

"Mercenary."

"Practical." Tenzin looked up at him. "Traditional human society has rejected their extended family over and over. Humans have taken their children, burned their camps, and treated them horribly. Why would they care about anyone who doesn't belong to them?"

Ben's vampire vision pierced the darkness, but he could detect no humans still wandering on the edges of the camp. The only humans awake were the ones currently serving the vampire guests. "I guess I can see your point."

"The Eastern Poshani are Radu's people. He was born to them, and he'll choose a successor from among their ranks."

"As long as we find the goblet for him." Ben let out a long breath. "Are you sure René doesn't have this thing and all his confiding in you was a big ruse to misdirect us?"

"He has no motivation to steal it," Tenzin said. "There is no gain for him. I think Vano has it."

"Why?"

"He's the sneakiest, and I think he hates Radu. René thinks Vano is the strongest, but he's not."

"No?"

"Strong and sneaky are not the same thing," Tenzin said. "René might think they are, but he is wrong."

For the hundredth time, Ben wondered whether Tenzin and René had slept together. There was clearly chemistry between the two, and René quite obviously was fascinated with Tenzin. "Okay, I know this probably is none of my business, but did you and René—?"

"No." Tenzin looked at him. "And why do you keep saying that my sexual partners—or possible sexual partners—are none of your business? They clearly are."

"Are they?"

She huffed out a breath and turned to him. "Are you deciding if we can be together?"

Ben crossed his arms over his chest. "I don't know what I'm doing with you most of the time."

Tenzin stared at him for a few long moments; then she grabbed his hand and dragged him to the nearest trailer, which was her own. She opened the door, pushed him inside, and followed him, shutting the door behind her.

Ben stood silently, waiting for her to speak.

"After I took you to Zhang, you sent me away." She turned and faced him. "You said you were 'done'—whatever that means— and that you weren't going back to New York and you weren't going to wait for me. But I said I would wait for you. And I have." She spread her arms wide. "So what do you want, Benjamin?"

*You!*

No, that wasn't it.

Okay, it was. But admitting that felt like defeat.

She asked, "Do you want me to wait longer?"

"No."

"Very well." She stood in front of him. "I dislike having to explain myself, but I am trying to... grow."

"New Year's resolutions?"

"Yes. I am here." She stood perfectly still. "This is *your* choice."

He didn't know what to say. He knew it was his choice. He knew she was giving him time. He just didn't know how to bridge the gap he felt between them. "Tenzin—"

"And to answer your persistent question, my sexual partners *are* your business because I assume you are feeling as territorial as I am. If you had sex with someone else right now when I am near, I would likely kill that person."

*Yes!*

Wait. No. That wasn't good.

He rubbed his temple. "That's not okay."

She stepped closer, and Ben felt the ripple of her power against his skin like a caress.

Tenzin spoke deliberately. "I am evolving, Benjamin, but I will never be human. I will never be tame, and it's long past time you admitted to yourself that you never will be either."

She left him in the trailer, staring at her empty bed.

BEN TRIED to keep his mind off Tenzin by keeping track of Vano the rest of the night, following him at a distance as he visited vampires, chatted with the cooks making dinner, and hovered around the bar where servers mixed drinks and carried wine.

Vano was among the vampire guests, but he wasn't a part of them. In fact, if Ben hadn't been paying attention, Vano would have melted into the background.

It was quite the skill, and Ben realized that Tenzin was right.

Vano was very, very sneaky.

An hour before sunrise as the nightly party wound down, Ben retreated to his secure caravan and called Chloe. "Hey, stranger."

"Hey." She answered the video call on her phone. She was in the middle of a crowd, and the raucous sounds of a party surrounded her. "Where are you?"

"No idea. Ukraine maybe? Where are you?"

"We went back to Monte Carlo." Chloe's face glowed. She walked away from the crowd and found a quieter place with red velvet draperies behind her. "We've been so many places. Oh my God, Ben, you cannot even imagine. Nice, Capri, Portofino—that was probably my favorite."

"Portofino is gorgeous." Ben picked at his shirt, which had

ashes from the bonfire on it. "The boats are amazing. You need to go to Rome though. You have Fabi's number, right?"

"Yeah, totally. I think we're kind of heading that direction, but just taking the lazy route since Gavin doesn't have a club there."

"Doesn't he?"

"No, he's got one in Naples though. Something about the VIC being more easygoing?"

Ben laughed. "Naples is bonkers. Great, but bonkers."

"Sounds like our kind of place." She leaned against a corner. "Miss you. I got used to having you around."

"I know. I'll be back soon."

"Don't you mean we?"

Ben looked down and traced the marbling in the table. "Nothing between me and Tenzin is settled yet."

"Why not?"

"I don't know. I need time."

"Fine." She rolled her eyes. "Make good choices," she sang.

Ben stared at Chloe.

"What?" she asked.

"You said, 'make good choices.'"

"It's simple but good advice."

*So you lost one choice and gained a thousand others. I didn't choose this life either; that is the nature of the world. We make the best of it, Ben Vecchio.*

Chloe was right. Tatyana was right. And Ben was a stubborn idiot.

He'd lost one choice and gained a thousand. He could be with his friends. He could be a big brother to Sadia and a son to Giovanni and Beatrice. He could live a life that would make them proud. He could guard Chloe and keep watch over all his human friends.

And someday he would have to say goodbye. But everyone faced that, human and immortal both. Humans survived it, and he would too.

He would meet new friends, extraordinary people who hadn't even been born yet. He would explore all the places he'd ever dreamed and others he didn't have the imagination to conceive of. He would watch Sadia grow up, and he'd see the world change and evolve before his eyes.

And he'd see all of it in a darkness that wasn't so dark anymore.

"Chloe?"

"Hmm?"

It was a new feeling, delicate as a freshly healed bone. But it was there. "I think I'm glad."

"For what?"

Ben swallowed hard. "Just to be alive."

Chloe's smile was incandescent. "Me too."

He put a hand over his eyes until he could steady his wildly careening emotions. "You knew I'd get here."

Her smile turned soft. "Yeah, I did. So did she."

"But I'm still angry." He cleared his throat. "And I don't know... How do you forgive someone when they're not sorry for what they did?"

Chloe blew out a long breath. "Okay, related question. How can someone be sorry for what they did if they truly believe they did the right thing?"

"Sometimes I really don't like you much."

"I know. I love you too."

## 30

Ben rose from bed the following night after a restless day of sleep. Something had disturbed him all night—some itching, aching feeling in the pit of his stomach nagged him like a pebble in his shoe. He checked all the email he could access, grabbed a thermos of blood left in the trailer, and looked at his most recent to-do list from Chloe.

Nothing was out of sorts. Nothing was on metaphorical or actual fire. His family was fine. His business was as expected.

What was wrong?

He called Tenzin. She answered after three rings.

"What?"

"How are you?"

She was quiet for a long time. "What do you mean by that?"

"I'm not trying to be complicated. I just have a weird feeling, and I'm checking on everyone."

"I'm fine. Don't worry about me."

"Right." Ben tried to think of the right words to tell Tenzin the realization he'd come to the night before with Chloe. That he was more than content with his immortal life. That he was *glad* to be alive. Glad that they had a chance to be more than they had been.

That he wanted to find a way to forgive her. "Tenzin, I was thinking—"

"Wait." She moved away from the speaker and her voice was muffled. "Not now."

"Is that him?" René DuPont's voice was unmistakable. "Tell him we're busy."

"What the fuck is René doing in your trailer at this hour?" Ben roared.

He threw his tablet across the room and rushed out the door, only to feel a hand throttling his throat as soon as he stepped outside.

The blow came without warning or preamble. A fist to the temple followed the hand at the throat. Ben felt himself lifted into the air and tossed into the side of the bus before he managed to speak a word.

His fangs fell and he caught himself from falling to the ground, but no sooner had he lifted his head than two burly vampires gripped his shoulders and locked their legs around his, forcing him back against the bus.

A pale, familiar face floated in front of him.

"Hello, Mr. Vecchio," Vano said. "I thought it would be a good idea to speak to you."

Ben bared his teeth. "Your men will let me go *now*," he forced past the hands at his throat.

Vano looked at him, and Ben began gathering the air to himself. He could feel it, like a great waiting storm over his head. Vano's men might have had the element of surprise, might even be faster, but Ben was elementally stronger than all three of them and Vano knew it, even if Ben's control wasn't ironclad.

Vano jerked his head to the side, and the Hazar guards released Ben. They floated to their master's side, flanking him in the air while Vano considered Ben from the ground.

"This aggression," Vano said. "It is unfortunate. But what

could I do? When I see the hired help following me around my own brother's camp like a gnat, it irritates me. I try to speak to a friend, I see you from the corner of my eye. I try to conduct some business, you are there. What do you want, Benjamin Vecchio?" Vano kept his hands in his pockets. "Or should I call you Benjamin Rios?"

"Do you think you're shocking? I remember you from Kashgar." Ben rubbed his throat. He cut his eyes at the two vampires. "I thought the Hazar protected guests of the kamvasa."

"Ah, but you are not a guest," Vano said. "As I said before, you are hired help. A servant. An errand boy for my brother."

"Sure." Ben knew Vano was trying to goad him by pricking his ego. "Whatever you say. I was also *invited*. Poshani hospitality doesn't extend to those invited to travel with them?"

The vampires with Vano looked uncomfortable.

Vano ignored the question completely. "Why were you following me?"

Ben frowned. "I haven't been following you."

It was clear Vano hadn't expected Ben to lie through his teeth.

The iron control on his face faltered. "You have been."

Ben laughed a little. "I mean... it's a pretty small camp. It's hard not to run into people."

"I saw you following me."

"Dude, a few days ago I didn't even know who you were." Over many years of being bullied by stronger opponents, Ben had realized that antagonists who attacked his ego usually had the most fragile egos themselves. "Just 'cause you saw me around doesn't mean I was following you."

"I saw you last night."

"I was *around*, but I wasn't following you." Ben glanced between the two vampires with Vano as if to say "*Are you hearing this too?*"

"When I was close by, you were watching," he said. "Waiting."

"For what?" Ben scratched the beard he'd been growing out. "I mean... wait, there's a thing happening, right?"

"A thing?"

"The festival?" Ben stepped forward and leaned into his Southern California surfer voice a little. It nearly guaranteed whoever was talking with him would dismiss him and think he was an idiot. "Like, that's why everyone is here, right?" Ben looked between all three of them. "You and Kezia and Radu. There's like a party or something, right?"

Vano was clearly irritated. His smooth face was wrinkled into an expression that said he'd caught a whiff of something foul. "Stay out of my business and keep to the silly amusements my brother plans for his guests. The festival is not for you."

"Interesting."

"What is?"

Ben stepped closer and used his height to subtly look down on Vano. "My uncle said you were smart."

Vano's men laughed and Vano smirked. "You should run along now, young Vecchio. Listen to your uncle."

Ben returned the smile and let the "surfer dude" fall from his voice. "Yes, very interesting."

Vano's gaze sharpened. "If I were you, I'd be careful to not become involved in things that could get you or your friends killed."

Ben had been keeping a strict leash on his amnis, but he allowed it to break free and the wind went wild. It knocked both of Vano's men off their feet and made his own ears pop.

Vano stood in place, but Ben saw him leaning. It was taking effort for the other vampire to remain standing.

"Right." Ben walked past Vano. "You really think *my* friends are afraid of *you*? That's a take. Not a good one, but it's a take."

Ben strode away from the scheming little asshole vampire, giving the man his back. He'd observed enough vampire body language to know that Vano would take it as the insult it was. *You worry me so little, I'll turn my back to you.*

Ben wasn't afraid, but he was irritated. Not only did he have a red spot on his neck, he thought he might be bleeding.

It didn't matter; he was focused on one thing: René in Tenzin's trailer minutes after sunset, clearly in the middle of something Ben had interrupted.

What. The. Fuck?

Ben nearly ran into René when he turned the corner. He brought himself up short, and it took every ounce of control he had not to twist René's head from his neck.

*Pop.* It would come off like a champagne cork. He could even throw it into the air in celebration. Look, everyone! The annoying little bastard is finally, really dead.

"Before you say anything—"

Ben's fist shot out and slammed into René's smug mouth.

"What the hell is wrong with you, Vecchio?" René's lip was bloody, but he wasn't on the ground. "You think this is going to impress her?"

"I don't care," Ben said. "I really don't. I've been wanting to do this for years." His left fist curled up and into René's solar plexus.

The vampire's breath collapsed and his body folded in two. He flew through the air, fifty yards from the clearing, and crashed into a large oak tree.

That felt good. Ben cocked his neck from one side to the other, releasing the tension that had gripped him since he'd heard René's voice on the other end of the line. "You just don't get it, do you?" He flew over and landed into a walk. "She thinks you're annoying."

René snarled and pressed his hands to the ground.

The earth reached up and tossed Ben from his feet. He stumbled for a second before he picked his legs up and floated through the air. "Nice trick."

"Yes, I have a few. Make sure you ask Tenzin about the rest."

Ben wasn't in reach of René, but he forced the heel of his hand out, aiming for the chin, and the air speared out and snapped René's neck back. Ben heard the crack and smiled.

"You idiot!" René snarled. "I am trying to help you."

"Yeah? How's that? You going to confess to being the thief?"

"I'm not the thief." René's lip curled. "You think I'd be helping you if I was?"

"I would not put it past you." Ben hovered a few inches off the ground. "Why are you here?"

He cocked his head at Ben as if to say *Really?*

"Don't tell me you don't have a theory," René said. "Tenzin—"

"Tenzin thinks you're amusing."

"I thought you said she thought I was annoying."

"That too." Ben crossed his arms over his chest. "She has a soft spot for thieves."

René rolled his eyes. "Clearly."

"I'm not talking about me."

"No? You should be. Don't pretend you're anything more than a thief, Vecchio. A thief who comes from thieves. You think your uncle trades for the manuscripts he finds? You think he buys them from auctions? You think Tenzin gained her wealth through honest means and the pittance of an assassin's wages?"

"What does that have to do with—?"

"You Vecchios think you are so noble." René curled his lip. "You all think you're better than the rest of us. You're not." René spat out his name. "Benjamin Vecchio, warrior of Penglai, Master of Iron in blah, blah, blah." René lifted his hands and the earth rose under him. "What are you but another immortal's creation? At least I make my own way in life and don't trade on my family's name."

"Because they're sick of you?"

"Because I have my own identity!" René thumped a fist against his chest. "Not theirs! Mine."

It was clearly a sore subject, but Ben still felt like making René bleed. "How attached are you to your left hand? Not your right—I know you're right-handed—but just your left one?"

One finger. Maybe two.

A thumb? Ben felt the edge of the dagger sewn into his pants.

"You think I'm the one who has the goblet?" René asked. "How naive are you? There is one master thief in this camp. One!" He laughed. "And it's not me, Vecchio. It's not you and it's not me."

Okay, René probably had a point. The only master thief in the camp was Tenzin. Ben kept his hands in his pockets. "You think she stole it?"

"Of course I do, and so do you. You've been holding her at arm's length the entire time you've been here. Why?" René sneered. "Because you know the truth. You know Radu is right. If the temptation was there, she would take it. She's playing with you! Tenzin plays by no rules but her own. She cares for none but her own. If the goblet was in front of her" —René reached out and made a grabbing motion— "she would take it without hesitation."

Hadn't she said it the night before?

*I will never be human. I will never be tame.*

"You keep trying to make her an ordinary woman," René said. "God knows why. She's not ordinary, Vecchio. She's a glorious monster, and she will never apologize for it. Why the hell do you think you're in love with her?"

"Fuck you." Ben flew away, leaving René in the shadow of the oak tree. He wanted to punch René's teeth in, but in his gut, he knew it wasn't because the man was annoying or grating on his nerves.

It was because he was right.

## 31

B en was waiting in her caravan when Tenzin returned from the dinner hour in the clearing.

"Hello." She hadn't been expecting him after she heard him fighting with René, had instead assumed he'd brood for some time.

"Hey." Ben stretched his neck back and forth. "Ran into René on the way over here. Got sidetracked."

"Yes, I heard. Does he still have all his limbs?"

"As far as I know."

"I did not have sex with him." She was distracted, disturbed by the scent of Vano on Ben and the faint scent of Ben's blood. Had he been wounded in his argument with René? Why did he smell like Vano? "René did stay in my trailer. He was telling me what he knows about Fynn, and the sunrise caught him."

"Yeah." Ben wrinkled his nose. "I can smell him in here."

"He was in the bed." She sat across from him at the table. "I haven't slept in a while."

"Stating the obvious," he muttered.

He didn't know. Ben could have no idea that she had been sleeping nearly an hour each day the first six months after they'd exchanged blood. Then it had faded away like a beautiful, forgotten dream. "Why are you here?"

"You losing patience with me?" His shoulders were tense.

"Is that what you're trying to provoke?" Tenzin wasn't losing patience, but she was mentally tired. "You want to fight."

She hadn't been able to fully meditate with René in her trailer. She didn't trust him that much, even if he was young and seemingly dead to the world. She knew she could rouse him if she needed him to be useful, which was the only reason she'd allowed him there in the first place.

Meanwhile, her emotional parries with Ben had been trying. He frustrated her because he had no idea what he wanted. Normally that wouldn't bother her, but for the first time in centuries—a thousand years, perhaps—she didn't know what she wanted either.

There was no balance between them anymore. Neither one could anchor the other, and she had come to depend on that anchor.

She was a creature of the moment, trying to imagine a future that depended on another person's whims. Ben could embrace her, offer his love again, and agree to pursue this strange new adventure with her. Tenzin was ready for that.

Ben could also cling to his anger like he appeared to be doing in this moment, resent her, and cut her out of his life for the next hundred years. She had every confidence he'd come back to her eventually, but Tenzin had truly hoped it wouldn't take that long. Life without him was far more tedious than she wanted.

Ben was angry about something, but he wasn't saying what it was.

"Tell me." She picked up a stack of notes she'd written during the day while René slept.

"What?"

She set the notes down again. "Tell me why you're angry this time."

"This time?"

"Yes. You're always angry, but this time it is about something specific." Was it Vano? His foolish obsession with René?

"Did you take the goblet?" he asked quietly.

"No." Though she wanted to. She really, really wanted to.

"I don't believe you."

"Is that supposed to surprise me?" She picked up her notes again. "You often do not believe me. You said you got a rubbing off the citrine goblet, but you never showed it to me. Is it in your trailer?"

"What do you mean, I'm always angry?" He stared at her intently.

"There is no hidden meaning, Benjamin. You have been angry since the moment I met you, and that anger has never waned."

He blinked. "That's not true."

"You hide it well, but it's always there." She paged through her notes, avoiding his eyes. He was a predator now—a part of him had always been a predator—and she didn't feel the need to provoke him.

"You're just making shit up now."

Tenzin sighed. "You can lie to yourself, but I am trying to be more honest with you, so don't insist I lie to you too."

His hand slammed down on the table and his anger spiked, filling the air around them.

Tenzin carefully set down her notes and raised her eyes. "Do not threaten me."

His amnis shimmered like heat off a desert plateau. "If I'm angry, it's because you took the most important choice in my life away from me."

"No." She shook her head. "That is not why."

"Fuck you!" He stood and walked away from the table, but

there was little room to move, even in a larger-than-average travel caravan.

Cursing was unusual for Ben. At least when he was arguing with her. He was balancing on a very thin edge.

"Benjamin, immortality does not change who we are; it only reveals it." She drew a careful breath. "You were angry when you were young. You were angry as a child. You were angry as a man. Now you are angry as a vampire. Do not blame this on me."

Violent energy rolled off him in waves. "I do blame you."

"I know you do."

"So why the fuck did you do it, Tenzin?" His rage exploded, the anger mixed with sorrow as his eyes turned glassy and red. "You took away the one person I needed to get through this."

His pain made her physically hurt. It brought her back to the night she'd flown over the ocean with his dying mortal body in her arms. The memory of rage and desperation threatened to reach up and choke her, but she forced it back.

*It is not about you; it is about him.*

"I'm here," she said. "I never went anywhere."

"But you ruined everything." He gripped his hair in both his hands. "Because even if I'm okay with this now, I can't trust you again. And I needed to trust you, Tenzin. I *loved* you. You were my best friend and my partner, and nothing makes sense without you."

His pain stabbed at her, sharper—keener—than her own. "I'm still here."

"Everyone wanted to know" —he began to pace— "why doesn't Ben want to be a vampire? What's his hang-up? Why is he being so stubborn?"

Tenzin let him rage.

"Do you know why?" He turned and shouted in her face. "I didn't want to be like *you*! Do you understand that? I didn't want to be a vampire because I didn't want to be cold and unfeeling and selfish. Like. You."

Tenzin swallowed the hurt. Ben was young and his emotions were going to be erratic; his control was on a razor-thin edge.

"I am selfish," she said softly. "And I can be cold. But I am not unfeeling. And being with you has made me less of all those things."

His smile was bitter. "Oh, I'm so glad I could be part of your modern humanization program."

She forced herself to speak. "I will never apologize for taking you to my father, but I am sorry that immortality has forced you to face the things you've been trying to hide from yourself. I know that is not easy or comfortable."

"*Fuck you.* You're so full of shit. You'll blame everyone and everything else to avoid your own responsibility."

"No. I have never done that." She considered her answer. "I have never done that about anything as important as you."

"You're a liar and a thief." He stepped away. "And I can't believe I thought we could be... more. That we could get past you betraying me. Betraying us."

"I am a thief, but I am not lying to you." She swallowed the ache in her throat. "And I am here when you need me. Always."

"I don't need you." He walked to the door. "And when this is finished, I want you out of my life. For real and for good this time. Just get the fuck away."

BEN FLEW to the forest next to the camp, hovering in the night sky and letting the air soothe his anger. It whispered along his skin, petting him and reassuring him.

Angry? He wasn't angry. Okay, he'd had a shitty childhood,

but he hit the jackpot when Giovanni adopted him, and he'd put that in the past.

His temper leeched into the darkness; the air absorbed it, enveloped it, and whispered it away. He closed his eyes and imagined being curled in Tenzin's loft in New York, her slight body pressed to his side, her low voice reading from a familiar story.

> *There was once a witch who desired to know everything. But the wiser a witch is, the harder she knocks her head against the wall when she comes to it. Her name was Watho, and she had a wolf in her mind...*

～

BEN SAW Radu in the clearing, under a starlit, cloudless sky.

"Ben!" Radu rose and called to him. "Come, my friend. Come join us."

Radu was sitting at the table with Kezia. A bottle of blood-wine was open between them, and Radu's cheeks were flushed. Ben had a feeling he hadn't only been feeding from the blood-wine.

He looked at them, two decadent immortals with servants hovering around them. He surveyed the other guests—rich beyond what he could imagine—tossing money at strangers to make themselves disappear into luxury while they escaped the chaos they'd likely caused in the outside world. Parasites indulging in games and wine and music every night in fairy-tale settings while others cleaned up their messes.

Ben was so tired of them.

"Radu." He sat and nodded to Kezia, trying to mask his disdain. "Kezia, how are you?"

"Contemplating how a fine bottle of schnapps ended up

spilled across my floor," she remarked dryly. "Do you have any ideas?"

Ben didn't feel like playing her games. "Are there earthquakes in this area?"

"Not usually."

Radu said, "But there are earth vampires, are there not?" He laughed and nodded toward René, who was glaring at Ben from a distant table. "One of whom you invited yourself."

Kezia smiled. "At your urging, if I recall."

"Was it?" Radu lifted his glass. "It's good to see old friends."

"Like Tenzin." Kezia looked at Ben. "I know you and Tenzin are old friends, are you not?"

"Whatever Tenzin and I are, it's definitely more complicated than friendship," Ben said. "Though I'm sure I haven't known her as long as you two have." He forced himself to smile.

"Yes." Radu pointed his glass at Ben. "In that you are correct. I told you..." He glanced at Kezia. "Tenzin is an accomplished thief."

*You have no idea.*

"Foolish men." Kezia smiled. "Tenzin only steals things that want to be stolen."

Radu snorted. "What *wants* to be stolen, my sister?"

She turned her eyes to Ben. "Some things."

He forced himself to ignore the glaring subtext. "Whatever her reputation, Tenzin has been a good partner in the art-acquisition business," he said. "Though obviously we only retrieve items for clients like Radu who are the true owners of a piece." He reached for an empty glass and helped himself to some blood-wine. "Like the icon."

Kezia and Radu exchanged a look.

"Of course," Radu said. "So wonderful to have it back in my collection."

"Yes," Kezia replied. "A sacred treasure should be with its rightful owner."

Ben turned to her. "Do you think so?"

"Absolutely." She pouted. "Now if I could just find a new bottle of schnapps."

Radu said, "Perhaps Tenzin could steal one for you." He laughed uproariously and slapped Ben on the shoulder. "I am joking of course."

He was definitely not joking. Radu still thought Tenzin had the goblet.

Ben noticed Vano lurking along the edges of the clearing. "Your brother is here," he said. "Should we invite him for a drink?"

"Oof." Kezia rolled her eyes. "Vano is the definition of that American phrase: *buzzkill.*"

Radu laughed. "I am afraid I have to agree. Vano is the businessman among us, Ben. He cares nothing for telling stories."

"Really?" Ben openly stared at Vano as the man stared back. "I don't know; he seems hungry."

Kezia said, "He is always working. Work, work, work." She rolled her eyes. "He is spending the week before Vashana asking the darigan for household inventory. Why? Let them relax!"

Radu waved a careless hand. "His motives are inexplicable."

"Perhaps he's worried they don't have what they need," Ben said.

"He should look to his own house," Kezia said. "For mine is well-provisioned."

Ben wondered if Kezia had as good a grip on her people as she thought. More than one revolution had started because the people were dissatisfied with the excess of their rulers. And he hadn't forgotten what Radu said when he first took the job.

*...if confidence is lost at any time, the mortal and immortal*

*members of the Poshaniya will overthrow that member and choose another.*

Ben didn't want to probe too hard. "Tell me about this festival," he said. "What does it commemorate?"

"It is a celebration of our sire's day of turning," Radu said. "During the first full moon of the summer, all the Poshani gather. It is a party of course, and a chance to catch up with friends and family."

"But," Kezia said. "The terrin—my brothers and I—we also take up important matters." She glanced at Radu. "This year is particularly important for our people's future."

"Oh?" Ben was curious how much she'd share.

"Outsiders should take no special notice," Kezia said. "You are invited for the parties, not the politics."

Radu cleared his throat. "Ben, what has been your favorite part of traveling with the Dawn Caravan?"

"Other than the company?" Ben lifted his glass.

Kezia and Radu clinked theirs with appreciative noises.

"Of course the company!"

"A good story will save a night," Kezia said. "And what else?"

"I love the music." He saw Vano headed in the direction of Tenzin's trailer. "Uh... the food has been great too. Just everything. I love the scenery."

"We are headed to a beautiful lake region," Kezia said. "You will enjoy it."

"Perhaps." Radu's voice was sharp. "The darigan, of course, decide where and when the caravan travels. They take many things into consideration."

"Yes." Kezia smiled. "We all depend on the wisdom of the darigan."

Ben lifted his glass. "To the wisdom of the darigan."

"To the darigan," Radu toasted.

The corner of Kezia's mouth turned up. "May they never burn us alive."

~

Tenzin hovered in a shadow, listening to Ben, Kezia, and Radu speak.

*"May they never burn us alive."*

Wow. Dark.

Tenzin wasn't worried about the darigan burning her in her sleep. She didn't sleep and she always had an escape plan when it came to any situation. Currently, it involved a very heavy cloak stored under her bed and the location of natural limestone caves within a few minutes' flying distance, should the need arise.

But why was Kezia questioning the loyalty of the darigan? Had something fundamental changed? The interdependence of the darigan and the Hazar was a foundational part of Poshani culture. What could disturb that?

Tenzin landed softly on the grass behind a kitchen trailer and started walking back to her caravan. She'd suspected Vano from the beginning, but now she was wondering just how much Kezia might be involved. Maybe it wasn't Vano trying to maneuver Radu out of the terrin. Maybe it was Vano and Kezia trying to make a trio into a duo of power.

She rounded the corner and sensed a large group just ahead.

Vano and some of his men if she had to guess by scent.

Interesting.

She hesitated for a moment and considered taking to the air. But seconds later, she felt something tight wrap around her ankles as a thin metal net enveloped her from head to toe.

What on earth?

Tenzin allowed herself to fall to the ground. She was curious what their plan was.

Vano walked out from behind her caravan. "A bird in a net."

Tenzin stared at him. "Do you actually think this will hold me?"

"It will hold you long enough."

Four men grabbed her.

Tenzin laughed as they lifted her on their shoulders and flew away. "The hospitality of the Poshani has been greatly overstated."

## 32

"Oooooh." Brigid's voice was pained. "She told you."

"Told me what?" Ben was in his room, an hour before sunrise, still brooding over what Tenzin had said.

"The anger thing. That's what reminded me so much of my life from the beginning." She moved from a babble of background noise into silence. "Now listen, I know you're probably—"

"I'm not an angry person, Brigid!" Ben was pacing again. He was very ready to be living in something bigger than his kitchen back in New York. The Poshani caravans might be the height of camping luxury, but they were still cramped. "She's completely off. I mean, I'm angry about *this* of course. I'm angry about her."

"I was going to say you're probably in denial."

*What the fuck?* Ben's mouth fell open. "You think she's right?"

"Right?" Brigid asked. "Of course she's right. Carwyn and I talked about it immediately after you turned."

Ben could only blink.

"Your childhood was shit, Ben. Your mother is a con artist and your father was abusive. You've told me that yourself. And childhood shouldn't be shit, so you have a right to be angry about that. I also think you have a little bit of a death wish and have had for quite a while. Which is related but another thing altogether, and I'm not a therapist." She took a breath. "Have you considered visiting Anne?"

"I don't need therapy!"

"Of course you fecking need therapy. We're all messes; we all need bloody therapy. You stole a vampire's wallet at age *twelve*. And then when he wanted to adopt you, you just went along with it. I mean, Gio's a good person, but did you know that at age twelve? Of course you fecking didn't. You don't think you had a death wish?"

"You're so completely wrong I don't even— Can we talk about Tenzin please?"

"Okay, but just so you know, she's right. You have a lot of unresolved anger."

"She said that becoming a vampire doesn't change who you are; it reveals it. And I don't agree with that. I think people do change. I've seen it."

"Everyone changes over time, but the woman's been alive for something like five thousand years. You don't think she has a fairly good perspective on this? I think she's right."

"You think becoming a vampire revealed who you really are?"

Brigid took a long breath. "I think becoming a vampire forced me to deal with the things I'd been avoiding in my human life. Because when you only have seventy or eighty years to live, you can put off looking at a lot of things too closely. You can fill your life with this and that, stay nice and busy, and if you really try, you can pretend you're happy with that."

Ben stopped pacing.

"But when you have hundreds of years stretching in front of you—possibly more," Brigid continued in a softer voice, "you can't push all those things away. You have to look at yourself for who you are. You have to learn to live with yourself. And sometimes that's shit, Ben. It's shit, but it's the only way to move forward."

Ben sat and stared at the blacked-out windows covered in works of art that literally hid him from the world outside. "I was telling Chloe last night that I was glad I was alive. Not just that I was okay with it, but that I was actually happy."

"Do you still feel that way? Think past your emotions right now and the fight with Tenzin."

"I think I do." He closed his eyes and tried to think clearly. "I'm all over the place, Brigid."

"That's normal. You're going through vampire puberty right now with the mood swings, and it's crap. You're processing everything faster, but your senses are stronger, which means there is literally more data coming in for you to process. To put it in technological terms, your system is overloaded. Your software hasn't quite updated yet, but it will. Eventually it will all even out." She muttered something under her breath.

"What?"

She cleared her throat and spoke so rapidly her words nearly ran together. "Getting a leg over helps, but I imagine that's a bit complicated for you right now, and a therapist definitely wouldn't suggest that, so probably ignore me, but it does help."

"Getting a leg over?"

"Sex, Ben! Sex helps. Jaysus, I'm Catholic—don't make me say it again."

Ben felt the urge to laugh for the first time in days. "I got it."

"Are you fecking happy to be alive or not?"

He thought past his anger. "Yes. I am glad to be alive."

"Then move on," Brigid said. "Face your anger and accept that it'll be a part of you for a while until you work through the shite you need to, and move on. Don't let it keep holding you back from having the life you want."

"How do I forgive her," Ben asked, "when she refuses to apologize?"

"She's not going to. Ever. From Tenzin's perspective, she was doing exactly the right thing."

He swallowed hard. "I can *kind of* see that."

"Then you just forgive her. Not for her but for you."

Ben couldn't speak. He was remembering a moment years before, a quiet confession in the sacred space between waking and sleep.

*I have been a hero and a villain in the same moment. If you live long enough, you'll understand what that means.*

"Just forgive her," he murmured.

"Tenzin's not perfect," Brigid continued. "Or perfectly wise. Feck, my husband is a thousand years old, and he's still clueless at times. He makes mistakes because he's learning to love me. And there's never been a me before, so it's a new situation for him. It's the same with you two. There's never been another Ben and Tenzin. The relationships you've had, the relationships she's had... They teach you, but only so much. Every person is a new world."

"So I just forgive her." Something about saying the words took a weight off his heart.

"Aye, you do. And the anger might come back, so you might have to repeat it to yourself every day for a year. Or a decade."

"Yeah." He cleared his throat.

"But you—of all the people in her life—know who Tenzin is. You know her better than anyone else does. This was not malice. She did the only thing she could."

He closed his eyes and nodded. "I have to let it go."

"Like a fucking party balloon." She whistled. "Whoosh. Float away."

Ben could feel the dawn coming. "I better go; I'm going to fall asleep soon."

"Call me after you've settled some things."

He rubbed his eyes. "You tired of being my guidance counselor yet?"

Brigid laughed. "You're like my little brother, Benny. I'm sure when you figure this all out, I'll think of a way you can repay me."

"I'm not going to give you any of my guns."

"Fuck yer guns, lad. I want one of Tenzin's swords."

～

VANO OPENED the door to Tenzin's trailer and tossed her inside with her feet and hands still bound, the metal net wrapped tightly around her body. She smelled the visitor in the trailer, but she didn't say a word to the vampire currently gloating from the open doorway.

"What do you think you're doing?" She asked from the floor. "I will be able to escape from this."

"Not before you fall asleep at dawn." Vano glanced at the horizon. "Which should be coming shortly."

Tenzin had no desire to share her secrets with Vano. If he thought she slept, she wouldn't spoil the notion. "Do you think Ben won't come looking for me if I'm not around tomorrow night?"

"By tomorrow night, it won't matter." Vano watched Tenzin's face. "You're going to disappear. But don't worry; I have no plans to kill your little pet. Doing that would attract the wrath of Penglai Island by mistreating a favored son. I have my businesses to think about."

Tenzin, on the other hand, could probably go missing and possibly no one would realize she was gone for a century or two. If they got rid of her things, even Ben might assume she'd just taken off.

"You're wrong," she bluffed. "My absence will be noted."

"If it comforts you to think so." He patted the edge of the doorway. "Sleep well, Tenzin. Such an undignified end for such a famed immortal. If I was sentimental in the least, I might feel for you."

"No, you wouldn't. You consider me an outsider and only have empathy for those people you consider your own." She shrugged as much as the metal net would allow. "I often feel the same."

"So we understand each other."

"Only if you understand that if anything happens to me, my mate will hunt you down and rip you limb from limb before he kills you."

"Your mate?" Vano smiled. "I know young Vecchio isn't truly your mate, just like I know that you've had a falling-out. Besides, the boy doesn't have it in him. He's soft. Pampered. Everything in this life has been given to him, even immortality." Vano's mouth twisted a little. "Power like that handed to someone who didn't even want it."

"Power like that should *only* be given to someone who doesn't want it."

"Spoken like a commander of the losing side." Vano examined Tenzin from head to toe. "Enjoy trying to get out of the net. I imagine you'll find it quite impossible."

He slammed the door, and she heard a lock snapped on the outside.

Tenzin began to twist and turn. Vano was right to a point. The metal net was thin and flexible; every time she tried to grab it, it slipped away. When she pushed, it flexed.

How irritatingly clever. She'd have to find out where he'd acquired it.

Nevertheless, it wasn't something she could break through quickly even with her immortal strength.

"Are you going to make yourself useful?" Tenzin asked. "Or are you enjoying the show?"

René stepped out from the shadowed corner where he'd been

hiding. "I admit, I am enjoying this." He slid his hands in his pockets. "Remind me; why I am staying in your caravan during the day? Oh, that's right, because you asked me to."

"Because you owe me," she said. "Who bailed you out in Singapore last summer, René? That's right, it was me."

"When this is over, you're never bringing that up again." He curled his lip and knelt next to her. "I don't even know what this is made of."

"It is some kind of metal fabric." She touched a piece between her fingers. "It's clever. Finely woven, which makes it harder to manipulate. I can't get enough leverage to tear it."

"Quite ingenious. How long do you think it would take you to get out without me?"

"More than an hour. Do you have scissors? Wire cutters?"

"Scissors, no. Wire cutters?" He pulled out a familiar-looking red knife. "I believe this has a small saw attached. That should do."

"Well done." She heard the knife tear through the fabric over her wrists. "Cut that and then get my feet."

"I'm taking this fabric."

"It's yours." She twisted her wrists and snapped the plastic ties that bound her hands. "I wouldn't suggest it for bedsheets."

Minutes later, Tenzin was free as a bird and sitting on the ground, staring at the door that Vano had locked. "His people are going to do something to the trailer during the day. Break it possibly. Try to drag me out."

René's eyes narrowed. "How do you know?"

"Why else would he tie me up in a trailer?"

"I can think of a few reasons to tie you up, but none of them involve murder."

"Boring," she snapped.

"Murder?"

"Your flirting," she said. "It used to be amusing. It's not

anymore."

He muttered something in French that she didn't care about translating.

Tenzin spoke to herself. "He doesn't know I don't sleep. Why would he?"

René's eyes went wide. "At all? You don't sleep at all?"

"You didn't know that?" Tenzin frowned. "I suppose not—why would you?"

He sounded nervous. "So the past few nights when you'd been asking me to sleep here—"

"I've been awake all day, yes." Something was tingling. Some unknown sense was setting off alarms. "Don't worry; I don't stare. Much."

"How the fuck—"

"Shhhh." She threw a pillow from the couch at him. "Shut up."

What was it? Vano clearly had a plan to get rid of her, so what was it?

René sulked in the corner. "Your caravan is much nicer than mine."

"I'm sure it is. Ben's is nicer still."

He rocked back and forth. "It doesn't shake as much as mine does."

"That's because—" Oh.

Oooooh.

She heard it then, the whisper-quiet business of the camp. The sun would be up within half an hour, which meant the darigan were setting about their business, retracting the braces that kept the trailers even, readying for the camp to move.

Except her trailer. No one was readying her trailer to move.

Tenzin smiled. "He's going to leave us."

René jumped to his feet. "What?"

"Relax." She waved him back. "This complicates things, but

it's not the end of the world."

"Some of us can't fly, Tenzin!" René was fuming. "Some of us have plans we've been working on for weeks that are more important your little feuds with Vano and Ben."

"You'll get your treasure," Tenzin said. "Didn't I promise?"

"Your deal was that I stayed in here during the day for some reason I now realize was *not* trying to make Vecchio jealous." René began to pace. "The deal was *not* losing the biggest potential score of my immortal life because you pissed off the wrong vampire." He started toward the door, but Tenzin was on him. She throttled him and sent him flying back into the bed.

"Sit," she growled. "Didn't I just say you'd get your treasure?"

"What is wrong with you?" René yelled even as his eyes began to blink longer with every minute. "You should be running outside and telling Radu what Vano did." He blinked harder. "You should be... tell Vecchio."

"Ben will be fine." The last thing Vano would do was hurt Ben. Too many people knew Ben was working for Radu. Not many knew that she was here though. Therein lay the brilliance of Vano's plan.

Utter silence told Tenzin that René had fallen into day rest. She walked over, bent over him, and slapped him hard across the cheek.

"What?" He sat up straight, his eyes wide. "Tenzin?"

"Just checking to make sure I can wake you when it's time."

"What?" He didn't answer because he slumped to the side, falling into day rest again.

"Never mind." She patted his shoulder before she dragged him onto the floor.

It was always good to have an earth vampire handy. That was why she'd lured René into her caravan. Not to make Ben jealous but to have another tool in her pocket.

Tenzin sat next to René and waited until the attack came.

## 33

---

Ben passed the day in a dreamless sleep. Nothing disturbed him. Nothing nibbled at his brain. He slept peacefully for the first time in months, and he woke with two certainties in his mind:

He still loved Tenzin. He didn't know if they could be together, but he also didn't know how not to love her. He'd said horrible things to her the night before, most of which he didn't mean, but he wanted to be with her if she was still willing.

Vano had the emerald goblet, and he was planning a coup against his brother and sister. The signs were all there. Kezia might be wise to it, but Vano was the ringleader and Radu completely underestimated him.

Which meant that Ben's only goal in the next week before the festival—other than trying to mend things with Tenzin—was to break into Vano's trailer and find the emerald goblet to prove to Radu that his brother was the source of the trouble.

He lay in bed, listening to the night birds waking. An owl hooted in the distance, and the strong scent of lilac told him that wherever they'd moved, flowers were blooming nearby.

Ben sat up and stretched, washed his face in the kitchen, and drank from the preserved blood in the fridge. He didn't love cold blood, but he didn't hate it either. Sometimes it was oddly, and grossly, refreshing. He'd stopped trying to explain why. He leaned against the small counter in the kitchen and listened to the birds.

Something was off.

Something was... wrong. It was too quiet.

Ben pulled on a pair of pants and walked to the door, swinging it open to reveal nothing but the sloping hills beyond his trailer and nothing else.

No fires. No musicians. No camp.

The Dawn Caravan was gone, and there was only the faint scent of something burning and a hint of kerosene in the air.

Shit.

SHIT!

What happened? Had Radu tipped his hand to Vano? Had he found the thief himself? He'd had an agreement with Radu. He wasn't supposed to back out without a single word.

Ben walked down the steps and turned in a circle.

When he saw the wreckage, his stomach dropped.

Beyond the oak trees, there was a single caravan smoldering, the body split open to reveal ashes everywhere. There was a mark on the side, a distinctive blue logo he remembered from the first night in her trailer.

It couldn't be. His mind couldn't process what he was seeing. It wasn't hers. It couldn't be. He raced toward the burned-out carcass, his mind rebelling at the images before him.

They wouldn't have burned her trailer.

This was an accident.

She hadn't been inside.

No, no, no, no.

Ben stood in the middle of ashes and yelled, "Tenzin?"

He looked to the swiftly darkening sky. Nothing.

Where was she? Because she couldn't be in the trailer and she couldn't be gone because he would feel it, right? He'd taken her blood. She was in him. If she was gone—

"Tenzin!"

Ben flew up and raced over the camp, scouring the air for any hint of her.

She wouldn't have left him. She wouldn't have just flown off. He flew back to the wreckage of the trailer and kicked through the ashes where the door would have been. His foot hit something hard and he bent down, lifting up a heavy metal lock burned black by the fire.

*No.*

He curled his fingers around the warm device. It was linked through the metal door mechanism. It must have been smoldering for hours, just like the ashes around him.

A padlock, basic tumbler. Easy to pick from outside.

Impossible to break from inside. Even for Tenzin.

Ben's mind shuffled through a hundred possibilities as he walked around the perimeter of the burned-out trailer, the padlock clutched in his hand. He could feel it searing his skin.

*She could have broken through the walls.*

*During the day?*

*She could have flown away.*

*In sunlight?*

"Tenzin?" He could hear the edge of panic in his voice. "Where are you?"

She couldn't be gone. It wasn't possible. A world without Tenzin didn't make sense. This was Tenzin. She had to have gotten away. She had to have a plan. She always had a plan.

The night sky was clear, star-filled, and silent.

"Tiny!" he screamed. "Where the fuck are you?" He turned in

circles. He took to the air again, racing from one end of the camp to another, but other than the occasional scrap of paper, there was nothing. It was as if the Poshani had never existed in this place.

He flew back to his trailer and looked underneath. Had she hidden there?

Nothing.

"Tenzin!"

She couldn't be gone. She couldn't be dead. He needed her.

Ben walked back to the wreck and began to dig through the ashes. He tore through the remains of cabinets and the odd swatch of fabric that had remained unburned, certain that at any moment he'd pull back a piece of rubble and see her impish grin.

*Got you,* she'd say.

"Tenzin." He began to speak. "Show me where you are."

More broken and charred cabinets.

Metal pipes.

Broken glass.

Twisted plastic, curled and cracked.

"What was the plan?" He stood and tossed the remains of the refrigerator across the clearing. "Where did you hide? You always have a plan."

If she had hidden, why hadn't she come back yet? He felt something wet on his face. He blinked hard and looked around.

The burned carcass of the trailer was torn apart, scattered across the clearing. The trailer chassis slumped to the side, broken and jutting from the ashes like metal bones.

*Vampires don't leave bones.*

"Fuck!" Ben gripped his hair and screamed, "This isn't funny anymore. Just *tell me where you are!*"

He didn't think about Radu and his caravan. He didn't think about the job. He didn't think about the humans who must have burned her trailer.

288

All he wanted was Tenzin. All he wanted was for her to be alive.

If she was so pissed at him she never spoke to him again, he'd be fine, he just needed her to be *alive*.

Be alive!

Ben fell to his knees, staring at the empty field of ashes.

Nothing.

No sound.

No life.

The air curled around him and cooled the tears on his face.

It wasn't real. It couldn't be. Was this how she'd felt? Was there an empty gaping hole in the center of her chest where his life had been?

*She can't be gone.*

*She can't be gone.*

She was Tenzin. The idea of her not existing didn't even make sense. She always had a plan. She *couldn't* be gone.

Silence.

The wind lifted him and turned him around. He felt the currents reaching beneath his clothes and pressing against his skin like gentle hands comforting him.

But Ben didn't want the wind; he wanted her.

His amnis was wild, whipping the air around him, churning the ashes on the grass. Confused and broken, the wind lifted him and turned him, raising him from the earth to the sky. It whispered to his amnis.

*I am here.*

*I am here.*

*I am here.*

*You are alive and I am here.*

The air stilled and the clouds scattered, revealing a blanket of stars.

"Benjamin?"

289

He opened his eyes and she was hovering over him. Her face was covered in dirt, not ashes, and her eyes were clear and calm.

His lips cracked when he spoke. "Am I dreaming?"

"No." She reached out and touched his face. "I'm here."

Choking back a cry, Ben reached up and pulled her into his arms.

## 34

Ben's mouth found hers and stole her breath. Tenzin had flown back to camp, prepared for his irritation and ready with explanations. She'd felt his amnis going wild from nearly a mile away. She'd flown faster, expecting to find him in a rage.

He hadn't been raging. He'd been grieving. He'd thought she was dead.

Tenzin pulled her mouth away, keeping both hands on Ben's ash-stained cheeks. "I'm here."

His voice broke. "You were gone."

"I flew away."

"I thought you were gone, Tenzin."

"I'm not. I'm here."

Ben clutched her closer and buried his face in her neck. He didn't speak. He didn't say a word, but his arms welded her body to his as if he was afraid for even the air to come between them.

"Ben—"

He cut her off when his mouth found hers again. He ran his fingers into the hair at her nape and gripped. Tenzin wrapped both her legs around him as they spun in space. She ran her fingers through his hair, drinking in the tactile sensation of his touch, his amnis embracing her, his mouth moving over hers as the air held them in its soft embrace.

Ben had kissed her before, but not like this. He'd been playful. He'd been angry. He'd been hungry.

This.

This was different.

There was still an edge of desperation to his touch, but his lips met hers over and over, drinking her in, savoring the taste of her, lingering a breath away, then taking her mouth again.

"You're alive," he whispered between kisses.

"I'm alive."

"You had a plan."

"I always have a plan."

His amnis built on hers like a storm gathering over mountains. Tenzin couldn't breathe, but she didn't need to. She didn't need to speak. For once, they didn't need to speak at all.

Ben guided them to the ground and led her to the trailer where he'd been sleeping. His was completely intact. As promised, Vano hadn't tried to burn that one.

She'd watched them drive away under the burning caravan. Watched them argue before they left. Ben's trailer had been intact and undisturbed.

Then René opened the ground to shield them from the heat and the flames.

Ben opened the door and lifted Tenzin from the ground and into the trailer, not even letting her feet touch the steps.

Tenzin snapped back into the moment. When he did things like that, she was wholly conscious of his physicality. He was a large man, far more muscular and solid than her slight frame.

An old voice hissed in her mind. *He could hurt you.*

*He could not,* a softer voice said. *He would not.*

Ben towered over her, running his fingers through her hair,

teasing leaves and branches out and tossing them away. With one arm, he reached over and flipped on the water nozzle in the small shower. Almost immediately, steam began filling the space around them.

He reached down and began to peel off her dirty clothes.

She reached for him. "Ben, I'm fine."

"Let me." His voice cracked. "I know you hate the dirt."

Tenzin nodded and allowed him to pull her tunic over her head. He gently pushed down her leggings, and she stepped out of them. Then she climbed in the shower. He tilted her head back and ran the water through her hair.

She felt the warm rivulets coursing down her body, washing away the dirt that had crusted to her. She stared at his bare chest, dusted grey with ash. Black streaks marked his torso. He was wearing only a pair of loose pants, and she could see the erection rising beneath them, but he was solely focused on her.

Ben took a bar of soap and ran it over her shoulders and down her arms. He rubbed soap in his hands and ghosted them over her breasts and her back, sliding his fingers over her skin.

"You're covered in ashes."

"I'm not hurt."

Tenzin put a hand over his heart, and it offered her two rapid beats before it fell silent. "I miss your heartbeat. Have I told you that?"

His voice was barely over a whisper. "No."

"I do." She closed her eyes. "I miss your beautiful dark eyes. I miss the way they used to look at me."

Ben's amnis, which he'd held so tightly as he bathed her, broke free and rushed over her. He fell to his knees, wrapping his arms around her waist as he fell. He pressed his cheek to her belly and his body shook. She felt everything. His panic, his grief, and his wild, burgeoning rage.

The water was going everywhere, but he didn't seem to notice.

"Come here. Don't be angry—come here." She lifted him to his feet and pushed his pants down before she pulled him into the shower.

He kicked the clothes away and climbed in, wrapping his arms around her body again and letting the warm water wash them both.

Ben bathed her as she washed him. The shower was tiny, and they were pressed together, but that didn't seem to bother him even though his body was far bigger than hers.

He washed her hair and skin meticulously, scrubbing every inch. She washed his chest and rinsed the ashes from his skin.

When they were both clean, he reached for a towel and wrapped her in it.

"Are we safe here?" he asked quietly. "Do you know where they went?"

"Yes, they're approximately seventy kilometers away. I didn't find any remnants when I went out to look. We're alone."

His voice was barely audible, even to her ears. "I thought you were dead. I didn't want to believe it—I didn't think it was possible —but for a few minutes I thought you were gone. And I can't..." He pressed his lips together. "I don't have words for what I felt."

Tenzin sat on the edge of the bed and watched him wrap a towel around his waist. His eyes had aged a hundred years since nightfall. There was an edge of darkness in his amnis that she hadn't felt before.

"Ben—"

"They tried to kill you." He looked at the floor. "Who?"

"Vano and his men. They didn't tell the other Poshani. I'm not sure what they told Radu, but the Poshani caravan was hours gone before they set the trailer on fire."

"I'm going to kill every one of them."

"Not tonight." She reached her hand out. "Come here."

He hesitated. "You're right. I've been angry with you and

with myself. I'm sorry for what I said last night." He put his hands on his hips, staring at the ground as he avoided her eyes. "I don't know how to be with you the way I am. I don't feel like myself. Most nights I wake up and I don't know who I am anymore."

"I know who you are," she said quietly. "I know you said you couldn't trust me, but—"

His harsh laugh cut her off. "Tenzin, I thought you were dead."

"I know."

He finally looked her in the eye, and any hint of humor was gone. "Do you think there's anything I wouldn't have done to get you back? Do you think there is a line I wouldn't have crossed? I know why you did it. Don't ever explain yourself again."

*One day you will be infinite.*

She fell into his amnis, the threads of darkness twisting around his natural warm glow. His scent changed, and she felt the predator in him wake.

Ben walked toward her and lifted her chin with his finger. He bent down and pressed his lips to hers with exquisite care.

Nothing could have seduced her more.

She reached for him, pulling him onto the bed, wrapping her arms around his neck and holding his body to hers. She shoved her towel off and reached for his, but it was already gone.

She pulled his body over hers, reveling in the weight of his muscle and bone, the length of his legs and the hard muscle of his arms. He embraced her, lifting them off the bed so he could slip his arms around her. His hands spread over her skin as he devoured her mouth, cutting his lips on her fangs so the heady taste of his blood flooded her senses.

His hands stroked up and down her back, one caressing the curve of her buttock while the other kneaded the small of her back. Her belly was pressed into his erection, and always there was the spark and seductive whisper of his amnis surrounding her, teasing her skin and stoking the growing storm.

"I love you," he whispered against her lips. "I never stopped loving you, not even when I hated you."

"I know." She gripped his hair and pressed her cheek to his, whispering in his ear. "I did not want to know what the world would be like without you." She turned her head and kissed the arch of his cheekbone. "I did not want to know what *I* would be like without you."

He turned to her and caught her lips with his own. This kiss was different again, a long and luxurious mating of blood and teeth and tongues that tasted of the different flavors of who he was and what he was becoming.

Ben was gold and fire, a gathering storm that held her so delicately she thought she might scream.

Tenzin nearly wept with relief when his hand moved from her thigh to between her legs. Her mouth fell open as his fingers slid up and down.

There was no hurry in this coupling, no violent storm of desire and anger and passion like what had swept them away after he woke. This was another new thing, another crystal moment she would hold in her mind.

He was a silent thief, stealing her breath and confusing her senses. There were too many things happening at once. His amnis kissed every part of her skin while his fingers danced her along the edge of an exquisite pleasure. His mouth took hers, over and over again, drinking in her blood while his tongue caressed her fangs.

She reached for him and wrapped her hand around his erection. "I want this."

"Not yet."

Tenzin wrapped her legs around his hips and rode his fingers and the hard press of his flesh until she was mindless and lost in nothing but him.

Benjamin's touch. Benjamin's scent. Benjamin's taste.

She couldn't remember a time she'd felt more present in her body. His blood seeped into her system, mingling his amnis with hers, and still she wanted more.

Just as her body began to convulse with pleasure, Ben took his fingers away, slid inside, and rode her through her orgasm, his fingers playing along her clitoris as he drove deep.

Yes. She wanted all that. And more.

He angled his body and gripped her thigh, pulling her closer as they rose off the bed and into the air.

He pulled away from her mouth and gave Tenzin half a smile as they rolled. "That's going to take some getting used to."

Her lips were swollen when she spoke. "Let me."

She pushed them down to the bed, Ben beneath her as she straddled him. The change of positions only sent him deeper inside her.

"Fuck." He arched his hips up as he gripped her hips, but even as he held them in an iron grasp, his thumbs fluttered delicately over her hip bones, tracing the lines of tattooing that marked her pelvis.

Ben looked down at their bodies joined together. "Beautiful."

"Yes." She lowered her torso to his and licked from his collarbone up to his neck as she rode him. "I want to bite you."

Ben's pupils dilated and his lips flushed. "So bite me." He angled his head to the side, exposing his neck.

"If I bite you, are you going to come?"

He groaned. "Yes."

"I want to come again." She pulled him up to sitting and put both his hands on her breasts, smiling when he immediately began caressing her sensitive nipples.

"Good." He bent to kiss her breasts.

"Bite me first."

Something came out of his throat that sounded like a growl, and he lifted his head. "Are you sure?"

She wrapped her arms around his shoulders and ground herself down as she laid her head on his muscled shoulder and bared her neck.

"I want your bite," she whispered. "Only yours."

He didn't have to be told twice. Ben's lips closed on her skin and his fangs pierced her neck, flipping her into another head-spinning orgasm as she felt her amnis enter his body. He grew impossibly harder as her muscles convulsed around his erection.

He drank deeply, pulling her blood from the vein like a starving creature. Then he licked the wound closed and locked his lips on hers. She tasted her own blood in his mouth, along with the hint of his own.

Ben grabbed her and lifted her up and down on his body, the combined friction and amnis whipping the air around them into a frenzy.

She heard something crash, and Tenzin thought the door flew open from the wind. The scent of lilac and new grass filled the air, but she didn't look. Her eyes were locked on Ben, and all she could see was him.

His cheeks were ruddy with her blood, and his strange grey-and-brown eyes searched her face.

"I want to bite you," she whispered again. "Say yes."

"Yes." He threw his head to the side and pressed her head into his neck. "I'm yours."

She licked his skin, warming it with her breath before she slid her fangs slowly into his neck.

"Oh fuck." He panted and groaned. "Faster."

She didn't rush. She drew out the pleasure, stroking the nape of his neck and the smooth skin of his shoulders, tightly stretched over straining muscles. His skin was gold, darker than hers.

How lovely.

When she began to pull from his vein, he came hard, shouting her name as his hand slammed into a cabinet, shattering it as his pleasure overtook him.

~

BEN LAY ON HIS SIDE, Tenzin in front of him, lazy from her blood and sated by pleasure as he surveyed the wreckage of the luxury camping caravan.

They were not going to be able to have sex in the loft for a while. Not unless they wanted to be impaled by weapons.

"Outside is good," Tenzin murmured.

"Right." He slid a hand down her side, tracing a finger over the tattooed lines that had taunted him.

The tattoos ran between her pelvic bones, but there were smaller, finer dots and symbols along her hips and trailing up her center toward her breasts. He could also see with his keener vampire vision the telltale marks that told him she'd born children in her mortal life.

Not tonight. He wouldn't ask tonight.

He could feel her in him, her amnis unexpectedly warm and threaded with an emotion so powerful and fine he understood why she had trouble putting it into words. Ben couldn't name it either. Love seemed woefully inadequate.

"I love you." Ben said it because even if she couldn't say it, she needed to hear it. He kissed her shoulder and cupped her breast. "I love you more than anything."

She didn't speak, but her amnis kissed him. It reached out all over his body and enveloped him in warmth.

"Even though I love you," he said, "I'm still kind of a mess."

"I know."

"I'm not... whole. I don't feel whole yet."

"I don't need you to be." Tenzin turned in his arms and looked at him. "I don't need you to have all the answers to be mine. I will take whatever part of you is ready, Benjamin. The rest of you has time to catch up."

He kissed her nose. "Sounds good, Tiny."

Her smile lit the room. "It's nice to see you again."

"You know I'm going to want to do this again in about an hour."

"Mmm." She lifted an eyebrow. "Newborn energy. I like it."

## 35

They left their shelter an hour before dawn. Ben and Tenzin stood over the wreckage of the burned-out caravan, and he felt his rage rising again.

"You're sure it was Vano's men?"

"They threw a very clever net over me and bound my feet." She looked confused. "I'm not sure why they thought it would hold me. Do they think I need to flap my wings to fly?"

"I admit it would be funny, except for the fact that they tried to burn you alive."

He heard Kezia's voice over and over in his mind.

*...may they never burn us alive.*

"If this gets out, no one will ever stay in the Dawn Caravan again," Ben said. "No one will trust it."

Tenzin shrugged. "Maybe. They could always deny it happened."

"Would anyone take the chance?" Ben turned to her. "Why? Why spoil the reputation of a valuable commodity like immortal trust when there are so many easier ways to get rid of us? And why leave me alive when they tried to kill you?"

"I believe Vano considered me the bigger threat. And I'm also known for disappearing for the odd decade or century, so if I go missing, it's less suspicious. You, on the other hand—"

"Newly turned son of Zhang Guo, nephew of a famous assassin and scholar. Yeah, I'd be noticed." He frowned. "Is it weird that I'm offended on your behalf?"

"It's nice that you care, but Vano's reasoning was solid." She shrugged. "I do tend to disappear."

He watched her. "But not from me. Not anymore."

"No." There was a slight frown between her eyes. "You've taken my blood twice now."

"Yes."

She looked at him. "If you take it another time or two, a more permanent mating bond will form."

"I know." He watched her carefully. "Does that bother you?"

"No." She didn't even hesitate. "As I said before, I am very territorial about you right now." She stared at the wreck. "I should tell you René was in my trailer when Vano threw me inside."

Ben froze. "Why?"

"Because I asked him to be there," she said. "When I told you that he fell asleep in there accidentally the other day, it was a lie." She turned to him before he could speak. "I apologize for lying to you."

Ben wanted to be angry, but an apology from Tenzin was too rare. "Why did you lie?"

"Avoidance. I did not want to cause a larger fight than the one we were already having."

Ben felt a piercing pressure in his ear. "But why, Tenzin? Why did you ask René, of all people—"

"Oh!" She walked into the wreckage and kicked aside a trio of pipes running the length of the trailer to reveal a gash in the earth. "He was insurance."

He stared at the trench. "Insurance?"

"It's always nice having an earth vampire around," she muttered, kicking a pile of ash. "Very useful creatures."

Ben's eyes went wide. "Wait, is René still under—"

"No, I flew him back to the caravan. He was quite grateful to be rid of me; not a fan of flying." She kicked aside the dirt. "I knew what they were planning once I smelled the kerosene. I broke through the floor when they walked away, waking René when we landed. You'll be happy to know I slapped him quite hard. He buried us under the vehicle, and as soon as the sun went down, he dug us out."

Ben stared at her. "You stayed underground with René fucking DuPont all day? Is he alive?"

"Yes. I was surprisingly calm when I was underground this time. I believe my irritation with René overrode my instinctual fear. He's surprisingly affectionate in his sleep. Very... handsy."

Ben cocked his head. *The fuck you say?* "Tenzin—"

"You're not allowed to kill him," she broke in. "Don't even think about it. He was and is part of the plan."

"What plan?" He spun with his arms held out. "We're in the middle of nowhere. We need to find a cave or something fast, because I do not trust that thing in daylight." He pointed at the trailer. "We have no plan."

"My Benjamin." She rose in the air, holding her hand out. "Of course we have a plan."

THEY TOOK shelter in one of the natural limestone caves in the area. Ben stripped the blankets and pillows from the trailer to make a pallet on the ground and grabbed the few belongings he had with him, leaving the electronics in the caravan, wanting nothing that Vano might be able to use to track him.

"Vano will believe I'm dead," Tenzin said. "With René back in the camp, no one will know he wasn't in his trailer last night."

"So you know where the Poshani are?" Ben felt the dawn coming.

"It wasn't hard since I knew their last location. I can travel faster than human caravans." She pressed him down into the pillows and blankets. "Sleep, Benjamin. I'll tell you the rest tomorrow night. We have time." She pressed a kiss to his mouth. "Sleep."

For the first time in his immortal life, Ben settled down for his day rest with Tenzin curled into his side. Her amnis ran through his blood, and her scent filled his senses.

*Sleep.*

Ben murmured, "'You must learn to be strong in the dark as well as in the day, else you will always be only half brave.'"

"I remember reading that to you." Tenzin laid her head on his chest. "You told me once that it was a greater compliment to be trusted than to be loved."

"I remember," he murmured.

"I trusted you to come back to me." She whispered something as he fell asleep, ancient words that crept into his mind and settled in his heart like a mantra.

"What...?"

"You'll learn," she said softly. "I will teach you."

THEY WATCHED the Poshani camp from a distance, surveying a landscape dotted with crystal clear lakes and ponds where water birds roosted in the long grass. The sky overhead was clear, unmarred by a single cloud, and the moon was waxing nearly full.

The circle of caravans and trailers was lit by the moonlight and torches. A large bonfire burned in the center, and Ben could smell the lingering scent of meat roasting over a fire.

"The festival will take place here in two nights, when the moon is full." Tenzin turned to look at him. "By that time, we will have all three goblets in our possession and we'll be able to expose Vano and his plot against Radu and Kezia."

Ben still had his doubts about Radu's sister. "How do we know Kezia doesn't know about this? She took Vano to Kashgar. She invited you to the caravan."

"Precisely because of that. They burned my trailer and believe they killed me." Tenzin nodded toward the camp. "I was Kezia's invited guest. Her beliefs would never permit it. She had no idea what Vano was planning."

"Are you sure?"

"Kezia and I both honor the Kali," she said. "And she knows I am a devotee of the goddess. Trust me on this."

Ben used the binoculars he'd stolen from the trailer. "Okay, but when we're done with this, you're going to explain the Kali thing. I thought you were an atheist."

"Why would you think that? I have a spiritual system; it's simply not as easily classifiable as yours."

"I'm nearly an atheist."

She laughed. "Being *nearly* an atheist is not a thing. You are a Catholic, like your uncle. Trust me, I recognize the signs."

"Can we discuss this later?"

"Just to be clear, I do not believe in marriage contracts."

Ben dropped the binoculars and glared at her. "Did I ask?"

"No, but it seemed relevant to the conversation."

"It's not."

"Okay." She leaned her chin on her hand. "I'm bored."

"You're the one who said we needed to wait for René."

ELIZABETH HUNTER

"I know. Right now Vano thinks I'm dead and you're gone. It's a great advantage." She pouted. "But it's boring to wait."

"If we weren't sitting in the middle of a forest, I'd think of something to amuse you," he murmured. "But we are and I'm not an exhibitionist. Looks like you're out of luck."

Tenzin swung her legs. "Are you going to return to New York?"

"Yes. It's past time I checked on the loft. God knows what you've done to it the past couple of years."

She didn't shoot him a quick comeback.

Ben glanced over to see her smiling. "What?"

"Nothing." She reached for the binoculars. "I want to see."

He handed them over. "They're setting up some kind of stage."

"For the ceremony."

Ben watched the flickering bonfire in the distance. "Why are they doing it? Radu, Kezia, and Vano aren't getting older. Why is it time to choose new leadership?"

"I don't know. It might not be all three of them—that would seem unwise. Maybe there is a timeline they agreed to when they became the terrin. But I believe any vampire choosing a successor will choose from Poshani candidates who present themselves."

"Only vampires?"

"Not necessarily," Tenzin said. "If a human proves to be the correct person to ascend to terrin, then that human would be turned. They are very selective about which Poshani become vampires and which do not, but new vampires are sired when it is necessary."

"So in theory," Ben said, "Vano holding two goblets means that he could choose a successor for Radu, and that person would be his ally and give him effectively two out of three votes?"

"Correct." She looked up from the binoculars. "Or alternately, Vano could choose two vampires who are his children, thus

306

retaining effective control of the entire clan. Or he could choose weak vampires and manipulate them. But control is the only motivation I can see for stealing Radu's goblet."

"Didn't someone tell me," Ben said, "that the Poshani decide their leaders in the end? That if a terrin was proven to be unjust or corrupt, the darigan wouldn't follow their lead?"

"Yes, but you can see how Vano has catered to the goodwill of the humans in the camp. I'm sure he has a plan to appease them."

"Shouldn't he want to cater to the darigan?"

"Not necessarily." Tenzin handed over the binoculars. "Catering is not leading, and every culture is vulnerable to demagogues if they show up at the right time. The Poshani need a leader, not a fairy godmother."

Ben's eyebrows went up. "A fairy godmother?"

"I believe the comparison is accurate. Chloe made me watch a series of movies featuring princesses' heroic journeys, and the fairy godmother trope appeared in most of them. I'm assuming they're old human attempts to make sense of vampires since many of the godmothers appear to fly or have other supernatural qualities."

Ben stared at her, unable to hide the smile on his face.

"What?" Tenzin frowned. "Have you seen these movies?"

"Princess movies? Yeah."

"I have thoughts about the mermaid movie. There are very unhealthy messages in it, and I don't believe Sadia should watch it."

He leaned over and pressed a fast kiss to her mouth. "I missed you."

"Yes, I missed you too." She lifted the binoculars again. "I believe I see René leaving something for us."

"We'll have to get closer and just pray the Hazar don't see us."

"See?" Tenzin hung the binoculars around her neck. "Catholic."

~

THEY PICKED up a bundle from the base of a birch tree.

Ben started to open it, but Tenzin stopped his hand. "Wait."

Her feet never touched the ground as she floated closer to the edge of the forest. She waited, motionless, while Ben stood in the shadows.

His amnis gave a pulse of excitement a second before she turned and floated back to him.

"Let's go."

"What—"

She put a finger over his lips, then took his hand and flew through the canopy, darting between trees and dipping low to skim over meadows and isolated ponds. The landscape was washed in an eerie white glow from the gibbous moon as they crossed the hills to find shelter in their cave.

They landed near a stream that cut through the narrow valley below where the cave was located.

"Do you know where we are?" Ben asked when they landed.

"I'm not certain," Tenzin said. "It's part of the traditional Poshani route. I would guess we are in the Eastern Carpathian Mountains, probably in Ukraine."

The moonlight created dappled shadows on the ground as Tenzin sat on a large rock and dipped her feet in the water.

"So" —she nodded toward the bag— "are you going to open it?"

Ben sat next to her. "As her majesty requests..."

Her eyes lit up. "I could get used to that."

He laughed. "Don't."

Inside the bag were a note, a gold bar, and three familiar rubbings.

"See?" Tenzin said. "I told you René was part of the plan."

"What are these?" Ben picked up the rubbings. One was

eerily familiar. "Are these... Does he already have the goblets? He only had one night."

Tenzin raised an eyebrow. "He'd been planning this for a while."

Ben was reluctantly impressed. "So René has the three goblets."

"Or he's been in their presence and knows where they are."

"And he's still at the camp? How do we know he's not tunneling to Paris as we speak?" *Like a gopher. A big French gopher.*

Tenzin took one rubbing from his hand. "The real value of the goblets is authority. René doesn't want that authority. He's spent his life running from anything that will require more than the most superficial commitment. He wants treasure."

"Don't lie. He wants the goblets too."

Tenzin shrugged. "I may have threatened to cut off various parts of his body if he took the goblets."

"I'm going to guess he was both afraid and oddly turned on by that."

Tenzin just said, "He is a very odd man."

Ben turned the gold bar in his hand. "Okay, so he wants treasure. Why is he helping us?"

"Because if he takes it without some major distraction, they'll know he has it and he won't have any peace, nor will he have a safe house when he inevitably pisses someone off again and needs a place to hide."

"So he wants to steal from the Poshani... but still stay friends?"

"I didn't comment on the likelihood of his plan succeeding or the probability of the Poshani figuring out who stole from them." She glanced up. "Which they will do. They will probably find out."

"So how are we getting away with it?"

"Silly Ben." She elbowed him. "You've been *hired* to steal for them. Which is probably the best hired job ever, in my opinion."

The wind turned, and a low rumbling sound came from over his shoulder.

Ben turned and his eyes went wide. "Tenzin."

"Yes?" She was reading the note.

"There's a very large bear right behind us."

"Hmmm." She didn't look up. "Does it have cubs with it?"

"I don't see any."

"Male or female?"

"I'm not going to ask." He reached for her arm. "You have the bag?"

"Yes, what—?"

Ben yanked her up straight into the air just as the bear's attention turned toward them.

Tenzin gave a whoop of pure joy and raced high into the air, arcing up and over Ben before she circled back to hover over his head.

Moonlight glinted on her fangs when she smiled. She held out her hand. "Fly with me."

He flashed back to a dream nearly forgotten. Him and Tenzin, skimming over white-barked birches, turning together, their blood and bodies linked in the air.

*This is what was always meant to be.*

It was as if he could hear her voice in his mind.

Ben rose and met her in the air, linking their hands as she drew him deeper and higher into the velvet-black night.

## 36

When Ben opened his eyes, Tenzin was staring at him. He jolted awake and sat up. "I didn't miss that."

"Miss what?"

"You staring at me while I sleep." He rubbed his eyes and sucked in a breath when he realized she was completely naked. "I admit I like this variation on the theme though."

Tenzin crawled up the pallet, straddling his legs as she kept her eyes on him with predatory intent. She wrapped her arms around his neck and kissed him full on the mouth, opening her lips to his as he placed both hands on her backside and squeezed.

"Mmmm." She squirmed over him and pressed her breasts into his chest.

"You like that?" Ben did it again.

"Yes."

He slid a hand over the curve of her backside, cupping her flesh and running his fingers along the crease of her thigh until he found her wet heat.

She pulled her mouth away from his and let out a long breath. "I do understand why so many women want to have sex with you."

"If you can think about that, I'm not doing my job right." He trailed his fingers up and down, learning the curves and secret corners of her body, taking his time as he toyed with her pleasure.

Her hands ran down his chest and her amnis teased him, kissing along his body where her hands and mouth couldn't reach. Whispers of air laved his skin.

"How do you make the air do that?"

She gripped his erection and began to kiss down his chest. "If you can think about that, I'm not doing my job right."

*Fuck.* "Do I need to be worried about fangs?"

Her low, wicked laughter only made him harder.

THEY RETURNED to the camp later that night, splitting up and remaining at a distance to avoid the Hazar. The preparations for the ceremony seemed to draw everyone's attention. Human voices became the dominant background noise through the night as the darigan erected more platforms and small stages. More and more wagons began to arrive.

Ben met Tenzin back at their perch in the fir tree. "Okay, what is our goal here?"

"We were hired to get Radu's goblet back to him," Tenzin said. "That is our goal."

"And Vano?"

"If everything goes according to my plan, Vano will be worse than dead. He'll be irrelevant."

Ben had to agree with her. For an egotistical asshole like Vano, irrelevance was a fate worse than death. "I think I'm going to try to get closer."

She shook her head. "You can't let them know you're still here. Whatever Vano told Radu—"

"That's exactly the point. We don't know. We need to find out what the rumors are and what the mood in the camp is, and René will know, but the note he gave us told us almost nothing. Probably by design."

"I wish there was someone slightly less self-interested we could trust."

He took a steadying breath. Brigid wasn't wrong when she said "getting a leg over" helped. Ben's head felt clearer than it had in months.

"I have a thought, but—"

"Tatyana?"

He turned to her. "How did you know?"

Tenzin glanced at him but kept her eyes on the camp in the distance. "You have good instincts. I believe she could be a reliable source, and she doesn't seem overly eager to curry favor with anyone."

"Even if they find me, it's not the end of the world. You're the only one Vano thinks is dead."

"I don't like it." She narrowed her eyes. "But I will admit that with all the other wagons and trailers arriving tonight, it is probably the best time for you to go if you're determined."

He kissed her quickly. "I'll be inconspicuous."

"Not with that amnis," she muttered. "We're going to have some lessons on moderating that."

"Are you saying I'm loud and flashy?"

"Like Giovanni wearing a cowboy hat."

He grinned. "I would be insulted, but you're cute when you're irritated."

She flicked her hand toward the camp. "Go. Try not to shout. If you're gone more than an hour, I'm coming after you and I'll probably destroy everything."

He snorted. "You say the sweetest things."

Ben flew off toward the twinkling torchlights in the distance.

*Time to act human again.*

~

THERE WAS ONLY one group of humans near enough to the forest that Ben felt like he could infiltrate and blend in. They were around his age, dressed similarly in dark pants and ordinary T-shirts. A few wore vests or light jackets over their shirts, but that wasn't a huge difference. Most had hair falling around their shoulders or pulled back in a knot and wore various lengths of beards. They looked like your average Eastern European hipsters.

The only problem? They were all speaking Poshani.

Since he was not a language expert who could pick up a foreign language in ten minutes, Ben waited until they began to walk back to the camp.

He trailed behind them, disguising the sound of his steps by directing the air around him, a highly useful tip Tai had taught him the year before. He stayed close enough that an observer would think him part of the group, but far enough away to keep the men from noticing him.

Once he entered the circle of travel trailers, he let out a breath. He quickly found a line of drying clothing and slipped on a vest; then he found a cap hanging on a hook at the end of a trailer. He pulled it down over his eyes, then walked to a solitary campfire burning in a cut-off barrel, using that vantage point to survey the camp.

Busy, busy, busy. If he wanted to get into the center of the trailers where Tatyana probably was, he needed to find an errand to run or a job to do.

He spotted the shovel and rake within minutes.

Okay, gross, but at least no one was likely to get too close.

When you had as many horses around the camp as the Poshani liked to have, you also had more than a little horse manure. Ben grabbed the shovel and rake, trying not to gag at the pungent scent of horse shit and piss. Sometimes being a newly turned vampire was a good thing. More than one of his immortal acquaintances had remarked that Ben still "walked like a human." He didn't know what that meant, but he was hoping they weren't just bullshitting him.

He began walking through the alleys between the rings of caravans, working his way, bit by bit, into the center.

No one gave him a glance.

Where had he always found Tatyana? She was usually near the humans cooking, seeming to prefer the company of humans rather than vampires. He scooped a few piles of manure along the edges of the inner circle until he spotted her.

"Vecchio!"

He tensed until he heard the accent. Ben turned and saw René walking toward him.

The man stopped a few yards away, seeming to examine a flower arrangement that had been erected near a music stage. "What the hell are you doing here?"

"We got your note," he murmured. "It told us nothing."

"It told you enough. Everything is in place. Come to the camp tomorrow night an hour before midnight. Meet me by the same birch tree where I left the gold."

"You're not the one in charge," he said. "What did Radu say about me and Tenzin?"

"Nothing. People come and people go. Vampires here don't ask questions."

"And Vano?"

"Playing his part. His people were the last to arrive today."

"Kezia?"

"Her people showed up the same day I returned to camp. They're coming from closer range."

"So all the Poshani are here now?"

"Yes."

Ben moved to another pile of manure. "And you have the goblets?"

"I have access to them," he said, strolling past Ben. "I have my own interests, Vecchio. Tenzin would do well to remember that." He curled his lip slightly. *"Merde."*

"Literally." Ben flipped a piece of manure toward René. It landed perilously close to a handmade leather shoe. "Oops."

"Tomorrow," he said. "Eleven o'clock. Birch tree. That's all you need to know. Now get out of here before someone sees you." René walked off, leaving Ben with the shovel and the rake.

He set them behind a portable toilet, then strolled through the outer ring of the camp, his hands stuffed in his pockets. Maneuvering closer to the kitchen area, he stopped to wash his hands before picking up a few chairs and moving them to where a man was pointing and shouting.

By the time he'd gotten close enough to Tatyana, he knew he was pushing his luck. He had to be close to an hour. The last thing the plan needed was Tenzin roaring in like a hurricane.

Tatyana was standing near the humans again, listening to them chatter as she sipped a glass of wine and observed the clutches of Poshani vampires and visitors in the most inner circle.

"Tatyana." He said her name barely over his breath, but she looked up.

"Ben Vecchio." She glanced around and walked toward him. "I am surprised to see you here, where you definitely should not be."

"Did Radu make my excuses for me?"

"He told us nothing. Only that you and Tenzin had chosen to leave the caravan. Is everything well with your family?"

"Yeah. I don't know if Radu knows what's going on." He spotted Vano speaking to some of his guards. "Stay away from Vano. He's dangerous."

"You tell me things I already know." She raised an eyebrow. "That man makes my skin crawl."

"Tomorrow night," he said, lowering his voice, "anything you can't live without, keep it with you. If you need to run, be light."

She narrowed her eyes. "What do you know?"

"Enough to know that something is coming and it could be violent."

Her blue eyes went wide. "This is the Dawn Caravan. Radu would never—"

"Radu would not," Ben said. "Others might."

She didn't say anything more, but she nodded.

"I like you," Ben said. "Take care."

"You smell like her now." The corner of Tatyana's mouth turned up. "Did you resolve your dispute?"

"You're very observant," Ben said. "You know that, right?"

Her smile fell. "That's what got me into trouble."

"Good luck." Ben tipped the edge of his cap toward her and sauntered slowly toward the edge of the camp again. He picked up a few more chairs and moved a few buckets, trying to keep from any appearance of haste.

He got to the edge of the clearing and walked straight into the trees. He heard a shout behind him, probably from a perimeter guard, but within seconds he was in the air, darting through the tree canopy as he and Tenzin had the night before, and in minutes he heard nothing but the wind.

## 37

Ben and Tenzin flew to the edge of the forest moments before they were to meet René the next night. Tenzin landed in a clearing and waited for Ben to land beside her. She looked to her right and watched him descend, her feeling of satisfaction immense.

He was beside her now, her blood in his veins, and his amnis knew hers. His light would never fade; it would grow and change like a jewel gaining facets with friction. His love for her was simple now, a seedling barely taking root.

What she felt for him?

*The love I hold has lasted as I have. It lives in my blood.*

She lived in Ben and he lived in her, joining the lives of those she had loved before. He existed with Nima, Stephen, and her children, residing among the names she'd chosen to forget and those she couldn't bear to speak.

He watched her watching him. "What?"

"This is right."

Ben frowned. "The job?"

"No. I mean, probably the job is right. I think our plan is solid, and if it isn't, we can always fly away and lie about what happened. I was talking about us."

He gave her half a smile. "Agreed. Not about the lying thing though."

"It's a minor lie." She lowered her voice and fell into step beside him. "René said he had *access* to the goblets?"

"Yes."

"You know what that means."

Ben said, "He's planning on us doing the dirty work."

"That would be my guess." She stubbed her toe on a tree root and had to remind herself why she wasn't flying.

*Act human.* What a ridiculous idea.

"We should stay together," she said. "He will attempt to separate us."

"Agreed. We stay together and we go after Vano and Radu's goblets. Let him get Kezia's."

"Yes."

She saw René in the distance, a flicker of movement in the shadow of the trees. He stepped forward when they approached. "You're late."

"No, we're not." Ben looked at the moon. "The festival hasn't started yet. Tell us where the goblets are."

René wasn't wearing black; he was wearing an elaborate costume that consisted of leather pants, a brocade vest, and a mustard-yellow cravat. On another man, it would have looked ridiculous. René DuPont was handsome enough to carry it off.

"You're wearing party clothes," she said.

"That would be because I am going to a party." He looked at them. "You look like you're going to a funeral."

"We all enjoy different kinds of parties, René." She walked past him and into the clearing, trying very hard to think about gravity.

Ben slipped his arm around her shoulders and sped up her

319

pace. "Nope. You're walking like a zombie, not a human. Just act natural."

Ben had a rhythm to his walk, a moderate swagger that she suspected came from being tall and sexually proficient.

"What kind of zombie did I look like?"

"The old, slow kind."

"That's not good." She leaned into him and followed his gait. "Is he behind us?"

"Yes. You don't really enjoy going to funerals, do you?"

"It depends on who died." She spied a group of Poshani watching them, but they were involved in a conversation that captured their attention before they could stare for too long.

René caught up to them. "Tenzin and I will go to Vano's trailer. Ben, you can go to Kezia's since you've already been there."

Ben frowned. "But Kezia—"

"No," Tenzin said. "Ben and I will take Vano's caravan; you take Kezia's."

"I do not agree." There was tension in René's voice. "Vano's trailer—"

"I'm sure has the bigger store of gold," Tenzin said. "Which we will leave for you. Trust me when I say there will be ample time for you to collect your prize once we have all three goblets."

René said, "I thought you were only hired to find Radu's goblet?"

"That was before," Tenzin said. "If we have all three, then we are in a far better bargaining position."

"And what are we bargaining for?" René muttered. "If you drag me into your—"

"Don't worry; it'll be great." Tenzin felt like skipping. This was going to be so much fun. "I think it's time for Vano to retire, don't you? And we're going to choose his successor."

~

THE CAMP HAD COMPLETELY TRANSFORMED for the festival. Music rang through the air, and the scent of food, flowers, and incense was everywhere. Ben saw reproductions of the Sara-la-Kali icon painted on banners and re-created in flower petals. Small statues of the saint decorated each caravan they passed, surrounded by peacock feathers and jars of honey. On each trailer or wagon, a sword hung over the front door, its hilt wrapped in a black scarf.

"So many flowers." Tenzin, despite the danger of the job, looked delighted.

Ben had to admit it was hard not to get caught up in the festivities.

Flowers were tucked everywhere. Cut and displayed in vases and glasses near the steps of each door. Hanging in baskets from roofs. Woven into crowns the Poshani women wore on their elaborately braided hair.

There were red strings tied on the corners of every caravan, some with small notes attached, some hanging in elaborate knots with paper flowers attached.

The bustling camp had turned into a crowded festival, and as soon as they entered the outer ring of trailers, not a single person took note of them. There were too many activities to distract them.

In the center of the camp, a giant bonfire had been lit and young men were taking turns leaping through the edges of the flames. Every attendee, human and vampire, trained their eyes on the spectacle, and loud encouragement and cheers rose every time another young man attempted a leap.

René guided them through the inner ring of vampire caravans. There were new trailers and buses, but Ben spotted Vano's sleek vehicle from across the clearing.

"We're not going for stealth," Tenzin said quietly. "It won't matter in the end. Everyone will know that we stole them."

René looked like he wanted to hit something. "Which is why you and I should—"

"Nope." Ben cut him off. "Tenzin's been planning this one for days. Just go with it, René."

Tenzin paused and looked up at René with wide eyes. "Do you think I would cheat you out of Vano's gold after you saved my life?"

René was unimpressed. "You mean after you trapped me in your trailer during the day and then used me to create a shelter from the daylight after your enemies tried to kill you? Yes."

"I'm very grateful."

"Clearly. If you're so grateful—"

"Ben and I will take Vano's trailer. You clearly know how to access Kezia's goblet since you have the rubbing. We will get the goblets—"

"Do you think I am an idiot?" René was fuming.

"—and *only* the goblets." She made an X over her heart. "I promise." Tenzin took Ben's hand. "Meet us near the kitchen wagon when you're done."

Without another word, Tenzin dragged Ben toward Vano's trailer, leaving René glaring behind them.

Ben let himself look over his shoulder. Just once.

René looked murderous.

He turned back to Tenzin. "I love how you work."

"I know."

They walked with purpose, which Ben had discovered over the years was the key to getting pretty much any place you wanted to go.

He spotted Vano's trailer in the distance, along with two Hazar guards near the entrance. "Ideas?"

"We don't want to attract that much attention." She nudged him. "Air."

Without another word, she took to the sky and dissolved into darkness. Ben stepped behind a trailer and called the air, lifting himself to the top of the caravan where Tenzin was waiting. He felt simultaneously hidden and exposed. The humans couldn't see them from below, but there were dozens of air vampires flying over the camp, jumping from one roof to another, laughing and visiting as the music grew louder and the dancing more rowdy.

"Just stay here for a moment," Tenzin said.

"Limited time."

"I know." She nodded. "Trust me."

In a matter of moments, Ben knew what she'd been waiting for. There was a show below, a fire juggler of some kind, and the man touched off a rocket that shot from the ground and into the sky, exploding overhead and grabbing everyone's attention.

"Nice." They kept an eye on the juggler, and when he was gearing up for another firework, Tenzin grabbed his hand. "Now."

They flew from their spot and alighted on Vano's trailer just as the second rocket exploded.

Tenzin put a finger to her lips and smiled. Then she slid across the roof to the plastic-covered air vent that was just small enough for a child to crawl through.

"There's no way my shoulders are going to fit through that," he hissed.

Tenzin frowned. "You're not going in."

"Vano thinks you're dead, Tenzin. If he finds you in his trailer—"

"He's not going to." She waited for the next firework before she ripped off the vent with her hands and handed the lid to Ben. "Be right back."

How on earth had René broken into this thing? Other than the vent that it took a contortionist—or Tenzin—to enter, it was a vault. He didn't see a crack or a seam. Ben was reluctantly impressed.

He waited on the roof, trying his best to appear like just another wind vampire hanging out on a caravan roof at the party, watching the fireworks light the night sky.

A few minutes after she'd disappeared, Ben saw Tenzin's hand pop up through the vent, holding a small bundle wrapped in leather. He grabbed it, stuffed it inside his jacket, and went back to ignoring the slight rocking beneath him as she moved around the trailer.

Five achingly long minutes after her hand first appeared, it popped up again, this time holding another bundle. Ben grabbed it and shoved it next to the other goblet before he scooted over and tried to help Tenzin out.

She lifted herself up and out of the vent, only to get stuck at her hips.

Ben frowned. "What's the problem?"

"I have no idea." She twisted and squirmed, but it just wasn't happening.

"What's going on?" Ben looked at her hips. "You didn't have a problem getting in."

"Maybe gravity helped?"

It was a tiny vent, but if she'd entered that easily...

Ben crossed his arms. "What's in your pockets?"

Her eyes went wide. "My pockets?"

He reached down and squeezed his hand through the side of the vent, reaching around her backside to feel a large lump that had definitely not been there before. "You have gold bullion in your pockets, Tiny."

"Do I?"

"Are you trying to tell me it just happened to fall in there and you didn't notice?"

"It's only twenty... thirty ounces. Maybe."

Ben squeezed one cheek. "Really?"

"In each pocket," she muttered. "Fine." She sighed heavily and dropped down again, only to lift a handful of small gold bars through the vent.

"Uh-uh." Ben wasn't taking Vano's gold. Sure, he was a bad guy, but Ben had been hired to find Radu's goblet. If he wanted to maintain a reputation as an honest operator, he had to stick to his principles.

"Oh, come on!" She popped her head out of the vent. "Will you just—?"

"I can't believe I'm saying this, but you promised René you wouldn't take Vano's gold."

She hung on the edge of the vent and pouted.

"Tenzin, we need to go." Ben could see the crowd beginning to break apart. "It's almost midnight."

She sighed deeply and dropped the gold on the floor; then she slipped from the vent with ease and nudged the vent back into place. "You're still no fun."

"That's not what you said when you woke me up tonight." He hooked his arm through hers. "Ready?"

They took off, stepping off the roof and gliding through the sky until they came to land across the clearing on a roof shaded by a large oak tree.

"What are we doing?" Tenzin asked. "We need to meet René."

Ben reached for the two pouches. "I may not be greedy, but I want to see them."

Tenzin crossed her legs and sat. "They're beautiful."

Ben unwrapped the first one, which was Vano's. It was encased in embroidered red silk. He carefully removed it from the padded sleeve and almost drooled.

The goblet was nearly a copy of Kezia's carved citrine, but it was crafted from a ruby the size of Ben's fist. The base was carved with a similar inscription, and the edges were smoothed from age.

"It's so beautiful."

"Look at Radu's."

The leather took a little longer to unwrap, but as it fell softly into the palm of Ben's hand, he felt the innate power in the ancient carved gemstone. He picked up the ruby in his right hand and held the emerald in his left.

"I feel like an emperor right now."

"I imagine whatever Persian king gifted them felt the same."

"Holy shit." He nearly groaned. "I get it."

"We can't keep them." Tenzin sighed. "Sadly. They are completely unique. And also completely foundational for Poshani culture. We wouldn't be robbing an individual, we would be robbing a people."

Ben handed her the ruby goblet. "One toast."

Tenzin took it and grinned. "If only we had some blood-wine."

"Cheers." Ben ever so gently tapped the edge of the emerald goblet to the edge of the ruby one. Then he leaned over and kissed Tenzin on the mouth. "We pulled off another one, partner."

"We stole it back," she said. "Now to get just a little revenge."

## 38

Stealing a scarf for Tenzin and a cap for Ben allowed them to blend into the crowd surrounding a central stage where three elaborate chairs had been placed. The middle chair was draped in gold and orange ribbons. The one on the left was draped in crimson, and the one on the left in vivid green.

Tenzin nudged Ben. "They don't look very happy."

It was true. Kezia, Vano, and Radu were conferring in the center of the stage, a circle of the Hazar gathered close around them. Ben could see Radu's expression, both worried and a little confused. Kezia looked furious, and Vano's eyes roamed the crowd.

"Do you think he suspects us?" Ben asked.

"I think he's thinking that someone double-crossed him. He suspects everyone."

Vano's eyes came to rest on René, who was lounging in a raised sitting area for the guests of the kamvasa. Ben spotted Tatyana not far from him, along with most of the other vampire guests. A few old faces were gone, replaced by vampires Ben didn't recognize. One vampire he did recognize was Oleg, the famous Russian fire vampire Tatyana had been hiding from.

Well, shit. That was inconvenient.

They were on opposite sides of the platform, avoiding each other. Oleg was only half watching the festivities—most of his attention was locked on Tatyana.

Tatyana, on her end, was completely ignoring Oleg. In the safety of the kamvasa, whatever disagreement they had couldn't be acted on. She was protected, but Ben saw her nerves in the tight lines of her jaw and neck.

Ben asked, "Why are the Poshani allowing guests in? I thought all the secret stuff happened when outsiders are gone."

"Any judgments or internal conflicts will be handled in private, but these" —she nodded to the vampires watching— "I'm guessing, are the witnesses. This is like an inauguration or a coronation. They need witnesses for legitimacy. Not a lot, but a few very trusted individuals."

"Like *René?*" Ben was incredulous.

"He probably paid someone for a ticket." She looked at Ben. "It would have been expensive."

"No wonder he doesn't want us messing his score up," Ben muttered under his breath.

At the base of the sitting area was a line of chairs, all with various humans and immortals sitting in them. All looked dressed to the nines with expressions wavering between confident and nervous.

"Candidates." Ben nodded at the line of seats. "The ones hoping to be chosen."

"They have no idea." Tenzin looked around the crowd. "This could turn ugly."

"We have to time it exactly right."

As if on cue, Kezia stepped forward and raised her hands. "My brothers and sisters, welcome to Vashana!"

A loud cheer erupted from the crowd.

"As all of you know, this is the Vashana Zata, a special night held only once every hundred years. Because of this occasion, we have invited a few trusted guests from the kamvasa." Kezia nodded to the raised sitting platform. "Our guests honor this trust and the privilege they have been granted."

Ben leaned down. "Meaning talk about our shit out of turn and be hunted to your grave."

"Exactly."

"This night will decide the next hundred years of leadership," Kezia continued. "Some of us may move on from our humble seats of servanthood—"

Hushed whispers from the area around the candidates, who appeared to be calculating their chances.

"—and some of us will remain, sharing the wisdom of the terrin with the newest member."

"That's smart," Ben said. "So they won't all choose a new member?"

"Despite my extraordinary wisdom and knowledge—"

"Not to mention your humility."

"—you know as much about this as I do." Tenzin glanced at him. "It sounds like you're correct."

Someone shouted from the crowd. Ben didn't understand much of it, but one word stood out as the crowd around them began to chant.

"*Dishana!*"

Kezia's face froze.

"*Dishana, dishana, dishana!*"

"The goblets," Tenzin said. "They're asking for the goblets."

The crowd grew in energy. Ben could feel it rising around him like a fog rising from the ground. The Hazar flew into the air, surrounding the crowd. The crowd quieted, and shouts turned to muttering and whispers.

"Sadly," Kezia continued, "the trust of the kamvasa has been breached."

Dead. Silence.

"Someone has used our hospitality against us," Kezia said, her eyes turning like lasers to the platform where kamvasa guests were sitting. "The dishana, the goblets gifted to our first terrin, have been stolen."

"No, my sister. Not stolen." Tenzin spoke, and as she did, she raised her hands and lifted Ben with her in a giant whirlwind.

Ben turned to her, shouting over the roar of the wind. "What are you doing?"

"Making an entrance!" She smiled wide and pulled the scarf from her hair, letting the wind whip around her, gathering a storm of flower petals from the crowd. "You have the emerald goblet?"

"Yes."

"Follow my lead."

Ben moved with her, adding his own power to hers until the air danced around them. They rose over the crowd and the stage, up and into the air, surrounded by a storm of flowers.

While Tenzin conducted the wind, Ben encased them both in a calm cushion of air.

"Are you ready?"

Ben pulled the emerald goblet from his jacket. "Ready."

She turned to him and locked her eyes with his. "Time to use that charm, *min shon*."

"Min what?"

"I'll explain later."

Ben felt the air easing. They landed on the raised platform, a cascade of flowers still whirling around them. As the blossoms settled, Ben walked over and raised the goblet to Radu. "Not stolen, my friend. Protected."

Radu's eyes went wide. Ben could tell he had roughly a thousand questions, but he stepped forward and held out his hand. Ben placed the emerald goblet in Radu's palm without hesitation, then turned to René.

"Monsieur DuPont?" Ben called. "If you would."

The vampire rose from his position on the platform and sauntered down the stairs. The crowd cleared for René as he walked up the stairs and across the stage until he reached Kezia.

Without a word, he took Kezia's hand, bowed deeply, and kissed her knuckles before he drew the citrine goblet from an inner pocket and placed it in her hand.

That left Tenzin alone in the center of the stage, holding the ruby goblet to her chest and staring at Vano, the vampire who had tried to kill her.

Vano stared at Tenzin and he didn't flinch.

"Shall I tell them, Vano, how I came to have this goblet in my possession?"

The corner of his lips twitched. "Because you are a thief. Hazar!"

Tenzin rose in the air, the goblet in her right hand. Ben rose with her and drew a short sword from his jacket. They hovered over the Poshani, their eyes trained on Vano.

"Long have I honored the Poshani and admired their hospitality," Tenzin said. "But four days ago, the trailer where I was promised shelter was abandoned, left behind when the kamvasa moved on."

"Vano told us you had asked to remain," Kezia said. "He showed us a letter signed by you and Benjamin."

"It was not written by us," Ben said. "Your brother lied to you."

The crowd all started to speak at once. Ben could hear some supportive voices, some who questioned them.

"And then, while I was in my day rest" —Tenzin's eyes rose to the platform of guests— "Vano's allies burned my shelter with me inside."

Every vampire on the platform rose from their seat, looking at the surrounding crowd with suspicion.

The Poshani crowd erupted in shouts until Radu stepped forward and raised a hand. "Brothers and sisters!" He glanced at the vampire guests. "There must be an explanation for this. Patience." Radu turned to Vano. "Brother, tell me our former guest is mistaken. That there has been a misunderstanding."

Vano might be a scheming bastard, but he couldn't hide the truth on his face. Ben watched Kezia's expression. He glanced at Radu, then at the crowd.

"There is no mistake," Tenzin said. "The ashes left behind prove my tale. Vano attempted to *kill* a guest of the kamvasa and lied to the Hazar and the darigan about it."

Vano's silence told his story.

Ben's attention was drawn to a disturbance at the back of the crowd. Men were shouting and pushing a man forward. He made his way to the edge of the stage, and his face was pale and drawn with worry.

"Who are you?" Ben asked.

The man glanced at Tenzin, then at Vano. "I am one of those whom Vano ordered to burn the caravan." He pointed at Vano, who was baring his fangs. "He told us the vampire inside had murdered a Poshani girl. That she was a murderer and the terrin had ordered her death for betraying our hospitality. He showed us a paper signed by all three. That is the only reason we followed his orders."

Kezia's face was grim. "The terrin made no such order."

Radu said, "I know of no murdered girl."

Tenzin stepped forward and raised her hands. "This is a mystery easily solved. Is anyone missing a daughter?"

There was muttering, but no one spoke.

"A mother?" Tenzin asked. "A sister? A *friend*? Have any of your women or girls gone missing?" After a long thread of silence, Tenzin turned to Vano. "I would *never* betray the hospitality of the kamvasa." She turned to Kezia. "As a daughter of Kali, I swear it."

Kezia turned to Vano and raised her finger. "You have betrayed us."

"She's lying!" Vano yelled. "They are thieves! I would never—"

"Why would she lie?" Radu raised the emerald goblet. "Our dishana have been returned to us. Only yours is withheld. Would thieves do that?" Radu looked at the Hazar. "Take him."

The crowd erupted in shouts and cries as the Hazar flew toward Vano and grabbed him by the arms and legs before he could fly away.

"You!" Vano screamed at Ben. "I let you live! I showed you mercy—"

"You tried to kill Tenzin." Ben rose and flew toward Vano. He flung the Hazar away from the vampire with a sweep of his arm; then he grabbed Vano by the throat.

For the first time since he'd turned, Ben gave in to the rage and the power that simmered just below the surface of his tightly controlled exterior.

Squeezing Vano's throat until the man couldn't speak, Ben hissed in the vampire's ear. "You're so smart, Vano. So tell me what I'm going to do right now."

Vano attempted to wiggle away, and Ben gripped the side his head and slid his thumb dangerously close to Vano's left eye socket.

"Give me a reason." Ben's voice was so eerily calm he barely recognized himself. "Shall I take an eye for a souvenir? Rip off an ear?"

Vano's response was only a gurgle.

"I can smell your blood," Ben said. "I hear it pooling in your mouth. Your lungs. How does it feel to swim in your own blood, you bastard?"

Vano's blue eyes burned into Ben's with so much hatred Ben was surprised he didn't feel a burn.

"If I didn't trust Radu and Kezia to do something far worse, I would rip your head from your shoulders with my two hands." He nodded at the hovering Hazar and shoved Vano toward them, but not before he felt the crunch of Vano's cheekbone as it collapsed under his grip.

Ben landed next to Tenzin on the stage and put an arm around her shoulders. "Radu, my friend, I believe I have met the terms of our arrangement." He nodded at the emerald goblet in Radu's hand. "Tenzin and I have protected the sacred goblet of the Poshani terrin."

*And I managed to hide the fact that it was stolen from you to begin with.*

Radu's eyes were glowing with satisfaction. "You have." He turned to Tenzin. "My dear Tenzin, you are in an unusual position."

Tenzin smiled a little. "That happens sometimes."

"You possess the ruby goblet of the Poshani terrin." Kezia stepped forward. "You are an old friend, known to the kamvasa." Kezia turned to the crowd. "Tenzin of Penglai, commander of the Altan Wind, daughter of the Kali, protector and bearer of the ruby dishana!"

The Poshani crowd, vampire and human alike, cheered around them. Some began shouting her name. Others threw flowers on the stage.

Tenzin turned to Ben. "This could be a problem."

"This was your plan, Tiny." Ben looked around nervously. "Think fast. I don't think we want to be stuck here for the next hundred years."

"Ideas?" She glanced around the festival and tried to smile. It looked like she was baring her teeth; unfortunately, that only made the Poshani cheer harder.

"You want ideas to get out of this?" Ben muttered.

"Please."

He racked his brain furiously for a way out.

Then he had it.

Ben bent and whispered in Tenzin's ear. She perked up immediately and walked to the edge of the stage and lifted both her hands. The crowd fell quiet.

"Poshaniya," Tenzin shouted. "You are kind and hospitable. You honor your guests and your history, and I would travel with you for a century if I could. But I am not suited for the honor of serving on the terrin."

Murmurs of dissatisfaction spread like a gathering wave.

"But there *is* among the kamvasa guests a woman of honor and cunning, a vampire who respects your traditions and has learned your language and your history." Tenzin turned toward the guests' platform. "Tatyana Vorona."

Tatyana stared at Tenzin with an expression Ben couldn't classify. Her blue eyes were wide but not shocked. She looked at Kezia and Radu, then at the crowd of Poshani gathered around the stage. Then she looked at Oleg and raised a single eyebrow.

No one spoke when Tatyana rose to her feet. She stepped delicately down the stairs, helped by four of the Hazar. She walked through the crowd and stopped to let a woman Ben recognized as one of the camp cooks place a flower crown on her head. They exchanged a few words before Tatyana mounted the stage.

She didn't look or speak to either Radu or Kezia but turned to the crowd and addressed the Poshani in their own language.

Ben leaned down. "Do you have any idea what she's saying?"

"Not really."

"Judging from her tone, I'm going to say she's willing but wants their approval."

"She's smart," Tenzin said. "She won't take her power for granted."

"That's what I was thinking." Ben watched Oleg, a vampire known as much for his power and fiery temper as for his cunning and determination. "I think Oleg is in love with her."

"Do you think so?"

Ben looked at the man watching Tatyana. "Yep. Pretty sure. He probably wouldn't admit it though."

"Well, that's an interesting twist." Tenzin looked at Oleg. "I don't see it."

"Maybe I'm wrong." He wasn't wrong.

He turned and saw Radu sidling up to them.

"Did you plan all this, Vecchio?"

"No," Ben murmured. "But when your brother left us behind and tried to kill Tenzin, we had to improvise."

"She's going to accept," Radu said. "It will be the first time in history that a terrin who is not Poshani holds one of the goblets."

A roar came from the crowd, and the Poshani started chanting Tatyana's name.

Ben slapped Radu's shoulder. "I think they're okay with it."

Flowers were thrown toward the stage, and Tenzin walked forward.

"Tatyana." Tenzin held out the ruby goblet. "I believe this is yours."

Tatyana looked at Radu and Kezia. Then at Ben. "This was you."

"Sometimes the wrong things happen to good people," Ben said. "And sometimes the right things happen to the right people."

Tatyana looked at Kezia and Radu. "I will never take this responsibility for granted. I will always look out for the most vulnerable."

Kezia looked at her brother and then back to Tatyana. "Then sister, take your goblet."

Tatyana took the ruby goblet from Tenzin's hand and lifted it to the cheers of the Poshani. She turned to Ben. "I won't forget this."

Ben and Tenzin stepped to the back of the stage as Kezia and Radu walked to either side of their new sister in the terrin. The Hazar surrounded them as the crowd cheered and music began to play.

"I'm not sure if that was a threat or not," Ben said quietly.

"Not a threat." Tenzin nodded at the new terrin. "She was looking for a home. She found one."

Ben looked around at the celebrating throngs of Poshani humans and vampires. "So, any idea where René got to?"

"Nope. None at all."

## 39

Ben woke at nightfall, Tenzin curled into his side. One hand was playing with the hairs on his chest and the other was tucked under his armpit.

"Were you trying to tickle me?"

"Yes. And now you're awake. It worked perfectly." She stroked her fingernails along his side, and Ben nearly doubled up in laughter.

"Stop." He'd always been ticklish, but he'd never slept with anyone who took advantage of it. "Don't tickle me."

"You're much harder to wake now. I have to discover new tactics."

He stretched up, throwing his arms over his head. "We're leaving tonight, right?"

"Don't you like our comfortable cave?"

"I want a proper bed, Tenzin. I'm taller than you and I actually sleep. I want to be comfortable and not cramped." He slid his hand down her bare back. "And beds have other desirable features we both might enjoy."

"Hmm." She propped her chin on his chest. "How about Venice?"

He put his hand on the back of her neck and pulled her in for a kiss. "I love you."

"We'll fly to the camp for a couple of hours, just to take proper leave, then we'll fly straight there. We can be there before daybreak."

"A few nights in Venice sounds perfect."

"I agree."

"Then we should probably go to Rome. I have a feeling Chloe and Gavin are about to send out the National Guard."

"I don't think they have any authority to do that in Italy."

"No?" He tweaked her chin. "Bummer. Did you know you're very cute?"

"You keep telling me that. Often followed by telling me that I'm irritating."

"Two things can be true at the same time."

"Ben."

"Tiny."

The corner of her mouth turned up. "I used to hate when you called me that."

"No, you didn't."

"I really did. I often thought about how I could injure you in nonpermanent ways when you called me that." She laid her head over his heart. "I have become accustomed to it now."

"Good." He stroked his hand through her hair and thought about all the nights they'd been apart. "Was it worth it?"

"What?"

"Whatever it was you had to give Zhang to make him turn me."

Tenzin looked up and straight into his eyes. "Yes."

No hesitation. No doubt. Not even a shadow of it.

"If you want to tell me—"

"I don't."

He stared at her and saw nothing hidden except the answer she knew he wouldn't give her. "Okay. I won't ask."

"Thank you."

"I'm still going to get angry sometimes," he said. "I'm still going to get mad that I'm not who I was, because I worked really hard to make that person."

"I understand."

"So don't forget this moment. And remember that wherever I go when I'm angry, I want to get back here."

Tenzin nodded. "I will remember."

"I love you." He gripped a hand in her hair. "And I will learn to love this life."

"Thank you."

"For what?"

She frowned. "For loving me."

"I didn't have much choice about it." He smiled and tucked a strand of hair behind her ear. "You just kind of worked your way in there."

"No," she said firmly. "Love—real love—is always a choice." She kissed the center of his chest. *"Baina min khar. Sha bol min yash."*

"What does that mean?"

She kissed him full on the lips, pressing her mouth to his over and over while she ran her fingers through his hair, trailed them along his jaw, and let them come to rest over his heart.

"It means that when you are angry, I will remember."

Tatyana, Kezia, and Radu sat at a table in the center of the camp, just next to the bonfire, watching the musicians on the stage.

"It will be the first time two women have been on the terrin," Radu said. "The Poshani are becoming very progressive."

Kezia and Tatyana exchanged a look.

"Oh yes," Kezia said. "Very progressive."

"We're still deciding what we will do with the Hazar and darigan who followed Vano," Kezia said. "But they have all been identified."

Radu looked at Tenzin and Ben. "I hope this does not affect your trust in the kamvasa."

Ben glanced at the full circle of trailers. "It doesn't look like you've lost any guests."

"Not so far," Tatyana said. "But if rumors start..."

"They won't have come from us," Tenzin said. "What happened to Vano?"

Radu, Kezia, and Tatyana stared at Tenzin with matching blank expressions.

"He has been dealt with," Radu said. "We appreciate your trust on this matter."

Oh yeah. Vano was super dead.

Ben nodded. "Of course. What will you do with all of Vano's businesses?"

"They remain part of his property," Tatyana said. "And the profit from that property employs and goes into the fund for all the Eastern Poshani. Radu and Kezia will help me to administer it until I understand the workings of the organization."

Radu said, "With your background in financial accounting, I have no doubt that you'll be an asset to all our people."

"There are needs," Tatyana said, "especially among the darigan. I believe I can be of some service."

Kezia rose and held her hand out to Tatyana. "Come. Let's visit some of the clan leaders while they are still gathered for Vashana. I will introduce you to everyone I know by name, and the old women will take care of the rest."

"So the same as every community." Tatyana smiled. "I already feel at home."

As soon as they were away, Ben said, "You know she was hiding from Oleg."

"Oleg is powerful," Radu said. "But now Tatyana is one of the Poshani. She learned our language before she ever joined us. Our people respect that. She acquainted herself with our history and has impressed our people with her humility. I will tell you that already, the Eastern Poshani will defend her to the death. She is their terrin."

"She won't travel with the caravan?"

"She is welcome anytime, but Vano's businesses are extensive and cross into Oleg's territory. There is no way they will be able to avoid each other, but he knows that she is ours now. He will have to respect that or suffer the consequences."

Ben sat back in his chair. "You're a good man, Radu."

He shrugged. "I have my faults like any other. The two of you..." He nodded and looked between them. "This is good."

"We've really got to stop taking jobs that lead to regime changes though." Tenzin sighed. "We're going to stop being invited anywhere good."

"Agreed."

Radu said, "Currently, I do not have any more work for you, but I do have a bonus." He withdrew a small lacquered chest and opened it. A row of gold bars lay nested in the bottom of the velvet-lined box. "The price Ben and I negotiated for the goblet has already been transferred to your account electronically, but this is for both of you, a thank-you for the inconvenience."

Tenzin's eyes lit up.

"I confess," Radu said, "Vano's gold stores were far less than I expected, based on his business empire and how much he had been withholding from the clan." Radu snapped the chest shut. "But what is there is yours. With Tatyana's skills, I have no doubt that the Eastern Poshani will be well provided for in the future."

Ben opened his mouth, but Tenzin grabbed his hand and

squeezed hard. "We will be honored to accept this," she said, "as an apology for the damage to my trailer and the... unfortunate incident that will never be spoken of again."

Radu looked relieved. "I do appreciate your discretion."

"Of course." Tenzin rose. "We should leave now. We're heading west tonight."

Radu and Ben both stood, and Ben held out his hand. "I would be happy to travel with you again."

"You are welcome anytime." Radu turned to Tenzin. "It was good to see you, Tenzin."

"I would say the same." She lifted the box and held it hugged to her chest. "We didn't move the trailers, but we did loot them a little."

"Understood. The darigan will take care of them. Do not even think of it." Radu reached under the table and lifted a backpack. "I nearly forgot this."

"Oh my God, my tablet." Ben hugged the backpack to his chest. "I don't even want to think about how many emails I've missed."

"Let's not think about that at all." Tenzin reached for the backpack and put the lacquered box inside. "Are you ready?"

Ben nodded and slung the backpack over his shoulders. "Radu, give our best to your sisters."

"My sisters." He smiled. "I do like the way that sounds. I will tell them. Safe journey, my friends."

Ben and Tenzin rose into the sky, waving at the Hazar, who flew alongside them until they had left Poshani territory. Then there was nothing in front of them except for scattered clouds and the nighttime sky.

"You realize," Tenzin said, "that if we hadn't let René take all the gold, we would have been paid so much more."

"You realize," Ben said, "that if René hadn't helped us get the third goblet, none of this would have worked out the way it did."

Tenzin huffed. "I suppose so."

"Leave it." Ben glanced over his shoulder. René was probably still in the camp, sewing Vano's gold into the lining of all his brocade coats. "I have a feeling we'll end up running into that annoying little bastard again."

THEY LANDED in the courtyard of Tenzin's home in Venice on the island of San Marco. The old palazzo was steps from the Assassin's Street, looking out over the rio di San Luca. The interior courtyard was filled with a trickling fountain and the orange tree was in bloom, filling the courtyard with a heavenly scent.

The house was locked up—Tenzin's caretaker Silvio was clearly not expecting guests—but Ben remembered where the keys for the utility room were stored. He turned on the power and the water.

"I'm really looking forward to a bath."

Tenzin was already lounging in the long gallery that led to the interior dock. "I thought that waterfall was a very good find."

"It was better than nothing." Ben flipped the breaker on, and the Moroccan lamps that lit the hallways flipped on. "But warm water cannot be beat."

In the corner, he spotted the old record player he'd found on his first trip to Tenzin's house. He lifted it from the storage room and set it on the gallery table before he plugged it in. He knew the records lived in the library, so he walked up half a flight to the first floor and opened the door.

The musty smell of books met his senses. Vanilla and leather. Mold, incense, and a hint of lemon oil. The familiarity of the smells allowed Ben to relax for the first time in weeks.

He walked to the far wall and grabbed a record in a faded white sleeve.

Perfect.

Tenzin was opening a bottle of blood-wine from the kitchen when he returned. He put the record on the player, and the crackling sounds of Louis Armstrong's trumpet filled the gallery. Ella Fitzgerald sang "Dream a Little Dream of Me," and her golden voice echoed through the marble hallways.

Tenzin set the bottle down and walked over to him. "Dance?"

Ben held out his hand. "We always dance to Louis."

Without another word, she stepped into his arms and Ben brought her close, wrapping his arm around her waist as he held her hand in his and swayed in the smallest hours of the night.

The city was silent as they moved in rhythm with the rising song. The music filled the air and floated over the water.

"Heaven," Ben whispered along with the music. "I'm in heaven."

"Heaven or Venice?" Tenzin pressed her cheek to his chest.

"Right now they feel the same."

"Your old room isn't light safe," Tenzin said. "You'll have to stay in mine."

Ben smiled. "You mean I have to stay with the woman I love and sleep in the grand entry hall that looks over the canal?"

"With the drapes drawn, it's light safe. There isn't a bed in there though. We'll have to bring a mattress up."

"I can handle that." Ben dipped her and kissed her neck. "You own a *palace*."

"It was a bargain in the seventeenth century. I had to put a lot of gold into this place to make it livable."

"Glad you hung on to it."

"Tell the truth." Her dimple peeked out. "Do you love me just for this house?"

"I mean..." He looked around. "It's not the *only* reason, but it helps to remember how loaded you are when you drive me crazy."

She laughed, and it echoed down the hallway, filling the house with music, laughter, and the quiet lapping of waves at the dock. The air was cool and dry, a perfect spring night in Venice, and the orange tree perfumed the air.

*Here.* Ben danced with Tenzin in the darkness. *Here right now.*

*This moment.*

He wanted to live in it forever. And now he could.

## 40

"You better have just escaped certain death," Chloe said. "Five days, Benjamin. Five. Days."

He frowned. "Wait, so you *want* us to have faced certain death?"

"I'm saying if anything less than facing certain death kept you from answering the nine thousand calls and messages I sent you... Plus I had to try to reassure your uncle and put up with Fabia freaking out. You really need to get to Rome because I swear that woman is paranoid about you after Shanghai."

Ben winced. "Well, if anyone has a right to be paranoid, it's probably Fabi. I'm fine. We're fine."

"We?"

Ben didn't know what to say.

*Tenzin and I made up.*

*We still have issues. We'll probably always have issues.*

*But...*

*I can't live without her. I don't even want to try.*

"We figured things out," he said quietly. "We're good, Chloe."

She was quiet on the other end of the phone.

"Chloe?"

347

ELIZABETH HUNTER

She sniffed. "Really?"

Ben rolled his eyes. "Yeah. We're good. We're more than good."

"Are you happy?"

Was he happy? He looked over at Tenzin, who was lying on her belly on one of the Persian rugs, her legs kicked up as she scowled at the screen of her portable gaming device.

"Thieving raccoons," she muttered. "Tiny, devious demons, both of you."

Ben smiled. "Yeah. I'm happy."

"I'm glad."

Tenzin threw her gaming device across the room. "Usurers end up in the seventh circle of hell, raccoons!"

"Yep." Ben watched the console bounce off the carpet. "Everything seems pretty much back to normal."

THEY SPENT four nights in Venice, sending texts to everyone who'd been panicking about them and catching up on emails while they enjoyed the solitary quiet of the city at night.

They didn't video call anyone. They didn't go out other than to fly over the lagoon at night and enjoy the evening air. They rested and enjoyed the quiet.

Unlike the bustle of daytime Venice, the nighttime city was calm and quiet, a perfect retreat from the intrigue and immortal machinations they'd been juggling for weeks. For the first time in two years, Ben felt refreshed.

He woke most evenings to Tenzin teasing him awake, kissing his neck or running her fingers across his chest.

She was far more tactile than he'd imagined she'd be. Maybe she was making up for lost time. She told him she hadn't taken a lover in the time they'd been apart, but even before then, it was rare for Tenzin to trust anyone enough to let them touch her, even in a nonsexual way. She was jealous of her personal space and didn't allow many others to intrude.

They were lying on the mattress Ben had dragged up from the first floor, and Tenzin was intent on tracing the muscles of his abdomen.

"Tenzin?"

She looked up, and her hair brushed the sensitive skin along his hip. Ben shuddered and grew hard again.

Tenzin looked down. "Your appetite is remarkable."

"I feel like I'm about sixteen again." It was true. He felt like he was going through puberty for a second time.

"Trust me" —she trailed a finger up his erection— "nothing about you reminds me of a boy."

"No, if anything, people are going to think I'm the cradle robber." It was true. To human eyes, Tenzin looked far younger than Ben did. Luckily, most vampires knew that looks were deceiving.

"Cradle robber." Her dimple peeked out. "That is an amusing idea."

He pulled her up and she floated over him, coming to rest on his chest.

"Hello." Ben slid his hands over her shoulders, down her back, and over her bottom before he reversed course and did it all over again.

She melted into him.

"I know you didn't take another lover," he said. "But did you have anyone who just hugged you? Chloe? Even Cheng?" Ben didn't like the pirate, but he did care about Tenzin, and Ben was starting to think she'd been completely touch-starved.

"Chloe forced a few hugs on me, but Cheng and I aren't currently speaking."

His hand paused. "Because of me?"

ELIZABETH HUNTER

"In a sense. He is not jealous—he knows our relationship was not comparable to what you and I share—but he did not approve."

"Of what?"

"Of my taking you to my father."

Ben frowned. "Really?"

"He thought I overstepped the limits of friendship." She looked up and into his eyes. "He could understand the impulse of the moment, but then I refused to leave you alone."

So Cheng was offended on Ben's behalf? That was... oddly honorable of him.

"I will say the following thing was kind of annoying," he said. "But I have to admit that if you hadn't followed me, I probably would have been worried about you."

Ben took a deep breath and tasted the air. He could smell the water in the canal, the scent of wool warmed in the sun, and above everything, Tenzin's blood.

The constant, comforting scent of her had quickly become the reason he took his next breath. He did not need to fill his lungs, but he did need her. It was a little frightening how much.

Tenzin laid her ear over his heart. "He did not understand what we are."

"Sometimes *I* don't understand what we are."

She didn't speak for a long time. "I think we don't have to be one thing. Humans try to classify everything because it makes life less confusing for them. But you are not human anymore."

"No." And Ben was learning to be okay with that. "Giovanni told me years ago that whatever we were, we were more alive together than we were separately."

"Hmm." Tenzin looked up and over Ben's shoulder, narrowing her eyes at something only she could see. "I think he was right."

He traced a finger along an old silver line that ran from her belly to her hip. "Are you going to tell me about them?"

She looked into his eyes and then away again. "Someday."

He nodded. "I'm not going anywhere."

"I know."

~

BY THE TIME they headed to Rome, he felt ready to meet the world again.

"We need a proper bed for that house." Ben looked down as they left Venice behind. "I'll call Silvio when we get back to New York."

They flew above the clouds and out of the swarm of insect life that hovered over the lagoon. When the city lights were only a twinkle on the ground, Tenzin set a relaxed pace. After all, it was only an hour or so to Rome.

"Where do you want to stay in the city?" she asked.

Ben frowned. "Giovanni's house of course."

"Because you have options now." Tenzin flew in front of him and turned, flying leisurely through the deep blue sky. "You should probably know about the safe houses now. Did Tai tell you?"

Ben knew there was probably nothing that would hit her while she was flying, but Tenzin flying backward still made him nervous. "Can you not?"

"Not what?"

"Um..." He was being ridiculous and thinking like a human again. "What are you talking about? Safe houses?"

"They're a little like human embassies, I suppose. Consulates? I'm not sure of the word." She shook her head. "They are little pieces of Penglai Island in different cities around the globe."

"Oh right," Ben said. "Yeah, like embassies." And that was a bird barely missing her shoulder. "Tenzin, can you just—"

"There are safe houses with facilities in all the major cities of the world." She completely ignored him and any random objects flying in her vicinity. The wind whipped her hair around in a riot while birds darted this way and that out of their path.

Ben asked, "So there's one of these safe houses in Rome?"

Tenzin did a barrel roll before she answered. "Where did you think I stayed when we were in Rome?"

Ben had never really thought about it. He stayed at his uncle's house near the Pantheon, and Tenzin was always just... around. Come to think of it, he'd never asked her where she stayed. "I always assumed you had a house."

"I don't have houses everywhere. How many houses do you think I have?"

"I mean, you have one in Venice, so I didn't want to assume—"

"Seventeen."

Ben blinked. "Seventeen what? Seventeen...?"

"Houses."

Ben's jaw nearly dropped. "You have seventeen houses?"

"More like twenty, but not all of them are houses. One is a cave in Bali and there's one in Turkey that couldn't be classified as—"

"*Twenty?*"

"Keeping in mind that not all of them are used regularly."

"How many do you use regularly?"

She shrugged and rolled again so she was flying above him. "Define regular."

He looked up. "If you were roaming around? Maybe once a year."

"Oh, then I only have five. New York, Shanghai, Venice, Tibet, and Fes."

"Fes?"

"Very few automobiles in Fes. I like it. I bought a house there only five years ago."

Ben muttered, "I had no idea."

Tenzin flew in front of his face, her eyes glowing. "I am telling you so many things, and I'm not worried about killing you! Chloe will be very impressed."

Ben couldn't stop his smile. "Good to know. So tell me about these vampire embassies."

She floated to his side again and rolled in the wind. "I don't know if other courts have them, but Penglai has bought property in cities around the world so that anyone in the court who needs access to a safe place has one in what might be hostile territory."

"And there's one in Rome?"

"There's one in all the major vampire capitols."

"So... Paris? London? Nairobi?"

"Of course. Buenos Aires, New York, Winnipeg."

"Winnipeg?"

Tenzin looked at him like he'd taken a blow to the head. "Where *else* would you put the vampire capital of Canada?"

"I mean, obviously Winnipeg," Ben muttered. "Don't know what I was thinking."

"So we can stay in the safe house in Rome if you want," she said. "Or we can stay near the Pantheon. I'm sure we'll be safe either place."

Ben sensed this was more about Tenzin than him. "Which place would make you feel more comfortable?"

She looked over her shoulder. "The Penglai house."

"Then why don't we stay there?" He sidled up to her and slipped an arm around her waist. "I don't mind."

"Fabia was very angry with me; I don't want to needlessly provoke her."

Ben had to smile. "New Year's resolution?"

"I think Chloe would be proud that I've done as well as I have."

"So is that why you don't want to stay at the Rome house? Fabia's my friend. She wants me to be happy."

"I think she is in love with you. I don't think she realized it before, but she is."

"I don't think so." He looked at her. "Fabi will be fine. I'm more worried about you and Beatrice."

"Beatrice has a right to be angry." Tenzin settled under his arm like a bird beneath a wing. "She wanted to change you herself. Her or Giovanni."

Ben couldn't dispute her, because that was probably a part of their anger at Tenzin. Maybe a big part.

"I will admit," he said, "when I considered the idea, I always thought it would be one of them." He took a deep breath. "And if that happened, I would be angry, but I would have you, and we'd work through it together. No matter what, I'd have you."

She floated up to his face and framed his cheeks with both her hands. She leaned forward and kissed him, lingering at his mouth until her amnis rose in his blood and he felt their connection like a thousand invisible threads binding them together.

Tenzin holding his hand in Rome, while Ben grieved the first time he'd taken a life.

Tenzin next to him while he piloted a truck of rotting vegetables through China.

Dancing through a sweltering summer night in Venice.

Laughing through an overly formal ceremony in Edinburgh.

He remembered a kiss in a cave that had almost taken his life, and a sword in China that had ended his mortality.

She had been there. For everything, she had always been there.

"If it had happened the way they wanted it" —he whispered against her lips— "I wouldn't be flying with you."

"No."

Ben kissed her again. "So I think things happen for a reason, even if we don't see the purpose at the time."

Tenzin smiled. "You really are Giovanni's son."

## 41

The safe house in Rome was not fancy, but it was nestled into a particularly green space bordered by the Tiber River and the Circus Maximus. The location was probably chosen because it presented the best balance of the elements that could be found in Rome, though Ben thought it also might have been because of the gelato place on the corner, which rivaled the one by the Pantheon in excellence.

Of course, it had been a while since Ben had gorged himself on gelato, so he decided that when Giovanni, Beatrice, and Sadia arrived in Rome, the best place to meet them was at Sadia's favorite cremeria near the Pantheon.

*"Tenzin!"* Sadia ran toward her favorite vampire, holding out her arms. "You're here! You're really here!"

Tenzin leaned over and grabbed the small girl, lifting her into a hug before she set her on her feet. "And you are very tall now."

Sadia huffed out a breath in the cool spring night. "Yeah. I am."

"Hi, gremlin." Ben felt like a whole lot of chopped liver.

"Hi." She hugged him around the waist and lifted her arms. "Piggyback ride."

"Are your legs not working?"

She threw her head back. "Pleeeeeease? I was on the plane for so long. Forever and ever."

Ben rolled his eyes; then he lifted his little sister and put her on his back before he walked over to Giovanni and Beatrice.

Giovanni was smiling with everything on his face. His mouth. His eyes. Even his hair looked happy.

Beatrice was smiling with her mouth, but her eyes looked concerned.

"Hey, B." Ben leaned over and gave his aunt a long hug. "I'm okay. We're okay."

"Mm-hmm." Her smile was tight, and her eyes kept darting to Tenzin over Ben's shoulder. "I want you more than okay."

He took her shoulders in his hands. "I am far more than okay."

His aunt examined his face. She pinched his chin between her fingers and stared into his eyes for a long time.

"Mama, what's wrong?" Sadia was hanging off his shoulders. *"Voglio il gelato."*

Beatrice allowed herself to smile. "Nothing's wrong, baby. Everything is good again." She clapped her hands and reached for Sadia. "Stop climbing on your brother and get down. You're a big girl, and your legs aren't broken." She took Sadia's hand, helped her down, and they walked to the cremeria, which was brightly lit in the dark azure twilight.

TENZIN WATCHED Ben and Beatrice as they chatted in line, waiting to buy ice cream for Sadia. Giovanni stood next to her, watching the evening crowd, from the elderly humans out for a stroll to the ancient vampire who sat on the wall bordering the Pantheon, trying to remain inconspicuous in the shadows of Rome.

"I can smell his amnis on you," Giovanni said. "You're nearly mated."

"It's too soon for that."

"No, it's really not." Giovanni glanced at her from the corner of his eye. "Does he understand what that means? Do you?"

"He's not a child, Giovanni. Neither am I."

"He's my child."

"He's your son; he is not your child." Tenzin watched Ben. She watched the strong, even line of his shoulders and the softness of his grip as he held Sadia's hand in his. She watched Ben's eyes as he measured the world around them, weighing every danger that might threaten the precious and vulnerable girl he'd claimed as his sister.

Mating was complicated. She had taken Stephen as a mate for political reasons. That blood bond had been planned and accounted for. It was never intended to be something permanent.

Would Ben want something permanent?

What had permanent ever meant to her? When life stretched into eternity, did creating permanent bonds make sense? The thought of taking a mate again, having her body and mind so entangled with another...

She wanted to be with Ben. Ben wanted to be with her. Did it have to be more complicated than that?

What they were was enough. For now.

Giovanni spoke softly. "My son looks peaceful."

"He still has terrible moments," Tenzin said. "But know that I will end any human or vampire who threatens his peace."

"He wouldn't want you to."

"That's why he is who he is, and I am who I am." Tenzin looked at Giovanni. "He is a good man. And a better immortal than either of us."

Giovanni smiled. "My sire spent years trying to mold me into the perfect vampire, the most excellent and ideal specimen of immortal life. Philosopher, warrior, scholar, poet, artist." He looked at Tenzin. "And five hundred years after he failed, a street child picked my pocket and became the man I could never be."

"He made himself," Tenzin said. "But you made that easier."

"You're right." Giovanni looked at his son. "He is better than either of us."

"Don't be so hard on yourself." Tenzin patted his shoulder. "You're really an excellent librarian."

Ben looked over his shoulder when Giovanni burst into laughter. His eyes met Tenzin's and held.

Philosopher. Warrior. Scholar. Poet. Artist.

If Benjamin Vecchio's canvas was the people he loved, then he was already a master.

*This is why he is necessary.*

He was still learning. She was still growing into her next life.

*One day we will be infinite.*

# EPILOGUE

*Three months later...*

B en froze midstride, his sword poised at Tenzin's hip.

She watched him, her head cocked to the side as she took the measure of his stance. He was loose, his hips relaxed and his arm poised to strike. The corner of his mouth turned up. He knew he had the advantage.

They'd set the rules for no flying, and with Ben's increased speed and reflexes, he was on the verge of besting her.

Again.

Unless...

Tenzin ran her tongue along her bottom lip and let her fangs grow.

Ben blinked, his eyes drawn to her mouth. "I know what you're trying to do."

She nicked the corner of her lip with her fang and let her blood well, and his eyes glazed over. "What?"

Growling, Ben slapped her ass with the flat of his sword before he leapt on her. "You fight dirty."

"That isn't a win!" she managed to yell before he tackled her to the ground.

His mouth locked on hers, and he sucked the drop of blood into his mouth. She wrestled him to his back, only to have him flip her over and spread her legs with one knee.

Were they wrestling or was this foreplay? She often had a hard time distinguishing between the two.

The low, happy growl that came from Ben's throat told her that it was foreplay.

Excellent. Sex would be much better than losing to him in another duel. It had happened twice now, and she was worried it would become a habit.

He had the advantage in strike distance now, and it was highly annoying. She had to stop agreeing to fights on the ground. It was far easier to fight dirty in the air.

She wiggled away from him and ran up the stairs, eager to see if he ran or flew trying to catch her. More and more he defaulted to flying, which delighted Tenzin.

The wind loved him. It danced around him in flight, played with his hair, and lifted him with a manic kind of glee. The wind had always been her comfort, but for Ben, it would be his joy.

Mood swings still happened, and Ben still had dark nights. He'd seen his father driving a cab on Houston Street three nights before and sank into a sullen mood he'd only shaken when he woke that night. She was hoping that challenging him to a duel he was likely to win would brush the last of the shadows from his eyes.

Judging by the low chuckle behind her, the idea had worked.

She flew up to the loft and crouched in the corner, daring him to come in.

Ben set his toes on the edge and hovered. "Tell the truth—you did that because I was going to win."

"You wish."

He smiled, and the beauty of it made her forget to breathe. Seeing Ben happy had become her obsession.

He fell on the mattress he'd dragged up to her loft and tugged her hand. "Come here."

Gladly.

She jumped on him, bracing herself over him as he stripped the clothing from her body. They rolled and tumbled in the bed, falling out once, only to have Ben float them back.

Their coupling was fast and full of laughter. Though Ben was still learning her body, he knew what brought her pleasure quickly and what would draw out sensual torment.

That night he wrapped her in his embrace and pinned her high on a wall, wringing a climax from her before he found his own release. It was fast and intense, and she took his blood as he came, drawing out his pleasure as long as she could.

They floated back into the loft and onto the new bed. Tenzin lay on him, aligning her body along his, skin to skin, as their amnis twisted and hummed.

She kissed along his jaw. "You're better tonight."

He played with a strand of her hair. "Sorry about the cranky mood."

"It's fine. You've put up with more than one of mine over the years."

"True." He didn't say anything more, even though it sounded like he wanted to.

She poked his side. "Speak."

"I've lived here for what? Five years? And in a city of eight million people, I've seen him three times. What are the chances of that?"

"It's really not that big an island. It is bound to happen." Tenzin wanted to say, *Shall I kill him for you?* But she didn't. That would probably be considered a backslide when it came to personal evolution. Chloe would not approve.

"We can move," she said. "We have options."

"I like New York. And Cormac has finally stopped giving me dirty looks when I run into him."

"Do you want me to find your father and strongly suggest he move back to San Juan?" *With amnis.* Not that she wanted to subject the lovely island of Puerto Rico to Ben's father.

"I don't think he'd do anything but make my grandmother's life miserable."

She laid her head on his chest. "Why does seeing him bother you so much?"

Ben didn't say anything for a long time. He stroked his thumb along her hip and stared at the ceiling. "Did you have children when you were alive?"

Tenzin stopped breathing for a moment.

He looked at her, and there was a challenge in his eyes. *You want me to show you mine? Show me yours.*

Poke. Prod. Stretch the skin and shed it. Leave the old behind.

Growth was painful, especially in moments like this.

"I had three children." She took a slow breath. "A girl who died and twin boys. I think possibly one of them might have lived to adulthood, but I don't know because I was abducted by raiders when they were babies."

The challenge in his eyes fled, and Ben wrapped his arms around her in an iron grip.

"My father is such a shitty person, and he still got to have a kid. I'll never have children, and I think I'd be so much better at it than he ever was. For some reason, in the past few months, that has been pissing me off. And then I saw him and it was just like... a slap."

Tenzin examined his expression. She sensed no hidden meaning or prevarication.

"It is ludicrous to say that you will never have children, because you are immortal now and you know that many of our kind adopt children. You don't know what your life will be like in ten years, let alone in one hundred or two hundred."

He stroked the back of her neck. "Would you have children again?"

"Not now, and not anytime soon."

He nodded.

"But I will not say never." She looked away. "It would be foolish to project like that."

"Okay." His hand stroked along her back.

Tenzin closed her eyes and felt his blood living inside her. She still hadn't told him that she'd started sleeping again. For a few blissful hours each day, she slept and dreamed. That, more than anything, had calmed the voices in her mind.

Often their days were spent like this, Ben falling asleep with Tenzin draped over him, either in the loft or the bedroom they'd light proofed when they returned to New York. Tenzin preferred that Ben sleep in the loft. She liked to sense his nearness even when she was awake or meditating.

That night they were supposed to meet Chloe and Gavin for drinks at the Dancing Bear. But then again, maybe they wouldn't.

She felt a burgeoning energy approaching, and a familiar scent blew through the open windows like a gust of night jasmine in the air.

Tenzin picked up her head. "Zhang is here."

Ben frowned. "What?"

It couldn't be. But it was.

"Zhang. My sire. *Our* sire." She sat up. "He is here." *What was he doing in New York?*

"Has he ever been to New York before? Are you sure?"

"I smell him on the roof."

She was about to fly out of the loft when Ben pulled her back threw a tunic at her.

"Clothing please. I know you don't subscribe to traditional

363

mores of modesty, but please don't make me crazy, even if it is your father."

She looked at him. "Is this another relationship parameter?"

He rubbed a small circle on his temple. "I can't believe we have to spell that out, but yes, Tenzin. Please don't randomly spend time naked in front of other people."

"That's a reasonable parameter." As was monogamy. Very few vampires as old as Tenzin subscribed to monogamy, but since she had no interest in sexual intercourse with anyone other than Ben, that was an easy request to agree to. Understanding the complex dynamics of an emotional and sexual partnership with one person was complicated enough. She didn't know how Arosh handled a harem, but he clearly had far more emotional depth than she could manage.

Tenzin pulled on a tunic and a loose pair of pants; then she flew down to the french doors that led to the roof. Ben was right behind her.

Just as she'd suspected, Zhang was sitting on a bench outside, his eyes roaming over the city.

"Extraordinary," he said. "Truly, I begin to understand Lan's fascination with the modern world." Zhang looked over his shoulder. "It looks like another sky has fallen to the ground, spreading its stars across the land."

Ben leaned against the doorway. "Yeah, it's pretty spectacular."

Tenzin didn't waste time on pleasantries. "What are you doing here? What is wrong?"

"A piece of unexpected information came to me two weeks ago." Zhang turned, and Tenzin was surprised by the tension she saw on her sire's face. "It affects both of you." He sniffed the air. "I see you have become sexual partners again."

Ben covered his eyes with one hand. "God, you two are so strange. I will never understand your relationship."

"That is none of your business," Tenzin said. "And it has no bearing on our relationship with you."

"Admittedly, this is true," Zhang said, "but I do hope you are both happy with the arrangement."

"Why are you in New York? I doubt it's to check whether Ben and I are having sex."

Ben groaned and sat on a bench. "You just keep saying it."

She spun on him. "*So* Catholic." Tenzin turned back to her father. "What is this about?"

"It's about Arosh," Zhang said, keeping his voice low. "I have sources who say he has found the bone scroll in Axum."

Tenzin felt as if her body had been hollowed out in an instant. "The bone scroll is a myth."

"No," Zhang said. "It is not."

"Aabmen—"

"I have seen it with my own eyes." Zhang's face was like a grave. "It is not a myth."

Zhang had seen it? It was as if she were seeing her father for the first time. How had he seen it? Where? If he had seen it, why had he not destroyed it?

Ben crossed his arms over his chest. "What's a bone scroll? And haven't we done enough for Arosh to last a lifetime? We found the Night's Reckoning. We ended the cold war between the West and the East. Isn't that enough?"

Zhang looked at Tenzin and spoke in the old language. "You haven't told him about Saba."

She responded in the same. "You didn't tell him either."

Ben walked over to Tenzin. "You're going to teach me that language because this" —he pointed between them— "is going to drive me crazy."

The bone scroll. It was a myth. She'd always been told it was a myth.

But her father did not lie.

365

Tenzin walked to Ben and looked him straight in the eye. "How do you feel about a trip to Ethiopia?"

~

THE BONE SCROLL
Elemental Legacy: Book Five
Coming Spring 2021

# ACKNOWLEDGMENTS

It's not easy to write a book during a pandemic.

Dawn Caravan was the first book I wrote in near complete isolation. Other than my husband and son, I spent time with no one else during the drafting. So for that reason, I want to give them special thanks for their love, support, and patience while I attempted to write this very difficult book.

Fictionally speaking, it's a lot easier to blow things up than it is to put things together. (Probably this applies outside of fiction too, but I've never blown anything up in real life, so there you go.) Night's Reckoning placed Ben and Tenzin at a crossroads, in the series and in their development as characters. I knew bringing them forward from that place of violence and transformation would be difficult, so I hope that Dawn Caravan met your expectations.

I love this book the way you love your most precocious child or your most mischievous pet. I love it hard, but I know what a pain in the butt it was to write.

I currently have one more book planned for this series, The Bone Scroll, but unlike other series I've written, this isn't necessarily the final chapter for these characters. So if you're a fan of

Ben and Tenzin, don't fear. I think there will be more stories to tell. I'll just have to wait and see what inspiration strikes me.

Many thanks to my incredible assistants, Jenn and Gen, who managed the weird transition to doing literally everything online, including juggling my neuroses and reminding me to eat.

Thanks to Emily and all the staff at Social Butterfly PR for their work helping my career and promoting my books. You are wonderful and I love you all. I'm proud to work with an organization like you that doesn't shy away from the hard stuff.

Thanks to my wonderful editors, Amy Cissell, Anne Victory and Linda at Victory Editing. Your excellence and professionalism make me a more confident and grammatical author.

Thanks to Damon and all the staff at Damonza.com who always manage to take a vague idea and create a stunning cover. You're magicians and I admire you so much.

And finally to the admins and members of Hunters' Haven, my Facebook home away from home, thank you for the love, support, and enthusiasm. All of you rock, and that is not a spoiler.

See you next time, friends.

Thanks for reading.

—EH

# ABOUT THE AUTHOR

ELIZABETH HUNTER is a *USA Today* and international best-selling author of romance, contemporary fantasy, and paranormal mystery. Based in Central California, she travels extensively to write fantasy fiction exploring world mythologies, history, and the universal bonds of love, friendship, and family. She has published over thirty works of fiction and sold over a million books worldwide. She is the author of the Glimmer Lake series, Love Stories on 7th and Main, the Elemental Legacy series, the Irin Chronicles, the Cambio Springs Mysteries, and other works of fiction.

ElizabethHunterWrites.com

## ALSO BY ELIZABETH HUNTER

The Elemental Legacy

Shadows and Gold

Imitation and Alchemy

Omens and Artifacts

Obsidian's Edge (anthology)

Midnight Labyrinth

Blood Apprentice

The Devil and the Dancer

Night's Reckoning

Dawn Caravan

The Bone Scroll

(Spring 2021)

The Elemental Mysteries

A Hidden Fire

This Same Earth

The Force of Wind

A Fall of Water

The Stars Afire

The Elemental World

Building From Ashes

Waterlocked

Blood and Sand

The Bronze Blade

The Scarlet Deep

A Very Proper Monster

A Stone-Kissed Sea

Valley of the Shadow

Glimmer Lake

Suddenly Psychic

Semi-Psychic Life

Psychic Dreams

(August 2020)

The Irin Chronicles

The Scribe

The Singer

The Secret

The Staff and the Blade

The Silent

The Storm

The Seeker

The Cambio Springs Series

Long Ride Home

Shifting Dreams

Five Mornings

Desert Bound

Waking Hearts

Dust Born

(newsletter serial)

Linx & Bogie Mysteries

A Ghost in the Glamour

A Bogie in the Boat

Contemporary Romance

The Genius and the Muse

7th and Main

INK

HOOKED

GRIT

Made in United States
Orlando, FL
03 September 2022

21953992R00232